DARK SECRETS ON DRESSMAKERS' ALLEY

ROSIE CLARKE

Boldwood

First published in Great Britain in 2024 by Boldwood Books Ltd.

Cover Design by Colin Thomas

Cover Photography: Colin Thomas

This book is a work of fiction and, except in the case of historical fact, any resemblance to actual persons, living or dead, is purely coincidental.

Every effort has been made to obtain the necessary permissions with reference to copyright material, both illustrative and quoted. We apologise for any omissions in this respect and will be pleased to make the appropriate acknowledgements in any future edition.

A CIP catalogue record for this book is available from the British Library.

Paperback ISBN 978-1-78513-159-2

Large Print ISBN 978-1-78513-160-8

Hardback ISBN 978-1-78513-158-5

Ebook ISBN 978-1-78513-161-5

Kindle ISBN 978-1-78513-162-2

Audio CD ISBN 978-1-78513-153-0

MP3 CD ISBN 978-1-78513-154-7

Digital audio download ISBN 978-1-78513-157-8

Boldwood Books Ltd
23 Bowerdean Street
London SW6 3TN
www.boldwoodbooks.com

1

LONDON, 1924

In the hours of darkness, the streets and lanes around Dressmakers' Alley could seem dark and frightening, but the two men creeping like shadows past shuttered businesses were not afraid of anything much, except the sound of a policeman's whistle and his pounding feet.

'This is the place,' the younger, shorter man said, stopping to glance at his companion, who was taller and heavier – a man just out of prison, a man hungry for revenge. 'I reckon if we smash that little window on the side, I can get my hand through and open the door. The daft bugger leaves his key in the back door. I need you to keep watch while I get in – and then we'll clear him out of cigarettes. Alf Harding banks on a Friday night, so with any luck, he'll have half his week's takings in his safe 'ere.'

The older man nodded, scratching at his frowzy beard. 'If it's the sort you say, I can open it in a minute. I used to be able to open almost any safe – but they've got better since I was banged up.' He muttered to himself, 'Twenty bloody years they give me... and I wouldn't be out now if I hadn't fooled 'em when they took me to the 'ospital...'

'You want ter be careful the bloody coppers don't come lookin' fer yer. Yer used ter live round 'ere, didn't yer?'

'Once...' the older man hawked and spat. 'I came lookin' fer that bastard Bert Barrow. Him what owns the clothes place in Dressmakers' Alley. He owes me.' He growled deep in his throat. 'That's the one I want ter do...'

'They've got that locked up as tight as the bleedin' Bank of England; belongs to some toff now I 'eard. Anyways, I told yer. Bert Barrow is dead. Dirty Sid done fer 'im, so a mate of mine said. Forget 'im and keep yer mind on what we're doin'.'

'Bleedin' lucky fer Barrow he is dead,' the older man said. 'I'd bloody make 'im sorry he was ever born.'

'Ain't no good bearing a grudge against a dead man, even if he did grass on yer.'

'I 'ate the bastard – and his bloody girls. Turned up their noses at me when I asked about 'im...' the taller man spat once more.

The younger man hushed him. He broke the glass in the side of the small newsagent's shop, muffling it with practised ease; then slipped his gloved hand through the hole, sought and found the key in the back door and gave a chortle of pleasure as it turned. 'One born every minute,' he crowed as he was able to open the door, allowing them both to enter. 'Easy as taking sweets from a baby.'

'Yeah, but there ain't much 'ere,' his companion said, following him in. 'I looked earlier and them shelves ain't full...'

'That's 'cos the new stock is still in boxes – 'andy fer us to carry away.' The younger of the two grinned. 'I might have better things lined up another night – but whether I let you in on it depends. Now go to the front and look through the blinds – make sure we ain't nobbled...'

'Yeah, all right – but where's that safe?'

'Behind the counter over there. It's a small one, but he's got it bolted to the floor, so we have to open it...'

'I told yer. I can do most of 'em...' The older man went through to the front and took a good look through the vertical blinds over the door. 'All clear – now show me that bloody safe...'

He was pointed towards it. It was concealed inside a wooden cabinet. Once the locked cabinet was prised open, the safe was found to be a simple number lock, and while the younger thief stacked cigarette cartons and some boxes of chocolates into three large haversacks, the elder pressed his ear to the safe and twirled the lock.

'How much longer?'

'It takes a bit of...' The cracksman gave a grunt of satisfaction as the safe clicked open. He shone his torch inside and took out a small bundle of notes. 'Only bloody twelve quid. I thought you said he kept money 'ere.'

'Maybe he didn't take much this week. Give it 'ere and we'll split it all later.'

'I want my share now – in fact, I think I'll just keep this. I'll give yer your share when you sell the fags and give me mine.'

The younger man growled in his throat. 'It was my con. I take the goods and split it wiv yer when we're done.'

'Make it worth me while next time...' the older man replied but didn't hand over the cash. He walked off unhurriedly, disappearing into the gloom of a wet night.

The younger man glared at his back as he went, but decided to leave it for now. He needed the cracksman's skills or he wouldn't have brought him along. Not every property was this easy to enter – and it was better working as a pair, safer. Besides, he knew the man he was dealing with was dangerous; he'd been convicted of burglary and assault, his victim an old man who had died from his injuries. It suited the thief to go along with him for now, but he didn't intend to be cheated or told what to do. He had a good thing going. A respectable working man during the day, his secret activities at night were gradually paying off his debts and he was building a business that would make him rich one day.

He despised the wretch who had helped him that night; he called himself Pug, but it was only a nickname, because of his broken nose. They didn't use their real names, because they could be overheard. To an incurious passerby, Pug appeared just an unwashed vagrant, but he was a man on the run from prison and, as such, could be relied on to do whatever was required of him.

A nasty smile touched the thief's mouth. He wasn't afraid of the older man's threats, because he knew that if it came to a fight, he was younger and stronger. His accomplice would be back, because you needed knowledge to know which houses were worth breaking into, when the occupants would be away and if a shop carried enough easily moveable stock to be worthwhile. There was not a lot of point in robbing a place for a couple of fivers. It was only the knowledge that Harding had just had a large delivery of cigarettes that had made that night's job viable. What they were really looking for was somewhere they could make a killing. Maybe Bert Barrow's old place would be worth investigating. They must hold some expensive stock there – and if that Miss Susie left the girls' wages there overnight, it would be a decent night's work... but he wasn't sure where he would shift that kind of merchandise. He'd have to talk to the fence he dealt with and hear what he had to say; it was much easier to rob to order because he didn't want to have to conceal any stolen goods on his own premises. In the eyes of his peers, he was an honest man and he needed it to stay that way, because everyone trusted him to enter their homes...

2

DRESSMAKERS' ALLEY, 1924

'Lilly...' Joe Ross entered the little flower shop on the corner of Dressmakers' Alley where his sister worked in the shop her husband Jeb had set up. 'How are you, love?' He was a tall man, well built with dark hair and eyes that could look as blue as a summer sky or as stormy grey as the winter seas, changing with his moods. Just now, they were anxious as he looked at the sister, towards whom he'd always been protective.

Lilly smiled at him, her hand pausing briefly on her rounded belly. She was younger than Joe by a few years, pretty, with soft hair that waved about her face and brownish eyes. She was also pregnant, but as yet it had hardly begun to show. 'We're both fine,' she confirmed. 'Stop worrying about me. I'm only arranging a few flowers and I have a nice comfy chair to sit in.'

'Jeb asked me to look after you while he's away for a couple of days,' Joe said and then frowned, his eyes darkening. 'I didn't want to scare you, Lilly – but there's a rumour going round the lanes that there's some bugger attacking young women on their own, taking their purse or whatever they have of value.'

'Yes, Winnie Brown told me earlier this morning,' Lilly replied with a little shiver. Several unpleasant attacks on women had occurred recently; thus far, the motive seemed to be robbery rather than anything else, but it was enough to make anyone uncomfortable walking alone. 'She pops in most days for a few fresh flowers for the reception at Miss Susie.'

'I thought I'd walk you home this evening,' Joe went on. 'We don't want you running any risks when you're in a delicate condition.'

Lilly went into a peal of laughter. 'I'm havin' a baby, Joe, and I assure you I'm not delicate. Thanks for the offer, my dearest brother, but Winnie said she would walk home with me. Several of the girls from Miss Susie live our way and we'll set out together.' The laughter left her eyes and for a moment there was pain reflected. 'I haven't forgotten what happened to me once before, Joe. I never shall, but Winnie says you have to fight back. She did when she was attacked by the same man that attacked me. She says she went for his eyes with her shoe and half-blinded him. I'll be safe enough with her. And don't forget what she did when that wicked man tried to murder Betty Ford... Winnie went for him with the fire tongs and held him off until you and Sam got there and then the police arrested him.' Betty managed the workshop at Miss Susie and she'd been attacked by the man behind the murder of her boss Bert Barrow. It was Winnie's bravery that had saved her from being strangled.

'Yes, there's safety in numbers,' Joe agreed, but his warm smile belied his anxiety. Lilly had been raped some years previously. For a while, it had devastated her, almost ruining her life. Joe had found the man who'd hurt her, and he'd given him a good hiding, but the devil had gone on attacking young women, including Winnie Brown, who had fought him off, until the police finally got him; he was now in prison, serving a lifetime sentence for rape and murder. Winnie was engaged to one of Joe's best mates, Sam

Collins, and she was a fiery one at times. Lilly would be safe enough with her. 'Well, if you're sure – but the offer is always there if you need me, Lilly.'

'Thank you, I shall remember,' she said and smiled. 'Are you taking Sibby out this evening?'

Joe had been going out with Sibby Thomas on and off for a while now. She was a girl from the Welsh valleys and had come to London in search of a better life. When her first job wasn't what she'd expected, she had turned to the Women's Movement and been sent to what was then Madame Pauline's workshops, to keep a sharp eye out for anything untoward, but by the time she'd applied, Winnie had already exposed the men who were keeping some poor girls prisoner on the top floor. Those poor girls had been kept against their will for the benefit of men who paid for their services, either in money or favours. Some had been released later by the police but others had sadly died. Nothing like that went on at the very respectable Miss Susie these days.

'Sibby says she has to wash her hair,' Joe replied, frowning. 'To be honest, Lilly, I am not sure I want to go on seeing her. I like Sibby, but I'm not thinking of marriage and she knows it's just as friends...' He shrugged. 'I always thought I'd fall in love – the way Sam did with Winnie, and you with Jeb.'

'You certainly shouldn't marry her unless it is what you really want,' Lilly said. She wished she could say more, but a customer had entered behind Joe. 'Yes, Mr Robinson. Have you come for the red roses you ordered for your wife's birthday?'

Joe nodded at her and whispered goodbye as she turned her attention to the customer.

'Yes, I have,' the gentleman said and Lilly excused herself to go out the back where she kept special orders. She returned with the bouquet she had made up earlier with a dozen beautiful and scented red roses and some white gypsum – or baby's breath as some folk called the sprays of tiny white flowers. 'Oh that looks wonderful, Miss Lilly,' he said. 'Rosemary will be delighted with these.'

'They are lovely and they smell gorgeous.' She smiled at him in her natural friendly way.

'No good having a rose that doesn't smell,' Mr Robinson said. He took out his wallet and paid her the price they'd agreed in advance. 'I knew I could rely on you. Some of the more expensive florists in the city don't seem to understand that roses must have a lovely scent. They look wonderful, but if they don't smell nice, they are no good to my Rosemary.'

Lilly nodded her understanding. His wife had been blind for some years and relied on scent and touch. She would see the bouquet through her fingers and smell their perfume. It made Lilly a little sad as she saw him walk away with the flowers, carrying them so carefully.

Working in the shop, Lilly got to know so many people. When she'd first started serving here, after leaving Harpers Emporium, in Oxford Street, where she'd been trained in the flower department, Dressmakers' Alley had seemed dark and dirty, but over the years since, it had improved and trade had grown.

Lilly knew that when Madame Pauline's had become Miss Susie, just over nine months earlier, things had begun to pick up. Almost at the same time, a new children's clothes manufacturer had opened on the opposite side of the road. Prior to that, several buildings had been boarded up, but extensive renovations were going on and some small traders had opened up new shops in the alley. Just up from Lilly, there was a sweet shop run by two young women who were sisters and further along still was a newsagent and tobacconist.

Almost every building in the alley was now occupied or being renovated prior to opening. The street sweeper kept the gutters clean these days and there was no longer a noisome smell during the warmer months, which was a good thing as it was May and although the rain had been incessant of late, it should soon be summer. Someone with influence had made a difference. Lilly suspected it might be Susie Collins' partner in the dressmakers' business who had instigated the changes. Lilly didn't know if the rumours were true, but she'd heard a whisper that it was Lady Diane Cooper, the darling of high society, wife to Lord Henry and mother of a beautiful little girl named Marie, who designed all the beautiful clothes made at the workshop of Miss Susie. Whatever, she could only be grateful for the changes that had brought many more people to the alley and a big increase in trade to her door.

Lilly smiled as she went back to making the gorgeous flower arrangements that would be delivered to a prestigious hotel in the West End of London. She had always hoped that such orders would come their way and often wondered who had recommended her talent to the manager of the Waverly Hotel. She thought it might be Susie Collins or perhaps Winnie, who had gone to a tea dance there, but she wasn't certain and didn't like to ask.

At a quarter to one, Lilly put the closed sign in the shop window and opened her back door to help Donald load his little van with the exquisite arrangements she'd made. He was the Waverly Hotel manager's son and worked in the hotel, doing all kinds of jobs.

'I reckon you've done us proud again, Lilly,' he said. 'Dad will be pleased. He wasn't sure at first, because of the area your shop's in – but the fancy West End shop he used before he was told about you let him down. Our visitors expect the flowers to be fresh and yours last most of the week; the ones we were having before were dead in two days.'

'These will last a week if properly watered,' Lilly told him with a smile. 'Your father likes his flowers extra fresh, Donald, that's why he buys twice a week, though I tell him they will last longer if he keeps them fresh.'

'He's afraid they might smell stale. Dad's a stickler for things being right.'

Donald loaded his van and waved a cheery goodbye.

Lilly returned to her shop and looked at the time. She would eat her sandwiches and make a cup of tea, and then open the shop again. She didn't have any more orders to prepare, but you never knew what might turn up.

On her way to work she'd bought a newspaper. Lilly liked to know what was going on in the world and just lately there had been lots of articles about the opening of Tutankhamun's tomb, which she'd found bewildering but also fascinating. She scanned the paper, but apart from some fashion pictures, there was just a lot of political stuff and an article about the terrible plague that had killed a lot of people in India in the previous month.

Lilly sighed and placed a fond hand on her stomach. Her baby wasn't due for months yet, but Jeb's and her brother's care for her was nice and made her feel loved. She would be glad when Jeb got back from his buying trip. He owned and ran a little curiosity shop in the Commercial Road, selling small items of old furniture, bric-a-brac and all sorts of glass and china.

She smiled as she thought of her hard-working husband. Jeb had started out as a barrow boy selling flowers and fruit, but he was ambitious. First, he'd found a shop where he could sell flowers, because he knew it was what Lilly wanted. Once Jeb had got the flower shop going, he'd started buying all sorts of bits and pieces, clearing houses of stuff others might think junk. He had taught himself about antiques, learning to recognise the age of a piece of furniture and the marks on silver articles. He still cleared houses for folk, but also he attended auction sales and he was building up a nice business.

'I want yer ter be proud of me, Lilly,' he'd told her recently. 'We shan't always live in a terraced house with a tin bath in the kitchen. We'll have a bathroom and a nice garden for the kids...'

'I just want us all to be happy,' Lilly had told him, hugging and kissing him. She'd kissed him as he left for the country-house sale. 'You come back safe,' she'd told him. 'I'll miss you, love.'

'Not as much as I'll miss you,' Jeb had said, grinning as he'd got into his battered old van and driven away.

Lilly missed him when he was off somewhere for a couple of days. As a rule, he popped in and out of the flower shop when he could, and he took her home at night.

She started to draw a basket of flowers. Lilly had found that it was a good idea to plan out the flowers she did for her hotel orders. She enjoyed coming up with fresh ideas and her sketches kept her busy for the rest of the afternoon, in between the three or four customers who popped in for small bunches of flowers.

It was just gone six when her shop door opened again and Winnie walked in, smiling at her. 'Are you ready, Lilly? Yvonne, Sibby, Val and Katie have gone on ahead to the pie shop, so we'll catch up with them there.'

'Yes, I'm ready.' Lilly picked up her basket, which contained her day's takings, putting the leather strap Jeb had made for her over her wrist so that it couldn't be easily snatched.

The young women went out together, Winnie waiting while Lilly locked her door. Across the street, an elderly woman was resting against the wall. She was wearing a moth-eaten fur coat and had an old pram piled with sacks by her side.

Lilly waved to her and called out. 'Are you all right, Rusty?'

The woman glanced her way, but didn't speak, instead pushing her pram down the alley.

'She is a strange one,' Winnie whispered. 'She asked for sixpence for a cup of tea the other day. I gave it to her, but she didn't thank me, just grabbed it and walked off muttering to herself.'

'Rusty has moods. She can talk for England when she feels like it,' Lilly told her. 'I think she knew rich people when she was young and on the stage – or so she told me...'

'She talks to you then?' Winnie stared after her. 'Was she an actress? You'd never think it.'

'Sometimes, when she is in a good mood, she tells me stories of when she was young; at other times she just walks off – but who knows what she has suffered?'

'No, I wouldn't want to have her life, sleeping rough and never knowing where the next meal will come from,' Winnie agreed. 'We're lucky, Lilly. When you think of the hard lives some folk have, it doesn't bear thinking of...'

Lilly nodded. They were just two working girls who didn't have much, but when you compared their lives to someone like Rusty, who was forced to wander the streets with no home, you just had to thank your lucky stars for what you'd got.

3

'Good morning, Susie.' Winnie looked up and smiled as her employer entered the reception area of the workshop the following morning. It was a bright, open area with two comfortable chairs for customers to sit and a shining mahogany desk set with a brass inkstand, a diary and a small vase of flowers. In the far corner of the room, a mannequin showed off an exquisite evening dress in a vivid emerald green silk. 'We had a telephone enquiry from a department store in Birmingham early this morning. I have written the details for you in the diary.'

'Thank you, Winnie,' Susie Collins replied. 'How many new clients have we heard from this month? Lady Diane was asking. Check and then I can tell her later.'

'I know already.' Winnie beamed at her. 'That is the sixth new enquiry so far this month. Three have already ordered – just small orders to try – and two said they would think about buying from us for their autumn range as they already have their spring and summer stock ordered.'

'That's not too bad. I will tell her when I see her this evening.

She is going to a grand ball in a private house and I shall help Meg to dress her...' Meg had been a parlour maid but Lady Diane had taken her on as her dresser when she'd asked Susie to manage the fashion business for her. Susie smiled. 'I might get to help bath Marie and put her to bed. Her ladyship likes to do that herself, even though Nanny disapproves. If she is busy dressing, I might get the privilege.'

'You love Marie, don't you?'

'She is so beautiful, Winnie. Marie almost killed Lady Diane when she was born, but that is all forgotten. We all dote on her.' There was a slightly wistful note in her voice, Winnie thought, as if perhaps she might like a child of her own.

'Is her ladyship truly well now?' Winnie asked and for the first time since her arrival, Susie really smiled.

'Yes, she is very well at last. It is hard to remember now how we feared for them both... for months.' A little shiver went through her and Winnie saw the dark memories in her eyes.

For the first few months, as Susie had battled to bring her ladyship's dream of her own fashion house to life, it had seemed as if Lady Diane would never recover her full strength, after the birth of her child.

Winnie had witnessed the deep grief in Susie's eyes all those weeks and months. She had done everything she could to help Susie establish the new business for her ladyship, going above and beyond what was expected of her as a receptionist, often doubling up as a seamstress after hours.

To begin with they had sometimes struggled to get orders out on time because it was hard to find girls with the required skill and dedication. Susie demanded excellent workmanship and would not be satisfied with anything but the best.

'Shoddy work would let her ladyship down,' Susie had oft

times been heard to say to her mother, brother, Sam, and Winnie, who lived with Mrs Collins now. 'She expects perfection for her designs and it is my job to see that nothing less than the best work leaves our establishment.'

Because Miss Susie was known to demand such high standards from her girls, several of the first seamstresses had left after a few weeks, preferring to work for less exacting employers. It was true the working conditions were much better than had existed when the workshop belonged to Bert Barrow, and the pay was fairer, too. However, some girls were just not prepared to work so carefully and some had to be dismissed. At one time, they had managed with Yvonne, three seamstresses, Betty Ford, their supervisor, and Winnie. All of them had worked long into the night to get those first few orders out, earning large bonuses.

Fortunately, the right seamstresses had found their way to Miss Susie and they could now take on larger orders and not have to work such long hours.

Susie paused as she opened the door into the main working area. A burst of laughter and happy chatter was heard and she looked at Winnie, their eyes meeting in shared enjoyment. A very different atmosphere now existed to the desperate silence that had been enforced when it was a sweat shop.

Winnie smiled as more than a dozen voices greeted Susie's entrance and then the door was closed. Susie liked to talk to her employees first thing in the morning and so they all had a tea break while she told them any news she had and asked how the orders were going.

Susie was, of course, a partner in the business. Lady Diane was their designer and it was her ideas that would make the business a success, but she did not visit the premises, except once fleetingly at Christmas when she'd brought a big hamper of gifts for the girls.

She'd looked so ill then, her beautiful face still pale and thin, but her smile had lit up the room as she'd thanked everyone for their dedication. Her girls had all been asked not to talk about the identity of their sponsor, as Susie described her, but Winnie knew that it was common knowledge in the alley that a wealthy lady was their designer.

Their merchandise was quite expensive, all original to them, and beautiful. Winnie had seen Miss Susie creations in the windows of all the bigger stores in London. Harpers had an exclusive line each season, because they had been the first to buy from Miss Susie, but most of the designs could be found in smaller shops now.

The telephone rang and Winnie answered in her best professional voice.

'This is Miss Johnson from Robinsons. I spoke to you last month about our autumn order. We have decided that we want to go ahead with the tweed costumes and the morning dresses we discussed. We will take all the lines in all sizes from a 36 hip up to a size 46 hip, in both colours for the dresses.' The tweed suits were only in a soft blue Harris material, the dresses in a choice of grey and midnight blue fine wool cloth, both with beautiful white lacy collars and long sleeves with turned-back buttoned cuffs.

'Oh thank you for getting back to me,' Winnie said. 'I think that is an excellent choice and bound to be popular with your customers. Did you decide about those evening gowns, too?'

'We thought they were a little expensive for us, unfortunately, but we love your daywear. The usual terms of a ten per cent deposit and payment on delivery?'

'Yes, thank you,' Winnie replied and smiled as the phone went down. She had written it all neatly in her order book. She would type it up now and send to the client so that no mistakes were made. This customer had bought last year, but this order was slightly larger.

She had just finished typing her invoice and was addressing the envelope when the door opened.

Winnie looked up and smiled as she saw her fiancé looking in.

'I won't come in, love,' Sam said. 'Do you need me to do any shopping for you – and what time do you want lunch?'

'Oh, Sam, you don't have to bother,' Winnie told him. 'I can do a bit of shopping on my way home this evening. I brought a sandwich with me...'

'I know – but I thought we might go for a cup of tea somewhere?' He grinned. 'You know what today is?'

'Of course I do.' Winnie smiled. 'I'll come to yours in an hour. Susie is here, so she'll sit here for half an hour while I'm out...'

'Right-ho,' Sam said, blew her a kiss and left.

Winnie answered the phone almost as the door closed behind him and took another small order – a repeat for a dress that they'd made for this summer. The client wanted another eight in the smaller sizes.

Winnie had replaced the phone and got up to take the order through to the workroom just as Susie came back into reception.

'I have an order for a repeat here,' Winnie told her. 'I think we have stock in hand for this – and I've just taken a big order from Robinsons for the autumn costumes and that range of wool dresses...'

'Good. I spoke to their buyer the day before yesterday and I wasn't sure they were going to order,' Susie said. 'When are you taking your lunch break, Winnie?'

'I thought in an hour's time? If that is all right for you?'

'Yes, just right. I have to go and see a supplier for a zip I ordered. It was delivered earlier but hasn't come in the right colour.' She frowned. 'I shouldn't be long. The wholesaler is within walking distance. I'll sit in for you while you have lunch.'

'I'm having it with Sam...' Winnie laughed. 'It is the anniversary of the day we first went out to tea. Sam wants to take me out for a cup of tea...'

'So he should,' Susie replied and smiled at her. 'I'll be back...' she began but waved and left as the telephone rang once more.

4

'I ordered the pale turquoise zips like this one,' Susie told the man in the office at Morrisons – the wholesaler she had been using for the past few months. She held it out for him to see. 'This is what you sent me...' She showed him a zip in a deep turquoise several shades darker than the one she'd ordered.

'That is the same zip – the number is ZX 63...' He pointed to the stock number on the packets – both carried the same number but were clearly different.

'Yes, but the dye is different,' Susie pointed out. 'This zip is needed for a silk dress and the deeper colour would show through the material.'

'That's rather strange,' he said, a puzzled look in his eyes. 'It is the same stock number.'

'I am not blaming you,' Susie replied patiently. 'I just need these zips in a paler turquoise as I ordered.'

'I'll have a look...' He went through a door at the back of the counter and shouted at someone.

Susie looked around the shelves; it was a treasure trove of items needed in the rag trade, as her business was known.

He returned after a few minutes with a large box, which he placed on the counter. He took the lid off and removed several zips, all of them the same colour as Susie had ordered. 'Are these what you wanted?' he asked. 'Seems they've changed the dye since then, but yours came in and were put to one side and the wrong ones were sent out to you. There are three dozen here, same as you ordered – do you want to return the others?'

'No. I can use them for something else, but I'm glad you have the ones I ordered.'

'That will be three pounds then, Miss Collins – and I'm sorry you were sent the wrong order.'

'I am pleased it has been resolved,' Susie said and paid for her extra zips.

He tied a piece of string around the box to make it easier for her to carry and Susie slipped it over her wrist.

'Is there anything else you need today?'

'No, thank you,' Susie replied. She bid him good day and left.

It was just another small problem solved, but it seemed there was always something. Running a business was much harder than Susie had dreamed and there were times when she wished she could go back to being her lady's dresser, thinking wistfully of all the times she might have been asked to look after little Marie.

It was as Susie approached the corner of Dressmakers' Alley and Silver Lane that she felt someone snatch at the box she was carrying. Startled, she swung round to see a man huddled in a dark and dirty overcoat that looked military. He was unshaven, with greasy hair and a dark complexion, his eyes glittering with menace. He was tugging furiously at her box, but because it was secured over her wrist, he hadn't been able to snatch it.

'Don't be foolish,' she snapped as he continued to try to pull it from her. 'It is only some zips and wouldn't be of any value to you.'

'Shut yer mouth and give me yer purse then,' the man demanded and produced a knife.

Startled, Susie screamed loudly and held the box of zips in front of her face to protect herself. She felt the knife being plunged into the box and out again, but then, just as she screamed for the second time, she heard a man shout and then running feet, and the brute attacking her heard it too.

'Bitch! I'll remember yer. Yer'll wish yer'd give me yer purse...' he hissed before making off down Silver Lane, with a couple of local men chasing him.

'Are you all right, Miss Collins?' another man's voice asked close by. 'I came as soon as I heard you scream...'

She turned her head and looked at the man who had spoken, recognising him as Eddie Stevens, the owner of the children's clothing workshop opposite Miss Susie. A little older than herself, he was a man with honest eyes and a nice smile.

'Yes, I think so,' Susie replied, shaken by the incident. She found she was breathing deeply and her hands were trembling. She managed to control them. She was fine; the box had saved her and the local lads had chased off her attacker. Susie took a moment and then said, 'I was just shocked because I never thought something like that could happen in broad daylight. He tried to get my box, but when I told him it was only zips, he wanted my purse and attacked me with a knife.'

'I can see where the knife tore the cardboard – at least it protected you.' Eddie looked at her in concern. 'You are sure you're unhurt?'

'Thank you, yes.' Susie nodded. She was shaking inside but didn't want to make a fuss. She gripped the box tighter to stop herself trembling. 'Yes, the box did its job, but I hope the zips aren't damaged. I don't think I can get any more of the same colour.' It was perhaps a stupid thing to say, but she was still in shock.

'Do you still buy from Morrisons?' he asked and shook his head as she replied in the affirmative. 'I order mine from a small factory that started up a few months back. They can dye your zips, silks, cottons and ribbons any colour you want, match them up for you, and they're far cheaper...'

'Really?' Susie looked at him with interest, her feeling of shock receding. Her head went up proudly. She wasn't going to let that brute's attack upset her.

'I'd be happy to give you the address for my supplier,' he said and smiled at her.

'Thank you. That is both kind and generous of you, Mr Stevens.' Susie smiled at him.

He inclined his head. 'Glad to have been of help...'

'I must get back. Winnie is waiting to take her lunch break with Sam.' She felt that if she didn't sit down soon, she might fall down.

'I'll pop that address over to your reception later,' he promised and they parted.

Susie walked on, conscious that although she often saw him going in and out of his workshops, it was the first time she'd stopped to say more than good morning to him in months. He always smiled and waved when he saw her arriving or leaving Miss Susie and she acknowledged him, but they hadn't become friends, although she knew he was friendly with Sam and Winnie. Perhaps because he'd hired some of her best girls when he'd opened. It had taken ages to find the right replacements.

Susie sometimes wondered if she demanded more than it was reasonable to expect, but Yvonne, her head seamstress, told her that good work was simply a matter of applying oneself and shoddy work wasn't to be tolerated.

'Don't worry, Miss Collins,' she'd said when Susie had been anxious that they would never find the right seamstresses. 'They will find their way to us in time and be glad to work for a house like this...'

'I don't think we can call ourselves a house.' Susie had laughed as she'd thanked her. 'We're not up to Worth's standards yet.' The Paris fashion house was renowned for its immaculate work.

'We're not all that far off, though,' Yvonne had told her. 'I don't think their seaming is better than mine. The embroidery is very fine and the cutting – yes, they might have the edge there.'

'Yes, I know.' Susie had employed Carl, who had worked as a cutter for Bert Barrow before she took over the workshop. He had brought in his young nephew, Simon, and was teaching him the trade. They were both skilled, but Susie wasn't sure that they could manage some of Lady Diane's latest designs, which would certainly require very skilled work. As yet, she hadn't commissioned two of the evening gowns, and she wasn't sure whether they would work, although she wanted to discuss it with Carl before she suggested any amendments to Lady Diane.

If they were in a position to deal exclusively with wealthy clients who commissioned a whole wardrobe for each season and did not wish any other lady to be wearing the same dress, the wonderful and daring creations Lady Diane had shown her recently would be immediately snapped up. Many of them could be slightly adapted to fit in with their range and the most popular lines were those favoured by the flapper girls with the flat-chested, dropped-waist look. Their most popular dress had been just such a design and sold several dozen. However, the two designs that were bothering Susie would cost in the region of a hundred pounds each to make and would therefore sell at twice that price in the shops. None of the stores that Miss Susie sold to had yet commissioned a gown selling for over a hundred guineas.

'I am sorry, Miss Collins,' Mrs Harper, of Harpers Emporium, had told her when she'd asked if another similar model appealed. 'I love it. If I was going to a special occasion myself, I might order one for my own use – but I don't think we could sell it in Harpers.'

In fact, the two expensive gowns they had ordered had in the end been sold at a reduced price to a customer who was going to a royal gala.

'I didn't move them to the sale rail, as I promised you I wouldn't,' Sally Harper had told her. 'But this lady is a regular customer for daywear and normally commissions her evening gowns from one of the big fashion houses. She asked if I would make a concession if she bought both and I said yes as none of my other customers had shown an interest.'

Susie had accepted her word and mentioned it to Lady Diane, but although she'd listened and seemed to agree that there was a limit to what they could sell, she had continued to design ever more expensive gowns.

It was strange, because at the beginning, the dresses had been more suitable for a middle range, affordable by women of comfortable circumstances. Susie distinctly recalled Lady Diane saying that she wanted to be able to produce beautiful clothes that the working woman could afford...

Shaking her head, Susie nodded to Winnie as she walked into the reception. 'I'll just take these through and then I'll take your place so you can get off, Winnie.'

Winnie thanked her and got up to get her jacket.

Yvonne looked up as Susie placed the box of zips on the counter. 'You managed to get them then?'

'Yes,' Susie said with a wry smile. 'I kept the others. I thought we might use them in those green wool suits.'

'Yes, possibly,' Yvonne agreed. She looked at the box, saw the damage and frowned. 'What happened?'

'I was attacked by some horrible man in the alley. Some kind of vagrant, I think. Fortunately, some of the local lads saw him off. I hope the knife didn't damage many zips...'

'Are you all right?' she asked, looking shocked. 'Would you like a cup of tea? You should sit down...'

'Yes,' Susie said and did. 'I would like some tea in a minute – are the zips all right?'

Yvonne had opened the box and was looking at them carefully. 'One has been damaged,' she said. 'We won't be able to use that, but the others seem to be all right.' She glanced at Susie anxiously. 'Are you sure you're not hurt?'

'I'm fine. No, really. It was a shock, but I'm all right now.' She smiled in a determined way. 'I will keep the damaged zip and see if I can have it colour matched, just in case. Mr Stevens has just told me about a new place that can match anything.'

'Good, because I think this dress will sell well...' Yvonne held up one she had finished all bar the zip. 'It is priced at five guineas, which means it will sell for ten – and I would buy it if I could afford it. This is one of the best we've done.'

The silky, pale turquoise dress had a low waist, a squared neckline with short sleeves and an elegant tie over the hips in a pristine white satin. They had taken an order for three dozen of the dresses so far and were hoping to get repeats once the dress was in the stores and selling.

'Yes, I love that one,' Susie agreed. 'I would buy it myself.'

'If you don't mind my saying so, Miss Susie...' Yvonne paused. 'I think we would increase our sales if we kept our daywear to this price range or below – and below fifty guineas for the evening wear...' She faltered as Susie's eyes narrowed. 'I am sorry if that offends you, but we're a small East End business and... well, if they can afford to pay two hundred guineas or more, why wouldn't they go direct to the big designers like Hartnell or Worth or...'

'You haven't offended me,' Susie said. 'I have been thinking along the same lines myself, but...' She shook her head. 'I shall mention this to Lady Diane. Oh, don't look so alarmed. I shan't mention your name. We need a clearer picture of what we are trying to do here.'

'I thought her ladyship wanted to bring beautiful clothes to the working woman,' Yvonne said. She picked up a sheaf of designs. 'These latest ones are all so expensive to make. Not many of the big stores will pay that for our clothes.'

'I agree,' Susie said, 'but it must be Lady Diane's decision.' She would speak to her and explain that although the latest designs were wonderful, they might be too expensive to sell...

When she sat down at her desk a little later, Susie saw a little smear of blood on her hand. The knife must have just caught her as she'd defended herself. For a moment she felt sick as she realised that she might have been seriously injured. Susie had known that other young women had been attacked in the area but it had never occurred to her that she would be attacked in broad daylight. He'd threatened her, too. Perhaps she ought to report the incident to the police. She decided she would do so on her way home.

5

Yvonne smiled as her twelve-year-old son John met her when she left work later that evening. It was his birthday and they were going to have fish and chips in the café behind the shop for a treat. She'd asked her son what he wanted and John hadn't hesitated. Fish and chips were a luxury for them, but Yvonne was earning more these days. She had made her son a pair of long trousers and bought him his first pair of smart shoes in tan leather. John was tall for his age and sturdy, with soft fair hair that fell across his forehead and intelligent blue eyes.

'Did you have a good day at school?' she asked as he came and took her shopping basket from her.

John nodded enthusiastically, his face alight with pleasure. 'It was lovely. We had drawing and games – oh and sums. Mr Atkins said there's going to be an Olympic Games this year in Paris and our athletes have a good chance of winning medals.' His enthusiasm was shining out of him. 'Then we read a book. It's called *Ivanhoe* and it is an adventure story from long ago. I liked it...'

'That's lovely, darling,' Yvonne said. 'I'm glad you enjoy school so much. Your teacher, Mr Jones, tells me you are nearly the top of your class in most things – but you don't like geography or spelling.'

'I'm not good at spelling,' John admitted ruefully. 'Mr Jones says I could be an artist or teach it in school, because I am good at showing other children what to do – but I told him I want to go to work as soon as I can leave to help you.'

'Oh no,' Yvonne said quickly. 'You would do better to stay on at school longer; if you work hard, you could be an art teacher. But you could find lots of jobs that you might like, because you are good at making things as well as drawing – and you won't be leaving for years yet.'

'Mr Jones says there are lots of jobs boys can do these days if they work hard at school. He says I am a bright pupil, Mum, and should stay on and take my certificate for higher education.'

'Yes, well, we'll have to see how you feel when the time comes,' Yvonne said and smiled. 'Look, here's our fish and chip shop. Let's hope there's a table for us in the café at the back.' It was a very popular shop, where you could buy your meal and take it home or eat in the large room at the back of the shop.

'I do hope so,' John said. 'It's special to have fish and chips out, Mum. Do you think we can have mushy peas and pickled onions, too?'

'I think we might,' Yvonne said with a smile. 'Oh, look – isn't that your teacher going into the café?'

'Yes, it is.' John laughed up at her. 'He has a lady with him. Do you think she is his girlfriend?'

'Isn't he married then?' Yvonne asked, hardly listening to the answer as she placed her order and was ushered through to the café at the back. It was a long room with several tables, all dark wood, and set with knives and forks, with pots of salt and vinegar and white paper napkins. They found a table in a corner and sat down. Yvonne had her back to the room, but

John had a good view of the other customers. 'What did you say, love?'

'I said Mr Jones held her chair for her and she looked all pink. I bet they're courting, Mum.'

'If they are, that's their business,' Yvonne said without turning her head. 'I thought he was married.'

'I told you, but you didn't listen,' John said. 'He had a wife, but she died and that's why he came to live in London, because he couldn't bear to go on living where he was.'

'That's sad,' Yvonne replied. 'Perhaps he has found a new life and a new friend and I'm glad for him if that's his story.'

'He is nice... He's looking this way... Mr Jones...' John called and waved at him.

'John, don't...' Yvonne reproved, but her son laughed and went on waving.

'He is coming over.' John's face lit up as the man approached. He was of medium height and build, his hair a nondescript brown and his eyes a soft grey. His mouth looked firm but was smiling. Yvonne made to get up, but he waved her down. 'Mr Jones. Mum brought me for fish and chips because it is my birthday.'

'Well, isn't that lovely,' he said and there was a faint lilt to his voice. His smile was gentle and genuine. 'I brought my sister for a treat, because it is her birthday too.'

John chuckled. 'Cor blimey,' he said. 'Mum, did you hear? It's Miss Jones' birthday too.'

'That was a nice thing to do.' Yvonne smiled up at the teacher. 'I hope you enjoy your supper.'

'We shall,' he said, hesitated, then, 'Could you pop into the school one morning or afternoon? I'd like to talk to you about John's progress...' He seemed to give her a message with his eyes.

'I am afraid I work from eight in the morning until six most days,' Yvonne said. 'It is difficult for me to take time off...'

'Well... I could come round on Saturday afternoon, if it is convenient – about five?'

'If you think it necessary...' Yvonne frowned. 'John isn't in any trouble, I hope?'

'Nothing of the sort. He is a bright lad, Mrs White.'

'Good...' Yvonne smiled a little awkwardly. He'd called her Mrs, but she'd never been wed. 'We mustn't keep you from your sister, Mr Jones.'

He nodded. 'Happy birthday, John,' he said, put his hand in his pocket and took out a florin. 'Is it all right to give John some money for sweets?'

Yvonne hesitated and then inclined her head. 'That is kind of you, Mr Jones. Thank you...'

He smiled, put the money on the table beside John, who smiled and thanked him, and went back to his table. Yvonne resisted the urge to watch him walk away.

'Wasn't that kind of him?' John said as she pocketed the coin. 'I shan't spend it on sweets, though. I am saving up for something.' He shook his head as Yvonne looked at him. 'I won't tell you – not yet anyway. It is a surprise.'

'You spend your money on yourself as you want,' Yvonne said. 'You don't get much pocket money, love.'

John earned a shilling a week cleaning the downstairs windows for his mother, and another two shillings for carting coal in for Mr Swarski, the old Polish man two doors down from them, and for cleaning the windows for two other neighbours – Mrs Harding and Violette, a French lady, who wore beautiful dresses that were years old and lived on a pittance. She had once been – to put it politely – a courtesan and her lovers had given her beautiful things. Those days were long gone, though she sometimes entertained Yvonne with tales of her life, when, before the war, she had travelled all over Europe with various wealthy men.

'I will tell you when I am ready,' John said and his face lit up as the waitress brought them two plates of fish and chips, with mushy peas, a plate of bread and butter, pickled onions in a little dish and a glass of orangeade for both of them. 'Cor, Mum, this is so delicious!'

'Yes, it is,' Yvonne agreed, her heart catching at the sight of her son's happy face. It had been a struggle to bring her child up alone with no husband, but she wouldn't change a thing. Yvonne had never been married; she'd given her love unwisely and been left in the lurch, but it hadn't made her bitter. She loved John and it was a pleasure to see him so thrilled over such a small thing – but, of course, it wasn't a small thing. It was a treat for them both. Neither of them got much in the way of luxuries and eating fish and chips in the café was exciting.

Listening to John's chatter soothed Yvonne after a hard day at her job. She loved working at Miss Susie, but it was exacting and she sometimes wondered if perhaps they were trying for too high a standard. She'd given Miss Susie a hint, but, of course, she knew that it was really Lady Diane who made the big decisions. She hoped that her ladyship wouldn't be annoyed when Miss Susie told her that some of her designs just wouldn't do for the market she'd said she was aiming for – not yet anyway. Perhaps in time, when they had gained a reputation for quality workmanship – but even then, there were only so many entitled and wealthy folk who could afford the creations Lady Diane was designing recently.

It might be the crossroads, Yvonne thought, as she ate her chips in silence and listened to John talk. They could go on with their first aim of bringing beautiful clothes to the market for working women – or they could go for the very expensive evening wear, but whether they could sell them was another matter. Unless, of course, Lady Diane was to put her name to her designs.

Then the novelty might just do the trick – but it still wouldn't be what they had set out to do...

'Mr Jones and his sister are leaving.' John's urgent tone broke into Yvonne's thoughts. 'Turn round and wave to them, Mum.'

Yvonne did so reluctantly, but both Mr Jones and his sister waved and smiled as they left.

'They didn't stop long,' John said, eating his last chip but making his orangeade last. He was in no hurry to give up his seat, even though there were customers queuing.

'Perhaps they are going to the pictures,' Yvonne suggested. She reached across the table and squeezed John's hand. 'If I get a bonus next week, I will take you to see a matinee at the Odeon on Saturday. I think the Keystone Cops and a Charlie Chaplin film are on.'

'I had a lovely birthday, Mum,' John said and smiled at her. 'One day when I am rich and famous, I'll take you to The Savoy hotel and we'll have tea...'

'Oh, and what put that idea into your head?' Yvonne asked, laughing.

'I heard one of our teachers saying that's what she'd like to do,' John admitted. 'What's it like, Mum?'

'Oh, it is a big posh place,' Yvonne said. 'I have no idea what it is like inside. I've never been – but I'd like to, so hurry up and get rich and famous...'

John went into a peal of laughter.

Yvonne got up and made her way out through the shop, her son running happily in front of her. It had been a lovely treat, well worth the extra hours she'd worked to provide the gifts she'd given John.

6

'So how are the orders coming along for the autumn range?' Lady Diane asked Susie the next morning as they settled down in her pretty sitting room, which looked out over an immaculate walled garden at her husband, Lord Cooper's, town house in Grosvenor Square. As warm sunshine poured in the long French windows, playing on soft peach and cream upholstery and exquisite gilded chairs, she presided over a tray of tea and home-made cakes that Cook had sent up for them. 'These little almond fancies are delicious, Susie. Please do try them.'

'Yes, thank you, I shall. Cook makes the most delicious tarts and cakes. You are very lucky to have her.' Susie had once been Lady Diane's personal dresser and still lived in her old room in the servants' quarters. Because she often helped Meg, Lady Diane's new maid, to care for her ladyship's clothes, they had decided it suited them both for Susie to continue as she always had for the time being. The only real difference was that she now had far more freedom to come and go as she pleased.

'Yes, we know.' Lady Diane smiled. 'I was recently speaking to Mrs Marchant – an acquaintance of mine, you may recall? – and she was in despair. Mr Marchant had complained for fully an hour about the dinner their cook had served them...' She laughed and then shook her head, her glossy dark hair tumbling about her face in deep waves, a gleam of mischief in her eyes. 'I must apply my mind to business, Susie. You are looking a little stern I think?'

'Oh, I hope not,' Susie replied. 'I am very happy that we have just had another large order for our daywear but...' She hesitated, then, 'I wondered if you had given me the wrong designs for evening gowns. These two would be extremely expensive to make – and I think we would sell only one or two...' She handed Lady Diane the two designs that Yvonne had cavilled at their producing.

'Oh dear me.' Lady Diane laughed gaily. 'I should just think so, Susie. I wondered what I'd done with these...'

'You didn't mean us to produce them in the workshop?' Susie's eyes widened.

'They would cost upwards of two hundred guineas each with the materials I have in mind. No, my intention for these was to ask Yvonne if she would like to make them for me in her own time. She might like to earn a little extra...'

Susie's brow cleared, feeling relieved. 'For yourself? I see. I am sure she would be delighted, my lady. Yvonne is always happy to put in extra hours. Do you have a special occasion in mind – a date she needs to have them finished by?'

'I thought the pale blue I might wear for an official reception we must attend on the sixteenth of June – and the other one, perhaps for our own ball this August...' She smiled at Susie. 'I have some exciting news for you, Susie. Matthew intends to propose to the Honourable Miss Pamela Fairley. You may have heard me speak of her parents? They have a large estate in Devonshire and a house in Hanover Square. We stayed with them in the country for a few weeks last autumn. Lord Henry and I expect to give a dance for their betrothal in August, if of course he is accepted.' Matthew was the eldest son of Lord Henry's first marriage, and now helped his father in all matters of business. Lady Diane was extremely fond of him, for he was always charming and considerate to her.

'I am sure he must be,' Susie replied. Matthew was handsome, good-natured, and wealthy in his own right, because of a bequest from his paternal grandmother. 'Was that the young lady he escorted to Lord Wentworth's ball last Christmas?'

'Yes... I was quite surprised when Lord Henry told me of his intention, for he is still young to marry...'

'Yes, though over twenty-one, so able to make his own decisions. When do you anticipate the wedding?' Susie asked and then, sensing something, 'Are you entirely happy about it, my lady?'

'Oh, she comes from a good family and is very beautiful – though I have found her a little cold in her manner, but perhaps she is shy...' Lady Diane sighed, a little pensive. 'I would think they will marry in the spring next year, perhaps.'

'If he loves her, she must be different with him.'

'Yes, of course.' Lady Diane looked at Susie for a moment, then, 'You have something on your mind, Susie. What are you thinking? Please tell me.'

'Oh, it was just a thought, when I wasn't sure what you intended with these evening gowns...' Susie shook her head. 'I don't think we could sell them as Miss Susie but... No, it isn't important.'

Lady Diane looked thoughtful. 'You were thinking that if I wanted to design expensive evening gowns, that were tailored to suit a particular lady with exquisite workmanship and materials, I would need to put my own name to them?'

Susie's mouth twitched with amusement. 'Am I that easy to read?'

'Yes, sometimes, to me.' Lady Diane laughed. 'We have been close for many years. I dare say you must often anticipate my thoughts.' Susie acknowledged the truth of this. 'I am not yet ready to go as far as to use my own name – but the idea is at the back of my mind. If the gowns Yvonne makes for me are well received, I may, in confidence, invite a few friends to place orders for similar gowns. In a year or two, I might then consider having a Lady Diane line of evening wear, which would be expensive to produce, exclusive designs.'

'Yes, I understand now,' Susie said, relieved. 'You love beautiful clothes and it must be tempting to design the very best quality – but, if we wish to stand firm in our aim to produce good clothes for the average woman, we must keep them below a certain figure or they will not sell.'

'It's just that the ideas keep coming. I think a lot of people will be looking for something with an Egyptian flavour, because of that truly wonderful find – such beautiful objects in that tomb.' The papers had been full of the exciting discovery by Howard Carter for months as the treasures of the Pharaoh's tomb were gradually brought to light and photographed, and anything Egyptian had become all the rage amongst the wealthy ladies of society.

'Ladies who can afford to indulge themselves, I dare say – but I doubt if many working girls would buy something they might only wear a few times...'

'Am I making it difficult for you, Susie?' Lady Diane asked apologetically. 'I do tend to get carried away by my designs at times, but I know we need to be original and stylish to make us stand out. You must tell me if you think some of my designs too fanciful.'

'Oh, they are all gorgeous,' Susie said, shaking her head. 'But perhaps we might use slightly less extravagant trimmings to bring down the cost of our daywear.'

'I do not know what to say.' Lady Diane was thoughtful, her lovely face reflecting her doubts. Her shining hair fell softly over her cheek and she brushed it back with an impatient flick of her fingers. 'Ten shillings must be a consideration for a working girl, naturally – but the buttons we selected and the velvet for the collar were so perfect, I hardly think it wise to change them...'

'Shall I see what I can find similar but cheaper and show you?' Susie asked. 'Or shall we hold to our original price?' She frowned. 'One of our customers told me she would place a larger order if the costumes were cheaper.'

'Then perhaps she should look for another supplier,' Lady Diane suggested. 'Unless we hold to our original ideals, we are nothing, Susie. Yes, I would like every woman to be able to afford my designs but...' She drummed her neatly filed fingernails on the little table beside her, her brow furrowed. 'Do you agree with me? Please, you must tell me if you think me wrong.'

'I do agree,' Susie replied. 'We set out to supply excellence and that is our ideal – but we have not achieved quite the level of orders for our autumn range as I'd hoped.'

'Even with the two orders you spoke of earlier?'

'Even so,' Susie replied. 'I shall investigate this new supplier and see what I feel about the quality of their materials, bring some examples to show you.'

'Yes, please do so,' Lady Diane said. 'Perhaps I am too demanding.' She sighed. 'I do want the business to be a success, Susie, and I promised I would not interfere in your decisions with the day-to-day running of the workshop. I will look at these examples – but if you decide that the change must be made, I will abide by your decision.'

'Thank you – but I want you to be happy with what we do, otherwise there is little point in it,' Susie replied. 'It may be that I can buy more cheaply without reducing the quality and, if so, that will solve the problem.'

Lady Diane smiled. 'Oh, Susie, what should I have done without you? I fear I am far too spoiled. You must do as you think best...'

A knock at the door interrupted them and, at her invitation to enter, it opened and Lord Henry came in. He was carrying his baby daughter wrapped in a beautiful soft wool shawl of white and smiling.

'Henry...' Lady Diane smiled, rose and went to greet them. 'You've brought Marie to me.'

'Nurse was on her way down, but I said she might give the child to me.' He smiled fondly at his wife. 'I fear she disapproved, but, after some persuasion, I was allowed to take her.'

Lady Diane took the baby in her arms, smiling down at her. Already, Marie had enough hair to see that it would be dark and wavy like her mother's. She was awake, her blue eyes wide with wonder as she stared up at her mother. 'She is getting heavier,' Lady Diane said, laughing as Marie waved a pink fist at her. 'See, Susie – see how beautiful she is...'

'Yes, she is gorgeous.' Susie smiled at the picture of her friend and employer with her beloved child. 'If that is everything, I ought to go,' she said, looking at the gilt clock on the mantel.

'Oh yes.' Lady Diane was nursing her child on her lap, cooing to her, Lord Henry looking on fondly. 'I am sure you are right, Susie – please do as you think best.'

Susie got up to gaze at the baby. She was indeed beautiful and would no doubt be spoiled by her doting parents. In most aristo-cratic households, children were seldom seen, and visits to their parents short and regimented by their strict nannies, but it was plain to see that even Lord Henry was besotted with little Marie. Susie did not blame him and somewhere inside her there was a longing and need she had hardly known she had until Marie was first shown to her. She thrust the thought from her mind. She had long ago accepted that she would never have the happiness of being a mother, for she had never wished, nor been invited, to marry anyone she could care for.

Dismissed, Susie left them to their private time. She had known that Lady Diane would agree eventually to the small changes she felt necessary at the workshop, but Susie would never make fundamental changes without her consent. However, she was a little anxious that the orders for the autumn range were not yet as high as she'd hoped. Susie wanted the business to succeed, otherwise she would feel that she had failed.

'You shouldn't worry so much,' Mrs Collins said after Susie had unburdened herself of her doubts. 'If her ladyship is happy, then so must you be, Susie. It might be that you cannot make profits for some time – but if her ladyship wishes to continue that is all you need bother your head over. I dare say she could stand a few losses if necessary – but it won't be, because you will make it work.'

'You always make me feel better, Mum,' Susie replied. 'Thank you for the delicious sponge cake and tea. I had best get back now...'

Mrs Collins caught her arm as she bent to kiss her cheek, looking up at her anxiously. 'Are you happy? I know you enjoyed looking after her ladyship, dressing her and caring for her. Do you miss it? Do you regret doing as she asked and taking on this business of hers?'

'I still help Lady Diane choose her clothes for special occasions,' Susie replied a little wistfully. 'In some ways, I do wish it was still the same, Mum – but his lordship begged me to do it when she was so ill after the birth of her child and she does enjoy her designing now that she is quite well again...'

'And?' Mrs Collins insisted.

'Nothing...' Susie smiled. 'Lady Diane told me that Mr Matthew is going to propose to a young lady and they will give a dance for them in August.'

'Now that is good news,' Mrs Collins said and smiled. 'He is a pleasant young man, Susie, and a big help to you with the accounts, I think?'

'Yes – and he showed me the easiest way to keep them.'

Mrs Collins nodded. 'Have you met his young lady?'

'No. She and her parents will no doubt come to the house for dinner once they are engaged. I have seen her mother – a very attractive lady.' She dropped a kiss on her mother's head. 'I really must go...'

Susie was feeling better as she left her mother's house. She could not explain the wistful feeling that had come over her as she'd watched Lady Diane with her daughter. Marie was such a beautiful child and... But no, she would not regret anything. Susie had chosen her life. Love and marriage had not come her way so she must try hard to find satisfaction in running the business Lady Diane had dreamed of.

Making up her mind to visit the new supplier and compare prices, Susie walked quickly and was soon at the junction of Dressmakers' Alley, Silver Lane and Clark Street. Clark street was wider and busy with delivery vans to various cafés and shops. She saw that another small business had recently started up, pausing to look at the notice declaring that it was to sell high-quality shoes.

As she stood there, Susie saw that the newsagents across the road had its windows boarded up. She frowned, wondering what had happened and then saw the owner come out to put a notice up saying he was still open. Susie crossed the street to speak to him.

'Good morning, Mr Harding. What happened to your windows?'

'I was broken into two nights ago,' he said, nodding to her. 'And I'm not the only one round here to be done over. Be careful, Miss Susie. You don't want to leave much cash on your premises. There have been a lot of burglaries lately around here.'

'Oh, I am sorry,' Susie sympathised instantly. 'Did you lose a lot?'

'All my stock of cigarettes and half a week's takings,' Mr Harding replied. 'I'd just had fresh supplies in...' He shook his head. 'Beats me how they knew.'

'It is worrying,' Susie replied. 'I hope it won't mean you have to close down.'

'I had some insurance, but they never want to pay up, do they? But I'll manage,' he replied. 'You make sure you keep all your doors and windows locked tight – you've got some expensive stuff...'

Susie thanked him for his concern and walked on. She'd known that some folk had been burgled in the area recently, but this was close to home – and she couldn't help wondering if it might happen to them. It was just one more thing to worry about...

7

Rusty swayed as she pushed her pram through ill-lit streets. Her mind was fuddled by two glasses of port and lemon, for she hadn't eaten much that day, but she knew where she was headed. There was a place at the back of that clothing workshop in Dressmakers' Alley. She'd discovered it one cold night in the winter. It had once been a coal store, but now it was just an empty shed, because the posh people who had taken over the premises had a better store for their fuel now. It had been safe and warm and she'd even left some of her bags there – but then he'd arrived, the man with the broken nose. Somebody had told her he called himself Pug, but she doubted it was his name. He looked to be the vicious sort and Rusty tried to stay clear of his kind. She'd found him sleeping there one night and he'd woken and threatened her with his fist.

She had money in her pocket, though. Rusty chuckled as she thought of the piece of old gold she'd been given when she was begging round the doors. The woman had given her a worn-out coat, which was fraying on the cuffs, but when Rusty had looked in the pocket, she'd discovered a hole – and deep inside the lining was a heavy gold brooch with a broken clasp. The money she'd got for it from the pawn shop had bought her several drinks and she still had some notes tucked in her clothes.

Rusty knew right off it was valuable. Once upon a time, she'd owned such beautiful things herself. As an actress – though never a leading lady – Rusty had been pretty and funny, and the men had given her gifts when she'd allowed them to take her to supper. Most had wanted to take her to bed, but she'd chosen her lovers with care, and she'd had a good life. She was smiling at her memories as she stopped walking. The back entrance to that Miss Susie's place was just ahead of her and, if *he* wasn't there, she could soon be warm and cosy for the night.

Hearing something, a slight scraping noise, she stopped in her tracks and peered into the darkness. Was that the flicker of a torch? Curious, and a little tipsy, she moved closer – and then she saw them. Two men at the back of the dressmakers' place; it looked as if they were attempting to break in, but the small window they were at had thick iron bars across it.

'I told yer it was as 'ard ter get in 'ere as the bloody Bank of England,' a voice said irritably. 'Come on, Pug, we're wastin' time. I know another place we can do…'

'Buggers! I'm owed…' another voice muttered as Rusty turned to leave, her pram rattling over a loose cobblestone. 'Who's there…?'

Rusty tried to run. She abandoned her pram and shuffled off as fast as she could, but her feet wouldn't move well enough. She was panting and frightened, because she knew those voices – and she knew they were bad men. Oh, Rusty knew secrets all right. That man Pug had a lot of them. He might think he was clever, but Rusty was a lady of the night, for she seldom slept more than an hour or so, wandering from place to place, trying to keep warm, to find somewhere safe, because the streets weren't. There were too many bad men around in the dark hours and Rusty saw them all; she saw what they did, the folk they robbed.

The big man caught up to her, grabbing her shoulder, and spinning her round to face him. 'You were spying on us,' he growled. 'Are you runnin' orf to the bloody coppers?'

'Why would I?' Rusty cried, frightened as much by the malice in his look as the iron grip on her arm. 'I ain't doin' nuthin' – just lookin' fer a place ter sleep.'

'I've seen her about,' said the man who had followed. He was smaller, his face covered by a muffler, but she knew him. 'Give 'er a clout, and let her go...'

'She's seen us, seen our faces... we can't let her go,' the bigger one said. 'We'll have ter get rid of 'er... Use that knife of yours to gut her.'

'I ain't goin' ter swing fer murder,' the shorter man said. 'You want her dead, Pug, do it yerself...' He turned his back and walked off.

Rusty tried to move. She knew that she had to get away, but her feet seemed glued to the ground and she couldn't move them. 'Don't hurt me,' she whimpered. 'I've got a few bob in me pocket. I'll give it ter yer – and I won't never tell.'

'I wish I could believe yer, but yer could ruin everythin'...' he said and brought his hand out from his pocket.

Rusty saw the flash of light on metal and screamed. She struggled and fought, begging for her life, but the hand was raised, a heavy instrument cracked on the side of her head and she felt blood on her lips, tasting it briefly, and then he hit her again. Everything went black.

* * *

The man called Pug stood looking down at her. He felt a twist of nerves in his stomach as he glanced uneasily over his shoulder. He'd never killed before – well, only in a fight, not cold blood. He felt panicked. Her body couldn't be left here. He must take it to the river, get rid of her, and her pram, too.

He threw his weapon into the pram and then lifted her body in after it. She weighed hardly anything and he was used to hard manual labour. Glancing round, he felt a shiver of unease. Had he been seen? He had a feeling there was someone in the shadows, but he dared not investigate. He had a muffler he'd pulled up over half his face now, so hopefully he would not be recognised. Not that anyone knew who he was. No one had recognised him since he'd turned up looking for revenge on Bert Barrow, but the years since he was here had aged and changed him.

He pushed the pram through darkened streets, heart racing, fearful of discovery, but saw no one. No one challenged him. No one screamed murderer. It seemed to take forever, his guilt haunting him, a shadow that would never leave him. Yet what else could he have done? The old woman had seen him. She knew him well. She'd heard them planning to break into that workshop – she could have brought the cops down on him.

Well, she wouldn't now.

He'd arrived at the river. He tipped her body at the edge and then picked the pram up and threw it into the water, his weapon with it.

He glanced around him, peering into the darkness, but he was alone, apart from a water rat sniffing at the river's edge. A bird called from somewhere and startled him, but no human was near. Grinning now, feeling a return of his confidence, he walked back the way he'd come.

After he'd gone, a man's shadow moved from the deep shade of a derelict warehouse. It walked to the water's edge and looked down at the face of the old woman. An indrawn breath was heard, a half-sob or a sigh of regret, and a muffled curse, then the shadow turned and melted back in the depths of the darkness.

8

Lilly was washing the window of her flower shop when Miss Susie walked past. No matter how often the windows were cleaned, they were soon dirty again and it had rained again during the night. It really was a wet month this May. Dark clouds chased across the sky and it looked as if her work might be in vain, but she liked the glass to sparkle when her customers came to look at the beautiful arrangements she had made and displayed.

She waved to Miss Susie, but she looked lost in thought and didn't see her.

Across the road, the street cleaner was sweeping the rubbish that blew into the gutters. Dressmakers' Alley often seemed to act like a funnel, the wind blowing through in a great rush, scattering litter everywhere.

'Would you like a cup of tea, Ernie?' Lilly called to the elderly man, who had leaned on his big brush for a breather. Sweeping the streets was a hard job, but he was glad to do it, for the few shillings he earned kept him independent and made sure he had a bed at night.

'Bless yer, Lilly.' Ernie's lined face lit up as he came across the road to her. 'Them windows of yourn look a treat.'

'Come through to the back,' Lilly said. 'I boiled the kettle a few minutes ago, so it won't take a minute to reheat.'

'Nay, lass, I'll wait here,' Ernie said. 'It wouldn't do fer yer posh customers to see me in there. You bring a mug out ter me and I'll leave it here by the door when I've done.'

Lilly didn't argue. She'd asked him to come in out of the chill several times when he was at his work, but his answer was always the same so it was up to him. She knew he had no home but spent his nights in a hostel or on a park bench if he didn't have his shilling to pay for a bed. He seldom had the luxury of a bath and clean clothes, which cost more than a shilling, but did his best to keep himself decent, when he could. Lilly felt sympathy for him, wishing she knew more of his story.

She made the tea as quickly as she could and took a mug of strong brew with two sugars out to him. He had taken the chance to rest for a while, his muffler round his ears as it had started to drizzle. He'd been looking tired, but his smile was something to see when she offered him the mug of hot tea and two ginger biscuits.

'You're a rare one, Lilly,' he told her. 'Go back inside, lass, and drink your tea. I'll leave yer mug by the door, as I promised.'

Lilly nodded and left him to it. She wished she could do more, but Ernie was proud, and perhaps not the worst off of her lame ducks. He wasn't the only one to linger outside Lilly's shop and Rusty, the bag lady, would stand and stare in for half an hour or more if Lilly was too busy to come out and offer her a mug of tea. Rusty had red hair with patches of orange and grey; it was wild and wiry and she wore a battered black hat on top with a drooping silk rose that she'd once been given by a fine gentleman, as well as a mangy fur coat. 'When I was young and beautiful and the gents queued up to take me to supper,' she'd told Lilly. 'I 'ad them all after me then...'

Rusty was only too happy to tell Lilly her story. She'd been an actress and had lots of lovers, but her beauty had long gone and she, like Ernie, had no home or family. However, Rusty did not work; she preferred to beg round the doors for rags she could sell, or play on the sympathy of those who had a soft heart, like Lilly.

Now she thought about it, Lilly hadn't seen Rusty that morning. That was unusual, because she came by at least once a day, on the chance that Lilly would have something for her.

* * *

Lilly was just finishing a beautiful basket of flowers when the shop bell rang and she went through into the front shop, smiling as she saw her brother, Joe. 'Would you like a mug of tea?' she asked him. 'I was just thinking of making one.'

'I wouldn't say no,' Joe said, following her back into the little room, where she boiled her kettle on a single gas ring.

'Lilly... I've got a bit of bad news...'

Lilly looked at her brother sharply. 'Not Jeb...?' she gasped, her heart jumping with fright. Had something happened to her husband? 'Has he had an accident?'

'Not to my knowledge,' Joe said, but he still looked serious. 'You know that woman who carries her bags with her in an old pram... Rusty? You give her tea and the odd shillin', don't yer?'

Lilly nodded, a tingling at the back of her neck. She could see by his face that something was very wrong, and she'd wondered where Rusty was earlier that day. 'Yes, I know her. What's wrong? Is she ill? She had a bad cough all winter...'

'She's dead, murdered...' Joe said and Lilly's face paled as she caught her breath at the shock. 'I'm sorry, lass. I thought you should be told...'

'How do you know she was murdered?' Lilly asked and sat down heavily, her legs suddenly shaky. 'Who told yer?'

'She was found down by the river last night and... her head was bashed in.' Joe took his tea and drank a big mouthful. 'I know it ain't a nice thing ter tell yer – but with Jeb away... I wanted to make sure you take care, Lilly. No walking home by yourself at night.'

'Why would anyone want to kill Rusty?' Lilly asked, distressed. Tears started in her eyes.

'The police seemed to think she might have been robbed – her bags were missin'...'

Lilly shook her head in disbelief. 'But she only has rags and a few bits, like her old tin mug. Who would want those?'

Joe shook his head. 'No idea – perhaps someone who had even less. She might have been given something good when she begged round the houses.' He frowned. 'Someone said he'd seen her yesterday evenin', in the pub round the corner – The Blue Ruin? He said she was drinking port and lemon. They cost more than a shillin'...'

'You think someone saw her and went after her to rob her...' Lilly couldn't go on. Her eyes were wet with tears now, her shoulders shaking.

'If she was given something she could sell for a few quid, she might have gone to the pub for a drink and... whoever killed her must have followed her out and taken his chance.' Joe looked grim. 'Some days you've got several pounds in your basket when you walk home. I don't want you ending up like that poor old woman, Lilly.'

A shiver went through her and she inclined her head. 'I'll be glad when Jeb is back.'

'When will he be home?' Joe asked her.

'He might get back tonight – or tomorrow.'

'I'll be here this evening,' Joe said. 'I'm not lettin' you walk home alone, Lilly. There's two of you to look after now, remember.' He smiled fondly at her.

'All right,' Lilly agreed. 'I've been walkin' home with some of the girls, but Winnie is meeting Sam this evenin'. They are goin' out to the pictures, so they want to get home and changed quick... Yes, thank you, Joe. I'll be glad of your company.'

'I will be 'ere at six,' Joe promised. 'You wait in the shop until I come.'

Lilly thanked him and then the doorbell rang again and she went through to serve her customer: a gentleman who wanted flowers for his wife's birthday. Lilly made him a beautiful bouquet and he went off with a smile on his face.

When she returned, Joe had left by the back door. Lilly gave a little shiver and relocked it. Normally, she didn't bother. She knew most of the people in the area, either by sight or by name. Most were friendly and she'd always felt quite safe, sometimes leaving the door unlocked when she was in the front shop. Now she thought it might be best to keep it locked for a while – until the murderer had been caught.

She wondered if it was the same man who had attacked some girls the previous week – and then there was the attempt to steal Miss Susie's parcel. It might be the same person, but it might not. Lilly was glad her brother was coming to fetch her and hoped her husband would be home from his buying trip soon. People must know that she carried cash with her on her way home from work. If there was a violent thief in the area, she couldn't be too careful.

Lilly's eyes were still damp with the tears she'd shed for Rusty. Poor, poor Rusty. She'd had so little. Why would anyone want to attack and kill her? She'd liked the old woman and always tried to give her something, even if it was only a mug of tea. Why did folk have to be so wicked?

* * *

'Have you heard about the murder?' Sibby Thomas asked Winnie when she got back from her lunch break. 'It was that old lady with the funny-coloured hair who used to walk by with all those bags in a pram. They found her by the river this morning...'

Winnie looked at her, a feeling of sick anxiety in her stomach. Just over a year ago, her own mother had been murdered for a silver coffee pot and she'd been suspected of the crime for a while. Only with the help of her good friends had she been cleared of any wrongdoing. 'That is awful,' she replied, her throat tight with emotion, perhaps as much for her late mother as the old woman she'd hardly known. 'Who told you, Sibby?'

'Joe Ross – you know, Lilly's sister...' Sibby bit her lip. 'We go out sometimes. I met him when I was on the way to fetch my shoes from the menders. I thought he might ask me to get wed – but he's a slowcoach and I go out with another feller now and then just to annoy him...'

'I know Joe,' Winnie replied. 'He's a good friend of Sam's. I wouldn't play fast and loose with him if I were you, Sibby. You might lose him for good.' A little shudder took her. 'That poor woman murdered – who would want to harm her?' She shook her head in disbelief.

'She was always asking for money or anything she could sell,' Sibby said with a shrug, obviously not much bothered. 'I kept well away from her – she smelled awful sometimes. But it makes you afraid to walk down the street, doesn't it?'

'Yes, it gives me the shivers,' Winnie agreed. 'You should be careful walking home at night for a while, Sibby. We all must until the police catch whoever did it.'

'I usually walk with Yvonne and others.' Sibby hunched her shoulder. 'Are you meeting Sam this evening?'

'Yes, he is taking me to the pictures.' Winnie smiled. 'We shall go straight home and get changed before the second showing.'

'I'd like to go to the pictures,' Sibby said wistfully. 'It's my birthday next week and I'd hoped Joe would take me – but he says he is busy that night.'

The phone rang beside Winnie then and she thrust the disturbing news of the murder from her mind, reaching for the receiver. 'Miss Susie – how may I help you?'

'Ah yes,' a female voice answered. 'Are you the young lady I spoke to earlier? Richards dress shop here – I was considering an order for those silk tea gowns...'

'Yes. I am Miss Brown. Can I take an order for you, Miss Sanders?'

'Oh, you remembered me... Well, yes. I have decided I will place an order for that tea gown I liked, in sizes 36 through to 42 hip. I will have it in both the blue and that pretty yellow silk I saw when I visited last week.'

'So that is eight of the silk tea gowns altogether,' Winnie said, smiling to herself. She had thought this order would come in and was pleased she was right. 'Was there anything else, Miss Sanders?'

'Yes, we have decided to take that pale blue tweed suit from the autumn range. We need all the sizes up to a 48 for that one. I think that will appeal to all ages – I particularly liked the buttons and the velvet collar...'

'Yes, they are lovely quality,' Winnie said. 'Thank you, Miss Sanders – that is seven of the tweed suit...'

'Oh, no. I think we will take two in each size,' came the answer.

'I am certain they are going to be popular and reordering isn't always as successful...'

'Thank you. I will put your orders in immediately. The tea gowns will be ready in two weeks and the suits later in the year – August delivery, I believe. We like a ten per cent deposit on all orders.'

'Yes, of course. I shall pay you as soon as I have your statement. Thank you...'

Winnie smiled as she replaced the receiver. That was the third order she'd been given for those particular suits that morning. It seemed as if the initial resistance to the price was gradually being overcome because of the quality. She would go through to the workrooms and give the order to Miss Susie as soon as she had typed it up. It looked as if the autumn range might be a success after all.

9

'I will leave you here,' Sibby said to Yvonne and another girl who had walked with her from the workshops. 'I'll be fine now...' She waved her hand to a young man standing on the corner of the Commercial Road. 'That's Rod Wilkins – he's been after taking me out for ages, but he always wants to go to the pub. I'd rather go to the pictures or a dance.'

'Yes. I'm saving up to take my John to the pictures,' Yvonne told her with a smile. 'Young boys always need something, though.' A small sigh escaped her. 'I don't mind a drink in the pub now and then – or I didn't when I was your age, but I wouldn't want to sit there night after night like some girls do...' Young women often accompanied their boyfriends to the pub for a night out. No decent young woman would dream of going there alone. 'If he is serious about courting you, ask him to take you to the cinema for a change.'

'Rod is good fun,' Sibby said, but her pretty face looked sulky. She had medium brown hair and hazel eyes, her mouth soft and sensual when she smiled. 'See you tomorrow...'

They parted company and Sibby ran to greet the handsome

young man, who had clearly been hanging around in the hope of seeing her. He greeted her with a grin and Sibby smiled up at him invitingly and then took his arm.

Yvonne walked on. Sibby was a good seamstress and a nice enough girl, if a little flighty. Yvonne was carrying a parcel of expensive material in her basket, intending to make a start on the evening gown Lady Diane had requested. The silk was so fine and delicate that she'd felt a thrill of pleasure just to touch it and thought the task set her an honour and the extra money would make her life easier now.

'Before Lady Diane asked me to work on her gowns, I had never seen anything as fine as this,' she'd told Miss Susie when the material came into the workshop. 'I'm not sure my work is good enough. I would hate her ladyship to feel she had wasted her money.'

'She was very satisfied with the alterations you made to her gowns when she was increasing,' Miss Susie had answered with a smile. 'Your work is always excellent, Yvonne, and her ladyship is not in a hurry. You will have plenty of time to finish it.'

'Oh, I shall love doing it,' Yvonne had assured her. 'And the extra money will be so useful. John grows so fast these days and he needs new shoes for school again.'

'Children are expensive,' Miss Susie had sympathised. 'My mother worked all hours for us when we were children – but we never went without much. Our clothes might have been from the nearly new stall on the market, but there was always food on the table.'

'Yes, that is most important,' Yvonne had agreed. A feeling of satisfaction had stolen over her then for she had managed to raise her son decently despite having him out of wedlock. She'd suffered insults and hardship to keep the child she'd loved, but she would do it all again. For years, she'd regretted the brief love affair with a man she had not known was already married until it was too late. His promises and declarations of passionate love had led a young Yvonne astray. She was now in her twenty-ninth year, John having been conceived when she was but sixteen.

'I'll leave you now, Yvonne...' Her thoughts were interrupted and she turned to the young woman who had walked silently beside her after they had parted from Sibby.

'Yes, you're home now, Sylvia. See you tomorrow.'

The girl smiled and ran across the street to the row of terraced houses.

Yvonne looked about her. She had only to walk round the corner and she was home. A couple of men were standing just ahead of her on the pavement, smoking and sharing a joke. Yvonne knew them both. They were finishing their cigarettes before going into their homes. One of them raised his cap to her as she passed and she inclined her head. She was safe enough now, nearly home.

All the chatter in the workrooms had been about the murder of the elderly bag lady. Most of the girls had known Rusty, at least by sight. Some were in the habit of giving her a couple of coppers if she asked, most were saddened by her demise, but all of them were aware of a dark shadow hanging over the lanes. The previous assaults on young women had not been serious, a case of theft of a purse was the worst thing to have happened – apart from the knife attack on Miss Susie, which most of the girls were ignorant of. The talk of a vicious murderer in the area had sent shivers down Yvonne's spine and carrying material worth a small fortune had made her uneasy, but she was home now.

The door of her house flew open as Yvonne approached it and her son came flying out. 'I've finished my homework,' he told her. 'What's for supper, Mum? I'm hungry.'

'Me too,' Yvonne said and ruffled his hair. 'We're having vegetable soup and Welsh rabbit on toast tonight.'

'I love melted cheese on toast,' John said. 'I filled the kettle for you, Mum. I know you like a cuppa when you get in.'

The kettle was nearly at boiling point on the range, which her son must have made up when he got home. She banked it with coke every morning so that it burned slowly all day, and John knew how to give it a poke and add some coal to get it really hot. The soup she'd made the previous day would reheat by the time she'd drunk her tea.

Her smile was loving as she looked at him. 'Did you have a good day, John?'

He nodded vigorously. 'We played cricket in the school field, Mum. Mr Wright says I'm good at all sports. He thinks I should take up running and run for the school. We have races at the end of the summer term. And football. I'm good at that too.'

'Well, you don't have to decide. You have at least another three years at school.'

'If I take my certificate,' he agreed. 'Perhaps I should go to work as soon as I can leave, Mum. Make it easier for you.'

'You will stay at school for as long as you need to,' she said. 'We manage perfectly well, John. In a year or two, you will know what you want to do with your life.'

John accepted this and got up to fetch the soup bowls as his mother went to stir the soup on the range, its delicious aroma filling the room. 'Maybe I'll be a train driver,' he said and she smiled.

'Yes, perhaps you will,' she agreed.

Hearing a knock at her kitchen door, she asked John to answer it, but before he could reach it, it had opened and her next-door neighbour poked her head in.

'That smells good,' she said. 'Sorry to be a nuisance, Yvonne, but could I borrow a cup of sugar?'

'Out of funds again, Maisie?' Yvonne asked but not unkindly. Maisie was the mother of six children. Her husband had a good job on the docks, but he was fond of his drink and too often Maisie got less than she needed in her housekeeping purse. She struggled to keep her family fed and clean, her youngest still a toddler, making it impossible for her to work. 'Yes, of course you can, but I'll want it back.'

Yvonne really had little hope that anything she allowed Maisie to borrow would ever be returned, but she liked her and understood all too well how hard it was to manage on very little money.

'I'll pay yer back one day,' Maisie said, producing an enamel mug, which Yvonne filled almost to the brim. 'Thanks, Yvonne. I'd keep an eye on young John if yer wanted a night out with yer friends.'

'Thank you, but I have work to do,' Yvonne said. 'I'll remember you offered, Maisie. Anything else you need?' She cursed herself for a fool as Maisie hesitated.

'Wouldn't mind a drop of that soup – if you've got plenty?'

Yvonne poured soup into two bowls that John carried carefully to the table. Seeing that there was a mugful left, Yvonne poured it into an enamel mug she seldom used and handed it to Maisie. 'I'll want that back...'

'I'll bring it round later...' Maisie promised and went off, carefully carrying her borrowed sugar and the mug of soup.

'You shouldn't let her take advantage of you, Mum,' John said after the door had closed behind Maisie.

'She can do with a bit of help,' Yvonne said. 'We're lucky, John. I've got a good job and I earn extra by working in the evenings. Charity begins at home. We shouldn't begrudge a little for a friend.'

'I don't,' John replied, polishing off the last of his soup. 'That was lovely, Mum. I just don't think she gives anythin' back to you.'

'Perhaps she will one day,' Yvonne said. 'I don't mind either way.'

John got up as she began to prepare the cheese, which would be melted with a little mustard and a drop of stout in a saucepan. Yvonne would finish the stout later, before she went to bed; it helped her to sleep on the rare occasions she treated herself. He cut two thick slices from the loaf, which was a day old. They would finish it up for breakfast as a bit of fried bread with some scrambled egg and she would buy a fresh loaf on her way home from work the next day. It was an economy they had always practised. John didn't mind that they had to be careful. He knew his mother worked long hours but wished he might help her more.

'One day I'll be rich and I'll buy you anything you want,' he declared as she buttered toast.

'Oh bless you.' Yvonne smiled, her eyes moist due to his expression of love. 'We're all right, my darling. I don't want anything I haven't got. Why should I when I've got you?' She took the lightly toasted bread and spooned the soft cheese onto it, the smell making her mouth water. 'Tuck in, John. I've got a dress to make for a lovely lady and then I'll be able to buy your new school shoes.'

* * *

John kicked at the bottle he'd found lying in the gutter just a few hundred yards from his home. None of his friends had yet made an appearance and he didn't have a football of his own. Mickey from number ten had a much-patched leather ball that they had to blow up with his dad's bike pump every time they played, but he hadn't appeared yet.

There were no fields or parks with trees he could climb in the vicinity and little a young lad on his own could find to do. He was just trying to decide whether he should knock at Mickey's door or go back into the house – but his mother had some expensive material spread out over the table and she'd asked him to go out and play for a while.

'No mates today?'

John looked up as the man spoke. He'd seen him around a few times, collecting money from the grocery shop at the end of the road, and from the betting shop in the back room at the Cock and Hen pub just down the road. That was illegal, of course, but no one told on the landlord, because most of the men liked a bet on the horses now and then.

'Nah, not yet,' John replied. 'Mickey's got the football so I'm waitin' for him.'

'You're Yvonne White's lad, ain't yer?'

'Yeah. Do you know her?' John asked, looking at him curiously.

'Seen her about,' the man said. 'My name is Tam – would yer like to earn a couple of bob?'

'Might do,' John replied, trying to hide his eagerness. 'I ain't doin' anything bad for it.'

'I just want to place a bet,' Tam told him. He took a piece of paper with something written on it and two white notes from his pocket. 'You know where to go? Tell Fred I want the lot on the nose. Can yer do that?'

John thought quickly. His mother would not approve of his placing an illegal bet for this man, but two shillings was a lot of money and it was easily earned. 'Yeah. I know Fred. He gave me a sweet once when I fetched a bottle of beer for Mickey's dad...'

'Fred's all right,' Tam agreed and grinned at him. 'Do this proper and I might find more jobs fer yer – earn a bit fer yerself, buy a football of yer own.'

John held out his hand for the money. 'What are these?' he asked, looking at the crisp white notes. 'I ain't seen one of these sort before.'

'That's a five-pound note,' Tam told him. 'Ten pounds I'm trustin' yer with, so yer better not let me down.' His eyes glittered with menace suddenly. 'You bring the bettin' slip back to me now. No runnin' orf with the money.'

'I won't let yer down, mister,' John said. He took the money and the slip of paper and ran off to the pub.

'I'll be waitin' 'ere...'

John didn't stop to look back. He was a bit scared of having so much money in his hand and stuffed it into his trouser pockets.

The Cock and Hen was busy and he could hear the sounds of raucous laughter from inside and smell the mixture of spilled stale beer and other less pleasant odours as he went round to the door at the back. There he hesitated, not quite sure what to do, but a man came from the toilet in the yard and looked at him suspiciously.

'What are yer looking fer?' he asked. 'Clear orf, kid. Yer too young ter be drinkin'.'

'I need to see Fred. Someone sent me...'

The man nodded, went in through the back door and yelled for Fred.

John shuffled his feet, half wishing he hadn't come, and then Fred came out. He smiled as he saw him.

'What are you after then, lad? Yer mum want a bottle of ginger beer?'

'Not today, Fred. Tam sent me...' He handed Fred the paper and the two five-pound notes. 'He said he wants the lot on the nose...'

Fred looked at the paper and the money and frowned, then back at John. It was a very large bet, far more than he was used to dealing with. 'You say Tam sent yer?' He shook his head over it, because it had never happened before. 'I wouldn't have thought... He must know somethin' I don't...' He looked doubtful for a moment, because although Tam was well known to him, this bet didn't sit well with him. 'All right. I'll lay the bet orf. I can't stand the loss of so much brass if the nag wins, which it didn't ought to – but why did he send you?'

'Dunno,' John replied. 'Said he'd give me two bob, so I agreed...'

'He's up to somethin',' Fred muttered. 'No skin off my nose. I'll give yer his slip. Take it back to him, lad...'

'Thanks, Fred.' John grinned as he took it. 'Easiest two bob I ever earned.'

Fred hesitated, then, 'I might have a few jobs if yer want ter earn a bob or two, but you'll have to work for them.'

'Thanks,' John said. 'I want to be rich one day so I can look after me mum.'

'Good on yer.' Fred smiled at him. 'Be careful what else you do for Tam, lad. Yer ma wouldn't want yer to get involved with his sort.'

'Thanks, Fred,' John said and scooted. He ran all the way back to where Tam was still waiting and handed him the betting slip. Tam gave him two shillings.

'I might have another job fer yer,' he said. 'Have yer got a bike?'

'No. Mum can't afford things like that,' John said.

'It would be better if yer 'ad a bike,' Tam said. 'I might 'ave one yer could borrow. I sometimes need a little parcel delivered, see. Only it might be a bit further away.'

'I'd do it if I had a bike I could borrow,' John said and then waved to his friend Mickey, who had emerged from his house. 'See you then...'

'Yeah, mebbe,' Tam said and walked off.

'What were yer talkin' to 'im fer?' Mickey asked as he tossed his ball into the air and caught it.

'Nothin',' John said casually. 'Just a bit of business...'

'Yer don't want nothin' to do wiv him,' Mickey said. 'Ma says he's on the fiddle – pinched stuff. He ain't the sort we want round 'ere.'

'Oh, I didn't know that,' John said. 'Come on, let's forget him. It will soon be dark and we shall have to go in...'

He forgot about Tam and the huge bet he'd placed as he and Mickey lost themselves in the joy of kicking a ball in the street, but later, in bed, John wondered what he'd done. Something told him there was more going on than he had any idea of and he wasn't sure he would do any more errands for Tam, if he should ask; he didn't want to get mixed up in crooked stuff.

10

Sibby watched as Rod played darts with his mates, stifling a yawn. He'd walked her home earlier, after she'd left Yvonne, arranging to meet her near the King's Head at seven, a respectable pub just round the corner from her home. He'd been waiting outside when she arrived, having washed, and changed her clothes; he'd told her she looked smashing and then taken her into the main bar, where they'd been greeted by four of his mates. It was a nice enough place, with individual tables and benches, and had a comfortable atmosphere; the kind of place where men took their wives or girlfriends on a Saturday night.

Rod had bought her a shandy and a pint of bitter for himself. He'd sat with her for about ten minutes until one of his friends asked him to have a game of darts. Since then, she'd spoken to him a few times and he'd bought her another shandy and a small pork pie, but most of his attention was for the dartboard and his mates. Not quite what she wanted or expected.

Sibby watched with amusement for the first hour or so. She wasn't exactly neglected, because several of the young men sat with her for a while and a couple of them tried flirting with her.

She glanced round the bar. The old oak panelling had been polished over the years and was very dark. The room smelled of beer and cigarette smoke, but most pubs did and Sibby was used to being taken there. Joe Ross had taken her dancing a couple of times and to the pictures now and then, but he too brought her to the pub more often than not. He normally sat with her and they had a couple of drinks and then walked home, enjoying a chat before she went into her lodgings.

Sibby liked him better than Rod, but he'd shown no sign of wanting to go steady or being in love with her. He'd kissed her goodnight on the cheek, but just a soft, careless kiss that anyone might give to a friend, and she couldn't convince herself that he would ever want to marry her. So, she had decided to make him jealous and she'd gone out with a couple of other young men; Rod was the latest, but sitting watching him laugh with his mates over a narrowly missed treble twenty made her realise he wouldn't be the sort of man she'd want in her life permanently.

'All right then?' Rod's slightly inebriated voice brought her out of her reverie as he sat down beside her. 'Do you want another drink?'

'No, thank you,' Sibby said. 'I think I'd like to go home now. It's past nine and I have work tomorrow.'

'We all do,' Rod said and there was a jeering note in his voice. 'I'm not ready to go yet – another hour until chucking-out time. I want another drink...'

Sibby watched as he shouldered his way to the bar and ordered another pint of beer. She wasn't sure how many he'd had, but she thought he was on the way to becoming intoxicated. Joe would never have taken her out and got drunk. Sibby realised that she missed him and wished she'd never tried to make him jealous, because it hadn't worked; he'd simply stopped asking her out.

Watching as Rod gulped his beer and then asked for a whisky

chaser, Sibby wondered what on earth she was doing. She was bored and she didn't want to be walked home by a man who was drunk and would inevitably try for more than a goodnight kiss.

She stood up, put on her light jacket, picked up her handbag and walked to the door.

'Sibby – where are yer goin'?' Rod's shout made her stop and glance back.

For a moment, she hesitated. If he'd come to her, she might have been persuaded to go back and wait for him, but one of his friends pressed the darts into his hand and he went to stand at the oche.

She went out as he threw his first dart, shivering a little as she felt the chill of the evening air. It was drizzling with rain and she turned her coat collar up and started walking. The street was light enough and she didn't have far to go but couldn't help glancing over her shoulder. A couple were walking in the other direction, but no one else was about.

Quickening her step, Sibby turned into her own road. In minutes, she would be home safe, but it was darker here and she hurried towards the house where she now lodged. It was as she reached the narrow passage that led to the back of the terraced houses that a shadow loomed up and a hand reached out and grabbed her.

'Bitch...' a hoarse voice muttered. 'I know you – one o' them workshop girls... stuck-up bitches...' A hand took her by the throat and she was aware of the stench of foul breath in her face as she struggled against him, the fear rising in her as she tried to scream again, and found herself unable to breathe for a moment. 'I'll get that other one next time...'

His hand moved from her throat to her hair, tangling in her mass of dark tresses, pulling and twisting, inflicting pain, but at least she could breathe again. His face was a dark blur in the light of a shadowed moon, his eyes glaring as she fought wildly. She could smell a strong unwashed odour and something more that was sharp and stung her nostrils.

'I'm owed, damn it. If I can't get my dues one way, I'll take them another...'

'Please...' Sibby pleaded, terror sweeping through her as he pushed his face close to hers. He was unshaven and had thick dark eyebrows above his glittering eyes, his nose squashed, as though it had been broken. 'Don't hurt me...' Her eyes were blinded by tears as she begged for her life. 'Don't kill me... please...'

Her fear overcame her, paralysing her so that she went limp, all the fight suddenly drained. He spat in her face and twisted her head to one side. She cried out as she was suddenly slammed back against the wall, her head hitting it hard. The blow was so severe that she lost consciousness and slumped to the ground at her attacker's feet. Her bag was wrenched from her hand and the assailant ran off, leaving her there for dead.

11

Winnie was answering the telephone when Miss Susie arrived the next morning. She stood waiting until she replaced the receiver, looking anxious and upset. Her manner was so odd that Winnie felt a shiver at her nape, because she knew that something must be wrong.

'Has something awful happened?' she asked.

'Yes. Will you come through to the workrooms, please, Winnie. I want all of the girls to hear what I have to say...'

Winnie followed her through, feeling a sick churning in her stomach.

Everyone stopped what they were doing as Miss Susie asked for attention. She waited until all the girls were looking at her.

'You may have noticed that Sibby isn't here this morning,' she said and Winnie felt a cold chill at her nape. 'I have been informed by the police that she is in hospital. She was attacked outside her home last night sometime after nine o'clock. Her head was bashed against the wall, causing a nasty gash and bleeding, and her bag was stolen. One of the other residents found her there at nine thirty when he got home from work. She was quite badly hurt and is expected to be in hospital for a while, but I am told that she will recover in time. However, she is lucky to be alive. This was a serious attack and we all need to be on our guard.'

There was a buzz of concern and everyone looked shocked and anxious. Sibby was liked despite her occasional sulks, and they all knew it might have been them.

'We sometimes walk home together,' Winnie said. 'Don't we, Jilly, Sylvia?' The two girls nodded in unison. 'But this must have happened later. Why was Sibby out on her own at that hour?'

'She met a man last night, someone she knew,' Yvonne said. 'Sibby thought he would take her to the pub for a drink.'

'She told me about him – if his name was Rod Wilkins,' Isobel, another of the seamstresses, said. 'He'd been asking her out – but if he took her, why didn't he walk her home?'

'That is what the police will be asking,' Susie said and wrote the name down. 'You said Rod Wilkins?' Isobel confirmed it. 'I will let the police know. The constable told me they will investigate any man she has been out with in the past few months, but it may not be anything to do with her private life. The fact that her bags were stolen seems to indicate it may be the vagrant who has attacked some of us before. And, of course there is Rusty's murder. The police are still investigating that, but they haven't got many leads as yet.'

'Yes – but the man who attacked Jinny – she's a friend of mine and was one of the first to be robbed – well, he didn't hurt her badly, just took her purse,' Isobel pointed out. 'To bang Sibby's head against the wall so hard must have been done with real violence. Might it have been someone different?'

'I mentioned that to the police, but they seemed to think that it was the same man becoming more violent. Possibly, if she put up a fight...'

'Do you think it was him who killed poor Rusty?' Isobel asked.

'She never had more than a few coppers, so why would he want to kill her?'

Susie inclined her head. 'I've been told in confidence that Rusty had several pounds in her possession that day. She had been begging and someone gave her a gold brooch. It may have been pinned to an old coat and overlooked when it was given to her, but, however, she came by it, she sold it to the pawnbroker at the end of Silver Lane. He gave her five pounds for it. Rusty then went to the pub and treated herself to a couple of port and lemons, which must have drawn her to someone's attention – if only because she never normally had enough to buy one. Of course, we don't know that was the reason – but the police think it might be.'

'Five pounds.' Jilly sighed. 'That is a small fortune to someone like Rusty – and to me...' The other girls gave a nervous laugh, relieving some of the tension in the room.

'It is a lot of money and a great temptation to a violent man who lives on the streets,' Susie replied thoughtfully. 'Rusty's death was a very sad occurrence – but I am more concerned that Sibby should have been attacked near her home.' Susie paused and looked at the worried faces. 'We must all be careful on our way to and from work – although this last attack was much later in the evening and the others have often been in daylight...'

'I can't imagine why she was alone at that hour,' Yvonne remarked as there was silence. 'Surely if she went to meet this Rod Wilkins, he wouldn't have let her walk home alone?'

'Perhaps she quarrelled with him,' Winnie said. 'Sibby hasn't been that happy since she broke up with Joe Ross. I think she regretted it a lot.'

'That is quite possible,' Susie agreed. 'This Rod Wilkins isn't much of a man if he let her walk off alone. Every local man is perfectly aware of the attacks that have taken place.'

The girls were nodding and murmuring to each other.

Susie smiled and suggested they all had a cup of tea before returning to their work stations. There was a feeling of unease they all shared. One of their own had been brutally attacked and that seemed to bring it all far too close for comfort.

'I saw the young man she went to meet,' Yvonne said to Susie before returning to the garment she had been working on. 'He looked to be perfectly ordinary and I would have thought she would be safe with him – but you never can tell.'

'No, you can't,' Susie agreed. 'I assumed it was the work of this vagrant who has attacked me as well as others – but it could have been one of the men Sibby had been out with recently, I suppose.'

'I don't think it would be Joe Ross,' Yvonne said and Winnie agreed.

'Sam knows him well,' she said. 'It wouldn't have been Joe – but it might have been this new chap she went to the pub with...'

The telephone rang in reception then and Winnie returned to her post. She took another order for the autumn range and was typing it up when Susie came through from the workroom.

'I am going to the silk warehouse,' she told Winnie. 'Was that another order for the autumn range?'

'Yes. Six of the morning dresses in fine wool suiting, six of the blue silk afternoon gowns and six of the tweed suits.'

'That is excellent,' Susie replied and frowned. 'You wouldn't risk walking home alone at nine o'clock at night, would you?'

'No, I wouldn't, not with that monster at large,' Winnie said. 'I've been thinking – perhaps Sibby fought back and that was why he hurt her?'

'Yes. He pulled a knife on me,' Susie said with a little shudder, 'just because I wouldn't give him my box of zips...'

'You were lucky the box protected your face,' Winnie replied with a little frown. 'I do hope they catch him soon. The police seem so slow at times, but they do usually get there in the end.'

'You are thinking of the man who kept those poor girls prisoner when this was Madame Pauline's?'

'Yes. The police seemed to me to bungle his arrest two or three times, despite the information they were given, but in the end, they got him – or they would have done if he hadn't been murdered by one of his own henchmen before they closed in on him.'

Susie inclined her head. 'That was a horrid affair, but I thought it was all over. We could do without this other business. It is uncomfortable for all the girls, Winnie – especially now that Sibby has been attacked.'

'It is horrid,' Winnie agreed with a small shiver. 'I like Sibby and feel a bit sorry for her. I think she liked Joe Ross more than he liked her. She hoped he would ask her to marry him, but he didn't, so she tried to make him jealous, but instead of getting angry and telling her she belonged to him, he just let her get on with it.'

'Oh dear, poor Sibby,' Susie said. 'It is a shame – but perhaps she was too impatient. Some men like to think about it before offering marriage. Sam told me he knew he was in love with you soon after you first spoke, but he couldn't see his way clear to marriage.' Susie laughed. 'Even now he is keeping you waiting, Winnie. You should tell him you want that gold ring on your finger.'

Winnie smiled. 'I wouldn't dream of pushing him,' she said. 'We'll marry when Sam is ready and that's fine with me.'

Susie looked thoughtful. 'You enjoy your work here, don't you?'

'Yes, I do. Sam says I can carry on until we have a family. I can always come back when they're off to school.'

'Yes, of course you can, if you wish,' Susie said. 'I'd best get off, Winnie. I need to see if the silk for those afternoon gowns has come in – and I want to order hooks and eyes to match the material, too.'

Winnie smiled as she went out, her hand reaching for the telephone as it started ringing again.

Susie was conscious of looking over her shoulder every now and then as she walked through the lanes towards the warehouse she needed. There was nothing untoward to alarm her and she reached her destination without incident.

Inside the warehouse, the smell of dye was intense, mingled with a strong odour of coffee. As she lingered for a moment at the reception, a door opened and the manager came out of his office, the smell of coffee much stronger, revealing its source. He stopped as he saw her and smiled.

'Miss Susie, how nice to see you again,' he said and offered her his hand to shake. 'How may I help you?'

'Mr Absalom,' Susie replied with a smile and took his hand firmly. 'I came to enquire after the pale blue silk I ordered – and to see what else you had in stock.'

'Ah yes, the blue silk. I believe it has come in this morning. I will enquire – but we do have some wonderful new stock in, if you would care to see?'

'Yes, I should, very much,' Susie replied as he released her hand and turned to show the way to the stockroom.

The next half an hour was spent pleasantly looking through a selection of high-quality silks and satin velvets. Susie found three that she thought would be just the thing for the winter collection and ordered several bolts of them. She was given a discount because of bulk purchase and, with his promise that her purchases would be delivered that very afternoon, she left and walked back towards the workshops. As she approached, she saw a small group of men standing on the pavement opposite Miss Susie.

'Just a moment, Miss Susie,' Eddie Stevens called to her as she was about to enter her own premises. He crossed the road and came to her, looking serious. 'I wanted to tell you – the police have arrested Ernie for the attack on Sibby Thomas...' He saw her blank expression. 'Ernie – the street sweeper...'

'No! That is ridiculous,' Susie exclaimed. 'How can they be so stupid? Ernie wouldn't harm a fly. He wasn't the man who attacked and stabbed at me in Dressmakers' Alley. Why on earth would they think he was the one?'

'Apparently, he had Sibby's bag when he was arrested. He told them he found it in the gutter and picked it up. It had been emptied of most of the contents and he was going to take it to the police station, but before he could, he was arrested and charged with the assault of a young woman...'

'That is so wrong,' Susie exclaimed. 'Is he still under arrest?'

'I think he must be. Joe Ross saw him taken in as he was leaving. They questioned Joe about his relationship with Sibby for nearly an hour, but he was at home with his mother, sister and her husband that evening and was able to prove it. Well, Joe came straight round and told Lilly about Ernie's arrest and she was up in arms. She has gone round to the police station and will do what she can to help him...'

'Oh, the poor man,' Susie said, frowning. 'Winnie was treated much the same when her mother was murdered – as if she would ever do such a thing. She isn't above defending herself and giving as good as she gets if attacked – but her own mother...' She shook her head. 'Thank you for telling me...'

'Will you sign a petition to say that we all vouch for Ernie?' Eddie Stevens asked her. 'We'll get a lawyer for him if we have to.'

'Yes, of course – and I will contribute if we need to pay a lawyer,' Susie confirmed.

Eddie Stevens' face lit up with his smile. 'Thank you, Miss Susie. The more signatures we can get, the more likely he is to get a fair hearing, poor devil. He must be frightened and bewildered.'

'From what I know of him, I wouldn't think he would be frightened,' Susie replied. 'Provided his stay isn't too long, and his innocence is established, I am certain he will treat it as a little rest and somewhere dry to sleep for a while.' She smiled as he looked at her in surprise. 'Lilly says he is very resilient and I think so too. I dare say he has a very interesting story if he cared to tell it.'

She met his wondering eyes with a smile and left him staring after her as she went into the workrooms.

Winnie had already heard the story and, like most of the workshop girls, had signed the petition. She greeted Susie with a shower of indignant words, protesting her belief in Ernie's innocence. 'I can't understand why the police would pick on him. He's always so polite to us.'

'Why do the police make such foolish mistakes?' Susie asked, shaking her head over it. 'The poor man has done nothing to deserve it, I am sure – and it certainly wasn't him that attacked me.'

'Nor would he have attacked Sibby,' Winnie agreed. 'I hope they have the decency to give him a cup of tea and feed him. When they arrested me, I had to wait ages before I got anything to drink and it was lukewarm. I hate tepid tea.'

'Me too,' Susie agreed, then, dismissing the subject, 'Our blue silk is being delivered this afternoon, Winnie – and I have ordered some gorgeous silk and silk velvet for three new models for the autumn/winter range...'

'Lovely,' Winnie said. 'I think I shall pop up and see Lilly in my lunch break. If we need to get a lawyer for Ernie, I might know just the man...'

'I'm not sure if...' Susie shook her head. 'Let's hope it isn't necessary...'

The telephone started to ring then and, as Winnie answered, she went through to the workroom.

'Oh, Miss Susie,' Betty Ford said, coming up to her at once. 'This bolt of linen has a flaw right through. I think it will have to be returned to the wholesaler and that means we haven't enough to finish those morning dresses.'

'Oh, that is a nuisance,' Susie said, glancing at the flaw, which looked like missed threads, some three stitches wide, running right through the bolt of material. There were several yards in the bolt and unless she could get a refund, it meant a loss. 'Can you remember when it came in and whether it was from Morrisons?'

'We had it in about January,' Betty replied. 'I'm not sure where it came from; it should have been checked at the time.'

'Clearly it wasn't,' Susie replied, frowning. 'In that case, I very much doubt we can send it back.' She fingered the material. 'The flaw is right in the middle too or we might have cut round it...'

'You might get some blouses out of it,' Betty suggested. 'I think Carl could find a way, but not those dresses, because of the full skirts.'

Susie nodded, looking at the material thoughtfully. 'We could make some blouses to go with that fine navy suiting. The skirt and bolero would look well over a tailored linen blouse.'

'The original design was for a silk blouse with very full sleeves,' Betty reminded her.

'Yes – but we could do a variation. It would make the one with the linen blouse cheaper to sell...'

'I think it would look better with a tailored blouse,' Betty replied and smiled. 'It's an outfit young women could wear for everyday then, rather than a special occasion.'

'Ask Carl what he can get out of it,' Susie said. 'We'll try one and see how it looks – and that means I have to find some more pale cream linen for those morning dresses.'

'Why don't you try Simpsons?' Betty suggested. 'I know you think Morrisons is superior, but they might have something similar in stock...'

'Simpsons were late with our orders three times last autumn,' Susie reminded her. 'I had to find supplies elsewhere – and Morrisons were so helpful.' Betty shrugged and Susie nodded to herself. 'Well, I shall try – perhaps on my way home.'

She went through into her office and took down the stock book, checking on the date and supplier of the linen. It had come through Morrisons in January and was ticked as being checked. Someone had skipped over their work clearly, but Susie wasn't sure who to blame. Betty ought to have checked it herself, but if she was busy, she occasionally deputised to one of the girls.

Susie put the stock book aside and fetched down her ledger to enter the amounts she'd paid for the new materials. It seemed for the moment that it was all pay out and not very much coming in – of course the money for the autumn range would all come in once deliveries were made, but... Sighing, she closed her accounts. Sometimes, she wondered where all the money went to.

12

'Did you manage to see Ernie?' Joe asked his sister when he called into the flower shop that evening after finishing his last delivery of coal. His face was smeared with black dust and it had got onto his shirt collar.

'Yes, they let me speak to him for a few minutes and I told him that none of us believed he'd attacked anyone and that if the police did not let him go by the morning, we would get a lawyer for him.'

'Was he very upset?' Joe asked in concern. 'I dare say he was frightened and shaken?'

'He was a bit upset that anyone would think him capable of such a thing, but I don't think he was frightened. Ernie knows he is innocent, Joe, and once the police think about it, I am certain they will let him go. He has told them his movements last evening and they have only to check them. He was in the pub until nine thirty, though he only ordered one drink, and then went to a hostel for the night.' Ernie knew the landlord of the Pig & Whistle in Mulberry Lane very well and was allowed to sit over his half-pint of bitter in the corner for as long as he wished on cool wet nights.

'What made them arrest him?' Joe asked, puzzled. 'Surely they must have had a reason?'

'Someone reported seeing him in the area last night – or, at least, they described a man of unkempt appearance, wearing a military overcoat...' Lilly looked anxious. 'He passed by the turning to Sibby's home on his way to the hostel and, I suppose might have had time to attack her, had he been so inclined – but why would he?'

Joe shook his head. 'It isn't likely. He gets on well with the girls from Miss Susie – with everyone. I mean, he doesn't say much unless you persevere, but he nods and smiles to us all.'

'I know some folk might think him rough and dirty, but he works hard at his job and the clothes he wears are probably all he's got, Joe.'

'Ernie was a soldier once and his overcoat was given him when he served his country, but there must be others who have them – many old soldiers are forced onto the streets through injury or infirmity. When they retire, they have no home to go to and very little money. Some have no family or friends and can only hope for a bed in a hostel and what they can earn begging on the street.'

'Ernie has never begged. He will accept a mug of tea and an occasional bun, but he doesn't ask – not like Rusty. She was forever asking for a sixpence or whatever you would give her. Poor Rusty...'

'Aye, she didn't deserve what happened to her,' Joe agreed grimly. 'I hope they don't think Ernie did that, too.' Joe didn't like what was going on in his area; there was always crime and violence in a big city, but this was his territory. 'Shall I walk you home, Lilly? Or is Jeb coming for you?'

Thankfully, Lilly's husband was now home again and could look after her.

'Jeb said he would be here by half past six,' Lilly told him. 'I have some more work to do yet, Joe. Do you see those frames? I have to make up another six of those ready to fill them with fresh flowers for the hotel arrangements for tomorrow. I'll be another thirty minutes or so.'

'Well, if you're sure Jeb is coming,' Joe said but still lingered.

'What is on your mind?' Lilly asked her brother, sensing that he was deeply troubled. 'Is it because of Sibby?'

Joe drew a sharp breath, making an agonised face at her. 'I feel terrible over what happened to her, Lilly. If I'd still been seeing her, she would never have been walking home alone at night.'

'I know – but it isn't your fault she was attacked, Joe. I don't know why she chose to walk home on her own – I think she went to meet some chap she talks to sometimes.'

Joe nodded. 'Rod Wilkins. The police had already interviewed him. He was in the pub until chucking-out time and with friends until in sight of his house. Apparently, she went off in a miff because he was playing darts instead of sitting with her in the pub...'

'Oh, poor Sibby,' Lilly said in sympathy. 'Jeb plays darts if we go to the pub, but only a couple of games. I don't mind, because he takes me out sometimes, to the pictures or for a meal. I know some men think it is fine to just leave their girlfriends sitting there with a drink all night.'

'Well, we all like a drink and a game of darts,' Joe said, 'but I wouldn't leave a girl sitting by herself all night if I'd asked her out.' He ran his fingers through his thick dark hair. 'I feel sorry for her – and a bit guilty. Should I visit her in the hospital, Lilly? When she starts to remember what happened, she'll feel so alone...' Air expelled from his lips in a soundless whistle. 'I don't know what to do, Lilly. I'd like to take her some grapes and ask her how she is – but if I do, she might think I want to get back together...'

'And you don't?'

Joe shook his head.

'How about you take me tomorrow night? If we go in together, I can give her the grapes and you can just pop in and then wait for me in the corridor?'

Joe's smile lit up his good-looking face. 'Thanks, Lilly. I know how busy you are – but I don't like to think of her alone and frightened. She is a nice enough girl but...' He lifted his shoulders. 'Not the one for me.'

'We'll go together. Then she will know she still has friends – but you don't need to be involved in that way.'

Joe thanked her, grinned a little self-consciously and left.

Lilly got on with her work, forgetting time as she worked the fine wire into different shapes that she would use to hold her beautiful flowers. She would add the fresh blooms in the morning after Jeb fetched them for her from the wholesale market.

Smiling as she imagined how gorgeous they would look once filled with roses, lilies and freesias with some greenery, she stood back and looked at the clock on the wall. It was almost seven and well past the time Jeb had promised to fetch her.

She stood, undecided for a moment, wondering what best to do now. Jeb had surely not forgotten and must have been delayed for some reason. He did sometimes lose track of time when he was engaged in his business. As he said, when folk were deciding whether or not to sell their bits and pieces to him, you had to be patient and go along with them.

'You can't just say take it or leave it, or they'd take offence,' he'd told her when he was late home for a meal.

Yet Jeb knew what had been going on in the lanes and would want her to wait for him.

She decided to make herself a cup of tea and went through to the back, boiling her kettle on a small gas ring she kept for the purpose. The brew made, she brought her mug through to the front shop and stood in the window, looking out as she drank it.

The time dragged, but by seven thirty, Lilly was hungry and tired. She decided to lock up and leave. For a moment, she debated whether to leave her takings in the shop overnight or risk taking them home. It was probably safer to leave them in the shop, she decided, taking her little money bag through to the back and hiding it amongst some empty cardboard containers.

Lilly went back through to the front, slipped on her jacket and picked up her basket. She locked the shop door and placed the key in her pocket and started to walk. At least it wasn't raining, but the night air was chilly and she turned up her collar to keep herself warm, walking as fast as she could but not running.

She had been walking for several minutes when she first heard the footsteps behind her. A nervous twitch at her nape made her shiver, but she resisted the impulse to look back. Another ten minutes and she would be home and in the warm.

At the junction of Silver Lane and Green Road, she paused as a van drove past, its lights fading into the distance as she stepped out. A hand clamped her shoulder and she jumped with fright, turning her head as her basket was suddenly wrenched from her hand and she was shoved hard, falling to her knees in the road.

It was all so swift that she really didn't realise what was happening until she looked up and saw the man disappearing round the corner. He had thrown her basket down and, when she recovered herself sufficiently to go after it, Lilly discovered that her small coin purse had gone, together with a packet of biscuits she'd purchased earlier that day.

Lilly felt a little sick. She was shaking, because the attack had brought back past memories – memories of an attack far worse than the one she'd just endured. Before she'd married Jeb, when she'd been working at Harpers Emporium, a man had attacked and raped her. As she fought to calm her nerves, she knew that this time she'd been lucky. All her assailant had wanted was whatever was in her purse – a couple of shillings only since she'd elected to leave her takings in the shop.

It took a few moments to stop shaking, but she wasn't hurt. She'd been luckier than Sibby; the assailant had merely stolen her basket but hadn't harmed her. Once she had time to gather her thoughts, Lilly discovered she was angry. Her fear had gone and she knew what she had to do, retracing her steps until she saw the lights of the local police station.

Lilly was home eating her supper when Jeb came in an hour later. He looked at her apologetically. 'I'm so sorry, Lilly. I was busy in the shop and I forgot the time. This chap came in and he had a whole house to clear, but he wanted me to look right away...' He broke off as he saw the look in her eyes. 'What? Did something happen?'

'I waited until half past seven,' she told him calmly. 'Then I decided to walk home. I was attacked at the corner of Silver Lane – my basket was snatched and I was knocked to my knees.' She saw the alarm and anger in his eyes. 'Don't get upset, Jeb. I am all right. I wasn't hurt – just a graze to my knees, as I told the police officer, but he stole my purse and some biscuits...'

'Lilly! I am so sorry.' Jeb came to her, kneeling down beside her to cup her face with his hands and look into her eyes. 'Are you all right, my love? I know how frightened you must have been after... Forgive me. I should have been there for you.'

'Yes, you should, Jeb,' Lilly agreed. 'I was sick with fear, but he didn't seem interested in hurting me – all he wanted was the money. I was lucky. Sibby was hurt badly and Rusty was murdered...'

'Don't! My God – if he'd hurt you. I'd never forgive myself.'

'Maybe there's more than one thief about,' Lilly suggested. 'Or... I don't know why I wasn't attacked. He just wanted my basket...'

'Your takings from the shop. I'll make it up to you...'

'It was just a few shillings. I left my takings in the shop. You can bank them for me in the post office tomorrow, Jeb.' She smiled and reached out to tussle his short hair with her fingers. 'It's all right. Don't look like that, love. I wasn't hurt – not like poor Sibby...'

'You might have been,' Jeb said and cursed. 'I shan't forgive myself in a hurry for letting it happen. I'll see it doesn't happen again.'

'It shouldn't be necessary, Jeb. I've walked home alone so many times but...'

'There is a monster on the loose,' Jeb said and the anger was back in his face. 'It's time we local men took a hand, Lilly. The police don't seem to know where to look for him, so it might be time for us to do something about what is going on.' He frowned. 'It may be more than one, because it is odd that you weren't hurt like Sibby... I just thank God for it.'

'Sibby works at Miss Susie – do you think that could have anything to do with it?'

'Why would it?' her husband asked, puzzled.

'I don't know – unless he has a grudge against the workshop or... or its owners. Remember, he pulled a knife on Miss Susie.'

'Yes... perhaps, but it isn't only those girls he's attacked.' Jeb sounded both angry and worried. 'The sooner the police find him, the better!'

'They arrested poor Ernie, but they will let him go now,' Lilly said. 'It wasn't him that attacked me because he was still in custody, so they must see they have the wrong man.'

'It doesn't prove he is innocent...' Jeb began but stopped as he saw Lilly's look. 'Of course whoever attacked Sibby might have another motive altogether. She has been out with a few blokes, hasn't she?'

'Yes, that is possible,' Lilly agreed. 'But I think the police have questioned them.' She smiled at him. 'I'll get you something to eat.'

'Oh, Lilly...' Jeb took her into his arms as she stood up. He held her close to him, kissing her hair and her neck. 'I am so sorry for what happened. Will you forgive me?'

'Yes, of course I will,' she said. 'But I think I'll walk home with Winnie or Joe until this is all over – just in case you forget me again.'

Jeb looked gravely at her. 'If anything worse had happened...' He shook his head. 'Sit down and finish your meal. I can get myself something.'

'Don't beat yourself up over it, Jeb,' Lilly said and kissed him. 'You can't be with me every minute and I wouldn't want to live like that – I faced my fear tonight, Jeb, and I found I was angry. It isn't right that a woman can't walk the street alone, even if it is night-time. We have rights and we should be safe in our own neighbourhood.'

'If I got hold of him, he wouldn't attack another woman,' Jeb said between his teeth. He looked so fierce that Lilly laughed and he relaxed a little as he heard her. 'I'd like to kill him!'

13

'Lilly attacked!' Joe Ross lit up like a fiery beacon when Jeb found him at his coal store the next morning. 'The bastard wants hanging! And I'd be the man to do it.' His fists clenched. 'The bugger! I hope he burns in Hell. How is she?'

'Surprisingly, she is all right,' Jeb told him. 'She said she was frightened for a moment, but it was all over so quickly and then she just got angry. She went straight round the coppers and told them she'd been attacked and robbed. I reckon she hopes it will mean they'll let Ernie go, but I ain't so sure.'

'Ernie never hurt anyone in his life,' Joe growled. 'That other bugger, whoever he is, wants stoppin', Jeb. He's killed once that we know of and there's Sibby in the hospital. If he isn't stopped, the next girl might not be as lucky as Lilly.'

'I think we should keep a watch,' Jeb said. 'Get enough of us local lads together to patrol the area. Not as a gang but within whistling distance. If we catch the bugger, we thrash him and then throw him in the river – sink or swim he won't come back this way.'

'I agree. I reckon Keith Harris and Steve Carter will, too. Both of them know someone who has been attacked and Keith was telling me earlier this morning that he'd like to have the bugger alone in his yard for ten minutes.' Joe's jaw hardened as he looked at his brother-in-law. 'I'd go to prison for it if I had to – but I won't put up with a rotten devil like him hurting our girls, Jeb.'

'You can imagine how I felt,' Jeb replied, a dark shadow of guilt in his face. 'It was my fault Lilly walked home alone. I got caught up with some business and couldn't get away. In future, she'll walk home with you or some of the other girls – and if I turn up, the more, the merrier.' His face twisted with real pain. 'If she'd been hurt, I couldn't have lived with myself.'

'I wouldn't either,' Joe muttered. 'Work is work, Jeb, but don't forget family comes first.'

'Yeah, I know. Don't think I'm not feelin' it, because I am. I'm lucky Lilly is still speakin' to me – but I won't have it happen again.'

'Not if we catch the bugger,' Joe said fiercely. 'Can't understand why the police haven't got him before this; he must be sleeping rough. You'd think they'd know where to look for vagrants.'

'Well, if they don't know where to look, I do,' Jeb said. 'I've got a bit of an idea what he looks like. Lilly says he wears an old soldier's coat, similar to Ernie's. He has a dark muffler round his chin and his hair is long and straggly, and he's unshaven but doesn't have a full beard.' He saw Joe's scepticism and grinned. 'Yeah, I know that description fits a dozen others, but there will be somethin' that marks him out. Most of them are drunk half the time, or they sit over a small fire and hug themselves to keep out the cold and misery – but this one thinks the world owes him something, and he seems to hate women. Leastways, he hasn't attacked a man that I know of...'

Joe nodded slowly. 'That makes sense,' he agreed. 'He won't be one of the ones who've given up. He has a grievance and he is determined to get his revenge.'

'Yeah, somethin' like that,' Jeb said. 'We have to try to find him, Joe, before he kills again. I'm goin' ter start by lookin' under the arches by the river. I'll mebbe ask a few questions if I meet someone who looks approachable.'

'Be careful,' Joe warned. 'Some of the vagrants look as if the wind would blow them over, but they can turn nasty – and they may carry knives.'

'I know, but a couple of bob loosens a lot of tongues,' Jeb argued. 'I feel sorry for a lot of them, poor devils. What have they got to look forward to? Nothing but cold, dark nights and wet days, very little food, and only a drink now and then to keep body and soul together, unless they go to the infirmary, or workhouse, as it used to be called – and the old soldiers don't qualify for a bed until they're on their last legs.'

Joe made a grunting sound in sympathy. 'I'd not want to end up in a workhouse myself, but they ought to do something for men who've given their lives to the service of their country. When yer think about it, you can understand why some turn to crime.'

'That's true enough. I'd say nothing if they swiped a bit of bread from a market stall or begged – but violence towards our women is too much.'

'Agreed,' Joe said. 'I'll talk to a few of my friends and we'll meet for a drink in the Pig & Whistle in Mulberry Lane – not tonight, because I've promised to take Lilly to visit Sibby in the hospital.'

'Right – on Friday evening then,' Jeb said. 'We'll have time to talk to a few mates and see if we can get enough of us to make it work. If the police can't keep our streets safe, then we shall...'

* * *

Joe was armed with a paper bag full of green grapes, which were sweet, because he'd tasted one before he bought them from the barrow boy, and a small posy of violets. Lilly had brought a magazine with pictures of fashionable ladies in it and articles about knitting and cooking, as well as a puzzle.

'I wasn't sure if Sibby would feel like reading stories,' she said to Joe, 'but anyone likes looking at pictures.'

He agreed, slipping a finger under his shirt collar that suddenly felt a little tight. 'Do you think the hospital will let us visit as we're not relations?'

'I doubt if Sibby has any family in London. She never talks about them and something she once said made me think she wasn't happy at home, which was why she came to take that job here.'

Joe was thoughtful as they got on the bus and paid their fares. It was only after they'd moved away from the stop that he said, 'Now that you mention it, she never did talk about her family much. Tell you what, Lilly. If they say it's only family allowed, we'll say we're her cousins.'

Lilly looked a bit disapproving but didn't refuse. 'I suppose we ought to have telephoned to see if she is well enough for visitors.'

'I think she must be,' Joe replied. 'Miss Susie rang them this morning and she told the girls that Sibby was conscious and would make a full recovery in time. Or that's what Winnie told Sam...' He shrugged his shoulder. 'It was a nasty bang on the head and she's lucky it wasn't worse. We were sayin'...' He broke off and took a grape from the paper bag, eating it and offering her one. She shook her head.

'You didn't tell me you'd seen Sam Collins,' Lilly murmured, her eyes searching his face.

'I've told you now. I knew I should see you this evenin', didn't I?'

'What are you keepin' from me, Joe?' Lilly asked, her gaze narrowing. 'You're up to somethin'. I can sense it. You're my brother and you can't hide anythin' from me.'

'Now why would I want to hide anythin' from my favourite girl?'

Lilly gave him a straight look. 'I'm your sister. I know you.'

'A chap has to have some secrets, even from his sister.'

Lilly snorted her disgust. 'I hope you and Jeb aren't planning anythin' stupid,' she said. 'I haven't forgotten what you did when I was attacked...'

'But we were warned not to interfere again by the coppers,' Joe replied innocently. 'Is it likely we would?'

'I hope not,' Lilly replied. 'I don't want either of you getting into trouble, Joe – you or Jeb.'

'We'll be fine,' he murmured vaguely. 'This is our stop. Come on, Lilly. Let's see if Sibby is up to visitors. We'll ask at the desk what ward she is in...'

* * *

As it happened, there was only one nurse on Ward 6 when they got there and she was busy tending to a woman who had just been sick and didn't even turn to look at them. Several patients had visitors, but Sibby was sitting up in her bed, which was almost at the far end, propped against several pillows. Her head was bandaged and her face badly bruised, her eyes closed as if she wanted to shut out the world around her.

Joe took one look at her and his heart caught with something between pity and tenderness. He liked Sibby, even though he didn't think he wanted to marry her, and it hurt to see her like this.

'Sibby...' he spoke gently. 'How are you, love?'

Sibby's eyes flew open, so surprised, her face a mixture of

disbelief and wonder that he'd come to see her, it made Joe feel he wanted to comfort her. He perched on the side of her bed, offering the flowers and fruit.

'Try one if you feel able, they're good. I've eaten a few...'

'Oh, Joe...' There was a little catch in Sibby's voice as she looked at him. 'You came to visit me. I didn't think you would...'

'Why not? We're friends,' he said. 'I don't forget my friends, especially when they've been hurt. I am so sorry, Sibby. How did it happen? Why were you walking home alone?'

'I went to the pub to meet... friends,' Sibby said, her cheeks flushed. 'Oh, it was a bloke who had been after me to go out with him, Joe, and you hadn't asked me for a while...'

'You had every right to go with anyone you like,' Joe told her gently. 'It wasn't him that hurt you?'

'No. He was playing darts. They all were. I got fed up and decided I would walk home on my own. It was only just round the corner and I thought I'd be all right... but...' She caught her breath on a sob. 'I didn't see him. He must have been in the passage between the terraces and he just grabbed me and attacked me. I don't know why, except...' She hesitated for a second, then shook her head.

'Did he steal anything from you?' Joe asked, taking her hand as it trembled on the bed covers.

'My bag,' Sibby said. 'I had a few shillings in it and... and I'm not sure, but I might have had my door key in there.'

'Did you tell the police that?' Lilly asked and Sibby inclined her head.

'Yes, I think so...'

'Then they will have warned your landlady to have her locks changed,' Joe said. 'I'll go round and make certain she knows.'

'Thank you...' Sibby was crying soundlessly, the tears trickling down her cheeks. Lilly took her other hand. She looked from one to the other. 'You are both so kind to me...'

'We care about you,' Lilly told her, but Sibby was looking at Joe, her manner so filled with a silent appeal, for forgiveness or love, that it was pitiful to see.

'It's all right, Sibby,' Joe said and bent down to kiss her gently on the cheek. 'I'll look after you when you leave here. I'll make sure you get home safe at night – but you must promise me that you won't take risks in future.'

'Oh, I do. I do promise,' Sibby said with pathetic eagerness. Joe squeezed her hand. 'They've said I can come home in a week or so...' She looked at Lilly. 'Do you think Miss Susie will let me have my job back?'

'I am sure she will,' Lilly said. 'You are a good seamstress, Sibby. You could get a job anywhere.'

'I like working there,' Sibby told her. 'The clothes are so lovely – and the money is better than a lot of places.' She frowned as she remembered, 'Although... that horrible man said something about the workshop girls – it made me think he had a grudge against us...'

'Why would that be?' Joe asked. 'Has he had a quarrel with one of the girls?'

'Not that I know of,' Sibby replied. 'Unless... Do you think it has anything to do with Mr Barrow and all that went on when his half-brother had those girls locked upstairs?' Mr Cyril Sinclair had used the top floor of the workshop as his private brothel, a place he could bring friends when he needed to repay a favour. He'd been a nasty crook and a murderer, and was now dead, killed by one of his own men.

'I doubt it,' Lilly said, but Joe was thoughtful. 'Maybe one of the girls told him to clear off. After all, they're not the only ones to have been robbed or attacked these past weeks.'

'If he is a vagrant – and from all the descriptions of him, it seems he must be – he probably has a grudge against the world,' Joe said. 'These men have their minds twisted by drink and whatever.'

'He smelled awful,' Sibby said. 'Like unwashed – and his breath was bad. I didn't see his face properly, but he was big – tall and bulky.'

'I've seen him in Dressmakers' Alley a couple of times,' Lilly corroborated. 'He wears an old army coat similar to Ernie's, but he is younger and much heavier. He's about your height, Joe, but a bigger build. He looks to me as if he might be a prize fighter or somethin'.'

'Well, let's hope he shows up again,' Joe said grimly. 'There are a few of us that want a word with him, whoever he is…'

'Joe…' Lilly said warningly, but he grinned and shook his head.

'No one harms my girls and gets away with it.' The words came out without him realising and as the light of hope and delight swept into Sibby's face, Joe knew she'd read more into them than he'd meant and cursed inwardly.

'Visiting is limited to an hour…' The nurse's voice cut into his thoughts. 'I am afraid time is up, sir – madam. You may visit again tomorrow, from seven until eight.'

'We'd better go,' Lilly said and squeezed Sibby's hand once more. 'Don't worry about anything, Sibby. The police will catch him soon and then we can all be safe again.'

'Thank you for coming…' Sibby looked at Joe with shy eagerness. 'You will come back, Joe?'

'Yes,' he confirmed. 'Not every night, but I'll pop in when I can.'

Sibby nodded, a suspicion of tears in her eyes as he touched her hand and walked away. At the end of the ward, he turned and waved to her. She was still watching him.

When they were out of the ward, Lilly looked at him. 'I thought you didn't want to get involved with Sibby again?'

'I can't just desert her,' Joe said, a faint blush in his cheeks. He raked his hair back from his forehead suddenly. 'I don't know what I want,' he confessed. 'I care about her, Lilly. It's true I'm not certain I want to marry her – but she needs someone to look after her.'

'Marriage is for a long time,' Lilly said. 'Be careful you don't throw your life away because you feel sorry for her.'

'Leave it, Lilly,' Joe said and felt he'd walked into a trap of his own making. 'I don't want to talk about it any more.'

14

———————

'Oh, this is beautiful,' Lady Diane exclaimed when Yvonne fitted the evening gown she had ordered on her. 'You have made it look exactly as I saw it in my mind. Sometimes, the clothes I design don't look quite how I thought they would – but this is wonderful.' A look of mischief entered her eyes. 'I know some of my acquaintances will be curious to know where it came from.'

'Shall you tell them?' Susie asked, seeing the look of pleasure in Yvonne's eyes. 'Or will you let them think it came from a French fashion house?'

'I shall tell them it was my own design and made specially for me by a very talented seamstress,' Lady Diane replied with a warm smile for Yvonne. 'I am not ready to disclose my links with Miss Susie yet. I think we have our hands full with what we are already producing.' She looked thoughtfully at them. 'I think in time we might have to open another establishment – to keep the two separate...'

'You mean run the expensive evening gown side of it as a separate business?' Susie asked with a little frown, feeling that might prove difficult to manage.

'If we wanted to make more expensive gowns, we would at the very least need a showroom and fitting room in a better part of town,' Lady Diane confirmed, a faint crease in her smooth brow. 'The ladies who would wish for exclusive gowns would not visit you in Dressmakers' Alley, Susie.'

'At the moment it would not be safe, my lady,' Yvonne said. 'There have been too many attacks on young women in the area.'

'Oh?' Lady Diane glanced at Susie. 'I knew one of our employees had been attacked, of course, poor young woman – but late at night. Have these attacks also happened in daylight, near the workshop?'

'A few...' Susie admitted. 'I was attacked myself, but I didn't tell you, because I saw no need to worry you. I was not hurt...'

'You should have told me,' Lady Diane replied. 'That is shocking, Susie. I should never forgive myself if you were seriously harmed. What are the police doing? Would it help if there were regular patrols in the area? Lord Henry will speak to his friend the chief constable...'

'That is very kind of you, my lady,' Yvonne said. Susie remained silent.

'It will be done.' Lady Diane nodded. 'Now – where were we? Ah yes, the matter of more expensive gowns. I think for the moment we will put that to one side, Susie. It seems that you have more than enough to contend with at present.'

'So for now we continue as we are?' Susie asked.

'Yes. My aim is still primarily to bring beautiful clothes to the working woman.' Lady Diane looked at Yvonne. 'We are very fortunate to have you. I know that you spent many hours working on my lovely gown and I can't thank you enough.'

Yvonne's cheeks were tinged with pink. 'I loved doing it, my lady. It was a pleasure and an honour to make such a gown.'

'I shall be the envy of my friends,' Lady Diane assured her. 'I have bought gowns from all the great fashion houses, but I don't think anything has surpassed this gown...' She gave a tinkling laugh. 'Of course I may feel that because it was my own design.' She turned in front of the mirror once more, admiring the long sleek line of the slender silk gown. The back dipped daringly with folds of soft silk draped to gently cover her lower back, and the diamanté straps divided into two with a little rosette of silver embroidery at the height of the shoulder. Tiny diamanté traced the scooped front and there was a trail of the shimmering beads down the bodice. 'It is so simple and yet so complicated. I know well the skill that went into this...'

'If there are no adjustments to be made, I will make a start on your ladyship's ball gown,' Yvonne said. 'That is a rather more intricate design – and I wondered how you wanted the skirt to look. From the design, I think you mean the underskirt to be fairly straight with the overskirt divided all the way down and drawn up over the hips with pleating.'

'Yes, it does look like that from the drawing,' Lady Diane agreed. 'What I require for my ball gown is that the overdress should be made separately, so that I can take it off like a coat when I want to wear the gown for a less glittering affair.'

'Ah, yes, now I understand,' Yvonne replied with a smile. 'Sometimes, at the workshop I am not certain how something is meant to go until I make one garment up. If your ladyship was there, I could ask, but I have to guess and then consult with Miss Susie.'

'Yes, it is a pity I cannot be more involved with the day-to-day business,' Lady Diane replied, 'but since my illness, after my darling little Marie was born, my husband worries about me. He is concerned that I do not overtire myself, though I am perfectly well now.' She smothered a sigh. 'In time I do hope to have more personal contact with you all – but for now I fear it is impossible.'

'Lord Henry does not want to lose you,' Susie said on a serious note. 'We came very close to it, my lady, and it shocked and distressed him.'

'Yes, I know. Henry loves me and I am fortunate,' Lady Diane said, smiling happily. 'Sometimes I feel a little confined by his concern, but as yet I tire easily.'

'You mustn't overtax your strength,' Susie told her. She glanced at the clock. 'We should be leaving, my lady. Meg will be here to dress you for your luncheon with Lord Henry at any moment – and Yvonne is needed at the workshops.'

'Yes, I have detained you long enough,' Lady Diane said. 'Once again, thank you, Yvonne. Susie will pay you for the hours I know you have spent making my beautiful gown...'

* * *

'Do you think her ladyship will ever open that West End establishment she spoke of?' Yvonne asked as they walked to the nearest bus stop. The bus was not long in coming and Susie did not answer until they were seated and had paid their fares.

'I'm not certain,' Susie replied as she tucked her purse away. 'I think in her heart it is what she would like to do – but I do not think Lord Henry would be pleased if she put her name to it. He would say it smelled of the shop.'

'I was surprised when I learned who she was,' Yvonne said. 'I love working on her special clothes, but I also enjoy making the Miss Susie ranges.'

'I believe her ladyship truly wishes to see young women with little money dressed beautifully,' Susie replied, 'but her notions of a modest dress are far beyond many a woman's purse.'

'Yes...' Yvonne smiled ruefully. 'I could never afford to shop in

Harpers or Selfridges, but I have made myself some clothes based on our designs, though in cheaper materials...'

'Have you?' Susie looked at her with interest. 'May I see some of them, Yvonne?'

'Yes, of course...' Yvonne faltered. 'I hope I haven't done anything wrong by copying them for myself.'

Susie looked thoughtful. 'You will not be the only one to do it. I should be surprised if that skirt and bolero set we're preparing for the autumn isn't copied within a few days of it being in the shops. Ours is made with a beautiful-quality silk and wool, woven suiting, but it would be equally as good in a wool blend I dare say.'

'Yes, I expect it would,' Yvonne replied. 'But the braiding on the hem and the bolero is expensive and a cheaper one would not sit as well on the curve of the bolero.'

'The silk sash at the skirt waist would be hard to copy in a cheaper material,' Susie said thoughtfully. 'The pleating is skilfully done and a cheap material might crease too much.'

'Yes, it would,' Yvonne agreed. 'I tried to make a similar sash at home, but the stitching wouldn't hold and the pleats opened. It definitely needs the heavier silk to make it look the way it was designed.'

'Yes, I know,' Susie said. 'That's why I'm trying to cut the costs with a cheaper blouse. The original silk one is expensive, but we have some linen that had a fault – well, you know. What do you think of the blouse we've made with it?'

'It is very well for everyday, but the silk blouse made it special.'

'Yes, I was afraid you might say that...' Susie sighed. 'Perhaps it wasn't a good idea after all.'

'We could make a plainer version of the bolero set, using the linen blouse. We could use that dark navy wool suiting we had left over from the winter range; the linen blouse would look good with that...'

'Was there much left?' Susie enquired uncertainly. She hadn't been aware of it until Yvonne spoke.

'Yes – several bolts. It would cost up at nearly half the price of the original...' Yvonne smiled. 'Since the ensemble will be copied cheaply within a short time, why don't we get in first with a cheaper version?'

'I suppose we could make up a few and see what happens,' Susie said. 'If the quality is still there in the making and design...'

'What would Lady Diane think?'

'I think you should make one up, Yvonne. I will take it and show her – and see what she feels. It might be nice if we did have a few cheaper lines... even if we put a different label in them.'

'It is what most manufacturers do,' Yvonne said. 'Those I've worked for in the past have their good range and also their cheaper ones and they usually put different labels in them.'

Susie laughed. 'Shall we call it the *Yvonne* range?'

'Now you're teasing me,' Yvonne said and blushed. 'It was just an idea, Miss Susie.'

'I know... and a good one. Make up an example for me, using materials we have in stock, and I will ask Lady Diane for her permission to go ahead with them.'

Susie spent the afternoon checking the bales of material on her stockroom shelves. She was stunned and amazed at how much was left of certain cloths. Of some velvet there was only enough to make trimmings for pockets, cuffs and collars, but they could undoubtedly use it for one of their autumn lines. However, when it came to the various bolts of silks and satins, she discovered there was enough to make several dozen dresses for the afternoons. How could she have over-ordered so much? She had not thought she would be so far out... and surely Betty had advised her to buy extra in case they had a run on certain lines.

Yvonne had the first bolero set in the navy blue suiting ready for Susie to take that evening. The girls had already made up two dozen of the linen blouses and the one hanging with the bolero set looked very well – more suited to the everyday working girl's life than the one with the silk blouse which had very full sleeves.

'This would sell in Harpers for six guineas,' Yvonne told her. 'The better-quality silk blouse would need to fetch eight guineas...'

'It looks very smart,' Susie told her. 'I will show it to Lady Diane tomorrow and hear what she has to say...'

Susie covered the ensemble in a sheeting bag to keep it clean – and to keep the design private until it was put on display in their showroom. She left the workshop and saw that Winnie was on the telephone. She looked flushed and, as she replaced the receiver, bubbled out her news in high excitement.

'I've just taken a huge order for a shop up north,' she said. 'The buyer is a friend of Mrs Harper – and she has bought all our autumn ranges in six sizes – two of each. She even ordered six of those expensive evening gowns you thought might not sell...'

'That is a marvellous order,' Susie said and smiled at Winnie's excitement. 'What is the name of the shop – and the buyer's name?'

'Mrs Rachel Bailey – and the name of the shop is Jenni's... I think she said it belonged to Mr Harper's sister... or had until she died...' Winnie looked at her, suddenly anxious. 'Do you think it was a genuine order?'

'Yes. Lady Diane told me that Mr Harper's sister died very young of something unpleasant. This Mrs Bailey must have taken over the buying. She is a new customer for us.'

'She came into the showroom yesterday while you were out and spent an hour or so looking at our new ranges and our old... Oh, she is buying some of our last season tea gowns, too.' Winnie screwed up her mouth. 'I thought she wouldn't buy anything when she just left like that, but she just told me that she spoke to Mrs Harper first, to make certain she had no objection to her buying the same range as Harpers have ordered.'

'It can hardly affect Harpers if the shop is in the north,' Susie said. 'Thank you, Winnie. The autumn range has really started to take off now. I must admit I was worried for a few weeks. I thought it might fail, but it cannot now.'

'I have been asked if we do any cheaper ranges,' Winnie said. 'At least half a dozen provincial shops have seen our leaflets and want to buy, but everything is a bit expensive for them. One shop is going to try some of the tweed suits – but the bolero set she particularly liked is too expensive for her to sell.'

'Well, that might change,' Susie said. 'I am going to Mother's now. Have you someone to walk home with this evening?'

'Yes. Sam is going to fetch me,' Winnie said and glanced at the heavy mahogany wall clock. It had just chimed the half-hour. 'He will be here at six. We are going to visit some friends after dinner, so you will be on your own with Mrs Collins. I hope you don't mind?'

'Of course not,' Susie said. 'I will see you for dinner...'

She smiled and went out, carefully carrying Yvonne's work over her arm. It was still light and people were still around, which should mean it was safe enough, though some of the attacks had been during daylight hours. In her pocket, Susie had some strong pepper, loosely wrapped, that she intended to throw into the assailant's face should she again be accosted by the vagrant.

As Susie passed the flower shop, Lilly opened the door and

came out to speak. 'I wanted to tell you that Ernie has been released,' she said, looking pleased. 'The police haven't exonerated him, but they said as he couldn't have been the one who attacked me, it is likely he isn't the one they want and they let him go – for now, they told him.'

'Oh, that's so unkind to add that,' Susie replied, feeling cross. 'It wasn't Ernie who tried to steal my box either. They should apologise to him, but I doubt they will.'

'I suppose they are still suspicious because he had Sibby's bag. I am sure he meant to hand it in – but at least they let him go.' Lilly laughed. 'Joe asked him how he felt and he said it was a nice little holiday and they fed him well...'

Susie chuckled. 'That is typical of him, Lilly. Ernie is an odd sort – you can never truly know what he thinks... that inscrutable look, as if he knows so much more than he is telling.'

'Yes,' Lilly agreed, much struck. 'I am certain he has a sad story, but he won't speak of it to anyone.'

'No, I suppose not...' Susie smiled. 'Well, we all have our secrets, after all. I must go. I am catching a bus and I don't want to miss it. I'd like some flowers for my mother tomorrow. See what you can find nice for me and I'll call in the evening...'

Lilly agreed and went back into her shop. Susie walked on and then caught a bus. She could have walked to her mother's home, for it was only six or seven streets further on, but carrying the precious outfit over her arm, she decided to take the bus instead.

So it was just a few minutes later that she walked into Mrs Collins' house and placed the linen bag carefully over the back of a settee at the far end of the room, before bending to kiss her mother's cheek.

'What are we having tonight, Mum?' she asked. 'If you need anything fetching, I can go.'

'No, my love. I got some lamb chops from the butcher this morning. They are in the oven and some nice jacket potatoes; we will have them with carrots, buttered cabbage and a lovely gravy I made.'

'What a treat,' Susie said and gave her a hug. 'You spoil me, Mum. Is that apple crumble I can smell?'

'Trust you.' Mrs Collins laughed. 'You always did love your apple crumble, Susie.' She smiled fondly at Susie. 'And how are things at work, love?'

'Oh, quite good at the moment,' Susie said and told her about all the extra stock she'd discovered on the shelves. 'It must amount to quite a bit of money, Mum. If Yvonne hadn't come up with her idea, I might have just let it be sold off cheaply.'

'You should find ways of using it all,' Mrs Collins advised. 'There must be remnants that could be used for collars and cuffs – or pieces of silk to make a blouse, to go under a costume jacket.'

'Yes, I think there may be,' Susie said hesitantly. 'I am sure we could use much of it up in other ways – but I must ask Lady Diane's permission to deviate from her original designs.'

'I don't see why you have to ask her every time,' Mrs Collins said. 'You were told to make a success of it by Lord Henry – I am sure he would think you should have a free hand in these decisions.'

'Yes... Lady Diane did say almost as much herself, but I prefer to ask her,' Susie said. 'She has a dream, Mum, and she has standards. I might make some money by slightly changing things, but I need her to be happy. If not, there is no point in it. This is all for her and I sometimes think she doesn't care if we make a profit. She simply wants to know her designs are being made up and sold.'

'That is just plain daft,' said the practical Mrs Collins. 'The world would soon flounder to a halt and we'd be in a right mess if everyone just took fancies into their heads. Besides, I know you, and if it fails, you will blame yourself... It is your happiness I care for more than her ladyship's!'

Susie laughed. 'You ought to know me,' she trilled, all her cares of the day floating away. 'You're my mum and I love you...'

15

'So, we're agreed then,' Joe said as he looked round at the small group of grim-faced men. There were eleven of them present, besides Sam Collins, who hadn't been able to come but had told Joe he was in. 'We'll take turns to walk the streets. There are twelve of us – so three shifts of four – two nights off and one on patrol.'

'How long for?' Norm Jackson asked. 'I don't mind 'elpin' fer a while, Joe, but I've a business to run. What are you talkin'? Weeks or months?' Norm ran a small café and was busy most nights, working long hours every day.

Joe frowned as he heard others mumble agreement. 'I know it is a big commitment – but it is difficult to say how long it will take to catch him. The attacks haven't been regular. The second we are concerned about was two weeks after the first – but this week there have been two, two nights runnin'. If that goes on, it won't be safe for our women or our kids.'

'If he touched my kid, I'd swing for him,' Norm growled angrily. 'I'm in, Joe. I was just wonderin' how long it would take to get the bugger and teach him a lesson.'

'The trouble is we don't know who he is or where he came

from,' Jeb said. 'I've seen him a few times, but he's not local. At least, if it's the man I think it is. I reckon he sleeps under the arches down by London Bridge. There's a lot of vagrants there at times – most of them old soldiers...'

'We could ask around. Some of the old servicemen are friendly enough,' Steve Carter put in. 'I set them on as casual labour unloading timber for me in my yard sometimes. If there's a stranger in their midst one of them will say.'

'That would be a help, Nobby,' Joe thanked him, using the familiar nickname. 'But we need to catch this devil in the act. Then, when we give him what for, he'll know why he is being punished. We want him gone – back where he came from so that our women are safe on the streets...'

'Probably just out of prison,' Norm said. 'Makes me wonder why he's picked our lanes for his attacks. If it's the man we think it might be, he's been seen loitering in Dressmakers' Alley a few times – what draws him there?'

'It might be something to do with the clothing business...' Joe said. 'Sibby says he muttered something about the workshop girls when he attacked her...'

'What can they have done to upset him?' Norm asked, shaking his head. 'Has to be somethin' more... if he has a grudge against women...'

'Maybe he didn't know it had changed hands. He may have thought it belonged to Barrow and have some grudge against him,' another man suggested.

'Why would he?' Nobby said. 'Nah, he's just a vagrant out fer what he can get. I reckon the police will pick him up soon enough.'

'I still think it's because of Bert Barrow...' the man repeated his accusation.

Joe looked at him hard. 'What makes you think that, Robbo?'

'Well, Barrow was in prison before he started the workshops,' Robbo muttered, his ears red as everyone looked at him, because he wasn't one who put his opinions forward as a rule. 'I don't know – just sayin' it might be he came to see Barrow and found it all changed... might be he thinks Bert Barrow owed him somethin'.'

'You could be right,' Joe agreed. 'I think he attacks women because they are easy prey. He may have a grudge against that place, because Barrow isn't around. If he is just out of prison, he likely has no home and nowhere to go. Maybe Bert Barrow promised him somethin'...'

'Well, he's not wanted round here,' Jeb said. 'We need to find him and send him orf with a flea in his ear before anyone else is killed.'

'Yeah, that's what we want,' a murmur of voices agreed. 'Now, can I get a drink? I'm dyin' of thirst 'ere...' Robbo complained.

Everyone laughed as Robbo went off to the bar. Watching him, Joe saw that Ernie had just approached the bar. He got up at once and followed Robbo, touching Ernie's arm as he stood patiently waiting his turn.

'Let me get you a drink, Ernie,' he said. 'Everythin' all right now?'

Ernie looked at him for a moment. 'Might lose me job,' he said heavily. 'If the council think I'm attacking women, they won't want me...'

'That's ridiculous,' Joe said. 'You're the best road sweeper we've ever 'ad, Ernie. If they try to turn you off, we'll get a petition up to stop 'em.'

'If they'll listen,' Ernie muttered darkly. 'Damned coppers poking their noses in where they ain't wanted...'

'Two halves of bitter please,' Joe gave his order, handing one glass to Ernie when they arrived and sipping from the other. 'We'll get you a fancy lawyer if we have to, Ernie. We won't let them put you away for something you didn't do.'

Ernie gave a snort of derision but nodded his thanks for the beer and moved away, choosing a small table in the corner of the bar where he could be alone and watch over proceedings.

Joe returned to his friends. 'Poor bugger,' he remarked, jerking his head towards Ernie. 'Might lose his job over this business. It ain't right and I shall be down there at the council offices complaining, if they turn him orf.'

'Won't do a mite of good,' Norm said. 'Council blighters don't give a damn about men like Ernie – give their health and often their lives as a soldier and what thanks do they get? I wouldn't go in the army unless I was forced, but I admire those that do...'

'Yeah, me too,' Joe replied. 'They wouldn't have me in the last war – too young and then said I had flat feet when I turned eighteen.' He finished his beer. 'I'm glad you're with us, Norm. I reckon if we keep a regular patrol for a while, we're sure to get him.'

'Sooner the better,' Norm replied. 'If I get my hands on the bugger, he'll wish he'd never come where he wasn't wanted...'

* * *

Joe visited Sibby in the hospital on Saturday afternoon. He found her sitting up in bed and looking much better, but when she saw him, she burst into tears.

'What's wrong?' he asked, feeling that queer little twist in his chest. 'You ain't worse, are yer?'

Sibby shook her head. 'They are sending me home tomorrow...' She gave a little sob. 'I'm scared, Joe. I can't go back to where I lived, in case he comes after me again.'

'He was probably just sheltering out of the rain and wind,' Joe tried to reassure her, but the tears kept running. 'I'll ask Mum if you can have our Lilly's room. She don't need it...' Even as Joe said the words, he cursed himself for a fool, but Sibby's face lit up like a beacon.

'Would she have me? I'd pay rent and keep my room clean – do the ironing for her too, if she likes. I enjoy ironing.'

'I'll ask her and I'll fetch you tomorrow afternoon. I can't in the morning, but I'll come in the afternoon about two.'

'I'll sit downstairs in the reception area if they want my bed,' Sibby promised, her eyes shining. She was looking at him as if he was her saviour and Joe knew he would have to find her a room elsewhere in the unlikely event his mother refused to have her.

He stayed talking to her until the end of the visiting hour and then left, telling her to wait for him the next day. Sibby nodded, watching him as he walked away. She waved when he looked back at the door. Joe nodded and went out.

For a moment, he leaned against the wall outside the ward, his eyes closed. The trap was closing round him and he knew it was of his own making. His mother would take Sibby in and fuss over her. She had been on at him for a while to marry and settle down, but he'd resisted. With Sibby treating him like a demigod and his mother watching and smiling over the romance, she would immediately suspect.

Joe shook his head to clear the thoughts. He'd got himself into this and had no idea how to stop the ball rolling. Yes, he liked Sibby as much as any girl he'd ever been out with, and yes, he did feel sympathy for her after what had happened, but he knew he wasn't in love with her.

He walked out of the hospital, his shoulders hunched, hands thrust into pockets, feeling like he'd walked into a minefield. It was almost dusk and raining again. The whole of this month it had done nothing but rain and would probably be recorded as one of the wettest Mays ever. Because of the gloom, he didn't see the figure hurrying towards him, nor she him, for she had an umbrella in front of her face to stop the rain driving into her. It brushed against Joe's shoulder as they collided.

'Oh, my goodness,' a woman's voice exclaimed. 'I am so very sorry, sir. I didn't see you. I am in such a hurry – I do hope I didn't hurt you?'

'No, nothing to speak of,' Joe said, staring into a pair of the bluest eyes he had ever seen in his life. Her hair was like spun gold, blowing wildly about a face so lovely it took his breath. 'I'm as much to blame...'

'How nice of you to say so,' the young woman murmured and a blush swept up her cheeks. 'I am very sorry – but I am late for work and Matron threatened me with death if I was late again this week...'

Joe chuckled. 'Surely it can't be that bad,' he said. 'But you get on, miss – I wouldn't want to be the cause of your demise...'

'No, that would be very bad,' she said and he saw the laughter in those blue eyes. 'Forgive me, I must go – but I'm Sarah Leigh and I work here...' She looked at Joe enquiringly.

He held out his hand and she touched it with the fingers of her free hand. 'Joe Ross,' he said. 'I'm a coalman – my own little business...' He felt his collar getting tight and wondered why he'd added that bit. Sarah Leigh was a well-spoken girl, a nurse, and out of his league. 'It was nice to have met you, Miss Leigh.'

'Yes, very. I am sorry. I must go,' she said and threw him a smile so sweet and natural that it stopped him from breathing for a second or two.

Joe stood staring after her as she ran into the hospital. He longed to run after her, to beg her to stay with him, spend the evening with him, but as his breath returned so did his senses. Sarah Leigh was too far above him. Even if there had been no Sibby, it was out of the question.

Joe knew that he'd never met a girl like Sarah before, never had a smile stop his heart – never felt so desperate with longing to take a young woman in his arms...

He walked away, trying to come to terms with what had just happened. Was he dreaming? Had he imagined a girl so perfect he wanted to spend the rest of his life making her happy?

The rain was coming hard now, soaking Joe's jacket and shirt. He was shivering with cold, feeling like he'd been through the ringer, his senses all over the place. He'd walked past his bus stop, on and on through the gathering night, hardly noticing what he did until he reached the end of the road that led into his.

Suddenly, he stopped in his tracks, threw back his head and laughed. He was moonstruck, daydreaming. A girl like that would never look at him – at least not in the way he'd like. She was beautiful but not for him.

As his thoughts cleared, he saw a man lurking under a lamp post just ahead of him – a man in an old soldier's coat. His thoughts came abruptly back to what had troubled him before the incident that had sent his wits scattering.

'Hey you!' he called. 'I want a word...'

The man looked at him and for a moment Joe thought he would take flight, but he didn't; he just stood there and waited. When Joe came up to him, he saw it was Ernie.

'Oh, it is you, Ernie,' he said. 'Sorry. I thought it might have been someone else.'

Ernie looked at him in silence for a moment, then, 'You're not the only one with a score to settle,' he muttered and then turned and walked off.

Joe stood watching him go. What had he meant by that? Had the council taken his job away from him? Joe would make it his business to find out if they had.

He turned into his road, his steps slowing as he saw the lights on in his house. His mother never went to bed these days before he was home. She'd been very ill a year or so back, hardly able to come downstairs, but she was much better now and she liked Joe to be in before she locked the doors.

He drew a sigh. Now he had to tell his mother that he'd promised to ask if Sibby could have Lilly's old room. Joe knew with a sinking heart that she would most certainly say yes.

16

Sibby was sitting on a chair near the entrance to the ward, clutching a small bag containing her things when Joe arrived the next afternoon. She'd done the best she could with her hair and put on a little pink lipstick. Lilly had taken her some fresh clothes earlier that day, telling her that all her possessions would be waiting for her at Lilly's former home.

'Joe will be in this afternoon to fetch you home like he promised,' Lilly had told her. 'Mum and me – well, we thought you might not want to wear the things you had on that night...'

'You're so kind,' Sibby had replied. 'I'd rather burn them than wear them again, even though the blouse was my best one.'

'Well, I should wash it all first and then see what you think when it's fresh and clean. It was a nasty thing to happen, Sibby, but it could have been worse.'

'You mean I might be dead or...' Her face had paled as she had seen the look in Lilly's eyes. 'You mean if he'd...?' Sibby hadn't been able to bring herself to say the words.

'It happens,' Lilly had replied in a flat tone, her eyes lowered.

'Well, I must go, Sibby. I have promised Jeb I'll cook him a pie for his dinner...'

After she'd gone, Sibby had wondered about that curious tone for a while, but then the nurse came and told her she was to get dressed and sit at the end of the ward and, in the excitement of waiting for Joe to fetch her and listening to the instructions about taking the pills she was given if she got headaches, she forgot. Sibby had suffered a few headaches in the last couple of days, but the doctor said it was due to the blow to her head and, unless they got much worse, nothing to worry for.

She jumped to her feet as Joe arrived, looking at him eagerly.

He smiled and held out his hand for her bag. 'I've borrowed a mate's van to take you home in,' he announced. 'Better than travelling on the bus... in case you feel a bit faint.'

'Thank you. I'm so glad your mum was able to have me, Joe. I didn't fancy going back to my old lodgings after what happened – but how did she take it when Lilly went to collect my things?'

'I went round myself,' Joe said. 'Your landlady was nice enough. Upset to think you'd been attacked like that, on her doorstep almost.'

'I thought she would grumble and say I owed her a week's rent...'

'She asked for that right enough,' Joe said with a wry smile. 'I paid her and she was fine about it then. Said she could let it again straight away to a young gentleman who'd been asking if she had a vacancy.'

'I think she likes gentlemen lodgers better than women,' Sibby said with a wry twist of her mouth.

'Mum says she is looking forward to meeting you,' Joe said, deciding he needed to explain. 'Mum has been very ill. She's able to do most things for herself. Ted – he's my eldest brother – and I do all the heavy jobs about the house, and Lilly does a lot of other small jobs, a bit of washing and ironing...'

'I could help with the ironing. I like that,' Sibby reminded him of her offer. 'I'd wash up and tidy my room as well – but I'm not much good at cooking. Mum died before she had time to teach me...' Her eyes were moist with unshed tears. 'I had to get away after that. My father... well, we didn't get on after Mum died. He was always angry and shouting at me if I was late back from my job. I worked in a corset factory, but I wanted to come to London and I took a job as a maid, but it didn't work...'

Joe nodded. 'You told me about that the first time I took you to the pictures,' he remarked. 'You like working at Miss Susie, though, don't you?'

'Yes, I do,' Sibby agreed. 'I'd best let Winnie know that I will be back next week. I might not start until Tuesday. Give myself a day to settle in...'

'Are you certain you feel up to it?' Joe asked gently as he opened the van door for her to slide into the passenger seat. The sun had come out and it suddenly felt like a spring day now that the rain had finally stopped. 'You don't have to worry about money for a while, Sibby. Mum will only charge you for your food – and not until you're on your feet again.'

'Oh, I ought to pay something for my room,' Sibby said doubt-fully. 'I don't want to be a burden to your mum, Joe.'

'She said if you're happy to do some of the jobs in the house, she will only need a contribution for your food.'

'Oh...' Sibby flushed. 'That is so kind. I was paying five shillings for my room and another five for my dinners and a bit of toast in the morning...'

'Well, you talk to Mum and she'll tell you what she needs,' Joe said. 'I live there and I pay the rent and provide the coal, as well as other stuff. Ted helps out if he can, but it's not often he has any spare cash, so it is mostly on me. Jeb gives Lilly plenty of house-keeping and she takes Mum a bag of shopping every Saturday afternoon. Buys her a few luxuries as well, like a new pair of fur slippers or some flowers.'

'Lilly is lovely,' Sibby said and smiled shyly. 'You are lucky to have a nice family, Joe. I always wished for brothers and sisters, but I was the only child. Mum was never well after I was born – or so my father said. He blamed me for her dying young...'

'Well, we'll look after you now,' Joe told her.

Sibby looked at him. He was kind and generous – and she'd missed him after they'd parted for a while, but in her heart, she knew he didn't love her. Her father had loved her mother. It was his terrible grief that had made him turn against Sibby. Joe had taken her out a few times, but she'd never felt the heat of passion in him when he held her. Other men she'd known had pressed her for more than a goodnight kiss; she'd felt the burn of their need and had known they wanted to make love to her. Sibby had never wanted to be loved by any of them, but she did want Joe to hold her and kiss her as if it meant something to him. It was her secret hope that he would ask her to marry him and it was because of his reserve that she'd quarrelled with him and looked for other young men to take her out.

She'd missed his easy-going smile and his gentle manner. She knew he wasn't always like that, but he reserved his rough ways for those that deserved it. Lilly had told her that Joe had been in a bit of bother for fighting more than once, but with her he was always considerate and kind. She loved him for it – but she longed to feel that he wanted, loved and needed her.

He was slowing the van down now, nearing a row of terraced houses. It was a nice little road and the houses all looked to be decent properties; their window frames and doors were painted often enough not to be peeling and although there were no front gardens, the white steps outside each door had recently been scrubbed. White net curtains hung at the front windows of the house Joe led her to, and, as the front door opened, she smelled flowers – or lavender furniture polish. The hall lino gleamed, as did the oak hutch and the hat stand, on which were hung a scarf and a lady's coat.

Sibby followed Joe down the hall into the kitchen at the back. It was a large room and furnished with a hotchpotch of chairs that didn't match, as well as an ancient but comfortable daybed against the wall, and a lovely old Welsh dresser filled with mostly blue and white plates and jugs, also cups and saucers and a variety of trinkets accumulated over the years. The black range had been recently polished and gleamed, and the long pine table had been set with a white cloth, plates, cakes on a little stand and cups. There was also a small vase of sweet-smelling flowers on the table, and the aroma of fresh baking in the air.

It was such a homely atmosphere that Sibby was reminded of her home when she was small and her mother was a capable woman, even though inclined to bouts of sickness. She blinked hard, her throat tight with tears and it was a while before she could focus well enough on the woman sitting by the range. She saw a woman of about fifty, dark hair heavily streaked with grey and a lined pale face, her eyes a faded blue. Those eyes were fixed on Sibby with curiosity and something more.

'Well, so this is Sibby,' Mrs Ross said at last, breaking the awkward silence. 'You are welcome, my dear. Won't you come and say hello to me? I don't get up unless I need to...'

Sibby went to her at once and took the outstretched hands in hers, kneeling down at her side on the slate-tiled floor. 'Forgive me, ma'am. I was so overcome... it is such a lovely room and feeling... so homely...' Unbidden, the tears trickled down her cheeks.

'You poor child,' Mrs Ross said and leaned forward to kiss

Sibby's cheek. She sent a look of approval towards her son, who was hovering uncertainly. 'Take Sibby's things up to her room, Joe. We'll have tea when you come down. I've made a seed cake and Lilly fetched me a new pot of strawberry jam. We'll have it with the fresh bread she made for me.' She looked at Sibby. 'Our Lilly makes the best bread ever, but only on Sundays. She is too busy the rest of the week, looking after that shop of hers... but that will have to change soon, when she has the baby.'

'Is Lilly having a baby?' Sibby looked at Joe, but his back was turned as he obeyed his mother and took Sibby's bag up to her room. 'She doesn't really show yet, does she?'

'Not yet, but she will,' Mrs Ross said with satisfaction. 'She says she wants to continue with the shop, but I don't see how she can once the baby is here... Besides, it is time she gave up work. It's not as if that husband of hers can't afford to keep her.'

'Perhaps Lilly will pay someone to help look after the baby,' Sibby said, rising to take her seat at the table when she was invited to do so, but a little shake of the head from Mrs Ross indicated displeasure.

'She ought to look after her husband and her child,' Lilly's mother said. 'She can pay someone to take care of the shop – until the child is at school, though by then she might have another one or two.'

'You wouldn't like to look after your grandchild?' Sibby ventured.

Mrs Ross looked at her and then got up to lift the kettle from the range, bringing it to the table to first warm the pot and then make the tea. Sibby saw that each movement was laboured.

'Forgive me. I didn't realise...'

'Until a few months ago I could hardly get down the stairs,' Mrs Ross told her. 'Yes, I would look after Lilly's little one – but I doubt I could do it.'

'Ah, I see.' Sibby moved forward to offer help. 'Shall I take the kettle from you?'

'Nay. I do what I can – a bit of cooking and tidying, but I can't be washing a baby's clothes. I send my sheets out and Joe's best shirts. I do wash his working things, but he puts them in the copper for me and I just rinse them when they've soaked long enough and he puts them through the mangle when he gets in. Lilly washes my bits and pieces for me...'

'I can use a mangle,' Sibby said. 'I can wash my own clothes – and do some of your things, if you wish.'

'That would be a big help. Lilly will not feel like it when she gets a bit further on.'

'I would be glad to do it for you. I helped my mother with all the chores...' Sibby caught back a sigh. 'I could iron Joe's shirts if you wished...'

'Well, you'll need to ask him about that,' Mrs Ross said. 'He pays someone to do them for him.' She picked up the large brown pot as Joe returned to the kitchen. 'I've told Joe I shan't charge you rent for the moment, but a few shillings will be needed for your keep. Now then, Sibby – how do you like your tea...?'

'She seems a nice little thing,' Mrs Ross said to Joe later, when he'd shown Sibby her room and returned to the kitchen. 'Eager to help and honest. Not as pretty as I thought she might be, but that's not important if she has a good heart.'

'Mum, I told you. Sibby is a friend. We have been out a bit and I like her – but I'm not at all sure that she will suit me...'

'Your brother was married before he was your age,' Mrs Ross said. 'I worry about you sometimes, Joe. I know I've been better of late, but with my heart the way it is, I could take a turn for the worse and be gone – and how would you manage then?'

'You're not going to die, Ma,' he said, using the name he had for her when in a teasing mood. 'Don't push me. I will make up my own mind when I'm ready.'

'Why did you ask if she could come here then?'

'Because she was frightened to go back to her lodgings. I do care for her – but perhaps I'm not the sort as falls in love...' His expression was unreadable at that moment, but something in his face made his mother fear for him.

'Joe, if you don't care for her, don't let her think you mean marriage,' she said. 'You're my son and I'd like to see you settled – but not if it would be wrong for you. Ted isn't that happy... He loves his children and maybe his wife, too – but she is a scold.'

'Sibby isn't like that,' Joe said and then frowned at his mother as they heard footsteps coming down the stairs. 'Well, I'm off to meet a mate. I'll be back late, so don't wait up for me... either of you.' He nodded to Sibby and went to take his jacket from the peg on the back door. 'I'll walk you to work in the mornin' if you're goin' in, Sibby.'

'Yes, I think I will,' Sibby said and watched as he left. She looked round the room and saw that it was neat and tidy. 'Is there anything you'd like me to do, Mrs Ross?'

'Not this evening. It's Sunday. I usually sit with a bit of sewing. I've got a machine in the best room. If you want to make anything for yourself, I can help you pin it on when you're ready.'

'I might make myself a new dress,' Sibby said. 'Isn't there anything I can do for you?'

'Just sit and talk to me – unless you want to go and visit a friend?'

Sibby shook her head. She didn't have many friends in London. The girls she worked with were nice enough, but she wasn't close enough to any of them to just pop round their houses without being invited.

'I have a few bits to wash,' she said. 'If you wouldn't mind.'

'Not on a Sunday,' Mrs Ross said again. 'You can hem this shirt I am making for Joe's birthday, if you wish – and sit here by the fire. While we work, you can tell me where you came from and why you moved to London.'

17

'I think you should have this...' The Honourable Matthew Cooper walked into Lady Diane's sitting room on Monday afternoon and handed her a small blue leather box. She had been sitting with her sketching pad, staring into the distance, and his words brought her thoughts back from their wanderings. 'Miss Fairley didn't want it...'

Lady Diane opened the box and saw a beautiful three stone emerald and diamond ring. Her gaze flew to his face as she understood what it was. 'Pamela refused your offer? Oh, my dear. I am so sorry...' She offered him her hand in sympathy and he took it briefly, giving her a twisted smile.

'Apparently, the match suited her parents, which is why I was permitted to escort her to various functions – but she told me that if I was thinking of making her an offer, I should understand her terms...' He looked at his stepmother, his expression a mixture of hurt and annoyance. 'Miss Fairley does not wish to make her home in the country. She requires a town house, where she intends to spend most of her year. She would be prepared to live on the estate during July, August and September, but that is all...'

'Oh, that was unkind of her, Matthew.'

'I believe she felt she was doing me a favour.'

'I suppose it was only fair to warn you,' Lady Diane said carefully, because she sensed his deep hurt, to his pride and perhaps his heart. 'Since you spend much of your time on the estate now... are you very disappointed, dearest?'

'Not as much as I thought I would be,' he replied with that twisted smile. 'It hurt, but perhaps more my pride than my heart.' He had not given his darling stepmother the full version of Pamela Fairley's rejection for he believed it would shock her. His intended had told him that she would do her duty and give him an heir but would then prefer to go her own way. A marriage of convenience was her ideal; it was not his. 'As you may imagine, I decided that I would not offer for her and I wished her happiness in her chosen life.'

'Well, you are young yet, and if she is not the lady for you, it is well that she spoke out,' Lady Diane said for he was not yet two and twenty. 'I dare say you will fall in love several times before you find the perfect wife, Matthew. I am sorry you've been hurt and my dearest wish is that you should be happy in your marriage, as I am with your father. I think Pamela is very foolish, but perhaps you are fortunate to have escaped so lightly. I have thought her a little reserved...' She indicated the chair next to her, hoping to distract him. 'Have a look at my latest design and tell me what you think...'

Matthew obeyed, this time with his natural smile of affection. He took an interest in his stepmother's business beyond that of a mere accountant. Looking at the gown she had been sketching, which had an Egyptian look, something that a pharaoh's wife might have worn, he nodded. 'Yes, I like it, Diane, and I am aware it is all the rage amongst the Flapper girls... but what is this...?' He had flicked over the page and seen something that caught his attention. 'Now, I like this very much!'

'Oh, that...' Lady Diane glanced at it doubtfully. The sketch was of a waisted jacket with military frocking and brass buttons, worn over a pair of culottes, very full and softly draped. 'It came to me, but I am not at all sure that it is of any use for Miss Susie. I doubt that it would sell in great numbers – and Susie is anxious that we should make a profit this year.'

'It would be perfect on ladies with the right figure – tall and slim. So elegant, Diane. You should certainly try it. Even if it is only a limited range... in fact, I think it should be.' He smiled and nodded to himself. 'Why don't you try a limited edition of some of your more expensive designs? It wouldn't break the bank to produce just a handful of them and sell them at a higher price. Even if you only sold one or two...'

'I am not sure Susie would approve,' Lady Diane replied. 'She was quite excited because she had discovered that we have large stocks of previously used materials on the shelves, which she says could be made up into a cheaper version of one of my designs. She thinks that we can produce a range using up these remnants and make more money...'

'You are not too happy about it?' Matthew guessed. 'Did you tell her so?'

'No, because what she says is sensible. If one of my designs proves successful, it will soon be copied in a cheaper version. Susie says we may as well do it ourselves – and I suppose she is right. A business should make money...'

'Yes, if you wish it to continue...' Matthew looked at her intently. 'Are you finding it difficult to come up with more ideas? Have you perhaps tired of it?'

'No! Oh no,' Lady Diane said swiftly. 'I love my work. I wish I might be able to be more involved with the production. Yet I do regret that we need to keep the costs low in the interests of making a profit... when clothes should be beautiful for their own sake...'

She had such a whimsical look on her face that Matthew threw back his head and laughed long and hard. 'Oh, dearest Diane,' he said, 'I am so glad I came to see you. Father was so lucky to find you.' His eyes sparkled with mischief and the hurt expression he had worn earlier had gone. 'How would it be if I take a look at the books and the stock register? Perhaps I can help find a way to cut the costs without lowering your standards?'

'Would you, Matthew? How kind you are...'

'I shall do so as soon as it is convenient to Miss Collins,' he told her. 'Then I must return to the country – unless Father has work for me here...'

It was at that moment that Lord Henry entered his wife's sitting room. He was frowning, but his expression lightened as he saw the smile in his son's eyes.

'Ah, there you are, Matthew,' he said. 'I came to ask if you still wish to continue with our ball in August, Diane?'

'Most certainly I do,' she said, smiling at him and then at Matthew. 'It will be a celebration of Matthew's birthday and my recovery from my darling Marie's birth. We haven't held a large party since I was unwell and it is high time we celebrated...' Her eyes twinkled at her stepson. 'It will show a certain person that we at least do not regret her foolishness.'

Matthew nodded. 'I shall leave you to talk,' he said and pressed her hand. Silently, she offered him the ring box, but he dismissed it with a jerk of his head. 'Keep it, Diane. I have no use for it. You may wear it or give it to a friend if you wish...'

'You might want it one day,' she suggested.

'No. If I fall in love again, I will buy her another ring,' he said and took his leave, closing the door behind him.

Lord Henry hesitated for a moment, then, 'He seems to have recovered from his disappointment.'

'I think he was merely dazzled – Miss Fairley is very beautiful,'

Lady Diane said. 'I think her cold – but it might be that she hides her feelings well.'

'It was a suitable match,' Lord Henry said. 'He was young to marry, as we thought when he told us of his intentions. Perhaps just as well, if his heart is not broken. I heard a rumour that... I shall not repeat it, but I shall not hide from you that I am glad he had the sense not to offer after she laid down her terms.'

'No woman in love would make such terms,' Lady Diane murmured. She had a good idea what he'd heard rumoured but would not press him to tell her. It was not her secret.

'Exactly.' He smiled and bent to kiss her cheek. 'I was fortunate, my dearest darling. I would have Matthew happy when he takes a wife – as happy as I have been.' He took her hand, looking at her anxiously. 'Are you certain you wish for this ball, my love? It will mean a great deal of planning on your part... all the invitations and decisions will be yours and you are already so busy...'

'I am quite well now, Henry,' she said and smiled as he took the chair Matthew had vacated. 'I have already made my lists and the invitations were to have been ordered when we heard from Matthew – now they must be changed for it is no longer in celebration of his engagement...'

'Then, if it pleases you...' He frowned. 'Will you invite the Fairleys?'

'Naturally; they are our friends,' Lady Diane said. 'Whether Miss Fairley will choose to come is a matter for her conscience... but I hope she does, and I hope that Matthew will be able to be happy despite her.'

'Why do you think she did it?' Lord Henry asked. 'Encouraged him to dangle after her for months – and then laid down those ridiculous terms, for living in town was not all of it, believe me.'

'We may never know,' Lady Diane replied, 'but I am glad that she was honest enough to tell him, rather than accepting his offer and then making his life a misery...'

Susie was surprised when Matthew walked into the workrooms that Tuesday morning. She was discussing something with Yvonne and turned swiftly as she heard a little gasp from the seamstresses. Seeing him, she smiled, murmured an apology to Yvonne, and went to meet him.

'Mr Matthew,' she greeted him gladly. 'I did not know you had returned to town.'

'Yes, I arrived yesterday morning,' he replied and offered his hand. 'Lady Diane told me you were a little worried about the accounts – would you like me to balance them with the stock you've discovered?'

'Could you?' she asked and, as he nodded, led the way through to the stockroom. It was lined with shelves that were almost completely filled with bales of expensive materials. 'The bolts of silk on that shelf have just been purchased and are not yet paid for. I am going to pay tomorrow and I have the money in the account. Everything else is on the books. Those four shelves are all new season – but everything else is left over from the past two seasons...'

'Rather a lot.' Matthew eyed them thoughtfully. 'Were the models these materials were intended for not successful?'

'Only one did not sell well,' Susie replied and pointed to two bolts of a dark green tweed. 'The rest all sold in fairly substantial numbers – and we did not have any cancellations.'

'How was it that so much extra was ordered?' Matthew wondered aloud.

'I am not sure,' Susie said, frowning. 'I discussed the quantity needed with Betty and with Yvonne – but then I was advised to order extra in case we had repeats and could not purchase it again. It seemed to make sense at the time, but so much has accumulated.'

Matthew nodded thoughtfully. 'I would say that the stock you have here might run into a few hundred pounds. That makes a big difference to your margins, Susie.'

'Yes, I realise that – and I don't know how I wasn't aware of the build-up until now, but for some reason or other, it didn't occur to me until the other day. I'm not quite sure what to do. Betty suggested we sell the remnants, but I think that would bring in a fraction of their worth...'

He nodded. 'It would be a pity to throw it all away. It makes good business sense to reuse what you can in other ways...'

'Yes, that's what I thought,' Susie said. 'I'm not sure that Lady Diane was happy about the idea.'

'She doesn't want to lower her standards,' he replied. He stood looking around him for a few moments. 'You sell her designs under the label Miss Susie, do you not?'

'Yes, we do...' Susie hesitated, then, 'I thought we might sell the cheaper versions as Miss Yvonne...'

His gaze moved to her face. 'I think that is an excellent idea. You could also then do a rather more expensive – shall we say, even exotic, range as Miss Diane...'

Susie's eyes opened wide. 'She would never agree... Lord Henry would not allow it!'

'Oh, I think my father is too good a businessman to veto something that would make you more viable.'

'But... are you sure we can do that?' Susie questioned. 'I mean... we are called Miss Susie. It is our label...'

'You are a clothing manufacturer,' Matthew told her. 'You are not haute couture; therefore I see no reason why you shouldn't have more than one range. Miss Susie for your main lines; Miss Yvonne for a cheaper range, based loosely on the same designs but with some differences; and the exclusive models that will be Miss Diane. You could make a limited range of perhaps half a dozen at first.'

'Is that what Lady Diane wants?' Susie asked dumbfounded.

'I think she may when I explain it to her,' he said and grinned. 'So that is your stock disposed of – though, if I were you, in future I would not purchase so much more than you are likely to need. Unless you were offered a bargain for taking a large amount...'

Susie was struck by this and then she laughed. 'Do you know – I think I might have done that a couple of times. Yes, it must be in the books... I believe it happened with some silk and... that navy suiting. I wasn't sure how much I would need and I thought it was a bargain.'

'I think I had best take your stock books and your account books home with me. I will check them this evening and return them to you in the morning, Susie – if you will allow me?'

'Of course, sir,' she said. 'If you could tell me whether we are likely to break even or if I must cut costs somehow...' She faltered as she met his slightly amused gaze. 'I do want to make this work for her... my lady.'

'It is the joy of seeing her creations brought to life and to know that others wear them that means most to her,' he told her. 'However, I am of your opinion that a business ought to make money, and we will make this work between us if we can...'

'Bless you, sir,' she cried thankfully and saw him frown.

'Have I not asked you to call me Matthew?'

'Yes, Mr Matthew but... I can't get used to it.' Susie laughed. 'I've worked for my lady for years and it doesn't seem respectful.'

'My father would no doubt agree,' he said and his slightly twisted smile made her catch her breath. 'I am of another generation, Susie. If we are to work together, it must be Susie and Matthew.'

'Very well, Matthew.' She took a breath, hesitated, then, 'Are we to wish you and Miss Fairley happy?'

His smile vanished. 'You may wish me happy, but Miss Fairley was not of a mind to become my wife...' He put a finger to her mouth as she would have exclaimed. 'I am not heartbroken. It was merely a mistake on both sides.'

Susie inclined her head but said nothing. He took her ledgers and left, walking through the workroom. She watched as he stopped and spoke to some of the girls as he passed, indicating their work, and clearly asking them if they enjoyed what they did.

'Well, what a surprise,' Yvonne said, coming up to her as Matthew went out. 'He is such a handsome young man, isn't he?'

'Oh yes, very. His father is the same,' Susie replied. 'In fact, his lordship has become even more attractive as he ages; it is the charm, I think.'

'Oh yes, very charming.' Yvonne rolled her eyes. 'He will make someone a wonderful husband – but not for the likes of us, or me anyway...'

'I am more than ten years his senior,' Susie said, laughing. 'Now, then, what were we speaking of before he arrived?'

'I was suggesting that the azure blue silk we have left over could be made up into silk blouses for the cheaper range we planned... if that is to go ahead?'

'I think it might now,' Susie told her with a little smile. 'Miss Yvonne, Miss Susie – and, perhaps Miss Diane... for a new expensive limited range...'

'She never will...?' Yvonne breathed. 'Surely?'

'We shall wait and see.' Susie smiled to herself. 'It would be a very limited range – but it is still to be decided...'

18

'Do you want to walk home with us?' Yvonne asked Sibby that evening when the girls were preparing to leave work.

'I could walk part of the way with you,' Sibby replied, looking about her as they left the workshop. There was no sign of Joe and she wasn't sure whether he would come to walk her home as nothing had been said that morning. 'I'm living at Joe Ross' home now with his mother and him.'

'Yes, someone said.' Yvonne smiled at her. 'I'll walk the rest of the way with you if you like, Sibby. I know it must be uncomfortable for you after what happened – even though that was much later in the evening.'

'Yes, it was… thanks, Yvonne. It isn't far after I leave you.' Sibby was disappointed that Joe hadn't come, but he seemed to be busy. If he wasn't working, he was out with his friends. She'd thought he might suggest they went out somewhere on Monday evening, even if it was only to the pub, but he'd just told them he was meeting a mate and gone. She'd spent another evening sitting by the fire sewing.

She hesitated, then, 'Do you ever go to the pictures, Yvonne?

I'd like to go, but I'm not sure who to ask. Most of the girls are courting...'

Yvonne looked at her for a moment and then nodded. 'If you'd care to go to the early house on Saturday. I've been promising my son a treat and I'd decided to go to the matinee this Saturday. You could come with us if you like.'

'Oh...' Sibby hesitated. It wasn't what she'd hoped for, but it was something. 'Thank you. Yes, I should like to come. Perhaps we could go for a fish and chip supper later?'

'I'm not sure I can afford that as well as the cinema tickets...' Yvonne said doubtfully.

'Oh, I'll pay,' Sibby said quickly. 'For our suppers. I don't pay rent now, just my food – and I do a few jobs round the house. I am doing some ironing this evening, I think.'

'I couldn't let you pay for John and me,' Yvonne denied her. 'We'll pay for ourselves and you pay your own. It would be nice to make a real treat of it. Yes, all right, Sibby. We'll do that...'

They had reached the end of the road where Sibby must turn off. She did so, refusing Yvonne's offer to walk with her. The back of her neck felt a bit shivery as she set off, but there were lots of people about and she realised she was being silly. The man who had hurt her would hardly try again when so many people were around, and, besides, it seemed that he'd attacked girls randomly. Joe and Lilly thought he was just a vagrant looking for money to fund his drinking habit.

She reached Joe's home safely. His mother was sitting by the range, on which a saucepan of soup was gently bubbling.

Mrs Ross looked up and smiled at her. 'Is Joe with you, Sibby? I thought he was going to meet you after work.'

'I didn't see him. I walked a part of the way with some of the other girls.'

'As long as you weren't scared – not that it is likely to happen again. Joe says he just attacks anyone who might have a little money. It is about time the police had him in custody.'

'I wish they would arrest him,' Sibby said, giving a little shiver. 'What can I do for you, Mrs Ross?'

'Nothing for the moment. We'll have supper when Joe comes in. I doubt he'll be long – but I'll make a cup of tea. If you're not going out, you might iron Joe's shirts later. I asked and he said it was all right.'

'I am going out on Saturday afternoon with a friend,' Sibby said. 'Yvonne and I are taking her son to the pictures and then for a fish and chip supper afterwards.'

'Well, that's exciting,' Mrs Ross said and looked surprised. 'You will spend all your wages in one go, Sibby. Still, you young things need a bit of fun sometimes.' She frowned. 'I hope Joe won't take himself off all evening again tonight...'

'Who is taking himself off?' Joe asked, coming into the kitchen through the back door and surprising them. He glanced at Sibby. 'You got home all right. I was busy delivering coke to the factory and couldn't make it in time to fetch you.'

'You're always working,' Mrs Ross told her son. 'We haven't seen you much since Sunday teatime...'

'I shall be out again this evening,' Joe said and looked at Sibby apologetically. 'I'm sorry I'm not around much lately – but what I'm doing is important.'

'And just what would that be?' his mother demanded sharply.

Joe hesitated, then bent to take off his work boots before walking to the table, pulling out his chair and sitting. 'We've got up a little group of us and we're patrolling the area – from Dressmakers' Alley to Mulberry Lane and as far as the Commercial Road in the other direction.'

'You're looking for the man who attacked me?' Sibby cried, her heart catching. She'd thought he was trying to keep out of her way. 'Oh, Joe! I had no idea.'

'We're taking it in turns – me, Jeb, Sam, Norm and several others,' he said with a little shrug as his mother frowned. 'I am on again this evening and then I have Wednesday off. I thought we might go to the pictures then, Sibby.' He looked at his mother. 'Would you like to come with us, Mum?'

'No, but thank you for the offer,' she replied, smiling at him. 'I'm content here in my own home with my sewing or a nice magazine to read. You younger ones should make the most of it while you can. Once you settle down to marriage these treats don't come often.'

'Do you fancy the pictures?' Joe looked at Sibby.

'Yes, please,' she agreed instantly. 'But why are you looking for that horrid man, Joe? What can you do if you find him?'

'That depends,' Joe replied. 'At least we can prevent him from harming any other girl.'

'And how will you do that – as if I couldn't guess?' his mother said. 'Joe, you shouldn't get involved, lad...'

Sibby too wanted to ask more, but at that moment the door opened and Lilly came in, followed by her husband Jeb. He was carrying a bulky package, which he took to a large dark wood chest of drawers, placing it down on the top.

'And what is that?' Mrs Ross asked as he began to take off the brown paper coverings to reveal a large shiny wooden box.

'It is a gramophone,' Lilly told them, laughing at her mother's expression. 'Jeb bought me one for my last birthday and I asked him if he could find one for you, Mum. It plays music and I've brought you some records I think you would like...'

'Good gracious me!' Mrs Ross exclaimed, distracted by the sight of Jeb winding the contraption. Lilly set a large black disc on it and placed the needle on it. Music started to play – a sweet sound that filled the room and made Lilly's feet tap. 'Do turn it off, Lilly. I can't hear myself think...'

'Oh, Mum,' Lilly cried, looking disappointed at her mother's lack of enthusiasm. 'There are several records. You can choose something you like.'

'I prefer peace and quiet,' Mrs Ross said. 'You will make my head ache. Take it away...'

'No, don't do that, Lilly,' Joe put in quickly. 'I will buy it – and Sibby can have it in her room. If she wants to play it up there it won't be too loud for you, Mum. We can bring it down sometimes in the evenings – and you'll get used to it.' He looked at his mother and she glanced down.

'Well, I suppose if you want it...' she said, grumbling. 'Lilly is forever wasting her money.'

Joe's eyes met his sister's across the room. 'It was a lovely thought,' he said. 'Mum will get used to it – and I've been wanting one for ages. We can take it in the parlour and dance to it, Sibby. Mum doesn't have to listen if we shut the door.'

Mrs Ross set her mouth but didn't say any more.

Lilly looked at her mother and then smiled at Joe. 'I'll give it to you for your birthday then, Joe, if Mum doesn't want it.'

'Oh, she'll enjoy it when she gets used to it,' Joe said. He gave his mother a look of reproach. Lilly was always doing something to help her and yet she never seemed to have a loving word for her.

Lilly nodded to Joe and turned to her husband. 'Shall we get back then?'

'No. You'll stay and have a cup of tea,' Mrs Ross said, her tone softer in response to Joe's silent reproach. 'It was a kind thought, Lilly. I just wish you two would think of the future and save your money. You'll have a child soon – and they're always needing somethin'.' It was as close to an apology as she would go.

Sibby smiled at Lilly as Joe carried the gramophone upstairs. 'I think they are marvellous things. I never imagined I would ever have one. Not that it is mine, but Joe has said I can play it...'

'I play ours whenever I have the chance,' Lilly told her. She moved the kettle onto the range to heat and the tea tray to a position in front of her mother. When the whistle let them know that the water was boiled, she made the tea and Mrs Ross was pouring it when Joe came back to the kitchen.

'You've given us some lovely records,' Joe said. 'Gershwin and Al Johnson – and there's a couple by Enrico Caruso, Mum. You will like those...'

'Shall I – why?'

'He has a wonderful voice,' Joe told her. 'He is the most popular Italian tenor and very famous. You must have heard of him.'

'Well, I might,' she conceded. 'Where did you hear him then?'

'I think the first time was at the cinema,' Joe replied, wrinkling his brow in thought. 'The reel had broken down and we had to wait ages before they got the film going again. Everyone was jeering and shouting for them to get a move on – and then they played some of his records...' Joe chuckled at the memory. 'It was like everyone was mesmerised and it suddenly went quiet, because we were all spellbound by his voice. I've heard several of his records since then; they play them up the Palais sometimes.' He looked at Sibby. 'You must have heard him?'

Sibby nodded. 'Yes, I think the last time we went they had his records on while the band had a rest.' The dance hall they went to sometimes normally played the most popular records in between sessions so that the band had a chance to refresh themselves.

Joe smiled at her. 'We might go one Saturday. It depends whether I'm on patrol or not...'

'You just be careful,' Mrs Ross said, frowning as she remembered what they'd been talking of earlier. 'I don't want you lying in a hospital bed – or worse.'

'I agree with Mum there,' Lilly said with a reproachful glance at her husband Jeb. 'I know we're all angry at what has been going on, and the police's slowness in catching him, but, well, just be careful.'

'I've told you not to worry, love,' Jeb said confidently. 'It's him that will be sorry when we catch him.'

Joe drank his tea. 'Well, I'm off,' he said, placing his empty cup on the table. 'I'll be late, so no need to sit up. Are you coming, Jeb?'

'I'm going to see Lilly home first,' Jeb said and looked lovingly at his wife. She smiled back at him and got up to clear the tea things, but Sibby was on her feet.

'I'll do it, Lilly. You get off home...'

'I'll leave it to you then.' Lilly nodded to her and then bent to kiss her mother's cheek. As she turned away, Mrs Ross caught her wrist.

'It was a kind thought. I just worry about you two – forever spending your money instead of saving for a rainy day.'

'Don't you worry about us, Mrs Ross,' Jeb said cheerfully. 'We're doin' all right. One day I'll be rich and then I'll buy us all a lovely big house with a garden – and one of them Rolls-Royce...' He grinned. 'I fancy a posh motor car.'

'Don't be daft!' Mrs Ross said, but she smiled at him. 'The big house with a garden sounds nice, though.'

Jeb grinned at her and took Lilly's hand, whispering something in her ear as they left.

Mrs Ross sighed and looked at Sibby as she carried the cups and saucers to the sink in the scullery.

'I just hope he doesn't get himself in trouble,' she said. 'They are both good lads, but inclined to be headstrong. Lilly should make sure she doesn't let him ruin it all...'

'I doubt he is likely to do that, Mrs Ross,' Sibby replied. 'They are both doing well with their shops.'

'As long as it keeps going,' Mrs Ross said. 'I've lived longer than any of you and I know the way things can change all of a sudden. My husband had a good business and we never went without… but then he got ill and died. The boys took his coal round over, but then the war came – and somehow things were never the same. Joe does all right, but he doesn't have a lot of money to spare.'

Sibby was silent. She wasn't sure if she was being warned or not. She joined Mrs Ross by the fire and took up her sewing, but after about twenty minutes of silence, she was surprised when Mrs Ross asked her if she wanted to go and play some records.

'I would like to try it,' Sibby said. 'If you're sure it won't disturb you?'

'You can put that Caruso record on,' Mrs Ross said. 'I might come to the bottom of the stairs and listen for a minute or so…'

'Yes, all right, I will.' Sibby jumped up and went eagerly up to her room. She selected one of the records and put it on the machine, then gently wound it a little and lifted the heavy head of the player so that it rested on the record. The rich sound of the famous tenor's voice flooded her bedroom, flowing out through the open door and down the stairs. She was certain Mrs Ross was there listening, even though she would probably deny it later.

Smiling to herself, Sibby drifted about the room as if she were dancing a waltz. It was such a treat to have music in the house – and a shame that Lilly's generosity had not been rewarded as it ought by her mother.

19

Sibby met Lilly the next morning as she was coming out of her gate and they walked to work together. Sibby told her that she'd played Enrico Caruso's records and that her mother had come to the foot of the stairs to listen.

'I am sorry she didn't accept it from you, Lilly,' Sibby told her as they reached the corner of Dressmakers' Alley. 'She was a bit unkind to you... and I know she liked the music. She told me I could play it whenever I wished.'

Lilly hesitated, then, 'Mum says things she doesn't mean, Sibby. I've learned not to take notice when she's sharp with me. She's had a hard life – but her bark is harsher than her bite.'

'Yes, I know. She is usually as nice as pie with Joe and his brother. To be fair, she's been fine with me.' Sibby looked at her awkwardly. 'I didn't mean to upset you.'

'I know.' Lilly nodded, looking sad, then, 'It is what it is, Sibby. She is my mum and I love her. Jeb gets upset when she hurts me. He says I should stop giving her things and stay away for a while, until she's ready to be proper with me – but I won't. I can't have her goin' short if I can help it.'

'I think you're lovely with her,' Sibby said and squeezed her arm. 'I like livin' with your mum, Lilly. She won't let me pay rent, so I help with the chores; I've been ironing Joe's best shirts, so he doesn't have to pay for them, then I either sew or go to my room. I can play music now and pretend I'm at a dance with Joe.' She gave a little giggle.

'Sibby...' Lilly looked a bit unsure. 'Don't hope for too much. Joe – I'm not sure he's ready to settle down yet.'

'Oh, I know that!' Sibby said quickly. 'We're just friends...' That's all they were right now, but Sibby cherished her dreams. One day he would wake up and realise that she would be a good wife for him.

'As long as you're happy...' Lilly hesitated but wouldn't say more.

They parted and Lilly went into her shop, while Sibby walked on. She reached Miss Susie just as Winnie came rushing from the other way.

'Oh, I'm late,' she gasped, out of breath. 'I went to the shop with Sam and we had a cup of tea... and then I realised the time.'

'It's not half past seven yet,' Sibby said. 'The church will strike...' Even as she said it, a bell chimed once for the half-hour. The alley was beginning to wake up, some of the businesses opening their shutters.

Winnie rushed in, taking off her jacket and fluffing her hair as she sat down at her desk.

Betty came through from the workroom and looked at them. 'I expect you girls here five minutes before your time,' she grumbled. 'Just because Miss Susie is a good employer, you lot think you can take advantage...'

'Sorry, Betty,' Winnie said. 'I know I'm a couple of minutes late – though our time is half past seven.'

'In Bert Barrow's day, you'd have been fined sixpence,' Betty said crossly. 'I had to answer that contraption, Winnie – and I took an order. It's for six of the blue silk tea gown. Mr Robinson... he says he will ring back to confirm later.'

'Oh, I am sorry,' Winnie said as Sibby disappeared into the workrooms.

Sibby couldn't hear what was said after the door closed behind her. She saw that most of the other girls were already at their stations, apart from Yvonne. That was unusual, because she was always one of the first to arrive.

Betty returned to the workroom, looking round as another of the seamstresses arrived. She frowned as she saw that Yvonne wasn't in. 'We are working on a new design today – or we were supposed to be,' she said as the girls hushed and looked at her. 'Yvonne was supposed to show us...' Her words drifted off as the door opened and Yvonne entered.

'I am sorry I am late,' she apologised. 'I was stopped by the police on my way here. There has been some sort of incident... I saw police officers and what I think was a doctor kneeling on the pavement...'

'Was it another assault?' Betty asked sharply. 'When did it happen?'

There was a little buzz of concern from the girls, but Yvonne shook her head. 'I don't know – I was diverted and made to go another way because they had closed off a section of Mulberry Lane. That's why I'm a couple of minutes late...'

'Well, forget about that now.' Betty's voice was edgy. 'What are we supposed to be working on today then?'

Yvonne nodded and went to stand next to her. 'I'm not sure if Miss Susie has told everyone yet – but we are introducing a new line of slightly less expensive daywear into our collection.'

A little bubble of speculation met her words and Yvonne smiled.

'We still want the same high standards of work from you, don't forget that – but we are going to make that bolero set from a fine wool suiting with a linen blouse...' She unwrapped the brown paper parcel she had been carrying and held the sample she'd made at home up to show them. 'It is the same style, so we all know what we're doing – but the waistband is plain and not pleated. We have used a cheaper braid on the bolero and the blouses have already been made up.'

'I like that better than the original one,' a seamstress named Ruby put in as Yvonne finished speaking. 'You could wear that at any time rather than just a special occasion.'

'Yes, that is perfectly true,' Yvonne agreed. 'This is the first in our new line – which will have a different label.'

'What will it be?'

'Miss Yvonne...' Her announcement was met with gasps and some laughter. She smiled. 'Yes, I felt the same, but it is a good idea to have a distinction between the different priced ranges.' She paused. 'We might also produce a far more expensive line one day, too – but that hasn't been finally decided as yet.'

'Are we big enough to expand, Mrs Ford?' one of the girls asked Betty, who was looking thoughtful.

'I've no idea,' Betty said grimly. 'When I told Miss Susie she needed to make cheaper stuff, she told me it wasn't what she wanted...'

'It will still be good quality,' Yvonne said. 'Make no doubt of that – we still do our best work. The cloth will be good, but we'll cut out some of the fancy stuff. We're going to make six models in the Miss Yvonne range and see what happens. If we get big orders for them, it might be that we could expand. We have a large stockroom upstairs and I suppose we might install some more workstations if we need more seamstresses.'

'We could do overtime,' one of the seamstresses said. 'I wouldn't mind working extra time if Miss Susie asked. I need the money for my daughter's wedding.'

'When is Shirley getting married then?' Sibby asked, a slight look of jealousy in her eyes.

'In September we hope,' Vera replied. 'She and Rodney are saving hard, but they don't earn much and we can't give them a wedding and all the furniture – but extra wages would help.'

'I'll make a note of that,' Yvonne told her. 'We don't know yet if overtime will be needed – but how many of you are willing?'

Most hands shot up.

Sibby waited and then raised hers reluctantly. She could do with more money but wanted to be free when Joe was ready to take her out...

* * *

'Did you know about the new range of daywear?' Sibby asked Winnie when they walked home together after work that day. 'Yvonne told us when she showed us what we were working on today – but I thought Miss Susie might have told you?'

'She said that they were thinking of making some changes, but she wasn't sure. No doubt she needed to discuss it with... her partner.'

'Who is her partner?' Sibby asked. 'Some of the girls think it is a society lady. They say they recognised her from her picture in the *Tatler* when she brought a Christmas hamper.'

'Well, they can say what they like, I suppose,' Winnie replied. 'But I think it best not to speak of things that don't concern us.

Miss Susie runs the business. Betty looks after the workshop and Yvonne is the head seamstress. I don't need to know more than that.'

'No, I suppose not,' Sibby agreed. 'Do you know what was happening in Mulberry Lane this morning, Winnie? Yvonne was late. She said it looked as if someone had been hurt, because the police had closed the lanes and she had to go the long way round.'

'I didn't see Sam this lunchtime,' Winnie replied. 'Miss Susie didn't come in and we were busy, so I just had a cup of tea and a sandwich at my desk.'

'I'll ask Joe this evening,' Sibby said confidently. 'He is taking me to the pictures. I would rather go to a dance, but he says we'll go one Saturday evening.'

'Are you back together again then?' Winnie asked. 'I thought you'd broken up?'

'We did and we didn't,' Sibby replied. 'Joe didn't ask me out and I got bored sitting at home, so I went out with some other men – just friends, really, though one of them wanted it to be more. I wanted Joe, but I thought he wasn't interested – and then when I was hurt, he was so kind. I couldn't face my old lodgings, so he took me to his home to live with his mum.'

'How do you like it there?' Winnie asked curiously. 'I heard someone say Mrs Ross has a sharp tongue – especially to Lilly.'

'She has sometimes,' Sibby agreed and frowned. 'Lilly says she doesn't take any notice of it, but I wouldn't like it. I don't think I'd want to live there if she was so off with me. She's all over Joe though... He gets what he wants, so perhaps that is why she is all right with me.' She looked at Winnie. 'You live with Sam's mother, don't you?'

'Yes, she is lovely. We talk and make clothes together – and she is teaching me how to cook. My mother never bothered to teach me much. I could cook some chops and boil vegetables, but I didn't know how to make a steak and kidney pudding. Sam loves them, and sausage and onion in pastry – he loves his dumplings with a stew, too.'

'I can't cook anything,' Sibby said. 'Do you think Mrs Ross would teach me?'

'You could ask her,' Winnie suggested. 'If she doesn't want to, I am sure Mrs Collins would. You could pop round on a Thursday night – that's my night for learning new things.'

Sibby's cheeks were pink with pleasure. 'Could I really? I should like that – but I will ask Mrs Ross to show me how to make her apple puddings. Joe loves those. They are different from apple pies, and the pastry is all soggy and sweet.'

'Yes, I know. Sam likes them, too. I prefer apple crumble with lots of custard, but he likes the puddings with brown sugar.'

They had reached the junction where their ways divided. Sibby said goodbye, looking around her nervously as she set off on the short distance to Joe's home. The streets were busy and lots of people were coming and going. There was no need to be nervous. For a moment, she wondered what had caused the police to block off Mulberry Lane that morning, and then she forgot as she went round the back of the house and saw Joe just taking off his work boots outside the kitchen door.

'These are black with coal dust,' he told her. 'Go in, Sibby. I'll be with you in a minute.'

Sibby nodded and went in. The kitchen smelled of a delicious pie cooking and some vegetables simmering on the hob.

Mrs Ross glanced at her and nodded. 'Dinner will be ready soon. Joe is taking you out tonight – so if you want to go up and get ready...'

'Shouldn't I help you?' Sibby paused uncertainly.

'Nothing much to do until I serve up. Go and change if you want to. This will be ready in ten minutes or so.'

Sibby shot off up the stairs, flinging off her work clothes in her bedroom and having a quick wash in the cold water from her jug on the washstand. Then she put on her second-best dress and tied it with a pretty sash at the side. It was a drop-waisted style, introduced by Coco Chanel and very much favoured by the flapper girls, with a squared neckline and short sleeves. She put on her best silk stockings and a pair of cream suede court shoes, flicked her cheeks with a dusting of face powder and added a little rouge to her mouth.

When she went down to the kitchen, there was no sign of Joe.

'He's gone to have a wash and shave,' Mrs Ross said. 'Put the cloth on the table and set it for me, Sibby. Then you can give him a shout. This is ready to come out now.'

She took the pie from the oven. The crust was a golden brown with a little pale gravy bubbling up from under it.

'Chicken pie with buttered cabbage and mashed potatoes tonight,' Mrs Ross said. 'I use a boiling fowl for my pies and they taste a treat. Tell Joe I am about to serve...'

Sibby went to the bottom of the stairs and called out to Joe. She heard a muffled reply but went up the stairs, thinking he might not have heard her. Approaching his door, she saw it was slightly open and paused. Joe was standing by his washstand, completely stripped, singing to himself. She could see the hard muscles in his bare arms and back as he washed himself. He had a lean beautiful body, despite a few dark bruises on his back and his neck where he lugged the heavy coal sacks. For a moment, Sibby was mesmerised and couldn't turn her eyes away, but then Joe turned and saw her.

A hot flush spread up into her cheeks as he frowned at her. 'I'll be down in five minutes,' he said sharply. 'Tell Ma to put mine in the oven...'

Sibby nodded silently, swallowed, turned and ran down the

stairs. Oh, if only he would ask her to be his wife. She could just see herself held in his arms, pressed close to that beautiful body... A little plan entered her mind. Sibby had seen Joe naked, perhaps if he caught a few glimpses of her with nothing much on, he might start to dream of her...

20

'Did you hear anything about what was going on in Mulberry Lane this morning?' Winnie asked Sam when he got in half an hour or so after her that evening. 'Yvonne was late because the police had blocked off the lanes and she had to go back and walk the long way round...'

Sam hesitated, then looked from Winnie to his mother. 'A girl's unconscious body was found about five this morning by a milkman making his rounds. She had been brutally attacked and left for dead... but she's now recovering in hospital, so I've heard.'

'Oh no! Not again.' Winnie felt sick and sat down at the kitchen table. 'It's attempted murder this time?'

'Yes. She was left for dead – not one of your girls. The police don't think she was local at all. I heard she had a recent train ticket from Scotland in her pocket. Her bag or suitcase was missing. Inquiries were made house to house and at all the local businesses, but no one knew who she was. The police seem to think she must have come to London looking for work and had nowhere to stay. She must have been on the street late at night, all alone...'

'Oh, poor thing,' Mrs Collins exclaimed. 'That is awful, Sam. How many attacks on girls is it now – seven or eight?'

'Including Rusty, yes, about that – she was killed though, by a single blow to the head...' Sam looked thoughtful. 'Constable Winston thinks her death may have been different. This latest girl was badly battered. Sibby was hurt badly, too, but most others got away with a few bruises. I'm not sure they are all related. I told Joe they didn't follow a pattern, but he's got it in his head it is this vagrant we've seen in Dressmakers' Alley...'

'Joe Ross?' Winnie looked at him. 'Has he got up a vigilante group again? You told me he did that when Lilly was attacked some years ago – and she had her purse stolen recently, didn't she?'

'Yes...' Sam looked at her warily. 'Now don't get upset – either of you. I did agree to help them, but only to patrol the streets for a few hours at night. I'm not in agreement with bashing the man half to death, whatever he's done. We've all got whistles to attract each other. All we need to do is catch him in the act and hand him over to the law. If we have witnesses, they will put him away for a long time.'

Winnie nodded. 'I'm not going to say you're wrong, Sam. I got impatient with the police when those murders happened last year. It took them ages to do anything and when they did, it seemed they were always too late.'

'They got their man in the end though,' Sam said. 'Well, after a fashion...'

'The police are slow but careful,' his mother told him. 'I don't want to see you in trouble, Sam.'

'I've warned Joe to be careful. If they wallop this man, whoever he might be, hit him a little too much – then it's them who will end up in prison.'

'You won't be that foolish, Sam?' Winnie said and he smiled at her.

'I don't want to throw my life away, Winnie. I've got too much to look forward to.' He reached for her, took her hands in his own and kissed them. 'Now, let's talk about us. I went to have a look at that new shoe shop in the lanes and I don't think it will make a sight of difference to my trade. What I'm thinking of setting up is boot-making for working men. Mending shoes will never bring a fortune and nor will making boots, but it will bring in that bit extra – and so I'm thinking we could be wed this autumn, Winnie. If you'd like it?'

'Of course I would,' she said and gave a little giggle of pleasure, moving in to hug and kiss him. 'I thought you were set on getting a bit more put by first?'

'I reckon if I put in a few extra hours during the week and concentrate on making those boots for customers who have asked for them, I can afford a wife and a family when it comes along.' He smiled down at her lovingly. 'Happy?'

Winnie nodded and looked at Sam's mother.

'I am so pleased for you both. It would be nice in September,' she said, already excitedly planning. 'The weather is often warm but not hot – and it gives you time to make your bride clothes, Winnie.'

'I might ask Yvonne to make my dress,' Winnie said. 'And I'll make some things for myself...'

'We'll go to see the vicar,' Sam agreed, 'and fix a date. We've waited long enough, Winnie, love.'

'Yes, we have – but you were worth waiting for, Sam.'

He chuckled. 'I'm supposed to be the one to say that...' He saw that she was reaching for her jacket. 'Are you goin' out tonight, love?'

'I'm going to Mary Winston's and then we're off to a meeting of the Women's Movement. Mary says she'll walk home with me afterwards. She isn't frightened. She carries a whistle and a pepper shaker with her and she says he'll get it full in his face if he attacks her.' Winnie frowned as she thought of something. 'How old was the woman who was attacked last night, do you know?'

'Not for certain, but I heard she was young – probably about your age, Winnie.'

Winnie nodded, looking thoughtful. 'All the girls who were attacked were young – twenty or less. Rusty was old but... I don't know why, but I think that was different somehow.'

Sam nodded. 'It doesn't fit the pattern, does it? I shall tell Joe that and see what he thinks. Perhaps these attacks aren't just the work of one man...'

'I'll speak to Mary this evening,' Winnie said, buttoning her jacket. 'Constable Winston often tells her things. I suppose there are a lot of criminals in London, but mostly they don't interfere with normal folks, do they?'

'Not if you don't stray into their world,' Sam agreed. He wrinkled his brow in thought. 'I reckon some locals know more than they ought about the burglaries we've been getting in the lanes, but it isn't my business what they do and I keep my nose out.'

Winnie stared at him in astonishment. 'Do you know any crooks, Sam?'

'Even if I did, I wouldn't tell you,' he said. 'We don't want to know about them, Winnie. You just forget I mentioned a word.' He squeezed her hand. 'Do you want me to walk with you to Mary's?'

'It is still light and I've got my pepper pot in my pocket.'

'You use it if anyone tries anything and then run...'

'All right,' she said and lifted her face for his kiss before saying goodnight to Mrs Collins. 'Don't sit up for me, Mum. I shan't be later than ten, but I know you like to get to bed earlier.'

'She is so independent, Mum,' Sam said, 'but I think she will be all right – the attacks haven't been in this area. We seem to be a bit far out for whoever it is.'

'Thank the Lord for that,' she muttered. As the door closed behind her, Sam's mother looked at him hard. 'Sam, I'm not askin' who or what or why – but if you do know anyone I wouldn't approve of, just stay clear. Do you hear me?'

'It's not me who's likely to end up in trouble,' Sam replied and looked concerned. 'He is a mate, or he was, and I would never want to see him get caught up in any bad business, but I have my suspicions. No one works harder than I do, but I never have money to spare – not more than a pound or two anyway. There's someone I shan't name seems to have plenty of it all the time. He's in business and perhaps he's good at it and I'm not but...' He shook his head. 'I don't think he's done anything really wicked, but he might have dabbled with stolen goods.'

'Oh, Sam! I hope it isn't anyone I know.'

'Well, it is only a suspicion,' Joe said. 'I don't know for sure.'

'You're not mixed up in anythin'?'

'No. I promise you.' Sam shook his head. 'I'll work for what I get or go without, Ma.'

She smiled at him. 'Good. I just want you and Winnie to be happy, and I know you work hard – and you have to look after me...'

'Susie does most of that these days,' Sam said and went to drop a kiss on top of her head. 'Whatever I do for you is a pleasure – but even for you, I won't handle stolen goods.'

'And you think this mate of yours has?'

'I think he might have,' Sam said and would say no more. The subject was dropped and Mrs Collins told him to fill the kettle.

'We'll have a cup of tea and talk about your wedding,' she said.

'One cup of tea and then I'll get back to work. I've got a pair of boots to finish for a customer for tomorrow.'

* * *

The talk at the meeting of the Women's Movement that evening was given by an American woman who was visiting England, especially to talk to the various branches of the Suffragettes. She was vivacious and told them lots of interesting stories about how the Movement was progressing in her home country.

'They seem to have got quite a bit further with their efforts over there,' Winnie observed to Mary as they left the crowded hall and began to walk home. It was chilly after the warmth inside, the rain having cleared off, at least for the moment. Women and some men were spilling into the street, laughing, and talking.

As Winnie and Mary walked along the Commercial Road, the smell from the pie shop was enticing. 'I could just eat a bag of chips,' Mary told her. 'I only had a sandwich this evening because Bill was on duty.' She glanced at Winnie. 'I think the police are after that man – the one who has been hurting young women and stealing their bags...'

'Does Constable Winston think it is all the work of one man?' Winnie asked, wrinkling her smooth brow in thought. 'It seems to me – and a few others – that more than one man might be doing these things.'

Mary nodded her agreement. 'Bill thinks that the old bag lady – Rusty, was that her name? – was killed by someone different. It isn't yet accepted by some of his colleagues, but he says it has a different look about it...'

'Yes, although now that young woman who came down from Scotland has been brutally assaulted, it muddies the water, doesn't it? One woman murdered – the other seven assaulted and robbed, two of them badly hurt. Why kill Rusty?'

'I can't see a reason why anyone would want to kill Rusty or attack the girls,' Mary said. 'I'm going to get a bag of chips, Winnie. Would you like some to take home?'

'I'd love a few, but I can't eat in the street and if I take them home, I'd need to warm them in the oven – and the fire will probably be let out or banked right down. So no, not tonight, Mary. I'll wait while you do, though…'

She stood outside the shop while Mary went in, shivering a little as she watched people walking by. An odd tingling at the nape of her neck made her think she was being watched, and, as she glanced across the road, she saw a man in an old soldier's coat with a muffler pulled up round his chin so that half his face was covered.

He looked straight at her and pulled his muffler down, mouthing something at her, grinning horribly, then turned and walked off.

Mary came out then with her parcel wrapped in newspaper. 'I got a bit of fish for…' she began when Winnie grabbed her arm.

'I saw him,' she said breathlessly. 'He was standing across the road, staring at me as bold as brass – the man they're looking for…'

'Which way did he go?' Mary looked each way, but the man had disappeared into the shadows.

'I don't know…' Winnie took a deep breath. She had tingles at her nape. 'I'm not sure what he mouthed at me – but I am sure he was threatening me.'

'Well, let him try,' Mary said grimly. 'I'm walking you to your door, Winnie. If that devil comes near us, he'll be sorry he ever saw us…'

'I'll defend myself,' Winnie agreed fiercely. 'Supposing he follows us and then comes after you when you leave me to go home?'

'I'll blow my police whistle first,' Mary said, 'and then I will pepper him.' She squeezed Winnie's arm. 'We're not going to let that so-and-so ruin our lives. If we dare not go anywhere without a man's escort, we'll be back in the seventeenth century. I won't let any man do that to me! Women have the right to walk the streets freely without fear of assault, or insult come to that.'

'No, I won't either,' Winnie replied, taking a hold of her nerves. It had been frightening for a few minutes, but the man had gone now. Mary was right. Women were fighting for freedoms and rights and surely one of those was to walk safe on the street whatever hour of the day or night it might be.

It was the next evening on the way home from work that Sam told Winnie the police now knew who had attacked the girl in Mulberry Lane.

'It was a drunk and he's been arrested, found in possession of her suitcase, too – still too drunk to know what he was doin' apparently.'

'So not the man who did the other attacks?' Winnie hadn't told him about the man who had looked at her threateningly outside the pie shop. Nothing had happened and she didn't want Sam fussing and saying she mustn't go to her meetings with Mary.

'Not according to the police,' Sam said. 'I talked to Constable Winston and he seems to think she is Nobby Carter's niece. She missed her train to London, came on a later one and when he met the one she was supposed to be on, he thought she wasn't coming...' He frowned over something and then shook his head. 'Nobby – that's Steve – says she lost his address somehow and thought she would stay overnight somewhere and then ring her home in the morning to ask her father where her uncle lived. He's in a right stew over it – says he'll kill the bugger who did it if they let him out...' Sam looked grim. 'I think he might, too. He was beside himself with anger. Never seen him that way. I told him to calm down and he looked as if he wanted to hit me.'

Winnie sighed. 'It's all horrid, Sam. Let's hope they've got the right man this time, but after the way they grabbed Ernie because he picked up Sibby's bag...'

'Yes, I know,' Sam told her. 'Us lads all still think that vagrant is behind most of it, but there are a lot of things that puzzle me.' He shook his head. 'All these robberies – and just at the right time, when folk have restocked or fetched the wages – or gone on a little holiday...'

'What are you saying, Sam?'

'It strikes me there is local knowledge... Mr Harding told me his safe was broken into, and he'd had a cabinet made to hide it...' Sam looked at her. 'How would they know to look there? And he'd just had a big delivery of cigarettes. I don't like to think bad things but...' He shook his head. 'I hope to goodness I'm wrong – for his family's sake.'

'You think you might know who is doing the robberies?' Winnie asked.

'I suspect, but I don't know,' Sam replied, looking worried. 'It was just something he let slip a couple of times – but why would he do it? He has his own business, same as me – but a different trade. It just doesn't fit the person I thought I knew.'

'Life doesn't fit neatly into slots the way it does in books or the films they make in Hollywood.' She smiled and kissed him. 'Be careful, Sam. If he thinks you suspect, he might be dangerous.'

'I might have said something...' Sam shrugged. 'I'll do my best to stay away from him. If he's a thief, he's no mate of mine.'

'You don't think...' Winnie met his eyes. 'The assaults...'

Sam stared at her. 'The attacks on women? No, I don't think so – I hope to God he isn't anyway.'

Winnie nodded. 'Are you going to work this evening?'

'I don't think so,' Sam said. 'We might go for a drink or just stay in and talk.'

'That would suit me.' Winnie smiled and kissed him. 'We've got a lot of planning to do if we're to be wed in three months' and three weeks' time...' She gave a little giggle of excitement and hugged his arm because all her dreams were about to come true.

21

'I have finished checking the books for Miss Susie, Diane,' her stepson Matthew said as he entered Lady Diane's sitting room early that warm afternoon in June. He placed the ledgers on a small polished table and smiled at her. 'Not quite in profit yet, but if you take the amount of stock accumulated over the first few months into consideration, not too far off. If the new cheaper range sells well, you should end the year by at least breaking even.'

'I suppose that is a good thing,' Lady Diane replied a little languidly. It had turned hot all at once, suddenly becoming summer after a wet dull May, and it had affected her, making her feel tired. She had not yet regained her full health, even though she liked to believe she had. 'Henry always says commerce is so tiresome and I think I agree.' She sighed as she glanced at the sketching pad beside her, a little downturn of disappointment on her lips. 'I have these wonderful ideas, but then I realise they will be too expensive for us to sell.'

Matthew looked at the exquisite ball gown she'd outlined and smiled. 'That would suit you very well – and I am sure some of your friends might like a gown of similar design. Why don't you try the limited editions, as I mentioned before?'

'Miss Diane?' she said doubtfully. 'Would it be suitable, Matthew? Do you not think people would realise that I had designed them? Quite a few of my friends know that I design my own special gowns. I have had hints that some would like me to do the same for them...'

'And if they do guess – would it be so very bad?'

'Your father might think so,' Lady Diane said carefully. 'If I am to reveal my involvement in the business – would it not make more sense to call the line Lady Diane?'

'Perhaps,' he agreed. 'However, Miss Yvonne, Miss Susie and Miss Diane fit well together – and it is less blatant. Father might not wish you to lend your title to a line of clothing, however exclusive it might be.'

'Yes, you are right, Matthew. I shall give it a little more thought,' she said with a smile and held out her hand. 'Sit beside me and talk to me, dearest Matthew. You go back to the estate tomorrow and will be there for some weeks – you will come up for our ball in August?'

'Yes, of course.' He squeezed her hand gently. 'I am sorry it is not to be an engagement ball – I wonder whether you would have held such an extravagant affair had I not thought to marry.'

'We still have much to celebrate, Marie's birth, Matthew's birthday and my recovery – and we must entertain our friends every so often. We are invited to so many society dinners, parties and balls. We could hardly do less.'

'You mustn't tire yourself too much. Father worries for you, Diane.'

'I know he does, but I am quite well really, just a little lacking in energy at times,' she replied. 'Tell me – how are you truly,

Matthew? I shall never forgive that girl for leading you on and then behaving so badly towards you.'

Matthew laughed. 'How much worse it might have been had she allowed me to propose and accepted me, giving me her terms only after we were wed. I believe she can have few natural feelings – and no affection for me.'

'She is a cold, proud beauty,' Lady Diane said in what was for her a fierce tone. 'Yet it is a good thing that she was honest, for you might have been very unhappy.'

'I cannot think the marriage would have lasted long, so she saved us both from the scandal of a divorce.'

'Now that would distress your father,' Lady Diane murmured with a little squeeze of his hand. 'I am aware that it is more common these days, but it is so sordid and unpleasant, Matthew.'

'I know – but I would not have stayed married to her,' he said and she saw a stubbornness she had sensed previously but not seen. He was, she realised, a stronger character than she'd known.

'Then we were fortunate,' she said. 'As long as she did not break your heart.'

Matthew stood up. 'My pride is severely dented,' he admitted with a wry smile. 'However, I shall live – and now I must leave you. I have some errands for Father and must be ready to leave early tomorrow...'

'I wondered if you might invite your father to visit the Olympics in Paris with you?' She smiled at him. 'In July might be best for there are some excellent British athletes taking part – Mr Harold Abrahams might win the 100m – or so your father says. I know he would like to watch some of our athletes, but I am not yet up to the journey and it would please him to travel there with you.' The Olympics had begun in May, but the track races would not commence until July.

'That is a generous and thoughtful suggestion,' Matthew said and looked at her fondly. 'Yes, I shall arrange it for July, for I believe it is then that the main events begin...'

'I am so pleased,' she said, smiling as he blew her a kiss and withdrew.

Lady Diane watched him leave and looked at her sketching pad. She gave a little sigh and got up, deciding to visit her darling daughter in the nursery for an hour or so, and then change for tea with her husband. Nanny might not be best pleased by the disruption to her routine, but Lady Diane had no intention of allowing the nurse to dictate their lives, even if it was a family tradition. Her daughter would spend more time with her mama than Matthew and his brother had been allowed with theirs.

'Henry says he thinks it can make very little difference if we use Miss Diane as a label for more expensive items,' Lady Diane informed Susie when they met the next morning. 'He thinks it is worth a try – since my true talents lie that way...'

'Oh, that isn't strictly true,' Susie exclaimed. 'The new bolero set we're making in the cheaper line is exactly what young working girls who wish to look smart but who cannot afford the Miss Susie range would like.'

'What do you think about the limited-edition range – where we just make one or two of a certain model...' Lady Diane arched an elegant eyebrow. 'Is it simply a flight of fancy? I know Matthew suggested it, but he did so because he knew I wanted to produce something like this...' She showed Susie the very daring jacket and divided skirt ensemble she'd previously only let Matthew see.

Susie took it and looked at it in silence for some minutes. 'That is wonderful – extremely modern and avant-garde. I think we could make it in either the top end of Miss Susie – or Miss Diane, if you decided to go ahead...'

'Very well, but we will do it as Miss Susie,' Lady Diane said. 'Cost it with the materials I've listed and make up three examples – in sizes 34 to 38 hip. I do not think it would look well above that size. I thought you could use the red velvet, the blue velvet and that military green suiting for the jackets. The trousers will all be the same pale cream in a fine crepe that gives the wide legs that fluid look when the wearer moves. Each jacket will have a different braiding – and they will all be exclusive, although the same design basically.'

'Supposing we get more orders. Are we to repeat them?'

Lady Diane looked thoughtful. 'That ensemble will not sell for less than a hundred guineas in the shops. I doubt many retailers will buy them or try to order them. I think we should offer them as an exclusive design to Harpers first and then to the more exclusive retailers, if Harpers is not interested – after all, it will only be an outlay of a few hundred pounds for the materials. If they do not sell, we will forget the idea.'

'And if I get asked for more?' Susie persisted.

'Then we will keep the same material for the divided skirt and change the jacket – colour, braiding, buttons. If we get orders, each one must be individual. It will be a job for Yvonne and any other you think skilled enough.' She hesitated. 'If we are asked for more, then we might think of introducing the Miss Diane range.'

'Most of the girls are almost as skilled as Yvonne.'

Lady Diane inclined her head. 'Then we shall try that ensemble. I have other designs in mind, but we'll go with this initially.' She showed Susie one or two new designs, including a short evening dress of gold silk edged with black beading that hung in a little fringe just below the knee. It had the popular Egyptian look that was all the rage just now and there was a black headband to complete the look. 'This one might be popular.'

'Yes, I am sure it will,' Susie said and placed the drawing with all its details carefully into her folder. 'I am excited with these new designs. It will be interesting to see what happens...'

22

'That is so elegant!' Yvonne exclaimed as she looked at the detailed sketches that Lady Diane had sent in. 'I should love to wear something like this...' She held it out in front of her, turning it this way and that before nodding. 'That divided skirt is so clever. As you walk, it will look like trousers, but when you stand or sit, it could be a slender gown.'

'Very different,' Susie said. 'It took my breath away when I first saw it – but I'm not sure it will sell. She isn't either – but it is an experiment. I can't wait to see it made up.'

'You could wear it with your figure,' Yvonne told her. 'You are taller than me and slender. It would look right on you – but I'd still like something similar...' She looked at it consideringly, knowing that her fuller figure would probably not suit the ensemble as it was shown.

'I want you to promise me you won't make yourself anything based on this design for at least six months,' Susie said. 'I know you do, Yvonne, and I don't mind – but these are special and we've no chance of selling a limited edition if you are seen wearing a cheaper version of the model before ours are sold.'

'I won't,' Yvonne gave her word. 'But I get ideas of my own, Miss Susie. Not copies exactly but something that triggers in my mind. I won't do it this time.'

'You are very talented at your work,' Susie said. 'Do you have any ideas that are not based on Lady Diane's?'

'Well, sort of.' Yvonne bit her lip.

'Bring me one or two examples in,' Susie said. 'Your ideas for the cheaper bolero set were good and Lady Diane may be too busy to produce all our models if things go her way. Besides, now that she is recovering her health, she will have a busy social life once more...'

'You mean I could have a say in the design of the Miss Yvonne range?'

Susie smiled. 'It might happen,' she replied carefully. 'I make suggestions, Yvonne, not decisions. Everything has to be approved by my lady. If we did decide to go ahead with something that was your original idea, you would receive a fee for your work.'

'I wasn't thinking about that, though I need as much as I can get with a growing lad.' She laughed and shook her head. 'One of his masters came to see me and told me John should be an artist, and he is talented at drawing – but his sports master says he is brilliant on the football field so he could do with some football boots.'

'John can draw?' Susie looked at her for a moment. 'Why don't you show him something you've made up and ask him to sketch it for you?'

'Well, I might,' Yvonne said. 'He has been saving up for a bike, or so he said, but the other day someone brought one to the house for him. It is old and has seen better days, but it means he can go to football practice when he wants now.'

'Well, talk to him, see what he thinks.' Susie smiled. 'He may think drawing dresses is daft, and if he does, just bring me in a sample of something you thought of yourself...'

* * *

Yvonne was thoughtful as she hurried home that evening. Miss Susie hadn't promised anything, but she knew that her suggestions went a long way with Lady Diane. Yvonne thought that perhaps her ladyship wasn't truly interested in the new, cheaper range; her talents were far more exotic and elegant – but Yvonne had often thought that it was possible to make beautiful clothes cheaper than the Miss Susie range. She made her own clothes for a fraction of the price and some of them looked equally as smart as Miss Susie's own.

When she got in, John was waiting for her. He'd banked up the range and put the kettle on so that it was nearly boiling. She smiled and thanked him and was rewarded by a big grin.

'It's your birthday tomorrow, Mum. I made something for you...' He indicated the table and, looking, Yvonne saw the card that had a picture of a woman in a beautiful ball gown and the words HAPPY BIRTHDAY MUM printed neatly at the top. Next to it was a wooden box that had an engraving of birds on the lid with a scroll of flowers and leaves, all of which had been carefully painted in bright colours. 'I thought you could keep bits and pieces for your sewing in it...'

'Oh, John, what a wonderful surprise,' Yvonne said, stroking the box with reverent fingers. Tears sprang to her eyes. He was such a loving boy and she was so lucky to have him. 'Why didn't you keep them until tomorrow, love?'

'Because we're always in such a rush in the mornings,' John replied with a grin. 'Besides, I've got another surprise for you tomorrow, Mum.' He laughed as she looked at him. 'No, I shan't tell you – but I'll meet you from work and we're going somewhere...'

'You mustn't spend all the money you earn on me,' Yvonne protested. 'I love what you've given me – the card and the box you made are beautiful. You're supposed to be saving for a new bike.'

'Don't need it now; I've got one,' John said promptly. 'Besides, you spend all your money on me, Mum – and I've been earnin' a few bob since I had my bike, runnin' errands.'

Yvonne smiled and ruffled his hair. He dodged back out of the way ruefully. John didn't like his hair ruffled, but she forgot and did it when she was feeling emotional.

'Dinner won't take long,' she told him. 'It's sausages and mash tonight with onion gravy.'

'Smashing,' John cried. 'I'm going to play football in the lane later, Mum. You don't mind, do you?'

'No, of course not,' Yvonne said, hesitating as she looked at the card he'd drawn. 'Do you think you could draw me in a dress I made, perhaps on Sunday? Miss Susie would like to see some of the things I make – and I thought you might be able to sketch one or two. I can see you have your own ideas too...' She picked up her card, which had been beautifully drawn in coloured pencils.

'I copied that from a magazine I found,' John told her. 'I've got it in my room. I think it's a fashion magazine.'

'Oh, where did you find that?' She looked at him with interest.

'I took a parcel to a shop in Mulberry Lane,' John said. 'The newsagent was putting a pile of papers and old magazines out for the rubbish and I asked if I could have it.'

Yvonne nodded; her gaze thoughtful. 'What made you want it?'

'It's what you do, Mum,' he replied. 'All my life I've watched you make lovely things – and I...' He shrugged. 'You won't let on to Mickey or the others what I do? They would think I was a sissy.'

'Of course you aren't,' Yvonne said proudly. 'You like to draw and you appreciate beautiful things – but lots of men do that; think of all the famous artists like Rembrandt and Van Gogh and... oh, I don't know, but there are lots and lots of them.'

John laughed. 'One day I'll go to the big art galleries and look at the paintings. I've seen them in books – in the school library, and the art master brought his books in to show us what true talent is...'

Yvonne poured the tea and drank hers, before cooking their supper. While she was busy, John went upstairs to his room, but came as soon as she called him. When he returned, he was carrying his sketch book and he showed her what he'd done.

'Is this what you want, Mum?'

Yvonne looked and felt a shock of surprise and pleasure as she saw a rough sketch of what was recognisably her wearing the dress she'd had on all day. 'That is so good, John,' she said, feeling a spurt of pride in his talent. 'Eat your supper and then you can go out for an hour or so – but don't be late. You still have school tomorrow.'

* * *

Tam was waiting for John at the end of the lane. He'd been smoking, but as John cycled up to him, he threw the butt down and ground it with his heel.

'Yer late,' he grumbled. 'I told yer seven and it's a quarter past.'

'I know, but Mum cooked tea and I couldn't come before. What do you want me to do tonight?'

'I've got a bit of business to do,' Tam said. 'I want yer to stand guard fer me and let me know if yer see anyone comin'. Yer can whistle, can't yer?'

John pursed his lips and let out a loud whistle. 'Like that?'

'Yeah, that will do,' Tam agreed and grinned. 'Come on, I've got my bike. Just follow me and keep up.'

'Where are we goin'?' John asked. 'I ain't keepin' cavey if you're going to break into someone's house.'

'Nah, nuthin like that,' Tam said. 'I'm goin' to a dog fight, see. Now there's some don't hold with it – so we need lookouts in case some interferin' busybody reports us to the cops.'

John was in the act of mounting his bike but stopped to look at Tam. 'I don't like dogs fightin',' he said. 'I don't mind placin' bets for you, and I'll take parcels wherever you want – but that's cruel.'

'Squeamish are yer?' Tam leered at him.

John's face was set as he dismounted.

'Like that, is it? Supposin' I take that bike orf yer if yer don't do what I ask?'

'Then you'll take it,' John said stubbornly. 'I don't want to come.'

Tam stared at him for a moment longer and then nodded. 'Suit yerself. Keep the bike. I'll need you on Sunday to run some errands, right?'

'Right.' John watched as Tam cycled off. He frowned, torn between his desire to keep the borrowed bike and earn a few shillings, and the sick feeling he had inside. Tam was a bad 'un. He'd suspected it right from the start, wondering just what was inside the packages he was asked to deliver from time to time. He'd been tempted to open one but never had, pushing his doubts away, but the suggestion that he should keep watch over an illegal and cruel dog fight had sickened him.

He rode round the streets for a while, because his mother would ask questions if he went back too early. John could just imagine what she would say if he tried to explain.

It was as he was riding down Gun Alley, just off Mulberry Lane, that he saw the man lurking in the shadows. John's instinct told him something was wrong and he braked, putting his feet to the ground. A young woman came out of the public house the other side of the alley and, immediately, the lurker moved quickly towards her and raised his arm to strike her from behind with a club.

John didn't stop to think. He remounted his bike and rode straight into the man's back, causing him to lurch sideways. The woman was alerted to the danger and screamed as she saw the tangle of boy, bike and a man in an old soldier's coat. Her screams were loud and within seconds two men came rushing round the corner. They went straight to her in concern. However, the woman was merely shocked but unhurt.

John's action had knocked the would-be attacker to his knees, but he threw John and the bike off and got up, racing away down the street. One of the men blew a whistle and started to chase after them, while the second man stopped to help John right himself and his bike.

'What happened?' the man asked John, after having made certain the woman was all right. Others had come from the pub now and she was being led back inside.

'He was going to hit her from behind so I rode into him,' John said and looked down at his bike, which had twisted so that the handles were at the wrong angle. 'If I've damaged it, Tam will go spare...'

The man looked at him. 'You're Yvonne's lad,' he said and John's head came up quickly. 'Are you talking about Tam Jones the Runner?' He was frowning as he looked at him.

'Do you know my mum?' John asked and the man nodded.

'I'm Jeb,' he said. 'I know your mum and most of the lasses from the workshop in Dressmakers' Alley.' He paused then, 'Do you run errands for Tam – carry stuff for him?'

John hesitated, then inclined his head. 'Don't tell me mum, will you?'

Jeb's gaze deepened. 'No, but you should know he's a wrong 'un, lad,' he warned. 'Be careful what you get mixed up in with him – you could get in a lot of trouble.'

John bit his lip. 'I know. He wanted me to keep watch at...' He shook his head because he wasn't a snitch, even if he didn't hold with dog fighting. 'I reckon I'll have to give the bike he lent me back – but he'll likely give me a clout for breaking it.'

'It's not broken,' Jeb replied with a smile. 'Leastways, nothing I can't fix. I'll come back with you now and straighten it for you – but then, if I were you, I'd give it back.'

'Yeah,' John said and sighed. 'Mum would be angry if she knew what I'd done.'

'Come on,' Jeb said. 'We'll go to mine and fix your bike and then you get orf home, lad.'

'Thanks, mister.' John looked at him consideringly. 'I reckon I know you – you are Lilly from the flower shop's husband.'

'Yes, I am.' Jeb grinned at him. 'Small world, ain't it, lad?'

John chuckled. He liked Jeb and, in his heart, he'd always known that his mother would say he shouldn't have accepted the loan of the bike for running errands. After all, there might be anything in those parcels he'd delivered – pinched stuff, guns, lethal knives, even drugs. John didn't know much about criminal stuff, but he'd sensed Tam wasn't on the level from the start.

23

'It was you, you bastard! I know it – so don't try to deny it...'

The two men were close to the dock area, where they had formed a habit of meeting prior to another break-in. The night was cloudy, a full moon obscured by dark shadows at that moment, but the mood between them sparked with danger, dark and foul like the stink from the river. Their uneasy partnership had never been without arguments, but now they faced each other, anger blazing out of the smaller man.

'Dunno what yer on about,' Pug replied and spat on the ground. 'I told yer from the start. I'll 'elp yer wiv yer jobs when yer need me – but what I do on me own is my business. So bugger orf. I don't need yer...' At that moment, the clouds rolled back and the moonlight shone on them. Unknown to either, a third man watched from the shadows.

'Tell me it wasn't you that beat my Christy and left her unconscious in Mulberry Lane...' the small man shouted, spittle forming on his mouth. 'I don't care what yer do – but if yer laid a finger on my girl...'

'What will yer do?' A harsh laugh escaped the heavier man.

'Bloody women, all the same. I despise and hate 'em. Never met one that wouldn't cheat on yer and empty yer pockets while yer slept.' He grinned, secure in his own conceit and strength, a little the worse for all the beer he'd consumed. 'If she was the mouthy one, she got what she deserved. Yeah, I gave her a clout, but she was askin' fer it, lurkin'...'

He got no further. The shorter man leapt at him, knocking him backwards, the swift action taking the bigger man off-balance and sending him down. As he jerked up, scrambling to rise, a hammer hit him full in the face. Pug put up his hands to ward off the blows, but he'd been in the pub for hours and was half-drunk, one of the reasons for his bragging attitude. The third and fourth blows caught the side of his head and blood spurted. As he fell back on his side, his eyes staring lifelessly at the river, the watcher walked out from the shadows.

'You shouldn't have done it, son,' he cried. 'I ain't sayin' he didn't deserve it but you should have let the law take its course. You could hang or spend the rest of your life in prison...'

The murderer turned to look at the newcomer. 'You!' he said bitterly, a harsh laugh on his lips. 'You've got some room to talk, you bastard.' There was anger and hatred in his eyes.

'I've told you before, I didn't kill your mother...'

'And I don't believe yer.' The murderer spat full into his face. 'All my life I've lived with it – the son of a murderer. That's what you gave us, your children; a lifetime of shame and regret. The nightmares I suffered as a kid – and the bloody orphanage they put me in; the bastards used us kids every night for months, years. Your fault. All your fault. Bugger orf – why don't yer run to the coppers if yer so lily-white?'

'You know I won't do that, son...'

The murderer watched as the older man walked away, sorrow in every line of his sagging form. Bitterness swelled in him. He'd shrugged off his past at the orphanage, built up a business and a reputation, and a nice little sideline in stolen goods – and then *he'd* turned up begging for forgiveness. It had made all the bitterness well up inside him again. He would never forgive his father for ruining his life.

Turning away from the scene of his crime, the murderer was so caught up with his bitterness that he failed to realise that he'd left his hammer lying close to his victim's body. He felt no remorse for what he'd done. None. He might be a thief, but that bastard had been attacking and hurting young women for weeks and that was one thing he couldn't abide. His mother had been murdered, found lying on her own kitchen floor, bleeding from the wound to the back of her head – and his father had gone to prison for it.

For a moment, he felt fear. Would his father go to the police and give up his son? No, somehow, he knew it wouldn't happen, and inside his head there was just a flicker of doubt. Was his father truly innocent? He'd refused to believe him when he'd begged to be forgiven for what had happened... but now, for the first time, he wondered.

24

'These are good, really good,' Susie said as she looked at the three sketches Yvonne brought after the weekend. 'Your son did them?'

'Yes, John has a talent for drawing,' Yvonne said proudly. 'He made me a wonderful card and a lovely sewing box he'd carved and painted for my birthday and then took me for fish and chips. His teacher told me he had an exceptional talent, but until I suggested these sketches, I really didn't know how good he could be.'

'And these are the dresses – or outfits, I should rather say – that you designed yourself,' Susie said, examining the dress and costume that Yvonne had brought with her. She was wearing the third outfit – a skirt and blouse with short puffed sleeves. 'I can see that you've vaguely modelled the costume on that grey one we sold last year, but the collar has shorter points and the sleeves don't have the frilled cuffs, but the dress is more like Chanel, but the big collar is different...' She nodded thoughtfully, then looked at Yvonne. 'Do you mind if I take these sketches and show Lady Diane?' She smiled and then reached into her pocket and took out a florin. 'Give this to John and thank him.'

'Oh, he will be pleased,' Yvonne said, hesitating, then, 'John made a confession to me the other night. He had been running errands for a man – I think he is local and, from what Jeb, Lilly's husband, told me, he is a small-time crook. He does errands for the real criminals – and he'd been getting my John to deliver parcels. Jeb told us he thought they could contain stolen goods or counterfeit money. There have been some false notes discovered in the East End recently – white five-pound notes.'

'Oh, that is unfortunate,' Susie cried. 'I have no doubt that you've told him it must stop – but the way these criminals use young lads for their dirty work is disgusting.'

'I think he understands it's wrong now – and he gave the bike back to this Tam on Saturday and told him he won't work for him again.'

'Good. We don't want him being arrested for handling stolen goods or counterfeit money,' Susie said.

Yvonne nodded, her face white at the thought. 'That would break my heart. I have told him that he must never do anythin' of the sort again, and he has promised, but he is disappointed because he earned a little money running errands.'

'Well, there are other ways of earning money,' Susie assured her. 'I am sure a bright boy like John will find a way soon.'

'Jeb told him he might have a few jobs for him. He's a nice man, Lilly's husband. I don't know what he could find for John to do, but he's told him to go to his shop with him on Saturday morning...'

* * *

Leaving the workshops, Susie walked down the lane to Lilly's shop. She intended to pay her mother a visit before keeping an appointment at a silk merchants. She entered the shop to find it empty and waited a moment before calling. Lilly came through from the back room then, sniffing and wiping her face with the back of her hand.

'I'm sorry,' she apologised. 'Oh, Susie, it is you...' She gave a little gulp. 'It's so awful and I'm not sure... It may be that your brother is involved. The police are arresting all of them...'

Susie felt a little chill at the nape of her neck. 'What's wrong, Lilly? Has something bad happened?'

'The police have found a body – a man's body,' Lilly replied in a hushed tone. 'It's that vagrant they've been looking for apparently... but he'd been beaten badly before he went into the river...'

'Dead?' Susie's cheeks paled and her knees felt weak. 'I know the men have been looking for him for ages – weeks, really. There was some wild talk about teaching him a lesson. Oh, my God! I hope Sam isn't caught up in it but...' She looked at Lilly's tear-streaked face. 'Have they arrested Jeb?' Lilly nodded. 'I am so sorry. What does he say? Was he involved?'

Lilly swallowed hard. 'He says not... Can you come through for a few minutes and we'll talk. I'll put the closed sign on the door and lock it...'

'Yes, I've got time. I was only going to get some flowers for Mum... but this is worrying.'

She followed Lilly through to her back room. There were two wooden spindle-backed chairs beside a bench strewn with flowers and bits of wire, where Lilly had been making her arrangements.

'It happened before the weekend, Thursday night – at least the police think it was then, because a report came in of an attempted attack on a young woman and a chase after her assailant by some of the local men...'

'That would be Joe and his friends,' Susie said, looking at her anxiously. 'Sam mentioned it. Joe got up this group to protect us all. Sam was involved with the patrolling, but he promised us he wouldn't get into a fight with the man. He was in favour of just following him and getting word to the police but...' She sighed. 'We all know what young men are like when their blood is up...'

'Jeb was so angry when I was attacked and Joe was fit to murder when Sibby was hurt. They said such wild things and...' Lilly gulped back a sob. 'I can't bear it if Jeb goes to prison. We were doing so well and there's the baby...' She placed her hands over her stomach protectively. 'If they say it is murder...' A shudder went through her and she had to sit down.

Susie looked at her in horror. 'Surely no court would convict them of murder for beating a vicious villain who had been terrorising young women? And there was Rusty's murder, too, don't forget.'

Lilly nodded catching back another sob. 'They warned Joe once before – and the man survived and was convicted of rape and imprisoned,' Lilly said after a moment, her hands trembling. 'If either of them was to hang for this...' She gave a little cry of despair, covering her face with her hands.

Susie put her arms around her as she wept. 'You mustn't get so upset, Lilly, think of the baby,' she said and hugged her. 'The police can't prove it was them, surely? We know what they planned, but the police don't – not for sure.'

'Jeb told me not to worry. He says he knows someone who will have him out of there – and he says he has an alibi for Thursday evening. He heard the woman scream when she was attacked – and he went to the rescue with Joe, but he stopped to make sure the victim was all right, and to help the young lad...'

'Young lad?'

'A boy of twelve rode his bike into the man we've all been looking for and knocked him down as he would have struck his latest victim on the back of the head. She was unhurt but heard the commotion and screamed her head off. After Jeb made sure the young woman was all right, he brought the boy to ours and mended his bike for him. He went home with him after it was done and talked to his mother – Yvonne from your workshops. After that, he came straight back to me.'

Susie nodded, her thoughts moving quickly. It didn't put Jeb entirely in the clear, although if the vigilantes had been after their quarry earlier and found him, Jeb couldn't have had anything to do with the beating. 'Your brother Joe went after that monster who has attacked so many young women – what does he say?'

'Joe says three of them caught up with him and...' Lilly faltered. 'He says they gave him a bashing and warned him if he came back to the area they would kill him, but... he swears he was alive when they left him.'

'Do you believe him?' Susie asked and Lilly hesitated.

'Yes. At least I want to, Susie. I don't want him or Jeb to be sent to prison or... or...' She couldn't finish her sentence because the tears were running too hard. 'But the police will probably think they're guilty. What can I do to help them?'

'For now you can't do anything,' Susie replied, frowning. 'Let's see if any of them get charged. If they do, we must find them a lawyer who can defend them properly. I know of a very good one, but I am not sure that he would agree to defend them. He helped Winnie but... hers was a different case...'

'I know,' Lilly said and wiped her eyes. 'If both of them should be brought to trial... I just don't know what we shall do and Mum will go mad when she hears.'

'I shouldn't say anything until you are sure,' Susie said. 'Meanwhile, you ought to open your shop, Lilly. You can't afford to lose your customers. You may need every penny you earn.' She put out a hand to squeeze Lilly's. 'We'll do all we can, I promise you, love.'

'Thank you,' Lilly said and blew her nose. 'I know I have to carry on, Susie, but it is hard when...' She shook her head, a look of determination settling on her pretty face. 'I have to for all our sakes...'

Susie smiled at her. 'I am going to buy some of your freesias for my mum, Lilly – but I'll be back later, and I'll call in to see if there is any news. Remember, you are not alone. We shall all be behind you – and if they try to make out Joe and Jeb and the others are evil, we'll make protests and do marches and whatever, until everyone knows that they are heroes.'

Lilly gave her a watery smile. 'You are a good friend, Susie. Thank you. I feel a bit better now.'

'Keep your chin up,' Susie said and went through to the shop, where she bought the flowers for her mother.

Leaving the shop, her smile faded. This could be a tragic affair for more than one family in the lanes. If Joe Ross and his vigilantes had murdered that man, there would be hell to pay...

25

'Tell me you weren't involved, Sam,' Winnie said when she went round to his shop during her lunch break. He was at his bench but looked up and smiled as he saw her enter. 'They've arrested Joe, Jeb and Norman Jones for the murder of that wretched man...'

'Jeb has a pretty good alibi if it happened the night the police say, though the body wasn't found until Sunday morning. Apparently, they think he'd been dead two to three days...' Sam met her anxious eyes. 'No, I wasn't there, Winnie. I was at home with you and Mum – at least I was from eight o'clock onwards. I worked late that night, didn't I?'

'Thank God,' Winnie said fervently. 'Have the police been to see you?'

'Not yet. I heard that the vagrant has been identified as Derek Norton and he has a criminal record.' Sam frowned. 'It doesn't look good for our lads, Winnie, because the police are bound to think it was one of us.'

'What on earth will Lilly do if both her brother and her husband get sent to prison?' Winnie shook her head. 'I'm sure they never meant to do more than give him a hiding – and most of us girls have felt safer knowing that someone was looking out for us...'

'I approved of the patrolling, but we should have just grabbed him and marched him to the nearest police station.' Sam looked grave.

Winnie sighed. 'I'm thinking of Lilly and her mother. Mrs Ross relies on Joe. If Joe is found guilty... and Jeb may not be in the clear despite his story of having stayed behind to help the girl and that young boy.' She looked at him anxiously. 'Yvonne says that Jeb did help her son with his bike and then brought him home. She is worried that the police will come after John for riding his bike at that man and knocking him down.'

'How could they – unless it is to thank him for preventing another attack?' Sam was indignant. 'If they'd done their job and arrested him long before this, none of it need have happened.'

'I suppose he must have given them the slip,' Winnie said. 'Constable Winston told me they were looking for him to question...'

'Maybe if they'd tried a bit harder, he'd still be alive.'

Winnie inclined her head. 'Oh well, I'd better get back, Sam. Will you be working late tonight?'

'No. I finished those boots, so I'll be home early. We might go out, just for a drink – or to the pictures?'

'I'd rather go to the cinema on a Saturday,' Winnie said with a smile. 'We could walk to the Red Lion for a drink if you like.' It was just a way of being alone for a while, a chance to talk and kiss on the way home.

'We'll go to the cinema this coming Saturday then,' Sam agreed and smiled, returning to his shoe mending as she went out. His smile disappeared as his thoughts turned towards the serious trouble that some families might soon be facing.

* * *

All the girls at the workshop were subdued as they left that evening. It was a relief to know that they could walk home safely and not be attacked, but violent death was horrid and some were shocked that local men were involved. Most of them walked by Lilly's shop without looking, feeling embarrassed and not knowing what to say.

Winnie went into the shop. Lilly looked awful, her face pale and her eyes red from where she'd been weeping. Her heart caught for her. She knew how frightening it was to be charged with a serious crime like murder, even when innocent.

'Any news, Lilly?' she asked, and when Lilly shook her head, 'I am so sorry. It is awful when you don't know what is going on. I hope they let them go soon. That wicked man deserved a beating. I'm sure they never meant for him to die...'

Lilly blew her nose. 'I don't know what they thought; they were all so angry, but I believed it just a lot of hot air...' She looked at Winnie. 'The police are bound to think one of ours did it, because of the patrols – and...' She faltered. 'Who else would have done it?' They looked at each other in silent fear, because a murder had been committed.

'Maybe someone else had a grudge against him,' Winnie said, frowning. 'If the police do charge either of them, you'll need a lawyer, Lilly. I know of someone, but I don't know what he charges...'

'I'm not sure what we can afford,' Lilly said and wiped her cheeks. 'Jeb was doing really well, Winnie. Earning more money than I've ever seen – but I think he puts it all back into his stock. I don't know if we have any cash put by...' She gulped back a sob. 'I'll have to look after Mum as well as...'

'I don't have a lot of money to spare, but I'll do what I can to help, Lilly.'

Lilly offered a half-smile. 'Thank you. A lot of people have offered to help. None of us have much money. I just don't know what they can do – but if there is anything, I'll ask.'

Winnie nodded, bought a few flowers for Sam's mother and left. She felt dreadful, because Joe and Jeb had been protecting all of them and if they had accidentally killed that awful man, they hadn't meant it to happen.

* * *

Sam was just packing up for the evening when the door of his shop opened and Constable Winston entered. He cleared his throat, looking uncomfortable as Sam glanced at him.

'Mr Sam Collins?' he said formally, though he knew Sam well. 'I've come to ask you a few questions, sir. I've been given to understand that you were one of a group of young men patrolling the streets at night recently?'

'Yes, Constable,' Sam replied evenly. 'We felt it necessary to protect our wives, girlfriends and sisters. There have been too many attacks on young women recently.'

'I agree with you, Mr Collins, but it is for the law to deal with these things.' Constable Winston cleared his throat again. 'Are you willing to come down the station with me to answer a few questions?'

'I could answer them here and now,' Sam told him. 'I was not on patrol on Thursday night. I worked until nearly eight and then walked home, where I remained with my mother and my fiancée.'

'That's as maybe, but what were you doing on Friday or Saturday?' Constable Winston looked at him narrowly. 'It seems, after examination of the body in question and further enquiries, it may not have been as a result of the beating on Thursday night that Mr Norton died...'

Sam stared at him. 'Not as a result of the beating...? I don't understand... Have Joe and the others been released?'

'For the moment, we have released our first suspects. They have all been warned not to leave the area and may still face charges of grievous bodily harm...'

'Well, that is certainly a relief,' Sam said puzzled. 'But why do you need me to come to the station?'

'If you will just come along with me, sir. We would like you to give us a statement – and to ask if you can identify something...'

Sam felt a coldness at his nape. Something was very wrong here and he had an uncomfortable feeling in his gut that there was more behind Constable Winston's polite request than he'd first thought.

'Yes, I will come,' he said. 'If you will wait while I lock up – and, please, if you intend to put me in the cells overnight, can you let Winnie and Mum know...?'

26

Lilly was at her mother's, sitting drinking tea at the kitchen table. Mrs Ross was staring angrily into space and the silence was taut between them. When the door opened, Lilly spun round and then jumped to her feet, crying out in relief as both Joe and her husband entered.

'Oh, thank God!' she sobbed and jumped up to hug them in turn, tears trickling down her cheeks. 'When did they release you?'

'Just a while ago,' Jeb said, holding her and stroking her as she wept into his shoulder. 'We didn't kill him, Lilly. I wasn't there when Joe caught him – but Norm was with him by then, and he swears Joe only knocked him about a bit and threatened that if he didn't clear orf, they would kill him next time.'

'He slunk off muttering and threatening us,' Joe told her. 'He was winded and his face was badly cut and bleeding, but nothing I did should have killed him. I thought I wanted to but, when it came to it, I couldn't... it felt wrong. We saw him go into a public house... and we told the police all this for a start. Well, now it seems they might believe us...'

'Thank goodness,' Lilly said. 'Are you in trouble for giving him a beating?'

'We might get charged with bodily harm,' Joe said. 'At least, I might. We told them Jeb wasn't there and Norm only helped me grab him...'

'You stupid fools!' Mrs Ross' sharp voice cut across his words. 'How dare you do something so stupid, Joe! What will happen to Lilly and me – and the baby if both of you end up in prison?'

'Ma...' Joe protested. 'It won't happen – and if it did, it would only be a few months. When the court hears what he'd been doing, they'll more likely give us a medal – he was the murderer not us...'

'Someone killed him, though,' Mrs Ross said, looking at him in a mixture of anger and sadness. 'You're not in the clear yet, Joe – or you...' She shot a look of disgust at Jeb. 'You have a wife and child to think about. You go off charging about, taking the law into your own hands like a pack of schoolboys, and look what nearly happened. You're grown men, both of you, and should be more responsible.'

'Ma...' Joe said. 'Stop it. We couldn't just stand by and let our women be attacked and frightened to go anywhere... He didn't deny it when we accused him. Just stood there sneering – but I wiped the grin from his face.'

'Patrolling the streets is what the police are for. I don't mind you scaring him off – but to beat him so severely...' She shook her head, but the tears had come now and her anger was done. 'You'd best sit down and let Lilly get you some supper, both of you.'

'They gave us a sandwich and a cup of tea,' Joe said, smiling now. 'Have you got food for us, Lilly – or shall I fetch pie and chips from the shop?'

'I'll make egg on toast and cheese on toast,' Lilly said. 'I didn't do much shopping. I couldn't...' She looked at them mistily. 'I was so worried about you both.'

'Well, it is over now,' Jeb soothed. 'Joe could serve a few months in prison for assault and be none the worse for it. We'd see his round kept going for him – and he did the right thing as far as most folk are concerned. I reckon he'd be a local hero when he came back...'

'I hope it won't happen,' Lilly said. 'I believe what you did was right, Joe. That awful man deserved a beating.'

'In prison is where he should be – and made to serve hard labour,' Mrs Ross said.

'I think he might prefer to be dead,' Jeb remarked. 'I was speaking to someone who served a harsh prison sentence not long ago. Twenty years hard labour he was given and it broke him...'

'What did he do?' Lilly asked, staring at him in shock.

'He was accused of murdering his wife,' Jeb replied. 'He swears he was innocent, that he came home from the pub one night and found her beaten to death on the kitchen floor. The police didn't believe him, because the neighbours heard him quarrelling with his wife before he went out – and they'd heard a crashing sound...'

'So he was sent to prison without real evidence?' Lilly asked, feeling horrified. 'Do you think he killed her, Jeb?'

Jeb shook his head. 'I am inclined to believe that he did what he said, pushed her against a chair that fell over with a clatter and that she was alive when he left her. Why would he maintain his innocence now that he has served his time? They convicted him of manslaughter rather than deliberate murder, but he had been broken by the time they released him after serving two thirds of his sentence.'

'How do you know him?' Mrs Ross demanded. 'You don't want to associate with that sort. Like as not, he's guilty as charged.'

'He isn't dangerous now; if he ever was,' Jeb said and looked thoughtful. 'He told me his story in confidence. I'll not give him away.'

'That sounds as if we know him,' Lilly challenged, but Jeb would say no more. 'A lot of folk were kind when they heard you were arrested, Jeb,' Lilly said, changing the subject. 'Susie Collins told me she would help me if... And Winnie was nice, too.'

'I'm sorry, love,' Jeb said and smiled as she put a plate of cheese on toast in front of him. 'I never thought anything like this would happen...'

'What I want to know,' Joe said as his toast was given to him. 'If it wasn't the beating that killed him – Derek Norton, they told us his real name was, though he called himself Pug...' He paused to take a bite of his toast. 'Then who was it that did for him...?'

'Derek Norton?' Mrs Ross half rose from her chair before sinking back with a shudder.

'What's wrong, Mum?' Lilly said, seeing her white face. 'Did you know him?'

Mrs Ross took a deep breath. 'Yes, I knew him. He was a bad one from the word go. A house-breaker, bully – and a rapist. They convicted him and he went to prison for twenty-five years. You wouldn't remember, Lilly, or you, Joe, long before your time. He caused a lot of trouble... oh, it must be nearly twenty-six years ago. I was just married...' She sat staring into space. 'If he's dead, then good riddance...'

Joe laughed out loud.

His mother looked at him and then smiled ruefully. 'Well, there are some that deserve what they get, Joe. I wonder what brought him back here. I wouldn't have thought he dare show his face round the lanes; there were a good many ready to kill him when the police arrested him all those years ago...'

'I think he came lookin' for Bert Barrow,' Jeb said, making them all stare at him. 'Someone told me he'd been asking everywhere for Bert Barrow when he turned up a few weeks back – and he hung around Dressmakers' Alley a lot...'

'Why would he come lookin' for him?' Lilly asked.

'Maybe they were in prison together,' Joe said thoughtfully. 'Bert Barrow might have owed him something... or maybe he wanted revenge...' He shrugged. 'We shan't ever know now, because they're both dead. But if he had a grudge against Bert Barrow, it might explain why he came back to the area. Not that anyone recognised him; I thought he was an old soldier.'

'He was never in the army in his life,' Mrs Ross said. 'I expect he took that coat off a real old soldier; it's what he would do...'

Silence greeted her words. Much remained a mystery, including who had killed Derek Norton – and why?

* * *

It was Joe who first heard the news that Sam Collins had been arrested for the murder of the vagrant known as Derek Norton. He was up early the morning following his release. He had deliveries to make and would need to work extra hours for the day wasted in a police cell.

At first, he couldn't believe it. Sam had been against the violence from the start and had agreed to help with the patrols, only on the condition that they just roughed the culprit up a bit and then hauled him off to the police station.

'Why would they think Sam would do something like that?' Joe asked Norm when he met him. Norm had been passing Joe's coal yard and pulled his van up when he saw him, coming over to tell him the news. 'Nah, they'll just question him and let him go, same as they did us...'

'I heard they've got evidence,' Norm said and frowned. 'He couldn't have been daft enough to do it – could he?'

'Doubt it,' Joe replied. 'Why would he, Norm? He came on patrol a few times, but that was just walkin' the streets, makin' sure no young woman was attacked.'

Norm inclined his head. 'Yeah, well, I 'ope yer right...'

Joe watched as Norm drove off in his van and then went back to loading his lorry with the sacks he'd been up at five to start filling.

Once Joe's lorry was loaded, he set out to make his first deliveries, which took him the best part of the morning, but then, instead of going straight back to the yard, he decided to call into the local police station.

He was saved the necessity of going inside to enquire when he saw Constable Winston leaving and went up to him. The police officer looked at him hard, but when Joe enquired whether or not Sam Collins had been arrested, he answered him straight.

'Yes, he has. He spent the night in the cells and is likely to be there for a while yet.'

'Surely you know Sam is the last one to commit murder? He might give someone a good hiding if they provoked him, as he did that bugger who murdered Bert Barrow and tried to kill Betty Ford – but he wasn't with us that night. I give you my word...'

A sigh issued from Constable Winston. 'I'm inclined to believe you, Joe,' he said. 'But after what you did, your testimony wouldn't be listened to – and they've got evidence.' He frowned and looked anxious. 'It is pretty strong evidence – and he's going to need a good lawyer.'

'What kind of evidence?' Joe demanded. 'I don't believe Sam would do it.'

'The murder weapon was found near the body. We are pretty sure it was used to kill Derek Norton and, it looks like the act may have been premeditated. If that is proven...' A spasm of anguish passed across Constable Winston's face. 'God knows what young

Winnie will do! They were planning their wedding for September...'

Joe stared at him in disbelief. 'Are you saying he could hang?'

Constable Winston met his shocked gaze. 'It is the penalty for premeditated murder. If it had been a spur of the moment thing he might have got imprisonment with hard labour, but...' A shudder went through him. 'God forgive me. I don't know how I'll face Mary or Winnie. Neither of them will forgive me for my part in his arrest – though, if it hadn't been me, it would have been another.'

'What is this evidence – this weapon?' Joe demanded. 'How can it prove Sam killed him?'

'You know I can't tell you that,' Constable Winston replied. 'I'd lose my job and find myself facing a charge if I did...'

'I don't care what you have,' Joe said, looking grim. 'Sam is innocent. I shan't leave it there, Constable Winston. Neither will his mates. We'll get a lawyer and we'll protest in the streets. If you send an innocent man to prison and see him hang, you're no better than murderers yourselves...'

27

'Susie, my goodness,' Lady Diane exclaimed as she saw her face later that same morning. Her eyes were red-rimmed and she looked dreadful. 'Whatever is wrong – is it your mother? Is she ill?'

'She will be if... Oh, my lady, I can't believe it,' Susie cried. 'My brother Sam has been accused of murder... a murder he didn't do...'

'No! How terrible.' Lady Diane stared at her in dismay and disbelief. 'No wonder you look tired to death. Did you sleep last night?'

'No, not at all,' Susie replied. 'I was at my mother's talking to Winnie about the wedding plans when the news came...' She swallowed hard, forcing back the tears. 'Some of the local lads had been arrested, accused of beating and killing this vagrant after he was caught about to attack another young woman. However, they were proven innocent when the landlord of the Cock and Hen testified that the man had been seen in his pub after the beating. The police then searched the area again and the murder weapon was found; it had fallen into a crevice and been overlooked the first time.'

'But I don't see why they arrested your brother...' Lady Diane was puzzled.

'It was his hammer.' Susie sat down on one of the gilt chairs in Lady Diane's boudoir. She never sat unless she was invited, but her legs felt weak. 'My mother bought it for him and it has his initials burned into the handle...'

Lady Diane stared at her in stunned silence for a moment. 'They are certain it was used to commit this crime?'

'They say that it bears traces of blood and hair...' Susie felt sick as she saw the doubt in Lady Diane's eyes. 'It is a claw hammer that Sam uses to draw out nails in work boots.' They looked at each other because a hammer like that would be a deadly weapon. 'He couldn't have done it. Sam wouldn't. He is innocent... I know it.'

'But the evidence is against him.' Lady Diane frowned. 'Does he recall losing the hammer – or might it have been stolen from his shop?'

'Sam doesn't think so, though he can't remember using it recently...'

'Does he not recall how long it is since he used it?'

'I don't know, my lady. I wasn't allowed to see him. Sam is engaged to Winnie, as I've told you before, and the only reason I know as much as I do is because Winnie's friend Mary's husband came to tell us the news. Constable Winston was the one who helped to prove Winnie couldn't have killed her mother...' Susie reminded her. 'He didn't want to tell us about the hammer but Mary forced him to – swore she would never speak to him again unless he did.'

'I see...' Lady Diane frowned. 'This is unfortunate for your family, Susie. I can offer the same help as I did before – but...' She gave her head a little shake. 'We must think positively...' She got up and went to her desk. Taking out a leather-bound book, she looked for a number and then sat down to use her telephone.

After a few moments, she was put through and asked to speak to Hugo Montford.

'I see...' she said as an answer was given. 'For how long?' She looked at Susie and shook her head. 'Oh... well, please pass on my good wishes for a speedy recovery. I must think about it. I will telephone again...'

'What is wrong, my lady?' Susie asked as she saw her distressed expression.

'Unfortunately, Hugo is in hospital undergoing an operation for appendicitis. He is likely to be away from his office for a month at least as it was an emergency and he... well, that is neither here nor there, though I am concerned, for he is a good friend.' She tapped her nails on the desk. 'I am not sure who to apply to. There is another lawyer, Mr Timothy Marsh, who works with Hugo, but he is younger and inclined to... Well, I would have preferred Hugo...'

'I hope to see my brother this afternoon,' Susie replied. 'If he has been charged, I must find someone...' She stood up. 'You will understand if I do not return this evening, my lady? My mother is in some distress and Winnie...' A slight smile touched her mouth. 'Winnie is furious. She says that if they charge Sam, she will get her friends at the Women's Movement to march and protest his innocence.'

'Perhaps they won't charge him,' Lady Diane said hopefully. 'Mr Marsh is a good lawyer, I make no doubt, but he does not have Hugo's quiet manner and authority... and he is expensive. I doubt he would give you better terms to oblige me, even though he works with Hugo.'

'I can pay for my brother's defence,' Susie said. 'I have

managed to save a few pounds over the years and, if need be, I shall spend every penny to see his name cleared.'

'It is such an unfortunate thing that his hammer was allegedly used to kill this man...' Lady Diane wrinkled her smooth brow. 'I am sure he is innocent as you believe, Susie, but a court needs proof and our belief is not likely to be accepted as proof of his innocence.'

'I know...' Susie's throat caught with emotion. 'I can hardly believe it. How can it have happened?'

'If you are allowed to see your brother, you must ask if he can recall the last time he saw the hammer – and whether he ever left it somewhere it might be found...'

'Yes.' Susie nodded her agreement. 'Someone might have taken it from his workbench at the shop. He works in full view of his customers – and, if he needed to go through to the back to fetch leathers, it could have been stolen while he was gone.'

'He must think if there was a time he left his bench unattended – or if there has been a break-in, of course.'

Susie looked at her intently. 'It has to be something like that, doesn't it? Otherwise, no one will believe Sam isn't guilty... no one who doesn't know him as I do.'

'I shall pray that it is the answer,' Lady Diane said, but again there was a flicker of doubt in her eyes. She wanted to believe him innocent for Susie's sake, but the evidence against him was strong.

Susie excused herself. She was fighting her anger and her distress as she went to catch her bus to the Commercial Road. From there, she would walk to her mother's home.

Lady Diane felt that the evidence was damning. Even though she trusted and liked Susie, she had wondered if Sam was guilty. Confronted with what the police called important evidence would a jury find him guilty?

But they didn't know Sam. Susie did. Her brother just wasn't capable of murder!

After spending the morning trying to cheer her mother's spirits, Susie was at last able to visit her brother in the cells.

'We haven't charged him yet,' the desk sergeant told her. 'He has been questioned and the officer on the case is putting in his report to the chief – but he will be detained for a while longer, miss – and if I were you, I'd be lookin' for a good lawyer for him.'

Susie inclined her head, forcing back the angry retort that sprang to her lips. Shouting her brother's innocence to the world wouldn't do any good and might result in her being refused permission to see Sam.

He was looking anxious when he was brought to the interview room, where a police constable stood by the door, arms folded with a grim expression on his face. Clearly, he believed they had a dangerous murderer in custody.

'Susie...' Sam sent her a look filled with apprehension and fear. 'Is Winnie coming?'

'Winnie wanted to come, but they would only allow one of us and she is too angry and upset.' Susie wanted to reach out and touch her brother's clenched hands, but she'd been warned that was not allowed. 'If... if they charge you, she is planning on causing trouble to arouse public sympathy. I've been talking to my lady and she has told me about a lawyer who might help us... if they bring this ridiculous charge against you.'

'You don't think I did it then?' He looked strained and white, and frightened.

'No, of course I don't,' Susie assured him. 'Why would you do something so stupid as to use your own hammer? You are not a fool.'

Sam smiled and for a moment the anxiety left his face. 'That is what I told them, but they think they have an open-and-shut case against me. They won't say if there are fingerprints on the hammer – but they must be there, if it belongs to me.'

'Can they test for fingerprints?' Susie asked in astonishment for she had never heard of such a thing.

'Oh, yes. I read in the newspaper that they already have a huge amount on record which they can check for likely suspects. I don't remember how many, but it was a big number – but it must take a lot of work to go through them all one by one... Besides, only known criminals would have their fingerprints on record.' He looked upset. 'They've taken mine – so I think they may have found prints.' He shook his head. 'I wasn't sure it was my hammer. I wanted a closer look, but they wouldn't let me touch it.'

'They must realise that if it is your hammer, your prints would be on it – that doesn't prove you used it to kill him. The murderer could have been wearing gloves...'

'True,' Sam said. 'If it is mine, it still makes me the most likely suspect – in their eyes anyway. You're my sister and you suffered an attack by him. So I had good reason to go after him – and I don't have an alibi for Friday evening between half past nine and ten, which is when they now believe the attack took place...'

'How can they know that – unless it was witnessed?'

Sam shrugged. 'They say he was seen on Friday at around nine. He went into a public house and asked for a drink of whisky, but he couldn't pay for it and there was a bit of an uproar as he snatched it and drank it. The landlord threatened him with the police and told him he was banned, but he ran off...'

'When... when was he found?' Susie asked, shuddering.

'In the early hours of Saturday morning, lying half in and half out of the river,' Sam replied. 'Because of the beating he'd had the previous day and the severe bruising, they first thought he'd been dead for some time longer than he had... but, apparently, they are now placing the time of the murder no later than ten Friday evening.'

'Where were you, Sam?' Susie looked at him in concern.

'On my way home from work. I'd promised Winnie I would take her out on Saturday evening – we went to a dance in the end – and I'd had a few rush jobs in, so I worked until nine thirty on Friday and then walked home. I got in just after ten, because Mum complained at the hour, scolding me for working so late...'

'Oh, Sam!' Susie looked at him in distress. 'If only you had been at home with Mum and Winnie as usual...'

'I know, but I often work late if I want to catch up. I was saving hard for our wedding...'

'Don't worry about the money for the lawyer. I have some put by and I will use it to hire him. We must find a way to clear your name, Sam. Can you remember the last time you used your hammer?'

He looked at her for a moment. 'I know I didn't have it on Friday evening. I needed it to remove some stud nails from a pair of work boots and I couldn't find it... but before that, I don't recall...'

'You brought it home to mend a window for Mum a while ago, didn't you?'

'Yes...' Sam looked at her thoughtfully.

'Could you have lost it on the way to work the next day?'

'No...' He shook his head and Susie frowned, because if he had, it might have helped to prove his innocence. 'I don't carry tools loose. I have them in my haversack – and I remember using the hammer on Thursday afternoon... but not after that...'

'You'll have to go now, Miss Collins,' the constable said in a stern voice. 'I must take Mr Collins back down to the cells.'

'Just a moment more...' Susie cast him a pleading look. 'Think, Sam – think hard about what happened between Thursday evening and Friday night when you needed your hammer and couldn't find it.' The constable was gesturing to her to leave and standing beside Sam, his hand on his shoulder as if he thought he was about to run.

Sam inclined his head, to tell her that he understood what she was saying, and then she was being ushered from the room.

She glanced back at Sam. 'Don't give up hope,' she urged. 'I shall find the best lawyer I can – and Winnie will come and see you if they allow it. We all love and believe in you.'

'Thank you,' Sam answered before he was hustled away by two burly constables.

Susie was taken through to the front desk and firmly shown the door. She left, feeling as if a dark cloud had descended on her. No doubt was left in her mind that her brother would be charged with murder. The atmosphere had been so heavy with suspicion that she knew they believed they had the guilty man locked up in their cells.

If only Sam hadn't chosen to work so late! He had no alibi and unless someone came forward to confirm that he'd left his shop at just after nine thirty, it was likely he would be found guilty. Susie knew she could walk from her brother's shop to her mother's home in less than twenty minutes. So it was just possible that Sam could have struck the lethal blow in that time, but he would have had to stumble across his victim, kill him and then run home. In which case he must have been out of breath and surely there must have been blood on his hands?

Had someone seen him leave his shop, it would be almost impossible for Sam to have done the crime. Yet how likely was it that anyone would have seen him at that hour? Most working folk would have been at home, preparing for bed. Only someone leaving the pub or returning from a night at the cinema might have seen him. Susie knew the chances were small, but she would talk to Winnie. Perhaps they could find a way of asking if Sam had been seen – an advertisement in the evening paper or some posters stuck up on walls and in the windows of shops.

It was a slim chance but it was worth a try, because unless someone came forward, Susie wasn't sure that even the best of lawyers could win her brother's freedom...

28

'If I'd known this would happen, I would never have got up that stupid patrol,' Joe said to Lilly the next morning when he stopped by and saw her cleaning the windows of her shop. 'I feel as if it is my fault that Sam is in the cells. I asked to see him, but they said he'd had his family visit and refused to let me.'

'It isn't your fault,' Lilly told him. 'I know you feel bad, Joe – we all do. I saw Winnie on her way to work this morning and she looked terrible, her eyes red and sore from crying. She said her friends at the Women's Movement are setting up a protest campaign. Sam is a decent man, and no matter what they say, Winnie won't believe he did it.'

'Can't see as that will do a lot of good,' Joe muttered and took his cap off, running his fingers through his dark hair. He left coal dust on his face and Lilly leaned forward to wipe it off with her cloth. Jerking his head back, he gave her a half grin. 'We have to do somethin', Lilly. Jeb and me – we both want to help pay for his lawyer...'

'Well, I expect Susie will pay for that, so you'll have to ask her,' Lilly said. 'Would you like a cuppa?'

'I'd best get on,' Joe said. 'Thanks all the same, Lilly. I've got my deliveries to do – but I can't help but think of Sam stuck in that police cell. If they find him guilty, I reckon he might hang...'

Lilly stared at him in horror. 'Oh no, surely not! Sam would never do anything like that, Joe. Everyone knows it.'

'Except the bloody coppers,' Joe replied morbidly. He shuddered. 'If they do, I'll never forgive meself.'

Joe went off and Lilly was about to go inside her shop when she saw Ernie leaning on his broom. He looked tired and she went over to him.

'Are you all right?' she asked the elderly street sweeper. 'I'm just about to make a pot of tea – would you like a mugful?'

He looked at her for a moment, his eyes weary. 'You're a lovely girl, Lilly. I'd appreciate that real fine, thank you.'

'Why don't you come into the shop and sit down for a while?' Lilly asked him. 'I've got some cheese sandwiches I made this morning, if you're hungry?'

Ernie hesitated and she thought he would refuse, but then he nodded. 'If you'll have the likes of me,' he said.

'Of course I will and glad to,' she said, smiling at him. 'I'll have the kettle boiled in a trice – and no one will touch your dustcart.'

Ernie followed her into the flower shop and through to the back. She filled her kettle and put it on her little gas ring to boil and then offered him a sandwich from a grease-paper packet. He took one and munched it hungrily while she got out mugs and milk and sugar. She offered him another sandwich, encouraging him to take it.

'I've got plenty. You're welcome,' Lilly said and then made her tea.

Ernie took another sandwich and ate it in silence, his eyes never leaving her as she moved about the small room. 'You remind me of my Rose,' he said when he'd finished his food and she handed him a mug of tea, just how he liked it with sugar and milk. 'She was a lovely lass and kind, my wife...'

It was the first time he'd ever mentioned his wife so Lilly hardly dared to speak. 'I'm sorry you lost her...'

'Aye, so was I...' Ernie stared morosely into his mug of tea for a long moment, then, 'She was murdered... hit on the back of the head when she was busy in her own kitchen...'

Lilly stared at him in shock. 'Ernie! I am so sorry,' she gasped as she saw the expression in his eyes – such a bleak, aching look that she knew how much he had loved his lost wife. 'Did... did they catch the criminal who did it?'

Ernie looked at her for some seconds in silence, then, 'They thought it was me,' he said. He drew a deep breath and she saw his hands were shaking; he looked really ill. 'We argued that night, Rose and me. I don't know why... something small and silly. I was tired. I'd come home from work and I was angry over something...' He gave a choking breath and his face twisted with remembered grief. 'I shoved past her and said I was going to the pub. I think a chair was knocked over, but she wasn't hurt...' Ernie's eyes met hers, bleak and lonely. 'I walked to the pub and I drank a pint and then I went home.' He was silent for a moment, his chest heaving as the emotion threatened to overcome him. 'I found her lying on the kitchen floor with a tea towel in her hand and her head bashed in...' A great shudder went through him. 'I fell on me knees beside her and cradled her in my arms. Crying like a babe I was – and that's how they found me. A neighbour came in, looked at us and went off screaming I'd killed my Rose...'

'Oh, how terrible,' Lilly cried, her heart going out to him. She'd always suspected there was something sad in his past, but nothing as terrible as this. 'What happened, Ernie?'

He closed his eyes briefly. 'I told them how I'd found her, but they didn't believe me. She was killed by one of my work tools; I'd left my bag lying on the floor – and the neighbour told the police she'd heard us arguing earlier and said there was a crashing sound.'

'But that is only hearsay...' Lilly cried indignantly.

'Aye, but it was good enough,' Ernie said. 'I admitted we'd quarrelled, for it was the truth, but I told them it was only a silly tiff – but they didn't believe me. They took my son and daughter into care. Everyone thought I was guilty – except my lawyer. He believed me, but the jury brought in a verdict of guilty – and I went to prison for twenty years. I was let out after fifteen for good behaviour and because they said someone else had confessed to the murder of Rose, when arrested for killing another woman.'

'Oh, Ernie...' Lilly's eyes were filled with tears of pity. 'You were in prison all that time for nothing...'

'Aye, I was,' he said grimly. 'They let me out and they gave me a full pardon and a bit of money, but what was that to me? I put most of it in the church box.' Ernie gulped his tea, clearly torn apart by his memories. 'My Rose was gone and I had no home, no friends. My daughter wouldn't even see me and my son thinks I'm a murderer. He lives not far from here, but he acts like I don't exist, despite the full pardon.' He smiled wryly. 'I used to be a master cabinet maker and now I sweep the streets...'

'I am so sorry those things happened to you,' Lilly told him. 'It was wicked – so unjust.'

'Yes, it was that right enough,' Ernie said and frowned. 'It's about to happen again, I reckon...'

Lilly looked at him, seeing a flash of anger in his face. 'You've heard about Sam then?'

'Aye, I have.' Ernie shook his head. 'It's a bad business, Lilly. I reckon they will charge him just the same way they did me all them years ago...'

'That is what we're all afraid of,' Lilly told him. 'Sam wouldn't do it – not in cold blood. If he'd seen that man attacking one of his victims, he might have fought him off, but he would never have taken his own hammer to murder someone.'

'Is that what they say – it was Sam's hammer?' Ernie asked and looked upset. He put down his mug and stood up. 'I'd best get back to my work.' He shook his head. 'I shouldn't have told you all that...'

'I shan't repeat it,' Lilly promised. 'Are you sure you're all right to work today, Ernie? You don't look well.'

'I'm well enough,' he muttered. 'Thank you for the tea and sandwiches. You're a kind lass...'

Lilly gathered the mugs and washed them before returning to her shop. She had some orders for arrangements to make, but she didn't feel much like doing them. Ernie's sad story had increased the anxiety she felt for Sam. If Ernie had been a victim of a miscarriage of justice, then it could easily happen again. Her heart went out to Sam's family. How on earth would they carry on if he was wrongly imprisoned – or worse?

29

'Why can't I see him?' Winnie demanded. It was the third time she'd been to the police station, but still they wouldn't let her speak to Sam. 'Sam couldn't possibly have been the one who killed that man... he just wouldn't do it.'

'That will be for a court to decide,' the desk sergeant told her. 'The only visits Mr Collins is allowed for now are those from his lawyer. If you want to know more, speak to his sister.'

'But I'm engaged to be married to him...' Winnie cried. 'I must be allowed to see him.'

'Well, you can't. He won't be here much longer. He will be moved to a remand prison in the next day or so... you might get a visit then.'

Winnie caught back a sob as the tears stung her eyes. 'Sam isn't guilty. You've got the wrong man. You should be out there searching for evidence, not charging him.'

'I must ask you to leave, miss,' the desk sergeant said calmly. 'If you make a nuisance of yourself, you might find yourself in the cells overnight.'

Winnie stared at him furiously but knew he wouldn't budge.

She flounced away, letting the door of the police station bang behind her. Her throat was tight with emotion and tears blinded her as she left and began to walk aimlessly.

If they found Sam guilty... Winnie shivered with fear. She loved him so much and couldn't bear to think what might happen to him. It had been frightening when she was accused of murdering her own mother, but Susie had got a fancy lawyer for her and Winnie had been freed on bail – and then Constable Winston had proved that she couldn't have done it and they'd caught the man responsible.

Supposing Sam was imprisoned for all that time – or even hung? Winnie leaned against the wall as the tears trickled down her cheeks. What was she going to do with her life then? She shivered despite the warmth of a summer's day and then her head came up. It wasn't going to happen if she could help it!

Winnie knew the power of protest. The Women's Movement had already scored several successes. She would gather enough support and make so much trouble that they had to release Sam! Surely the evidence was circumstantial. Just because Sam's hammer had been used, it didn't make him guilty. If she could bring the details of his unfair arrest to the public eye, enough fuss might be made that the police were forced to look for the real culprit.

Winnie knew that some folk would think the hammer was sufficient evidence, but she was in no state to think clearly. In her desperation, she'd turned to what she knew – the power of solidarity. She must try to whip up public support, jog people's memories of what they might have seen without realising it. Susie was set on getting a fancy lawyer, well, that would help, and Winnie would talk to him – but first she would talk to the girls at the office where she'd worked for almost a year before going to work as a seamstress. The members of the Women's Movement would stand by her.

Rosalind, and Marie Jessop, Andrea, Claire... perhaps Mary Winston, and then there was that new girl... Winnie had only met her once at an evening meeting. She thought she was a nurse, but Rosalind would know. Rosalind had helped her when they were looking for that evil man who had kept young girls prisoner at Madame Pauline's when Winnie worked there. Rosalind enjoyed having something to march and protest about. She would know the names of all the girls most likely to help Winnie.

Winnie's tears dried and her shoulders squared as she turned in the direction she needed to go. Miss Susie could do without her for a day. Winnie would get something planned, something to help free Sam.

* * *

Betty Ford looked up as Susie walked into the workshop. 'Winnie hasn't turned up,' she said with a grim look. 'I know she's upset, but I've had to spend half the day answering the phone – and it isn't my job. Yvonne is doing my job as well as her own and if this goes on, we shan't get the orders out in time.'

'I'm here now and I'll answer the phone,' Susie said. 'I told Winnie she could take some time off if she needed it.' She lifted her brows as Betty glared at her. 'Sam is innocent and will be proved so, Mrs Ford. It is understandable that Winnie should need a little time to come to terms with what has happened.'

Susie might feel that Winnie's plans to involve the Women's Movement were unnecessary, but if it gave her something to do, then perhaps it might help – and they were both so desperate to help Sam, that anything was worthwhile.

Betty mumbled something that Susie couldn't catch but went through to the workroom.

Susie sat down at the reception desk and closed her eyes for a moment. She put her hands to her face, leaning her elbows on the desk and sighing. She had just come from an interview with the lawyer Lady Diane had told her was the best they could get while Hugo Montford was ill in hospital. Mr Timothy Marsh was in his mid-thirties, attractive, and Susie had disliked him on sight. He had an air of arrogance that made her feel he was looking at her from some great height, and though he'd said he was willing to take the case, she'd felt that he had no great belief in her brother's innocence. For two pins, she would have left his office and looked elsewhere for help, but even as she had prepared to stand up, he'd looked at her and said, coolly, 'I am the best you'll find, you know, Miss Collins. I win nearly all my cases...' He'd smiled in a self-assured manner, then, 'Even when I don't particularly think the clients innocent...'

Susie had sprung to her feet, wanting to strike him at that moment, but something had made her say, 'Will you take Sam's case? I've been told you are the best – apart from your partner, who is ill.'

He'd laughed then, suddenly seeming more approachable. 'Yes, I know I'm second best, Miss Collins – and yes, I will take your brother's case.' He'd invited her to sit down again, made some notes and then dismissed her. 'I have another appointment I must keep. I will get back to you as soon as I've seen your brother, Miss Collins – but if they've charged him, I doubt I can get bail. He may have to stay in the remand prison until his case is heard.'

Susie had drawn a sharp breath. It would be sheer torture for Sam – just as it was for her, her mother and Winnie. 'Thank you,' she'd said and held out her hand. He'd taken and held it, smiling at her.

'We shall find a way,' he'd promised and for a moment Susie had felt a lifting of her spirits, because she'd felt as she looked at him that he would.

She hadn't been able to do more than nod and leave him.

A man had been sitting in the outer office, shifting uneasily, and fidgeting in his seat, and Susie had thought that if ever she'd seen a guilty man, it was him. It had made her smile for some reason, but she'd only gone a short way after leaving the office when she had felt a return of her doubts.

The evidence against Sam was circumstantial, but the fact that his hammer had been used to kill a man was a big hurdle to climb and she wasn't sure that even Mr Timothy Marsh could pull it off.

The telephone rang beside her, pulling her out of her thoughts, and, putting on her most professional tone, she answered. Life had to go on and she still had a business to run, though at the moment nothing but Sam's fate seemed to matter...

30

'When are you going to take me dancing?' Sibby asked Joe before he left for work the following Thursday morning. Several days had passed since Sam Collins was arrested and she was bored, tired of all the long faces. 'You promised to take me last Saturday and you didn't...'

Joe looked at her pouting face and scowled. 'It wasn't exactly the right time, Sibby. I was under suspicion for murder – and, with Sam in prison for a crime I'm damned sure he didn't do, I don't feel like dancing.'

Sibby looked at him sulkily. 'You promised,' she said. 'It's not my fault if you do daft things and get yourself arrested... and why it matters so much to you that Sam Collins is in prison, I don't know. I'm bored spending every evening at home with...' Her voice died away as she saw the look in his eyes.

Joe was angry now. He'd gone after that vagrant in the first place mainly because his attack on Sibby had put her in the hospital. He'd felt obliged to bring her to his home, because she was too frightened to return to her lodgings, but he was damned if he was going to be dictated to by a girl that he knew very well he didn't love. 'Well, find some friends to go out with,' he said sharply. 'I've got other things to do. Winnie is getting up a petition for people to sign and there will be protest marches and posters that need putting up – and I've promised to help.'

'Surely you can spare time to take me out on Saturday night?' Sibby's voice rose to a whine. 'I thought you cared about me, Joe Ross...'

'I care about a lot of folk,' Joe replied coldly. 'One of them is my mate Sam – and on Saturday I'll be with Winnie and the others protesting outside the Houses of Parliament.'

'That's not fair. Just because...'

'Damn you, Sibby!' Joe's temper snapped. 'Stop being so selfish and think of someone else for once. Winnie must be goin' through hell...'

Sibby huffed and walked out, leaving Joe to finish his mug of tea.

His mother came in from the scullery, a look of disgust on her face. 'I thought she was someone you cared for when you brought her here,' Mrs Ross said. 'She's not the sort of girl I'd hoped you'd marry, Joe. She does a few chores, but grudgingly most of the time – and she spends most of her evening up in her room playing that wretched gramophone – or goes out with friends.'

'Don't start, Mum,' Joe pleaded. 'I've had it in the ear from Sibby – but for the moment I can't think about myself or the future. Sam is in prison and it's my fault – and don't go sayin' it ain't, because I know the truth. It was me that got everyone riled up. Sam wouldn't have joined the patrols if I hadn't pushed him into it.' He sighed and ran his fingers through his thick dark hair. His eyes fixed on her bleakly. 'If he hangs, I'll not live with myself...'

'Don't be daft,' Mrs Ross said but looked alarmed. 'If the man is innocent, the law will find it out.'

Joe glared at nothing in particular. 'I'd like to know who pinched his hammer.'

'What do you mean?'

Joe shook his head. 'Stands to reason. If his hammer was used, someone else had it. How did they get it? It must have been taken from his workbench when he was out in his back room. He keeps his leathers there and it's possible someone took the hammer when he was fetching leather for a repair...'

'He would know it had gone, surely?' Mrs Ross looked at him. 'Why are you so certain it wasn't him? He laid into that bloke who killed Bert Barrow, didn't he? I don't say he intended murder – but...'

'You mean he had it with him and... came on that Norton bloke by chance and... then what? Sam wouldn't have deliberately gone for him with a hammer. He might use his fists, but creep up and hit him on the back of the head? Never.'

'Oh well, I don't know,' Mrs Ross said, deflating suddenly. 'I just don't like to see you in such a taking, Joe. Sayin' as you couldn't live with yourself...' She shook her head. 'What about me and your sister – to say nothing of that girl? I might not like her much, but she's taken it into her head that you mean marriage – and I thought so too until this mornin'.'

'I know. I was sorry for her,' Joe confessed, shame-faced. 'She's lonely – and I do like her, but... I think of her more as a sister or a cousin I'd look out for...'

'Then you shouldn't let her think you mean to wed her,' his mother scolded.

Joe looked at her for a moment, then sighed. 'I know. I didn't promise marriage, but I did say as I'd look out for her, so...' He hunched his shoulders. 'I'm trapped and I don't know how to get out of it.'

'I'll get rid of her for you if that's what you want,' Mrs Ross told him.

'No, that wouldn't be right,' Joe said and laughed ruefully. 'I'm hoping if she gets bored enough, she'll go off herself, Ma...'

His mother snorted her disgust. 'Men! You're all great lubies! Well, I won't interfere if you say not, but I think you're a fool. You'll find yourself wed to her if you're not careful.'

Joe gave her a regretful grin, shrugged on his work jacket and left. He had several deliveries to make, though trade was slowing down as the warmer weather took hold. Coke was the main seller now, for kitchen ranges that had to be kept going despite the heat of the summer for cooking, and small businesses that used high burning fuels for their furnaces and ovens.

In the summer, he normally found himself extra jobs to make up for the slacker trade in the coal yard. Joe could cart heavy articles on his lorry and he was a carpenter of sorts. He could mend gates and fences and window frames and was often in demand for the small jobs that builders couldn't be bothered with.

He'd promised to have a look at a broken fence that morning and because the gentleman in question wasn't an early riser, he'd had a leisurely breakfast for once. As he walked down the street, he was thoughtful. Joining Winnie's protest march and pasting posters up on walls for her wasn't enough. Winnie was hopeful someone would have seen Sam working late in his shop and come forward, but Joe knew that was a long shot. That hammer had to be at the scene of the crime somehow – but how had it got there? Joe puzzled over it, turning various ideas over in his head. He stood for a moment as it came to him like a blinding flash and he pictured what had happened in his mind.

'I'd stake my right arm that was the way of it...' he said aloud, causing a passerby to stare at him in alarm. Joe shook his head. 'It's all right, mate. Just somethin' I thought of...'

He started walking again, going over the idea in his head, and he could see just how it had happened. He would swear that Derek Norton had sneaked into Sam's shop when he was out the back and pinched that hammer, probably intending to use it if he was attacked again. Perhaps someone else had attacked him – another vagrant or... whoever... and in the struggle the hammer was wrenched from his hand and used against him.

It must be something like that, Joe reasoned to himself. Sam wouldn't have used it or gone after Derek Norton; he had no reason to. The man had already been warned to clear off. Someone else had got into a fight with him and either they had stolen the hammer or Norton had used it to defend himself but found it turned against him.

For a moment he was tempted to go down the station and tell Constable Winston what he believed, but then he chanced to catch sight of Ernie.

Ernie was leaning against a low wall, perched on it as he smoked a cigarette. Joe went up to him. For a moment, he thought the old street cleaner would walk off without speaking, but then he put his cigarette out against his dustcart and slipped the butt into his overcoat pocket.

'Still got yer job then, mate?' Joe said with a grin.

'Yeah.' Ernie looked at him oddly. 'Thought they might turn me off, but they didn't.'

'I'd have given you a job,' Joe said cheerfully. 'But this suits you, doesn't it? I reckon you must see a lot when yer walkin' the streets cleanin'.'

'Sometimes,' Ernie agreed with a nod. 'I've seen a thing or two and mebbe some as I shouldn't...'

'I was wonderin',' Joe said. 'Last Friday... were you in Dressmakers' Alley or nearby?'

'Might 'ave been.' Ernie's gaze narrowed as he looked at him. 'Somethin' I ought ter have seen then?'

'My mate Sam is in the cells for somethin' he didn't do,' Joe said. 'That so-and-so Derek Norton who was attacking girls was killed with Sam's hammer. If Sam didn't do it, someone pinched his hammer – and I reckon that someone was Norton himself. I reckon he took it to defend himself and I think he was attacked and used it but...' Joe shrugged. 'So I wondered if you'd seen Derek Norton hanging around near Sam's shop that day, or anyone else.'

'Might have done,' Ernie said. 'Any particular time, was it?'

'It would have had to be on Friday I think...'

'Yeah, well now you mention it, I did see Norton hanging around near Mr Collins' shop on Friday, just around lunchtime...' Ernie said and then coughed. He turned his face towards the wall and took out a crumpled rag from his pocket, holding it to his mouth. His paroxysm of coughing lasted for several seconds and before he returned the rag to his pocket, Joe saw bloodstains on it. 'Sorry,' Ernie muttered and took a small bottle of liquid from his pocket, swallowing a mouthful. It made him choke, but after a minute or so, his normal colour returned.

Joe stared at him in silence for a few seconds, then, 'There was blood on the rag, Ernie. You're ill...' He saw Ernie's glare and put out a defensive hand. 'I'm not interfering, but have you seen a doctor?'

Ernie's glare intensified. 'Nothing they can do,' he muttered, taking another sip of what Joe now saw was whisky. 'I know it ain't good for me, but I'm dyin', so what does it matter?'

Joe was stupefied for a moment, then, 'I'm sorry. I had no idea, mate. Is there anywhere you could go – for treatment or just to be looked after?'

'I don't want to die in an institution,' Ernie muttered. 'They won't do much for me. I prefer to take my chances on the street. Shan't see another winter out.'

'If I can do anything to help...' Joe offered, feeling useless, because what could he offer? 'Buy you a hot meal or a bed for the night? Mum would get you food any evening if you come to the house, somewhere to sleep, too, if you'd like?'

Ernie's look was chilling as he said, 'You can't do anything for me, Joe Ross – but I might be able to do something for you...'

'Ernie...' Joe began but he held up his hand to stop him.

'I'll think on what you said.' Ernie nodded and then turned his dustcart and trundled off down the road.

Joe watched him for a moment, then remembered his appointment. If he wasn't careful, he would be late.

31

'I'm not sure demonstrating outside the Houses of Parliament will do any good,' Susie argued when Winnie told her what she had planned for that Saturday. 'I can't see the police will just suddenly let him go because you parade with placards proclaiming his innocence.'

'It's just the start,' Winnie said. 'Sam has been falsely accused and charged with a murder he didn't commit. I know his hammer was the murder weapon, but it doesn't mean he is guilty, and they should let him out on bail...'

'Mr Marsh has tried, but it was refused,' Susie said, looking at her in sympathy. Winnie's face was showing signs of sleepless nights – something Susie was also feeling. 'I can't stop you demonstrating, Winnie, but I won't come. I need to be with Lady Diane on Saturday. Mr Marsh thinks the posters are a good idea. If someone saw Sam working late, it would help to prove he couldn't have killed that man.'

'Whoever did it deserves a medal,' Winnie said fiercely. 'Norton was evil and he deserved what he got, but my Sam is innocent.'

'I believe that as much as you do,' Susie replied. 'I told him to try to think if he had lost it or noticed it was missing...'

'Knowing the police, they wouldn't believe him. I don't think Sam was anywhere near the man when he was killed,' Winnie said with a stubborn look. 'He would surely have had blood on his hands when he came in and he didn't – his clothes too would have bloodstains. None of them have.'

'Have the police asked you any questions like that – or asked to see his clothes?'

'No, they haven't,' Winnie said still angry. 'If they had any sense, they would do so, but they just want him to be guilty...'

'I must tell Mr Marsh that they made no enquiries about bloodstains.' Susie made a mental note. 'I am seeing him again this evening. He is going to visit Sam this afternoon and hear what he has to say. I just pray he thinks he can find a way to prove his innocence.'

* * *

Leaving the workshop a little later, Susie saw Eddie Stevens exit his own business and come across the road to meet her.

'Miss Collins,' Eddie said. 'I'm glad I caught you. None of us in the lanes believes that Sam is guilty. I was working late on Friday night myself and I saw Sam leaving his place at about twenty to ten. He works so hard...'

'Twenty minutes to ten?' Susie looked at him, her heart giving a great leap. 'Are you certain of the time, Mr Stevens? It is important – because Sam was home just after ten and it takes more than fifteen minutes to walk to my mother's house.'

'Quite certain, because I looked at my pocket watch when his lights went out. I was in a hurry and wanted to get to the pub before ten and I'd decided to lock up myself only a few minutes earlier...' He grinned at her. 'I needed to buy a bottle of whisky for my uncle's birthday...'

Susie hesitated, then, 'Would you stand up in court and swear to that, Mr Stevens?'

'Certainly. If it would help...'

'I think it would help quite a bit,' Susie told him. 'It still doesn't explain why Sam's hammer was used as a murder weapon, but it might make all the difference when it comes to the trial because he couldn't have done it and got home in twenty minutes.' She smiled at him, feeling her spirits soar. 'Thank you so much for telling me. I am seeing the lawyer I engaged later and I will tell him. He may come and ask you for a signed testimony...'

'Yes, of course. I am always here and I will go to the police station and tell them what I saw.'

Susie thanked him and set on her way once more. The fact that he could confirm Sam's story of working late must surely help. It must be proof that he couldn't have done the murder. She had not believed that anyone was likely to come forward to testify to seeing him, but it seemed that a miracle had happened. For a moment, tears pricked her eyes, but in her heart, she knew Sam wasn't out of the woods yet – there was still the mystery of how his hammer came to have a man's blood and hair on it...

'Thank you for meeting me here,' Timothy Marsh said, glancing round the busy Lyons' Corner House. 'You can be sure of good service here; the food is eatable and no one bothers about anyone else. We can talk and not worry about being overheard...'

The restaurant was busy; the nippies were everywhere with their notepads and their laden trays. Mr Marsh had ordered tea and cakes and within minutes it was brought to their table.

'You saw Sam,' Susie said, looking across the table anxiously. 'How was he? Is he bearing up?'

'I believe he is the better for my visit. He was, I think, a little despairing before I discussed the case with him, Miss Collins. However, I feel we have a good chance. Especially now that this Mr Stevens has come forward. If your brother was seen leaving his shop at twenty to ten, there is no possible way that he could have committed a murder and returned home to arrive just before ten.'

'Winnie says there was no blood on his hands or clothes – but the police haven't even asked them.'

'I dare say they know the answer they would get if they did...' He saw her face and his thin brows lifted slightly. 'No mother or future wife is going to say yes he had blood on his hands, is she?'

'My mother wouldn't lie,' Susie said hotly and his hands came up, fencing her off in a laughing manner.

'Perhaps she wouldn't – but most mothers lie through their teeth for their sons, especially those who are as guilty as hell.' Susie glared at him but said nothing. 'However, I am of the same opinion as you, Miss Collins. Now that I have spoken to him, I do not believe that your brother killed this Mr Norton. Who was, I understand, a thoroughly nasty piece of work. I would imagine he had many enemies from the criminal fraternity and I intend to use that in our defence.'

Susie's anger drained away instantly. She took a sip of her hot sweet tea. 'Thank you,' she said when she had recovered her composure. 'I was afraid you would think Sam guilty.'

'I am not a fool. I learned from my first time in a police interview room that there are guilty men and innocent men accused falsely. It isn't always as clear-cut as that, but in this case, I firmly believe that Sam is innocent – and I intend to prove that.'

Susie nibbled a scone, the tension going out of her for the first time in days. 'I just pray that you can,' she said. 'I think Sam's hammer must have been stolen, but how or when, I can't think.'

'I asked him about that,' Mr Marsh said. 'He thinks he had it on Thursday when he was repairing some boots, but doesn't remember seeing it after that...'

'Did he leave the shop empty at any time, without locking his door?' Susie's brow wrinkled in thought.

'He told me that he left the front shop and went to fetch leathers from the back room twice during Friday, once in the morning and once in the afternoon. He didn't lock the front door at either time...'

'Then someone could have gone in and taken the hammer?' Susie sat forward eagerly.

'Sam wasn't sure about that,' Mr Marsh replied. 'I suggested it and he said the bell should ring when the door opens. He doesn't recall it ringing when he was through the back...'

'Perhaps he just didn't hear it... or the church bells were ringing...' Susie bit her lip. 'It must have happened that way. I don't see how else it could have...'

'No, that is the problem and why the police think they have a tight case against him,' Mr Marsh agreed. 'If I proposed that in court, Sam would be cross-questioned and asked about the shop bell – if he heard it ring when he was out the back...'

'Sam would tell the truth,' Susie replied, her heart sinking.

Mr Marsh nodded. 'I believe, like you, the hammer was taken somehow, but when and why did your brother not hear the bell?'

Susie swore beneath her breath and then blushed. 'Forgive me. I hoped it was the answer.'

'It would be so convenient,' Mr Marsh agreed. 'To your knowledge, does your brother have two claw hammers?'

Susie thought for a moment and then inclined her head. 'Yes, I think he might – but only one has his initials on it. Mum gave it to him as a present when he started the shop.'

'Why then would he have two?' Mr Marsh looked at her.

'Because the one Mum gave him isn't as heavy or as strong as the one he bought when he could afford it...' Her eyes met his and she felt puzzled as she saw a gleam in his. 'I don't understand...'

'If Sam preferred his other hammer, then it may well be that he used that one on Friday morning. He could well have mislaid the one with the initials at any time. I will ask him for particulars when I next visit him, which I am afraid will not be for two weeks.'

'Oh.' Susie felt a surge of frustration. 'That is a long time to wait...'

'I am afraid I have double the workload at the moment with Hugo in hospital, but don't worry, I shall still be working on the case.' He looked at her consideringly. 'Do you have a key to your brother's workplace?'

'Yes, but...' Susie met his eyes. 'You want to know if there is another claw hammer on the bench. Yes, I could go and look – take a photograph of it if you wish.' Susie didn't own a camera, but she could borrow a small box camera from Lady Diane, who used it often to take pictures of her daughter.

'That would be a good idea and the sooner, the better.' He folded his hands in an arch, looking at her over the top. 'Perhaps your brother lost the hammer a while ago and didn't want your mother to know. Has he bought a new rucksack recently?'

'Yes, I think he did.'

'Have a look for the old one,' Mr Marsh suggested. 'If there is a hole in it, bring it to me. We must build up a case for his having lost this wretched hammer – perhaps he brings work home sometimes?'

'He used the hammer to fix a window that was sticking for Mum a few weeks ago,' Susie said. 'I asked him if he could've lost it, but he said no...' Her eyes flew to his. 'He wouldn't say that just to protect Mum's feelings surely?'

'Who knows? – but it may have been lost without his knowledge. It is a thread, no more. We need proof, but if we can build the probability of it being either lost or stolen – and also prove that he had no time to attack and kill Mr Norton, perhaps a jury would return a not guilty verdict. It is often a matter of persuasion, which is where I earn my money.'

'Yes, I see,' Susie said and looked at him. 'We haven't discussed terms as yet, Mr Marsh. I will find the money to pay for Sam's defence no matter what...'

A smile touched his mouth. 'I am very expensive for criminals who can afford to pay me from their ill-gotten gains, Miss Collins – but I think you will find my terms for an innocent brother quite reasonable.'

'Thank you. If you could let me have some idea...'

A little laugh escaped him. 'I wonder if you will pay. My terms for restoring your brother to you are that you take me to dinner at The Savoy. Nothing more. Nothing less.'

Susie gave a gasp. 'You are mocking me!' He couldn't mean it, surely?

'No, not mocking,' he said and leaned towards her. 'Do you know that you are beautiful when you are angry, Miss Collins?'

Was he flirting with her? Susie felt the warmth of embarrassment in her cheeks. Why would he make such an offer? 'No, no, I couldn't accept. You will please tell me the normal terms...'

'No, Miss Collins, I shall not,' he murmured a glint in his eyes. 'If you want me to represent your brother in court, that is my price...' A smile lingered on his mouth. 'Come, come, Miss Collins – is a dinner so much to ask?'

Susie stared at him for a while in silence and then dipped her head. 'I think you quite foolish to demand such a price,' she said, feeling a little dazed. 'However, a dinner it shall be.'

He offered his hand and she took it. He held it tight for one second and then released her. 'Good, that is a bargain.' He summoned the nippy and paid the bill. 'I must go – but please stay and finish these delightful cakes if you will. I shall speak to you after my next visit to Sam...'

Susie sat where she was and watched him leave. It was the most ridiculous bargain she'd ever heard of, but, in truth, she would have paid any price to see her brother free and happy again.

32

Winnie could hardly believe how many people had turned out to support her. Not just folk from the lanes, but her friends and colleagues from the Women's Movement, some of whom were wearing their tricolour sashes and parading with protest boards.

POLICE BRUTALITY
INNOCENT MAN ARRESTED
WOMEN SAY EVERYONE IS ENTITLED TO A FAIR HEARING

'Thank you,' she said to Rosalind, who she knew had gone to a lot of trouble to get the message out to many of their fellow members. Some of the ladies protesting had come up from the country just for the occasion. At a guess, Winnie thought there must have been upwards of five hundred people, marching up and down in front of the Houses of Parliament. She wasn't sure that they all knew what they were protesting about, but they were here, supporting a member of their movement. Some of the women had suffered false arrest and brutality at the hands of both police and prison officers, who had force-fed them to break their hunger strike. They hardly cared why they'd been summoned; it was merely an excuse to protest against what they saw as an unfair society. However, there were also local men and women here to support Sam, because they knew him and did not believe him guilty.

'I wish I could do more,' Rosalind said. 'We all know your Sam wouldn't kill anyone in cold blood. Besides, we haven't turned out for a protest in ages, so everyone thought it would be a good idea to remind our friends in parliament that we haven't gone away and we shan't until we win equal rights for women.'

Winnie nodded, smiling at her friend. It helped to know that she had supporters who would stand by their convictions. Susie had placed her trust in a fancy lawyer she'd found, but Winnie was haunted by the fact that Sam was still in custody and had been transferred to a remand prison to await trial. She knew how he must be feeling, the despair, fear and anger going on in his head. She had suffered a night in the cells, but Sam had been there for more than a week now and would most probably be there for months before his case was brought to trial.

Winnie went to stand in the front line of protesters who were shouting out their slogan of 'Free Sam Collins. Innocent man arrested. Free Sam Collins...' She joined in the shouting and saw that the police had arrived. A crowd of bystanders had gathered to watch and a few seemed to be considering whether to join in. She noticed that a police officer was talking to Mary Winston, trying to discover whether he could get the protesters to move on, but she was shaking her head.

'I say, this is quite fun, isn't it?' a girl's voice said beside Winnie. 'It's the first time I've been on a protest march. Are we going to parade outside Buckingham Palace?'

'We might if we don't get arrested before then,' Winnie replied. She looked at the attractive young woman. She too had thought some of the protest marches she'd been on would be fun, but for her this one was deadly serious, perhaps even a matter of life or death. 'I've seen you at the office briefly – I don't know your name, sorry...'

'I'm Sarah – Sarah Leigh,' the girl said and smiled at her. 'I only joined recently. Are you Winnie? I think it is your fiancé who has been wrongfully arrested, isn't it?' Winnie nodded. 'I'm really sorry. When I said this was fun, I didn't mean – I know it can't be for you...'

'I knew what you meant,' Winnie said. 'It is so unfair. I know Sam didn't kill that man, but just because his hammer was used, the police have charged him with murder.'

'That is only circumstantial, surely,' Sarah said with a frown. 'I don't know Sam, of course, but Rosalind told me that he was a decent man – and she told me something similar had happened to you, once. My father says a lot of the suffragettes have been badly treated by the police and the government. I wanted to join, because it isn't fair.' She hesitated, then, 'I know this march isn't about the movement, but some of us felt it was a good excuse to make our strength felt.'

'I expect that is why we have such a big crowd,' Winnie said. 'I don't care why they are here – if it brings attention to Sam's case, it must mean he will at least get a fair hearing – don't you think?'

'I think in the past there have been many cases of injustice, where men didn't have proper defence.' She hesitated, then, 'I might know someone who could represent him in court if you need a good lawyer, Winnie.'

'Sam's sister has found someone, but thanks.' Winnie saw several police officers coming towards them. 'They are going to try to move us on now. It might get a little rough. If I don't see you again, try not to get arrested...'

The police had arrived in sufficient numbers and were linking arms, trying to force the protesters away. 'Come along, ladies,' one of them said not unkindly. 'This is a matter for the justice courts, not you...'

'Free Sam Collins!' Winnie shouted. 'He is innocent. Police brutality...'

Several voices took up the chant. One of the police officers drew his truncheon and a yell of anger was heard from the back of the crowd.

'Police brutality... kill the bastards!' The voice was a man's and came from the crowd of bystanders, not the protesters.

The cry was taken up from all sides, however, and Winnie felt herself being pushed forward by angry protesters trying to get to the front of the crowd. She was pushed against a police officer, who immediately grabbed her by her wrist and clapped a pair of handcuffs on her. She was dragged off towards a police Black Maria and bundled into the back. Behind her, she could hear sounds of shouting and screaming and it sounded as if the peaceful march had suddenly become an angry mob as people fought against the men in uniforms who were now wielding their truncheons left and right.

'She is one of the ring leaders,' an officer said of Winnie. 'Grab a few more of them and then we'll break this protest up.'

'We have a right to protest peacefully,' Winnie cried but was ignored as another woman was thrust into the van with her and then half a dozen more, one after the other. 'What are they doing out there?' she asked a woman wearing her suffragette sash.

'They are charging us,' the woman said and showed her where she had blood on her face. 'Why? We were perfectly peaceful. They had no right...'

Someone had incited the trouble, someone who was not a member of the protest itself.

Winnie scowled as the door of the police van was slammed

and then they were driven away. 'They don't like it when we tell the world what brutes they are...'

One of the women was sobbing, but most were in a defiant mood.

'If they put me in prison, I shall go on hunger strike,' the woman wearing the sash declared.

'They will force-feed you,' another woman warned. 'Best to keep quiet and stick to our story – a peaceful march and the police started the fight. That way, they will let us out after a night in the cells...'

Winnie nodded. Her wrists hurt where the police officer had manhandled her into the van. She wished Mary Winston was with them but knew she had been trying to pacify the crowd and stop it developing into a riot, so perhaps she would escape arrest.

Winnie bit her lip. The march had seemed such a good idea – but she had no way of helping Sam if they put her in prison, too.

* * *

Sarah was caught up in the push that the line of officers made against the protesting women. She found herself trapped as the protesters at the back surged forward and had a feeling that some of them were men who had come intent on causing trouble rather than helping free an innocent man.

Suddenly finding herself thrust back and falling to the ground, she was saved by a strong pair of arms. 'Don't worry,' a voice said. 'I'll get you out of here...'

She felt the protection of his arm about her as he forced their passage through the rioting crowd to a clear space, but instead of stopping for breath, he continued supporting her until they were far enough away to be clear of the trouble.

Sarah looked up at the man who had rescued her, staring for a moment as she tried to recall when she'd seen him before. Then, like a blinding light, it came to her. 'We've met before,' she said and laughed. 'Last time, you almost knocked me over – this time you saved me from being trampled... Joe... it is Joe, isn't it?'

'Yes, it is,' he said and smiled at her. 'You're Sarah. We met at the hospital. You are a nurse.'

'Yes, I am,' she replied and her eyes met his in wonder. 'I hoped... but we never met again. I didn't think it would happen...' A little trill of laughter escaped her, her smile lighting up her eyes. 'How on earth did you see me in all that madness?'

'I didn't know it was you at first,' Joe admitted; the wonder in her eyes was reflected in his. Incredible that fate should throw them together in this way. 'I saw a woman stumble and came to help – and then... I knew it was you.' He drew a deep breath. 'I can't believe you're here... that I found you in all this...'

'Well, I can only say thank you,' Sarah murmured, shivering a little. 'They are arresting a lot of the women, aren't they? I haven't seen one man arrested...'

'I expect they know that without the Women's Movement, the protest will falter,' Joe said. 'It was a bigger turnout than I expected when Winnie said what she intended.'

'I think some were just louts out to cause trouble,' Sarah replied. 'I thought it would be fun and the Women's Movement is always ready to protest about what they see as injustice – as well as supporting Winnie – but I never expected it to end like this...' She looked up at him, laughing and breathless all of a sudden, the noise and chaos seeming to fade away as their eyes met.

Joe nodded. 'After that ordeal, let me buy you a cup of tea. It must have been quite scary just now.' He offered her his arm. 'We could find somewhere quiet. I think we should talk, don't you?'

'Yes, I do,' Sarah agreed, her hand resting in the crook of his arm. 'I'm so glad you were here, Joe...'

'Me too,' Joe told her. 'Let's find somewhere we can be quiet for a while...' They smiled as they walked, Joe on the kerb edge of the pavement, protecting her from harm as a gentleman ought. 'It's... as if it was meant to be...'

'Yes. Something told me I must come today – and now I know why.'

* * *

'So, tell me about yourself,' Joe said as Sarah poured tea for them both in the little café. 'How do you know Winnie and what made you join the Women's Movement?'

'I met Winnie properly for the first time today,' Sarah said. 'I joined the movement because my father supports it. He says it is long past time that every man and woman over the age of twenty-one had the vote. My father believes that women should think and act for themselves. He came from a privileged background,' Sarah told him. 'But he has egalitarian ideas, which was why he allowed me to become a nurse. My mother said I should stay home and marry a man of substance, but Dad says I should see something of the world first.'

'And have you?' His eyes dwelled on her face, watching the play of emotions.

'I've been to France and Italy. I might go to Austria next year, but...' She sighed and shook her head. 'To be honest, I would just as soon be here. I enjoy my work. I like helping people, even though Matron doesn't think I'm very good at it...' She laughed and Joe smiled.

'I am sure you would be good at anything you wanted to do.'

She was so open and honest and he knew that the emotions she'd stirred the first time they met had not been mistaken. She was adorable. Listening to her was like being in an enchanted dream for Joe; she was a beautiful shining light, full of laughter and bubbling over with her love of life, but the more she talked of her family and friends, the more fascinated he became, though deep down inside he knew that the social gap between them was too wide. Her father was well off, a respected lawyer, her mother a vicar's daughter, and she was educated, clever, beyond him in every way.

At last, when he'd been silent for a while, she said, 'You haven't told me much about you, Joe. You're a coalman with your own business and you do odd jobs in the quiet season – but what do you like? Are you interested in music or the theatre – or football?' Her eyes seemed to dance with mischief. 'My father loves cricket, but my younger brother is mad for football.'

'I like football,' Joe agreed. 'I like cricket too, but I rarely get time to watch a match – that's an all-day thing...' Sarah nodded. 'I like music, all sorts, and dancin'...'

'I love to dance...' Sarah's eyes met his and he knew what she was asking. 'I don't often get the chance...'

'I could take you,' he said at last, 'if you'd like that?' He knew he was daft because this could never be more than a brief inter-lude, but he couldn't just walk away now. He just wanted to sit there and watch her face as she talked. She showed her emotions so openly, laughing and then sad, her beauty so much more than skin-deep.

'I would like it very much,' Sarah said. Their eyes met and held and Joe couldn't break away. He found himself smiling. It was fool-ish. She was too far above him. Nothing could ever happen between them, but he was caught fast in a silken web of delight and the need to see her again.

* * *

After tea, Sarah wanted to go to the offices of the Women's Movement, where she said she'd been told to report back. 'We'll be contacting people to see who has been arrested and working to set them free...'

Joe walked her there and she looked up into his face, touching his arm. 'You will come on Saturday? To the address I gave you?' she asked and he nodded.

'I'll be there at seven, and I'll call at your home for you,' he agreed and left her to go into the office, where lights were already blazing.

Joe was thoughtful as he walked home. He would meet Sarah, because he couldn't help himself, but he knew in his heart that it could only lead to tears. Her family would never allow her to go out with a mere coalman and once they'd seen him, they would probably forbid her to meet him again.

33

Winnie was at her desk in reception on Monday morning. Susie looked at her as she entered. Her brother's intended wife was looking pale, her eyes red-rimmed, but otherwise her usual self.

'How are you?' she asked. 'I didn't hear you'd been arrested until I popped in to see Mum on my way here this morning. Was it awful?'

'Not too bad,' Winnie replied. 'They treated us pretty well considering, but I think they knew it wasn't the Women's Movement that started the fight. There were some professional trouble-makers mixed in with the genuine protesters – and we got a lot of publicity. The papers are full of it this morning – have you seen the headlines?' Winnie pulled out a national paper she'd purchased on her way to work. There were large headlines on the front page of *The Times* and several inside, all of them favouring the protesters over the police.

'I know. I bought a paper after Mum told me,' Susie said. 'They do mention Sam a few times, but most of it is anti-police, aimed at the government. One reporter is calling them brutes of the first order.' She smiled at Winnie. 'I think the tide of public opinion is turning in favour of the Women's Movement, but I'm not sure it helps Sam much.'

'No, I know...' Winnie drew a long shuddering sigh. 'When they arrested us, I thought we might be charged with public affray and given prison sentences, but I think the police felt it would be bad politically – because we were peacefully protesting until that idiot charged at us. And if I had been charged that wouldn't have helped Sam one bit.'

'No, it wouldn't,' Susie agreed. 'I'm not saying you should abandon your ideas, Winnie, but it might be better to carry on with your petition rather than gather a large crowd outside public buildings.'

'Yes. I was talking to a lady who was arrested with me. She suggested a petition that I could take to the Prime Minister, Ramsay MacDonald – or even King George. She says she knows some people who are knowledgeable about how to get innocent people free – they've done it on behalf of suffragettes who were badly treated in prison.' Winnie shook her head. 'That law – you know, the Cat and Mouse... where if a woman went on hunger strike, they let her out of prison and then rearrested her so it started all over again, and then the force feeding...' A shiver went through her. 'It's wicked how some of them have been treated in the past.'

'I agree.' Susie sighed. 'At least we have one piece of evidence in Sam's favour. He was seen leaving his shop and the time was later than he thought – which means he just didn't have time to commit a crime like that, because he was home by ten. Mr Marsh thinks that will help and if we can discover what happened to Sam's hammer, it should help to clear his name.' She was intending to visit Sam's shop that evening before she went home, to see if she could find the second hammer.

'I do hope so,' Winnie said fervently. 'If... if he was sent to prison for a long time, I don't think I could bear it...' She swallowed hard, blinking back her tears. 'I miss him, Susie.'

'Yes, of course you do. We all do... but Mr Marsh seems confident that he can help when it comes to court, so...' There was silence for a moment, the silence of fear and frustration. 'I'm afraid it means he may have to stay in prison for quite a while yet. Winnie. Unless some new evidence comes to light, there will be a trial...'

Winnie sniffed and blew her nose.

Susie knew she was struggling against her feelings. 'Would you like a few days off?'

'No!' Winnie was definite. 'I'd go mad, Susie. I want to be here doing my job. I know I can't do much to help Sam, but if I just give in... We'll need our money to pay for his defence.'

'That is taken care of,' Susie replied. 'Don't worry over that, Winnie. I've already agreed it.'

'Sam won't let you pay. You've had to work hard for your money, Susie.'

'I can afford the price I've been asked,' Susie said with a little twist of her mouth. 'You should be thinking about when Sam comes home. If I were you, love, I wouldn't wait any longer. I'd get married as soon as the banns are called.'

'Oh, if only...' Winnie gave her a watery smile. 'You're a good friend, Susie, and a lovely sister.'

'I'll ask Mr Marsh if you're allowed to visit Sam in the remand prison. I'm not sure. You may have to wait for a while longer...'

The telephone rang then and Winnie answered. Susie left her taking what sounded like a large order and went into the workrooms. There was a hushed silence and then Yvonne said, 'We all want you to know how sorry we are about Sam, Miss Susie – and none of us believes he would kill anyone.'

'Thank you.' Susie managed to keep her voice from wobbling

as the emotion welled up inside her. 'Sam would never murder anyone – the police have the wrong man.'

There were murmurs of agreement and then everyone went back to work.

Yvonne was about to return to her station, but Susie touched her arm.

'Come through to my office,' she invited. 'I have something to tell you...'

Yvonne followed her into the small room, not much more than a cubicle, where Susie kept her accounts and various bits and pieces.

'I've shown those garments you made, along with the sketches, to Lady Diane and she thought they were just what we needed for the cheaper collection. We shall produce a range of six pieces next season. We will use good-quality materials but not as expensive as those we use for the Miss Susie range.' She smiled at Yvonne. 'You had obviously based most of your ideas on the Miss Susie range so they are not originals. However, Lady Diane wants to pay for your work, Yvonne – and she suggests a bonus of five pounds for each of your adaptions. If you were to come up with some original designs, it would be more.' She heard Yvonne's gasp and arched one eyebrow. 'Is that satisfactory?'

'Oh, I never dreamed you would pay me for my ideas,' Yvonne told her, clearly excited. 'I thought Lady Diane might be cross because I had used her designs to make some clothes for myself.'

'No, not at all,' Susie said, smiling. 'She feels that three ranges would tax her ingenuity as well as her strength. You know she has only just recovered enough to begin going out socially again. While she loves what she does, she would find the cheaper range less enjoyable and is content to leave it to you and me to come up with models for the new season.'

Yvonne's excitement shone from her eyes as her fingers moved as if they were impossible to control. 'If it is a success' – she breathed – 'I could earn perhaps as much as forty or fifty pounds extra a year...' She shook her head in wonder. 'I've never had that much money, Miss Susie.'

'I think it might be more,' Susie told her. 'You have talent, Yvonne, and so does your son. You will need to make the garments and ask him to sketch them as before.'

'Oh, he'll do that all right, and I'll share whatever we earn with him,' Yvonne said. 'I can't thank you enough for taking this to Lady Diane. I can't believe I'm to be paid so much... it is like a dream...'

Susie laughed at her pleasure. 'I think my lady was relieved. Mr Matthew suggested the extra ranges to her as a way of making more money and she agreed, but I think she thought it might be too much for her – as it would. If you become our designer for the cheaper range... well, in time, who knows where it might lead.'

Yvonne gave an almighty sniff, swiping at her cheek with the back of her hand. 'And you persuaded her to let me do it – with all the worry you've got on your shoulders. Running this place and your mother worried to death over your brother.'

'We all are,' Susie confirmed. 'However, that doesn't stop me doing my work. I gave Lady Diane my word that I would run this place for her and I have to go on... whatever happens.' Susie looked grave. 'She has her troubles too, for all she is the wife of a rich man who indulges her.' She shook her head as Yvonne looked in enquiry. 'No. It isn't for me to discuss, but never think that being rich means someone's life is pain-free, Yvonne, because it doesn't.'

'I suppose not,' Yvonne said. 'I'd better get back to my station, Miss Susie. We have an order to get out – and one of our girls hasn't come in today.'

'Did anyone let us know why?'

'No. It's Sibby...' Yvonne told her. 'She is a bit of a sulker. I know she was in hospital for a while and it upset her – it would anyone, being attacked like that – but she's always been moody.'

'I do hope she is all right and won't make a regular thing of staying off work...' Susie said. 'After all the attacks on girls these past weeks, it makes you wonder...'

'I expect she'll turn up tomorrow,' Yvonne said.

Susie nodded and sat down at her desk as the seamstress went back to the workshop.

Susie picked up the orders for the last few days, glancing through them. The Miss Susie range was beginning to sell really well at last. She wondered whether it would have been wiser to stick to one range, but Mr Matthew had thought Lady Diane needed to be able to express her taste for the exotic and she had certainly given Susie some beautiful sketches. Her latest included some long, flowing scarves with flags and symbols of the Olympic Games, which was now well under way. She had also suggested a shawl with prints of Parisian attractions.

Susie considered how they would make up the latest models and frowned. She had been going to ask Sibby to work on them with her, as she was one of the best seamstresses. It would be a pity if she were to prove unreliable, but perhaps she was simply feeling unwell...

* * *

Yvonne managed to get the last of the orders done by working late herself. Susie helped and they had everything ready to be pressed and packed the next day. When they left the building, most of the other girls had already disappeared from sight, all of them having worked overtime for which they would be generously paid.

Yvonne and Susie walked to the end of the alley together. The light was still on in Lilly's shop and they could see she had a

customer. As they parted at the junction of Dressmakers' Alley
and Silver Lane, Yvonne turned homeward. She hadn't told her
son she would be working late and hoped he hadn't got bored and
gone off on his own.

She'd been walking for some minutes, lost in thought, when
she caught sight of Sibby talking and laughing with a man on the
corner of the street that led to Joe Ross' home. He was dressed in a
sharp suit of pinstripe cloth and had shoes that Yvonne always
thought of as co-respondent, which meant they were flashy.

'Sibby...' Yvonne waved to her, wanting a word, but she turned
away and walked quickly in the opposite direction. 'Be like that
then...' Yvonne commented crossly. She would have a few words
when that young madam decided to turn up for work.

She walked quickly home, breathing a sigh of relief when she
saw her son playing football in the road outside their home with
one of his friends. Now that the nights were lighter, he preferred to
be out in the street rather than sitting at home.

'You're late, Mum,' he said. 'I was a bit worried...'

'We had an order to finish,' Yvonne told him with a smile.
'Come inside now, love. I've got some nice pork chops for our tea.'

'Ooh, I love chops,' he said, waving at his friend. 'Be out again
later, Mickey...'

Mickey nodded and carried on playing, kicking the ball against
a wall.

Yvonne looked at her son with loving pride. He'd worried her
for a while when she'd discovered he'd been running errands for a
known crook, but he'd stopped when Jeb told him it was a mug's
game.

'I've got some good news,' she told him as she took off her
jacket and John went to move the kettle onto the hob for their tea.
'You know those drawings you did of me in my dresses?' John
nodded. 'Well, we've been asked to do some more and I'll be paid

for each one – and I'll give you a share of the money, John. You can save up for that bike you want, love.'

'Mum!' His face lit up like a beacon. 'I was going to tell you – Jeb says I can help him in his shop on Saturdays, because he trusts me. He says if I work hard and do what he wants, he'll find me a bike at a cheap price and he'll help me do it up so it is as good as new.'

Yvonne smiled. 'So what does he want you to do, love?'

'He says I can polish bits of silver and brass, make them shine – and, if I like the trade, he'll take me on as his assistant when I leave school...'

'Don't you want to draw – or play sport on Saturdays?' she asked.

'I can do that on Sundays and, in the evenings, too,' John said. He looked at her. 'I know my teachers told you I could be an artist or a footballer, Mum – and I might one day, but Jeb says there's good money to be made in buying and selling old stuff. He'll teach me – make me his partner when I'm older...'

'He never said that...' Yvonne laughed, her eyes quizzing him.

'No, not yet he didn't,' John agreed. 'But he will, Mum. You'll see – him and me get on real well. He likes me.'

'That doesn't mean he'll make you his partner...'

'He might,' John said with a giggle. 'I like Jeb, Mum. I didn't like Tam much. He wasn't honest like Jeb...'

'I like him too, and Lilly. She is his wife.'

'I know that,' John said. 'She gave me one of her rock cakes. They are good people, Mum. Don't say I can't work for him on Saturdays, please.'

'No, I won't say that,' she said. 'Just think carefully about what you want to do when you leave school, John. I think you might find there are other things you'd rather do – with your art, for instance. You have a wonderful talent. If you could design clothes... do sketches of dresses, like you did for me, there might be a good career for you at a dress manufacturer.'

'That's not a job that's fun,' John said and laughed.

Yvonne smiled and started to cook their meal. She sipped her tea as she turned the chops over in the pan, watching them turn a delicious golden brown. Her son didn't know how talented he was, but he would be safe enough working for Jeb on Saturdays for the time being. It would be good for him to have a male role model in his life.

34

After leaving Yvonne, Susie let herself into Sam's shop. It felt cold and deserted and made her shiver. She lit the gas lights in the front and went through to the back room. Her brother kept all his supplies here and it smelled strongly of leather. There were piles of it everywhere, as well as the boxes of special nails he used for his work. She could see no signs of any tools so went back into the shop where his work bench was, his high stool behind it. On the bench were the moulds that he set the shoes on to work, some leather soles and heels he'd cut with his sharp knives, and his tools all neatly set out in little trays, as well as a pair of shoes that were half-finished.

Susie saw the heavy claw hammer lying on the bench almost immediately. She'd borrowed a box camera from Lady Diane and she took several photographs, hoping that the light would be good enough for pictures. She considered taking the tool to her next meeting with Mr Marsh but decided against the idea. Sam's hammer should be left in situ so that the police could check for themselves. It wasn't evidence in itself, but showed he had another hammer, which might account for him not missing his favourite one. Each small piece helped to build a picture that would prove Sam's innocence.

Just as she was locking the door after her, Susie heard the sound of a man's footsteps and turned to see Eddie Stevens approaching. She smiled and, when he stopped to speak, told him what she'd been doing.

'That's it, Miss Collins,' he said. 'Do whatever you can to help Sam. I spoke to the desk sergeant and he took my statement, but whether he believed me or not, I can't say. If you ask me, that lot have made up their minds, whether the evidence is there or not.'

'I know – but Mr Marsh says a jury has an open mind and he thinks Sam will be proven innocent, despite the hammer. I appreciate your help, Mr Stevens – whatever happens.'

'I do hope it will be so,' Eddie said and hesitated. 'I wouldn't mind if you called me Eddie, Miss Collins. Most folks do...'

'Oh – well, my name is Susie,' she said and laughed. 'I am sure you knew that...'

'I'm not one to take liberties, Susie,' he said and smiled at her. 'It would be nice to be friends, though, don't you think?'

'We are neighbours and should be friends,' Susie agreed. The church clock struck loudly, making her jump. 'Is that the time? I must go...'

'That clock is always five minutes fast,' Eddie said. 'That is what made me check my pocket watch the other night. They never manage to get church clocks right, do they?' He touched the silver watch in his breast pocket, taking it out to check the time and nodding. It was a very handsome watch with engraving on the case.

Susie laughed and disclaimed and they parted: she to hurry for her bus and he to enter the public house just down the street.

* * *

'Did you find what you needed?' Lady Diane asked when Susie was helping her undress later that evening. It was Meg's evening off and Susie enjoyed slipping into their old routine, though these days they were friends rather than mistress and maid.

'Yes, I found Sam's second hammer, and took pictures of it,' Susie replied. 'I am not sure it means much, but Mr Marsh suggested it...'

Lady Diane sighed. 'I do wish Hugo had been available. I visited him this afternoon. He has a private room in a nursing home while he recovers, but he was very uncomfortable still.'

'I am so sorry, my lady. We were all grateful to Mr Montford when he helped Winnie.'

'I told him he should retire and he was cross with me.' Lady Diane's eyes sparkled with fun. 'He isn't much older than me, you know, fifteen years perhaps – but his manner would lead you to think he is in his dotage. Poor Hugo needs someone to stir him up, but he doesn't have a wife.'

'Perhaps he is happier as he is,' Susie suggested.

'Nonsense! Every man needs a wife to look after him, even if they think they don't. Lord Henry had no intention of marrying again until I came along – and look how much happier he is now.'

Susie burst out laughing. 'Oh, my lady. Of course he is happy. He has you...'

'Yes, that's what I said.' Lady Diane gave a delightful gurgle, but then her laughter dimmed. 'I cannot help worrying for Matthew. I sometimes wish he had not chosen to live in the country all by himself...'

'I am sure he has friends and lots of people looking after him, my lady.'

'He does, of course – but I fear he is suffering despite what he would have us believe.'

'I felt sure his proposal would be accepted,' Susie replied. 'He is so charming and kind – as well as being attractive.'

Lady Diane nodded. 'His charm comes from his father, as do his looks – I think his occasional reserve comes from his mother. I have been told she was inclined to be stand-offish with anyone she didn't care for.'

'I have heard whispers, my lady.' Susie was silent then and Lady Diane said no more, merely wishing her goodnight.

'And don't worry, Susie,' she said as Susie reached the door. 'I am sure Mr Marsh will prove your brother's innocence.'

Susie thanked her and went away to her own room.

Alone in her room, Susie prepared for bed and then knelt beside it. She bowed her head in prayer. 'God bless Lady Diane, Lord Henry and Mr Matthew,' she said softly, adding in other names who were important to her as she prayed fervently. 'Please, please, God, let there be justice for Sam. Please don't let him die for something he didn't do...'

A tear slid down her cheek as she got into bed and pulled the covers up around her. Susie had never asked for much in her life. She'd considered herself lucky to have a good job and a family who loved her as she loved them. The long hours she'd worked for little money had never worried her, and now that she was earning considerably more, she had no desire to go out and spend it on herself. She enjoyed buying little gifts for her mother and some-times Winnie or Sam – but she longed with all her being for her brother to be exonerated and free.

Unless that happened, she was not sure she could carry on despite wanting to please Lady Diane...

As she was gradually falling asleep, she thought about her chance meeting with Eddie Stevens. She had resented him when he had opened his business across the street, but it seemed that she had misjudged him. He'd asked to be friends and the least she could do was to call him by his first name.

For a moment, she thought of Timothy Marsh. All her hopes for Sam's freedom were placed on him. She could only hope that he was right when he said he was certain a jury would listen to the evidence and find there was no case – apart from that wretched hammer...

* * *

Lady Diane was nursing her darling little Marie when Matthew walked into her sitting room the following day. She smiled and put the sleeping baby into her cot, inviting him to sit on the little armchair opposite her. He bent to drop a kiss on her head, peeped at Marie and then sat.

'She grows more beautiful every day,' he said. 'Like her mother.'

'Flatterer.' She laughed. 'Tell me, dearest, what may I do for you?'

'Father told me I should find you here,' he said. 'What are you making?' He glanced at a piece of delicate silk she'd obviously been working on earlier. 'Something for Marie?'

'Oh, no, just something for the business. I'm not sure if it will work, so I thought I would just try putting one together myself. Susie normally does that, but she has such a lot on her hands just now.'

Matthew frowned. 'Father told me about her brother – do you think he did it, Diane?'

'No, I don't believe so. Susie is adamant he couldn't have. I am hoping he will be proved innocent. Now, what brings you back to London?' She gave him a direct look and he smiled.

'Would you believe I came just to see you?'

'No, I should not,' she replied with a twinkle in her eyes, but it faded as she saw something in his face. 'You look troubled. Have you spoken to your father – is it the estate?'

'No. Everything is well there,' he said. He reached into the breast pocket of his smart coat and took out a letter, hesitated and then handed it to her. 'Read it and tell me what you think...'

Lady Diane began to read the letter but looked up at him in surprise. It was from Pamela Fairley and personal. 'Are you sure you wish me to read this, my dear?'

'Yes please. I know Father wouldn't understand... please, Diane.'

She read it through to the end and then some passages over again before looking at him. 'She is asking you to forgive her, Matthew. She says that she has reconsidered and would be happy to live in the country with you...'

'Yes – but why?' he asked and she saw something in his face that told her he had not been as unaffected by Pamela's rejection as he'd let her believe. 'Why suddenly now?'

'She says she realised afterwards that she cared deeply for you and knows she was selfish to demand such things of you...' Matthew nodded. 'Do you still care for her?'

'I think... perhaps,' he admitted. 'If I am honest with you, I believed myself truly in love, though I denied it...'

'And now you are not sure?'

'I think I could still love her – but I have to know why she wants me to ask her now when she didn't before. I don't think I believe her...'

'And you want my opinion?'

'Yes...' He hesitated then, 'You know so many people, Diane. Have you heard anything I should know?'

She was silent for a moment. 'I cannot tell you what to do, Matthew. Only you know whether you still love her enough – but I have heard rumours...' Her gaze was serious. 'I believe her parents are anxious to see her wed and there has been some talk of marriage to a man much older than Pamela...'

'Do you think... could she be in trouble?' He looked shocked, white-lipped.

'Not in the way you might imagine,' Diane said, hardly wanting to say more but aware that if she was silent, he might make a terrible mistake out of sympathy. 'I heard a whisper that she was discovered in an embarrassing situation with... an older woman...' She looked at him anxiously and saw his hand clench on the letter she had returned to him. 'It... it happens, you know, dearest. Some married ladies I know have these little...' She shrugged her shoulders. 'Shall we say affairs of a certain nature?'

'Oh, my God!' he exclaimed. For a moment, he looked shocked and then he suddenly laughed. 'That makes perfect sense. I see now why she wished to live separate lives once I had my heir...'

'At least she didn't marry you and deceive you,' Lady Diane said softly.

'I must be grateful for that I suppose,' Matthew replied grimly.

'What will you do?'

'Throw the letter into a fire and forget it. If I marry, I want a woman I can love who will love me – as you do my father, Diane. I have seen the happiness you bring him, dearest Mama, and I will settle for nothing less.'

'I am sorry I had to tell you. I know it must give you pain...'

He shook his head and she said no more. He would deny it as he had the first time, but it was there in his eyes. 'Please, I would prefer that my father knows nothing of this letter,' he said, thrusting it into his jacket.

'Of course, dearest. It was in confidence. I am sure you will find a woman who adores you one day. I have no patience with her...' Pamela should never have allowed him to think she would

welcome his offer and the letter was a cruel act of self-preserva-
tion. Unless she was married quickly, Miss Fairley would find
herself at the centre of a scandal, quite possibly ostracised by
society.

'Perhaps,' he said lightly. 'I have a little business in town for
Father and then I shall return to the country. Do not worry for me,
Diane. I feel much better now I know the truth.' He smiled then, 'I
have arranged a visit to Paris the week after next. We will spend
five days at the athletics, before sailing home. It will be a surprise
for Father and we shall be back long before your ball.'

Lady Diane inclined her head. He had taken her suggestion to
visit the Olympic Games. Well, it would give him something to
think about for a while. She had no doubt he was suffering, but it
would fade in time. He was young – perhaps too young for
marriage. She smiled and held out her hand. He kissed it and
left her.

She picked up her needlework and then threw it down impa-
tiently. She was fond of her stepson and angry that a girl she had
always thought of as cold should have hurt him. To have sent such
a letter! It was beyond bearing. She could only hope that
Matthew's heart was not irrevocably damaged.

* * *

Susie found Lady Diane in a reflective mood that evening. She
smiled at the woman who had been her personal maid and was
now her trusted partner but could not confide the reason for her
present mood of sadness.

'Are you well, my lady?'

'Yes, quite well, dearest Susie,' Lady Diane replied. 'Just
thoughtful.' She looked at Susie. 'And you – you have so much on
your mind, I know…'

Susie suppressed a sigh, forcing her fears for her brother to the back of her mind. 'I wanted to tell you that there is a decided upturn in orders for the autumn range.'

'Ah, that is excellent news,' Lady Diane replied. 'I am working on some new ideas for our spring and summer ranges for next year, but I... Well, something distressed me earlier today and I have abandoned my work for the moment.'

'I am so sorry,' Susie said instantly. 'Is there anything I can do?'

'In this instance, I fear not.' Lady Diane smiled. 'It is not my problem but another's. Sometimes, there is just nothing one can do to help, even though one wishes there were.'

'Yes, I know,' Susie agreed. 'Winnie is distraught at the moment, but refuses to take time off work. I think it is frustration because there is just nothing she can do.'

'That is exactly how I feel...' Lady Diane gave a little sigh. 'I wish we were not going out this evening, but Lord Henry is looking forward to it. I must get ready. Will you ring the bell for Meg, please Susie?'

'I could help you,' Susie offered and looked a little sad, as if she missed the intimacy they had shared when she was Lady Diane's personal dresser.

'You could, but it is Meg's job now,' Lady Diane said. 'If you look in my sitting room, you will find some material and the sketches I was working on. I had cut the pattern and was hemming it in place... perhaps you would do that for me, if you have nothing you would prefer to do this evening.'

'No. I am not visiting my mother. I spoke to her earlier.' Susie smiled. 'She is bearing up better than either Winnie or I because she is convinced that right must out.'

'I am glad she has such faith,' Lady Diane replied. 'I do hope she is proved correct for all your sakes...'

Susie had rung the bell and Meg entered the bedroom. The time for intimate conversation was over and Susie took her leave.

Lady Diane allowed Meg to dress her, then sat alone for a few moments before going up to the nursery to kiss her little daughter goodnight. Having spent a few moments with Nanny, discussing Marie's present health, she left and went to greet her darling husband with a smile on her face. Matthew had not shown his father the letter from Pamela Fairley, for he'd known what his father's reaction must be to the woman who had let him down so badly. He'd spoken to her in confidence and although it was uncomfortable not to be able to discuss it with Lord Henry, she would keep Matthew's secret. The girl had not used him well. If Lady Diane chanced to see her at any social affair in the future, she would give her the cut direct. It would be better to ignore her as if she didn't exist than to rain down upon her the very just anger that she felt over that wretched letter.

The girl had tried to use and deceive Matthew, hoping that his feelings for her would extricate her from the scandal she'd brought on herself. If her parents had their way, she would shortly be safely married to a man many years her senior, which was not in itself necessarily a bad thing, except that the man in question was not a pleasant person. His reputation was far from respectable, and Lady Diane would have felt sorry for Pamela's plight if she had not tried to use Matthew, giving him hope that his very real affection for her was returned. Had he rushed off to offer for her, he might well have been trapped in a marriage that could only lead to unhappiness. He would no doubt recover and think himself fortunate to have escaped such a fate, but he was still young enough to be sensitive and unsure of his own charms.

'You are very quiet this evening, my love?' Lord Henry said as they settled into the back of the comfortable car that was taking them to their social engagement at a friend's house. 'You are not unwell?'

'Not in the least,' she excused herself with a little laugh. 'Forgive me, dearest, I had something on my mind, but I shall put it aside.'

'I suppose it was one of your wretched designs,' he teased. 'I am not sure why I ever agreed to this venture of yours...'

'It was because you love me,' she responded and placed her hand over his. 'Because you spoil me and give me everything I want – and I am the luckiest wife in the world.' She looked up at him lovingly and he bent his head to kiss her softly.

'I know I am lucky to have you,' he said softly. 'I dare say I know who put the idea of a trip to the Olympics into Matthew's head?'

'I thought it might please you?'

'It does – though I would have liked you to accompany us. I do understand it might be too much for you.'

'I promise you I am well, but such a trip might prove too much for me and I do not wish to leave Marie just yet, though I know she is perfectly safe with Nanny – perhaps another year,' she told him and he smiled and nodded. 'Are you thinking of holding a shooting party at the estate this autumn, Henry? You did not do so last year because I was unable to come with you – but I think you should this year. We ought to hold an open day, too, for the local people and our tenants. We could go down the week after our dance and invite friends of Matthew's, too.'

Lord Henry nodded and then frowned. 'I shall not invite Fairley, though. I've heard something about his girl... Do not ask, Diane. You would be quite shocked, my love.' He looked grim for a moment. 'I shall tell you that I think Matthew had a lucky escape there...'

Lady Diane murmured agreement, holding her smile inside.

Lord Henry was still a little old-fashioned. He sought to protect his young wife from something he would consider sordid, not dreaming that she'd known of it for longer than he. She loved him for it and wouldn't have him any other way, though had it been anything that did not concern Matthew so closely, she might have teased him to tell her.

'Good. I shall enjoy a little stay in the country this autumn,' she said. 'I will give you a list of the ladies I should quite like to have stay with their husbands and, if you choose, you shall invite some of them...'

'Minx,' he replied lovingly.

She laughed, knowing that he had probably guessed that she meant to invite some of the prettiest young women she knew. Matthew might have a broken heart, but he would enjoy the company of lively young women and it could only help him to heal.

35

Winnie was at her desk that Friday afternoon. It was the first week of July. Sam had been under arrest for nearly three weeks now and each day seemed like a year, making it hard for her to smile, despite the beautiful weather. The sun was shining, seeking its way into the reception area, despite the blinds they'd pulled down to protect the silk dresses on the mannequins from fading. She had just taken an order and was writing it down when the door opened and a bell rang.

'Just a moment,' she said without looking up. She finished her order and glanced up, a shriek of relief mixed with excitement leaving her lips as she saw who stood there. 'Sam!' she wailed as the tears sprang to her eyes. 'Oh Sam, my love...' Jumping up, she rushed to him as he held his arms open. They clung to each other with a desperation born of enforced separation, kissing and hugging, both crying. It was a few minutes before Winnie looked up at him, her eyes shining through the tears. 'Sam, how? They let you go? Is it... is it all over?' He nodded. 'Truly?'

'Winnie love,' he said and reached out to stroke her hair back from her wet cheeks. 'I'm free – cleared of suspicion.'

She gulped back a fresh burst of tears as the feeling of joy almost overwhelmed her. 'But how? They told us you'd been charged and were in the remand prison.'

'I was there for a week and a half,' Sam confirmed and a shiver of pent-up emotion went through him, his eyes bleak with remembered grief. 'I thought I would be convicted and then this lawyer came to see me again and said he'd got some evidence that made it impossible for me to have done it, but he still thought it would be a while before he could get bail...'

'Susie found him for you,' Winnie said gazing up at him, hardly able to believe he was here with her. 'What happened next?'

'This morning, I was told there had been a further development and this afternoon the lawyer came back and told me the charge had been dropped and I was free to go – an innocent man.' Sam shook his head. 'I could hardly believe it, Winnie. The police wouldn't tell me what had happened – but in the cab coming home, Mr Marsh told me that he'd been about to get bail for me when someone walked into the police station and confessed to the murder...'

'No!' Winnie stared at him in shocked disbelief. 'Someone actually told the police that they had killed him – that horrid man? Who was it?'

'You won't believe it...' Sam shook his head sorrowfully. 'I don't believe it myself, Winnie – but the police believe him, so they let me go.'

'But who? It wasn't Joe Ross or – or Jeb?'

Sam shook his head. 'You've seen him in the alley most days, Winnie. Pushing his dustcart and sweeping up the litter...'

She gasped and instinctively rejected the idea. It couldn't possibly have been that quiet, polite man they all trusted. 'Ernie! Surely not? Why would he do it? How did he get your hammer?'

There must be some mistake – and yet his confession had set Sam free. Her conflicting emotions whirled as she tried to find an explanation in her head.

'That is my thought also, Winnie.' Sam looked grave. 'He says he found a hammer lying in the gutter – or that's what the police told Mr Marsh. He didn't know it was mine and he didn't intend to murder Derek Norton – but Norton was drunk and bragging about killing Rusty. Ernie told the police that he did it in a rage because Rusty was his friend...' Sam looked upset, disbelieving. He drew a deep breath, then, 'I understand why he might go for that bugger if he was bragging about killing her – but I'm not sure he has the strength to do it.'

'He doesn't look that strong. In fact, Lilly thinks he's ill... but he might have been strong enough in a fit of rage, especially if he cared about Rusty.' Winnie couldn't help but agree that Ernie didn't look capable of violent murder. She'd seen him speaking to Rusty sometimes in the alley, but hadn't known they were close friends. 'Oh, poor Ernie.' She looked at Sam, dismayed and distressed; something wasn't right about all this. 'I'm grateful he confessed and I'm glad you're free, Sam – but I can't help feeling sorry for him.'

'I feel the same,' Sam assured her. 'I like him and I still can't believe he did it, even though he's confessed to it.' He rubbed at the bridge of his nose as though he had a headache. 'He must have or he wouldn't have confessed, but it doesn't feel right to me...'

'Oh, Sam...' Winnie snuggled up to him. 'Don't let's think about it. Just be happy that you're free.' She could feel his tension and knew he was still suffering from the ordeal he'd endured; these past days, locked in a cell and accused of murder, not knowing that people were working to free him, must have been sheer torture.

'Mr Marsh says the police knew they'd made a mistake after

Eddie Stevens came forward and told them I left my shop at twenty to ten. I didn't have time to do it – and Constable Winston told them I wasn't the sort to do it, but they wouldn't listen. Mr Marsh says that he would've have got me off when it came to a trial... but...' He frowned. 'I've thought and thought how I could have lost that hammer, Winnie. I don't remember for certain when I last used it – but I thought I had it on Thursday. I didn't bring my tools home that night... but I can't recall seeing it on Friday morning.'

'Could someone have taken it from the shop and then... oh, I don't know, dropped it in the gutter?'

'I suppose they might have,' Sam replied with a puzzled look. 'I fetched stuff from the back a couple of times that morning...' He shook his head. 'The truth is, I don't know, Winnie. Someone got hold of it somehow...'

'Maybe Ernie did find it – or perhaps he took it and didn't want to admit it as it makes the murder premeditated...'

Sam met her anxious gaze. 'If he did that, he's not the man I've always thought him.'

'Perhaps we were all mistaken in him,' she said. 'Oh, don't let's think about any of it, Sam. Have you seen your mum?' He nodded. 'Good. Let's go and tell your sister that you're free...'

'Is she here?' Sam looked towards the workshop.

'I think she is in her office,' Winnie said just as the door to the workshop opened and Susie came rushing out.

'I just heard from Mr Marsh...' She looked at Sam and burst into tears. 'Oh, I'm so glad... Sam, Winnie, I'm so glad for you both...' She came up to them swiftly and put her arms out to embrace them both so that they all hugged in a circle. 'I couldn't believe it when he just telephoned and told me... It is like a miracle...'

'I can hardly believe I'm free,' Sam told her, kissing her wet cheeks. 'Thanks for all you did, Susie. That Mr Marsh is a decent bloke. He says he'd have got me out even if Ernie hadn't confessed.'

'That is the only bit I can't understand,' Susie said. 'He always seems a pleasant man to me, a bit reserved unless he knows you. He gets on with Lilly well, but it just shows you never can tell...'

'You think he did it then?' Sam stared at her hard.

'Of course. Why would he confess if he hadn't?' Susie looked surprised. 'Surely you don't think he did it for any other reason but his guilty conscience? He waited to see if they let you out and when they didn't, he knew he had to tell the truth...'

'You can't know that,' Sam objected, clearly uncertain.

'Oh, but I do,' Susie said. 'Mr Marsh has agreed to represent him. He told me that's what Ernie said... and he thinks he can get him off on compassionate grounds. Rusty was his friend, so he was driven to sudden anger when Norton boasted of murdering her for her windfall...'

'There you are then,' Winnie said relieved. 'Just forget him, Sam. We've got our lives back...'

Sam looked at her and his worried frown eased, some of the tension leaving his body. 'Aye, we have, and we're goin' to make the most of it, love. If you still want to marry me, I reckon we should do it right away. No sense in waiting any longer... unless you'd rather not?'

'We'll be married as soon as the banns are called,' Winnie said. 'Yvonne has finished making my dress – but I'd get married in my old one if she hadn't...'

Sam laughed and swept her off her feet, swinging her round and then kissing her. 'I'll go and see if I can get a special licence,' he told her. 'I'm in no mood to wait three weeks for the banns, Winnie. We'll be married in church if we can, but if not the registrar office.'

'You'll be married in church properly,' Susie told him. 'You get that licence, Sam, and we'll find a church that will marry you next week or the week after...'

* * *

Sam left Winnie and Susie at the workshops and walked round the corner to his own little shop. It was a long time since he'd left it and it felt strange for a moment as he went in, silent and cold. He'd thought he might never see it again.

Sam drew back the blinds and went into his back room to pop the kettle on the gas ring. He heard the church clock strike as he filled his kettle. He didn't have any fresh milk but kept a tin of the condensed sort in his cupboard. Once his tea was made, he would make a start on that repair he hadn't finished – but he'd kept his front door locked as he didn't want customers in yet. He needed to be alone to work, to find his own way back from the hell of prison.

He took the large mug of hot tea through to the front shop and sat down at his bench, frowning as he tried to think what he'd done with that wretched hammer. Sam was pretty certain he hadn't lost it, despite Susie and Mr Marsh suggesting it to him – and he didn't see how anyone could've entered when he was through the back and stolen it.

'Bugger it,' he muttered to himself and finished the tea. He reached for the shoe he was mending and clumsily knocked it to the floor. When he looked down, he saw it had rolled right under his work bench. Annoyed with himself, he got down on his knees and reached for the shoe, but the first thing he touched sent a frisson of recognition through him and as his fingers curled around it, he gave a cry of satisfaction. He picked up the dropped shoe and placed both on the bench – a half-finished job and his claw hammer with the initials SC burned into the handle.

'I knew I hadn't lost it!' Sam exclaimed, looking at it for several minutes with pleasure. And then it struck him. His hammer had been here all the time. The one the police had as evidence was not his; they'd jumped to conclusions and he hadn't been allowed to pick it up and examine it properly.

It wasn't his hammer that had killed Derek Norton!

Sam gasped and then started laughing. It was a shock reaction, something near hysteria, letting go of all the pain, anger and grief he'd stored inside. All he'd been through and it wasn't his hammer! He laughed and laughed and then he cried. Then, as the storm of emotion passed, he shook his head, puzzled and confused. His hammer had not been used in a murder, so if Ernie had picked it up in the road, it belonged to someone else with the initials SC – and who the hell could that be?

Sam sat and thought, and then he knew. He knew who the murder weapon belonged to – a man who was usually called by a different name but, in reality, had the same initials as Sam. Nobby Carter – whose real name was Steve. He was a carpenter by trade and... Sam suspected something more by night.

What should he do about it? Sam used his hammer as he completed the repair he'd been working on the night he was arrested. The familiar action was soothing to his soul, allowing him to think clearly. Ernie had confessed to the murder – but had he really done it? Why else would he confess? The police hadn't been looking for anyone else. They would never have suspected Ernie.

Something wasn't right. Suddenly, Sam felt cold all over. If Ernie had confessed to a murder he hadn't done, he must have his reasons – personal reasons that Sam couldn't know. What dark secrets lay in his past?

The thoughts churned in Sam's head. For a long time now, he'd had his doubts about Nobby Carter. He'd seen him taking stuff into the premises of a known fence late at night when Sam had been working long past his normal time. He'd seen evidence that he had more money than a small businessman normally earned, seen it in new bikes for Nobby's two sons, the good clothes his wife wore and the newish van he'd bought for his work, but he hadn't been sure that anything unlawful was going on. And he recalled seeing Ernie speaking to Nobby twice in the street; they had been having a disagreement, though the anger was all on Nobby's side.

Something nagged at Sam's thoughts – something to do with Nobby and Ernie – but he couldn't work it out. He shook his head, almost certain he was right – that in some way Nobby was behind all this... Sam was pretty certain his one-time friend was a thief; could he also be a murderer?

What was the right thing to do? Sam just didn't know. He would tell Mr Marsh where he'd found his hammer – but should he tell him that he was almost certain he knew who the murder weapon belonged to? The uncertainty plagued him.

Supposing Ernie didn't kill Derek Norton, but Nobby had? Nobby had a wife and children to support. If their sole provider was arrested – perhaps hanged – what would they do? It would ruin their lives.

Ernie was old. He probably didn't have a lot of time left to him. Yet even a few years or months were precious. Why would he give it up if he was innocent? To protect someone? There was far more to this than Sam could fathom. What did Ernie know that he didn't? Sam couldn't guess. He liked Ernie, passed the time of day with him, and gave him a shilling for a cup of tea now and then – but surely that wasn't enough to make him sacrifice what life he had left to him? If he was making the most noble sacrifice that any man could make, by giving his life for another – there must be something that was more important to him. His secret... so did Sam have the right to force it into the open?

Supposing that the murder weapon did belong to Nobby Carter. That still didn't prove who had used it. Ernie, who had picked it up in the gutter and used it in a rage, as he'd confessed? Or Steve Carter, who had perhaps set out to murder in revenge for the attack on his niece?

'Oh bugger it!' Sam cried. He didn't know what was right – but he didn't fancy letting an innocent man go through all it would mean if he said nothing. He was going to have to show Mr Marsh the hammer. Should he also tell him of his suspicions as to the identity of its original owner? If he kept quiet, an innocent man might spend his last days in prison – and if he spoke up, his erstwhile friend, a husband and father, might die at the end of a rope...

36

Susie looked at herself in the mirror as she got ready for her dinner date that evening. She was wearing a gown of midnight blue velvet that had a slender skirt and long sleeves that ended in a point on the back of her hands. The neckline was a three-cornered slash of silver satin embroidered with pearls and it was stunning. Lady Diane had insisted on giving it to her when she'd told her where she was going.

'But this is part of the new collection,' Susie had protested. 'It is far too expensive for me.'

'It is my gift to you,' Lady Diane had said. 'When I designed it, I knew it was perfect for you, Susie. I've never thanked you properly for everything you've done for me. You made my dream come true and I know how hard you've worked.'

Susie had felt she ought to refuse the extravagant gift, but she couldn't. It was perfect for dining at The Savoy and she owned nothing to compare with it. She had bought herself a pair of silver evening shoes in a fit of extravagance, for which she felt terribly guilty, but they made it a perfect ensemble. After all, she reasoned, she could keep the dress and one day she might sell it – an exclusive design like this would still have a value in years to come, so even though she might only wear it once, it wouldn't be wasted.

She was feeling excited and not a little nervous as she went downstairs to the hall. Fox, the footman, had been instructed to invite Mr Marsh into Lady Diane's parlour, because she'd wanted to speak to him and thank him personally. Unknown to Susie, she'd intended to tell him she would pay his fee, but in that he'd frustrated her by telling her there was none. Lady Diane had had no chance to press him for Susie arrived looking magnificent in the splendid gown. She'd contented herself by thinking that her dear friend looked every bit as lovely as she'd expected, her dark hair swept back off her face with combs that sparkled with diamanté. Susie had refused the loan of diamond hairpins from Lady Diane, but her own looked pretty enough. She wore no other jewellery but didn't need it.

'You must take good care of her,' Lady Diane told Mr Marsh as he turned to look at Susie with a stunned expression on his face. 'She is very important to me, you know.'

Mr Marsh promised solemnly that he would do so. 'She will come to no harm this evening,' he said with a grin that gave him a slightly daredevil look, his eyes glinting with what could only be mischief.

'I would expect nothing less from a gentleman,' Lady Diane replied.

'Meg will look after you this evening,' Susie said. 'We have our regular meeting in the morning.'

Lady Diane nodded and Susie smiled, taking the arm he offered. As Fox opened the door for her, he winked at Susie in a saucy manner and she could hardly keep from laughing. She could imagine what the household would be thinking – Susie

Collins, from parlourmaid to Lady Diane's dresser, then her partner in a business that might one day prove profitable and now dressed up like a lady and off to The Savoy for dinner. No doubt Fox would take a good look at the Daimler car that waited outside, complete with chauffeur, and report back to the kitchen.

'And what are you smiling about, Susie?' Timothy asked as he slid into the back seat of the sumptuous car after her. It smelled of new leather and, faintly, cigar smoke. 'I hope you like the car – it belongs to my uncle...'

At that, Susie had a fit of the giggles.

Timothy looked at her, highly amused. 'Tell me,' he demanded, 'what is so funny?'

'The look on Fox's face when he saw me like this and then the car. I can just imagine what he is saying below stairs now...'

Timothy laughed. Susie liked the warmth of it. 'He will think I am fabulously rich and that you've got yourself a good catch...'

'I doubt it,' Susie replied. 'He will be thinking that I've thrown my reputation to the winds and will be a fallen woman by morning.' As Timothy looked into her eyes, she felt heat sneaking up into her cheeks. 'No, no, don't look at me like that – I just found it funny because he will know that Lady Diane's erstwhile parlourmaid couldn't possibly expect anything more...' Her skin prickled as he continued to look at her. 'Fox doesn't know that we made a bargain just for tonight.'

'Were you her parlourmaid?' Timothy asked and reached for her hands, removing one of the long gloves and turning her hands over. 'These hands have not done menial work for a while...'

'No, of course not. I became her dresser and now her partner... Oh, I shouldn't have... You won't speak of it?'

'Did you imagine that I didn't know? I work in the same chambers as Hugo, Susie. I know she made you a partner in Miss Susie.

She is your designer and you run the business...' He smiled and stroked her wrist with one finger. Susie knew she ought to remove her hand from his grasp, but couldn't make herself because she liked it. 'I would keep her secret for her sake – and my uncle's. You knew that Hugo was my uncle?'

'No, I didn't,' Susie replied, surprised. 'May I put my glove back on please?'

'Let me do it for you,' he said and did so, expertly.

'You've done that before?'

'Oh, yes,' Timothy said. 'I have a mother and two sisters – neither of whom can manage it without help. My father died when I was twelve, so I have tended to look after them.'

'I am sorry you lost your father so young,' Susie said, glad of the change of mood as he had released his hold on her. 'That must have been hard for you?'

'It was hardest for my mother. She never remarried...' His eyes had lost that mocking look. 'Uncle Hugo managed everything. There wasn't much money, but he saw to it that we were looked after. I had the proper education for a man destined for the law, and my sisters were provided with small doweries and are both safely married. I look after my mother now...'

'I would never have guessed it.' Susie found herself liking him more, her heart caught with sympathy.

He laughed. 'Did you imagine I was rich like Uncle Hugo? One day he will leave me a part of his fortune, my sisters will also receive something. He has no wife or children of his own, so he thinks of us as his, but for the moment I am a hard-working lawyer – and I do work hard, believe me. Uncle Hugo allows me to use his car when he doesn't need it... for meeting important clients...' Now the sparkle was back in his eyes. 'I am looking forward to this evening. I don't often get treated to a meal at The Savoy...'

'Then we're both imposters,' Susie said and smiled. 'I've never been there in my life. It will be a marvellous experience. Thank you for suggesting it as your fee.'

'I didn't do anything much,' he replied, sitting back at ease. 'I would have though... but now I have another man I have to prove innocent...'

Susie's smile dimmed. 'Do you believe him innocent?' she asked, a little surprised. 'But if Ernie didn't do it – and Sam didn't – who did?'

'That I have yet to discover, but I shall,' Timothy replied. 'I think Ernie is protecting someone. He may refuse to retract his confession and he has the right to remain silent if he wishes – but I'd like to know who he is protecting and why.'

* * *

Susie thought that she'd never enjoyed an evening so much. The soft, hushed atmosphere of the exclusive hotel and the décor which was Art Nouveau with a touch of the newer Art Deco looked as if it had been freshly done or refurbished and gleamed with a dull gold and the pale colours of spring. The chairs were comfortable, especially when they removed to the lounge to have coffee.

Timothy offered her a cigarette from a silver cigarette case but she refused.

'Why not try one?' he asked with that gleam in his eye, which could be a little devil-may-care at times. 'You might like it.'

'I might like it too much,' Susie said. 'My father smoked thirty a day when he was young and the doctor told Mum he thought it might have contributed to the lung disease that helped to kill him.'

'I see. In that case...' He replaced the case in his jacket pocket and when she blushed and said that she hadn't anything against him smoking, he smiled but left it where it was. 'Smoking has bad connotations for you, so I can wait...'

They enjoyed their coffee with a liquor after the most delicious meal of shrimps in a delicate cheese sauce on thin crispy toast, duck done in a red wine sauce with tiny roast potatoes no bigger than a thumbnail, tiny carrots in butter, minted peas and honey-roasted baby turnips and where they had come from at this time of year, Susie had no idea. For pudding, there was such a variety that neither of them had known what to choose, but Susie had decided on brandy snaps with cream and strawberries with a drizzle of butterscotch and Timothy chose an individual bread and butter pudding made with cream, dried fruit and nuts and drizzled with strands of warm toffee.

'I think that was the best meal I've ever had here,' he said when they had finished their liquor, causing Susie to look at him sharply.

'I thought you said it was a treat for you to come here?' she asked, looking at him intently.

'I said it was a rare thing for me to be treated. I do bring Hugo's clients here sometimes, but the bill goes on his expenses account.'

'Oh...' She couldn't tell from his expression whether it was the truth or not, but it didn't seem to matter. They'd drunk wine with their meal and a brandy liquor with their coffee and she was feeling a little mellow, though not foolish, or drunk. Perhaps a little tipsy. However, when the waiter brought their bill, Timothy attempted to take out his wallet, but she forestalled him. 'This was your fee – remember?'

He allowed her to pay the bill, which might have taken her breath away had she not made sure she knew what to expect. She had more than enough notes in the little silver bag Lady Diane had loaned her and paid it without a blink.

Timothy laughed. 'I could get used to this – would I make a wealthy widow's gigolo, do you think?'

'I have no idea what you mean,' Susie replied with a reproachful look, though of course she did.

'Yes, you do. You're not a prude, Susie, or you wouldn't be here this evening.' It was still a little unusual for a single woman to dine out with a man who was not of her family, though not unheard of since the war had broken many of the old bonds that had previously fettered female behaviour.

'What do you mean?' She glared at him. 'If you think—'

'I don't,' he told her. 'I know you're a decent woman – but I don't think you're as starched up as you try to be. However, time will tell.'

'I think it is time we were leaving...' Susie couldn't look at him. She wasn't sure why he was trying to provoke her, and he certainly was.

'Good grief, yes,' Timothy said, looking at his pocket watch. It was gold on a gold chain with a small topaz fob at the end. 'I have to travel tomorrow, so it is time I was tucked up in bed.'

He escorted her from the hotel to the car, opened the back door and smiled. 'George will drive you, home, Susie. Forgive me, I must go in the opposite direction. It is very rude of me and I promise I won't do it again...' He leaned forward and kissed her briefly on the cheek. 'I had a wonderful evening, Susie. I look forward to seeing you again. I will telephone in a few days when I've caught up with myself.'

'Goodnight, Timothy,' she said as the door was shut and the car moved away. She waved at him from the window. 'I had a lovely evening, too...'

* * *

As she undressed for bed, Susie was feeling sleepy. She had enjoyed her evening so much, though Timothy's behaviour when they were having coffee bewildered her. He'd seemed as if he wanted to push her – to find out who she really was beneath the cool, calm manner she normally adopted. Then, as if he had suddenly tired of it, he'd packed her off in Hugo Montford's car with the chauffeur and promised to be in touch.

Susie yawned as she slipped between cool sheets. She liked him. Found him interesting and amusing company. They'd talked a lot about music and books and history over their meal. Some of it she could answer intelligently, the history was beyond her; she'd never studied it at school beyond the third year, leaving at fifteen to enter service. However, she lived in a house where there was a wonderful library and had long ago been given the freedom to read what she chose. She enjoyed romances and plays, sometimes period farces, and there was always music in the evenings. Lady Diane would play the piano, but she also had a gramophone, on which she played lots of modern music from the cinema. So Susie heard both popular and classical, though she'd never been to the opera – and listening to Caruso she thought she might like it.

'You would like *Madame Butterfly*,' Timothy had said confidently. 'There are many beautiful operas – and the ballet, too. Have you ever been?'

Susie had looked at him, one eyebrow arched. 'I was a lady's maid until last year. When would I go to the opera or the ballet?' she'd asked, laughter in her eyes.

As she was falling asleep, Susie wasn't sure what she felt about Timothy Marsh. On the way to The Savoy, he'd had her believing he worked for a pittance for his uncle, but he was clearly perfectly at home in the expensive hotel – and she'd noticed his pocket watch was gold. Was he deliberately leading her up the garden path, and why?

She hoped he wasn't lying to her about everything, because despite her initial dislike of him, she was now feeling very differently. Susie had never fallen in love. A lot of girls in service did so and had to leave when they married – or got themselves into trouble by an illicit love affair. Susie had never been tempted.

Not until that evening.

37

'We can be married in All Saints, Newby Road, next Saturday,' Sam announced that Monday evening when they were all sitting round the kitchen table. 'I've arranged it for half past two – and we can have a bit of a do in the King's Head nearby... It won't be as fancy as it might have been if we'd made plans sooner, because I'm not sure we'll get a wedding cake...'

'Well, that's where you're wrong,' Mrs Collins said, smiling at him and Winnie. 'I've been baking cakes and storing them, adding a little brandy for some weeks now. I've got three tiers and all I have to do is ice them...'

'Oh, Mum,' Winnie cried and went to hug her. 'Thank you so much. I had no idea.'

'You don't know all my secrets,' Mrs Collins said, laughing at the pleasure on their faces. 'We'll have whatever the pub can put on, Sam – then I'll prepare a little supper in the evening for family and close friends. Lilly and Susie will help me. So who are you going to invite? We don't have much in the way of family, no aunts, or uncles – but quite a few good friends.'

'Mary and Bill Winston for a start,' Winnie said. 'My aunt Hilda. I'll ask Yvonne and Lilly – Rosalind and one or two others from the Movement... if that's all right?'

'Yes, of course it is, love,' Sam said. 'I'll be asking Jeb and Joe Ross and Bernie Watson. I was in the army with him. He's not from round here – but that's about all I need...'

'What about Nobby and Norman?' Mrs Collins said. 'You are good friends with them.'

'I might ask Norman, but he isn't much for weddings and stuff.'

'Not Nobby?'

'No – not him,' Sam said and frowned. 'Oh, I should ask Eddie Stevens – and any wives or girlfriends they want to bring.'

'What about Mr Marsh?' Winnie asked, looking at him curiously. 'I think you should ask him, Sam, even if he says no.'

'Yes, of course you should,' Mrs Collins agreed. 'Susie will come, of course. I wondered if you might ask Lady Diane and Lord Henry – or Mr Matthew. He is in the country but might come up for your wedding.'

'I don't know him,' Winnie said. 'I could ask Lady Diane and Lord Henry, but I am sure they wouldn't come and – and it looks as if you're hoping for a gift...'

'Nonsense!' Mrs Collins replied. 'I was in service for a short time. I asked my lady to my wedding and she came. She was at the church and stopped to toast the bride and groom. I don't say they would stop long, but they might just like to pop in. I think you should ask a few more of the workshop girls, Winnie, just to the pub do. Her ladyship might like to have a few words...'

'It might be too expensive,' Winnie said looking hesitantly towards Sam, but he smiled and shook his head. 'No, I've saved enough for a good do, Winnie. I agree with Mum. I'd ask more myself, but... Do you want to ask any of your neighbours, Mum?'

'I'll ask Violet and Jeff from next door,' Mrs Collins said.

'They've been good to me over the years – but it should be your friends, Sam. Why not ask Nobby? You two were as thick as thieves once...'

'Not any more,' Sam replied. 'Don't ask, Mum. I know things, but I'm not sayin'.'

'All right, I shan't push you – as long as you're happy, love.' She looked him up and down. 'What about a suit? I know Winnie has some nice things, but your only suit won't do, Sam.'

'I'll either hire a good one or buy a cheap one,' he said. 'I have to go up the West End on Wednesday to see Mr Marsh about something. I'll get some clobber then.'

'That's leaving it late,' Winnie said, but he smiled and shook his head.

'There will be something,' he said. 'Don't worry, love. I hired a suit when Jeb got married and it looked good.'

'Yes, it did,' his mother agreed. 'I'd forgotten about that...'

'I only had that wretched demob suit,' Sam said with a grimace. 'And I couldn't afford to buy one, so I hired a nice one. I shall probably do it again. After all, I mostly wear a blazer and slacks when we go out. Even to the dancin' at the Palais. Most of the lads prefer 'em to a formal suit.'

'Well, you can invite Mr Marsh to the wedding when you see him.' Mrs Collins smiled. 'Lovely. I've waited for this a long time, Sam – and Winnie. All I want now is to see our Susie settled and happy...'

* * *

'Thank you for seeing me, Mr Marsh,' Sam said when they met at Hugo Montford's offices. 'I know how busy you are...'

'You said you discovered your hammer in your shop. Your sister had a look round – but she was looking for a second hammer, which she found. Where was this one?' He looked at Sam's hammer, which showed signs of having been used over and over again.

'It had rolled under the bench. Susie couldn't have seen it there. I knocked a shoe down and had to go on my knees to get it – and there it was. I didn't think I'd lost it...'

'Well, this is the final proof if we'd needed it, and I'll be sure to put it in my report for the police.' He looked at Sam, gaze narrowing. 'You didn't come here today just for this – did you?'

'No – but I'm not sure...' He hesitated.

'It is a criminal offence to withhold evidence if you have some, Sam.'

'I think I know whose hammer it might be at the police station,' Sam said reluctantly. 'He has the same initials as me, though he doesn't go by his name...'

'Would that be Steve Carter – known as Nobby locally?' Timothy asked with a lift of a fine brow.

Sam was flabbergasted. 'How did you know that?'

Timothy smiled. 'I have my way of discovering things people want to keep secret,' he said. 'You know that he came from the north when he was a small child – though his accent is more Londoner than anything these days.' He paused, watching Sam for his reaction.

Sam just shook his head. 'You know more than I do,' he said. 'I knew he came from away, but he was only a kid when he was sent to an orphanage in London.'

'His family didn't want him or his sister; she was adopted, he went to an orphanage. His father went to prison for murder – a murder he didn't commit,' Timothy said. He laughed as Sam's eyes widened in shock. 'I guessed something and went searching for answers and this time I was lucky.'

Sam stared at him. 'I still don't know what it means. I don't know if Ernie is protecting someone or...'

'I think he is protecting his son,' Timothy replied. 'Have you ever wondered about Ernie's second name?' He nodded as Sam's eyes met his in disbelief. 'Ernie Carter – convicted of the murder of his wife, Rose. He was released and given a small amount of compensation when another man confessed to six killings, one of which was Mrs Rose Carter. He was hanged – but that didn't help Ernie. His prison experience broke him – and then his daughter would have nothing to do with him. She refused to believe he was innocent...'

'So he came to London a year or so ago to look for his son and found him...' Sam nodded. 'But it doesn't explain why he gave himself up; it wasn't Nobby who was arrested, it was me...'

'I think Ernie Carter is an honourable man,' Timothy replied. 'He couldn't let an innocent man be punished as he was – and he doesn't have long to live. I doubt they will ever get him to trial...'

'But...' Sam struggled with himself. 'If it wasn't my hammer, it might have been Nobby's. Who used it, Mr Marsh? Was it Ernie or his son?'

'That is the last secret I have to uncover,' Timothy replied, frowning. 'I don't think Ernie will tell me, even if I give him all the facts. I think he will take his secret to his grave.'

'What will you do if he refuses to change his confession?'

'I must abide by his decision,' Timothy replied gravely. 'No court is going to try him as sick as he is; it will be dismissed on the grounds of ill health. I'll put in a doctor's report and ask for clemency. However, he might still be sent to a kind of prison. He will probably die in an institution – perhaps even before his case comes to court.'

Sam's fists clenched. 'It doesn't seem right...' He hesitated, but the words wouldn't be denied. 'Nobby is a thief and a murderer. I'd swear I'm right, Mr Marsh. We used to be friends, but I saw him with a bag of silver items. He took them to a known fence and sold them, came out looking mighty pleased with himself and bought a new van the next week. He works hard, but he can't earn the sort of money I've seen in his pocket – wads of fivers. I reckon he might have worked with Norton and they fell out over somethin'...'

'That sounds about right,' Timothy agreed. 'We both know it, but even if it could be proved it was his hammer, he could claim he lost it. Besides, his father won't change his mind. I suspect that he may well have witnessed the murder and knows his son is responsible.'

Sam nodded. 'I can understand why he might confess now. He was sent to prison for a crime he didn't commit. His children were separated and his son was sent to an orphanage far from home. Ernie feels he owes Nobby something...'

'Yes, I imagine that is more or less it,' Timothy agreed. He arched his shoulders as if a great weight was on them. 'Frustrating, isn't it? In a way, it is the most noble thing I've ever encountered – and yet it is a waste. The father is worth a dozen of the son.'

'I am sorry for it,' Sam said. 'I like Ernie and he has surely suffered enough?'

'Yes, one would think so.' Timothy closed the file in front of him. 'Well, at least we have you free with your name cleared, Sam.'

'Yes – and I'm to be married on Saturday,' Sam said, pushing the thought of Ernie from his mind. 'I know it is short notice, but we'd both like it if you could come, Mr Marsh.'

Timothy extended his hand and they shook. 'I should be delighted to attend. Where and when?'

Sam told him the details and they parted. At the door, he turned back. 'If you wanted to bring a young lady...'

'No young lady,' Timothy replied, smiling. 'Not yet, though I've hopes.'

'Well, thank you again,' Sam said and went out.

He walked briskly towards his bus stop, feeling so much lighter. Mr Marsh had the same ideas as he'd had and it felt good to know that he wasn't keeping a secret. Unfortunately, the knowledge that Mr Marsh had uncovered wouldn't help Ernie much. To voice their suspicions to the police without proof – and without Ernie's permission – might cause a huge problem. Sam was uneasy with the thought that someone he knew so well was a murderer – but he couldn't do any more.

But there was one thing Sam could do...

Nobby was just leaving his house when Sam caught him. As soon as Nobby saw Sam, a guilty flush rushed up his neck into his cheeks. For a minute, he seemed thunderstruck and then, he mumbled, 'Sam – can't stop. Talk to you another day – but glad to see yer out. Knew yer hadn't done it...'

'Of course you did,' Sam said and the look in his eyes was stone cold. 'I know what you did – and I know a lot of other things the police might be interested to hear...'

'Don't know what the hell you're talkin' about...' Nobby blustered as Sam moved towards him, blocking his escape as he tried to reach his van.

'I can't think what kind of a man would let another die for him,' Sam said, disgust in every breath. 'You would've let me hang – and you'll let him take the rap for...' Sam looked into his face, reading the guilt and panic there. 'Your father?'

The shock and fear in his face was all the proof Sam needed. 'The bastard deserves all he gets...' Nobby pushed him aside, wrenching the van door open. 'You're bloody mad, Sam Collins. You can't prove a thing...'

'Maybe not, but I know,' Sam said, his eyes never leaving Nobby's as he stood aside to let him go. 'The police make mistakes, but they get there in the end – and now I can prove it wasn't my hammer that killed him... I don't reckon it would take much for them to put two and two together. So just watch it and stay clear of me, because I'm not a snitch, but any friendship we had is dead.'

38

When Sam asked Joe to stand up with him for his wedding as his best man, he was chuffed to bits and full of it when he got home that evening after a hard day's work.

'I thought he might ask Jeb or Norman,' Joe told his mother with a grin. 'I reckon that's a compliment, don't you? I thought he might hold a grudge because of what he went through, but he don't blame me a bit.'

'Nor should he,' Mrs Ross said, looking at her son fondly. 'It wasn't your fault the police picked the wrong man.' She was thoughtful for a moment. 'What will you wear? You hired a suit for Lilly's wedding, didn't you?'

'Aye, I did,' Joe agreed. 'I think I might buy one this time...'

'It's cheaper to hire,' his mother replied. 'If you go to the thirty-shilling tailor, the cloth isn't likely to wear well.'

'I thought I might go up to the West End,' Joe said. 'Get myself a decent one – about five to ten pounds should cover it.'

'Where in the world did you get that sort of money to fritter on a suit?' Mrs Ross looked at him with dark suspicion, but Joe just laughed.

'I work hard, Ma,' he said. 'If I'm not delivering coal, I'm doing other jobs – and Mr Sampson the builder has taken me on for the whole summer as a labourer. I'll go to him from seven in the morning to three thirty in the afternoon, and then I'll do my usual rounds...'

'You'll kill yourself working all hours,' Mrs Ross exclaimed. 'Joe, don't be daft. There's no need for you to work yourself silly, lad.'

'You'll never have time to take me anywhere,' Sibby said. She'd sat quietly listening to them talk, but now Joe turned to look at her, frowning as he saw she was sulking again.

Joe hesitated. Why did she continue to cling to him despite his efforts to let her down gently? 'I did tell you to make other friends, Sibby. I may not be around to take you out in future – I have other plans.'

'You always have.' She pouted her disappointment.

'I'm not the only bloke, you know. Find someone else to take you to the wedding. I'll be busy.'

'Winnie hasn't asked me,' Sibby said with a flash of temper and Joe understood the reason for her mood. 'She has asked several of the girls from Miss Susie, but not me.'

'I expect there is a limit to what Sam can afford,' Joe said reasonably. 'I've told you before, I'm not interested in goin' steady.'

Sibby hunched her shoulders at him. 'I don't think you care about me at all, Joe Ross.'

Joe was silent for a moment, then, 'I'm sorry if you got it into your head that I was keen on you, Sibby. We can be friends, but that's all there is to it – and if I choose to work harder so I can get on a bit, that's my business.'

Sibby stared at him for a moment, then rushed out of the room. They could hear her feet pounding up the stairs and then her bedroom door slam.

Joe hesitated, turning as if he would follow.

'Let her be, Joe,' his mother warned. 'It was time you made it clear. She'd set her heart on bein' wed, though I'm not sure she'd have been happy even if you had put a ring on her finger. Sibby wants to be out with friends and dancin'. She thinks she wants to be your wife, but she wouldn't settle here with me. I've seen girls like her – and I've seen them married and miserable, because they get bored and want more excitement. It leads to trouble, Joe.'

'I can't marry her, Mum. I don't love her.'

His mother nodded, her eyes thoughtful as she studied his face. 'Found someone, have you?'

Joe shook his head. Sarah was not someone he would discuss with his mother. He knew that he wanted to see her, to be with her – that he wanted so much more. He also knew it wouldn't – mustn't happen, for her sake. 'When I've got somethin' to tell you, I'll tell you,' was all he would answer for now.

Joe shrugged on his jacket and went out. He needed to get a message to Sarah, to tell her that he couldn't meet her on Saturday. He had written a letter and sealed it, addressing it to Nurse Sarah Leigh. It explained that he was standing up with his friend and asked Sarah if she would meet him the following Saturday instead. Joe had intended to keep the appointment, but to tell her that it could not continue, because he wasn't good enough for her. It would have to wait for a week because Joe wouldn't refuse his friend's invitation. He caught a bus to take him most of the way to the London Hospital. He would leave the letter with the porter and hope that Sarah would get it and understand.

* * *

In her room, Sibby flung herself on her bed and sobbed for half an hour. Joe was mean and cruel and she hated him now. She'd thought she loved him, but he'd let her down too many times. All he cared about was work and his friends. He didn't care about Sibby even if he said he did – not how she'd wanted him to, anyway.

Sibby finally stopped crying and started to think. She didn't want to stop here any longer. It was boring just doing chores and talking with Joe's Mum. Mrs Ross was all right to her, but disapproving if Sibby went out and got back late. Sibby wanted fun and to go dancing – and she'd met someone who had already taken her for a nice meal of fish and chips as well as the cinema. He'd told her she was beautiful and promised he would give her nice clothes and presents if she would be his girlfriend. She'd taken a day off work to be with him and he'd driven her out to a place by the river, away from all the hustle and bustle of the East End. They'd had some delicious food at a pub and then Rory had given her a silver necklace and some high-heeled leather shoes. He'd told her to put them on, admiring her pretty legs.

'You would look wonderful in fancy clothes and nice jewellery,' he'd told her. 'You ought to have the best of everything, Sibby.'

'I wish.' She'd sighed and pouted up at him. 'I don't earn enough for that, Rory.'

He'd reached for her hand then, stroking the fingers and she'd laughed, because he was so romantic and charming. 'If you come and live with me, I'll give you lots of pretty things,' he'd told her. 'You'll be my girl, Sibby – and I'll look after you.'

Sibby had felt like a princess, but she'd been brought up to be decent and she knew Rory wasn't offering her marriage, but she'd still hankered for Joe, hoped for marriage. Now, she knew it wasn't going to happen.

If she went to live with Rory, it wouldn't be forever. Sibby knew that instinctively. When he was tired of her, she would be one of those bad girls – no chance of ever being married. She could have a lot of fun for a while but then...

Sibby washed her face and then put a little rouge on her cheeks. If she went with Rory, she would have to give her job up and find something else. She couldn't bear her friends to know what she'd done. Her stomach clenched with fear and she shook her head. She couldn't do it... because if she started that kind of life, she could never go back. Yet the prospect of pretty things, someone to take her dancing and care for her was enticing. Rory said he loved her and had never loved anyone else. If she let herself believe that, she could have such a good time – while it lasted.

Sibby put on her best jacket and her high heels. She went down the stairs and out of the front door. Mrs Ross called to her, but she ignored her. She was going to find Rory.

39

The wedding was perfect, all their friends gathered at the church, including many they hadn't been able to invite to the reception. Laughing and cheering as the groom and then the bride arrived, they all wanted to wish them well, after the ordeal they'd been through.

The sun shone all day, but there was a slight summer breeze preventing it from becoming too hot. Winnie looked beautiful in a dress Yvonne had made for her in cream chiffon over a satin underlay. It was styled in the shorter fashion, coming just below her knees, had a dropped waist with a satin sash, and some beading round the squared neckline; the sleeves short and puffed. Her headdress was a tiara of silk flowers on a headband, with a short lace veil that framed her dark hair, and she wore a small silver locket at her neck.

Inside, the church was packed with friends, many of whom had come through the Women's Movement and who were not invited guests but just wanted to wish Winnie good luck on her special day. She had a bridesmaid, Lilly Ross, who wore a pale lemon dress she had made for herself and a little straw hat festooned with silk roses.

For Winnie, the ceremony passed in a blur of sunshine piercing stained-glass windows, long shards of bright colours reflecting on the sombre stone of the ancient church. She had never felt so happy, so sure that what she was doing was right. It was as if she was being carried on a golden cloud, her smile as bright as that orb in the sky. Her whole being just sang with joy as Sam lifted the little veil and kissed her and she knew they were man and wife.

Afterwards, they left the church to the sound of bells ringing and her friends cheering. Winnie's eyes felt wet with happy tears. She hadn't known she was so popular in the Movement and it overwhelmed her that so many people had come to wish her happy. She was given lucky horseshoes tied with blue ribbons and lots of small gifts, which Joe, Susie and Lilly gathered up for her and carried into the pub where the reception was held.

Lady Diane had come with Nanny and baby Marie, decked out in a beautiful lace dress; also, Sally Harper, who had given Winnie and Sam some crystal glassware. Lady Diane explained that Matthew and Lord Henry were in France for the Olympics but sent their good wishes. Her gift was a prettily wrapped parcel of old lace and some gorgeous linens.

Some photographs were taken by Rosalind at the church and more inside the pub when the guests were gathered. Winnie tried to thank everyone, but there were so many well-wishers. It was fortunate that the pub had prepared a generous buffet of sandwiches, little pork pies, pickles, sausage rolls and sweet tarts, as well as some cream sponge cakes and the large, iced cake that Mrs Collins had made, because Winnie was sure Sam hadn't invited half of the people who crowded in. It didn't matter. There was wine for the toasts, and for others a cup of tea or a glass of beer. Somehow it all went round and everyone was happy and chatting away, smart ladies from the Movement at ease with the East End mates Sam had invited. It was just a joyous occasion and they all made the most of it.

* * *

The evening supper was much quieter. Just a few close friends and family, but every bit as happy and perfect. Mrs Collins had held one tier of the cake back, which was fortunate as the rest had been eaten at the reception. She had prepared a large piece of cold pork and a gammon, which were eaten with pickles, jacket potatoes and a trifle to follow. Everyone helped with the clearing up afterwards, and Susie stayed on until the last to help her mother. She was staying overnight, but after that, Mrs Collins would have the company of her neighbour's teenage daughter until Sam and Winnie returned from their honeymoon.

When they left in a taxicab at around nine that evening, Winnie tossed her bouquet over her shoulder as tradition demanded and it was caught by Rosalind, who laughed and said there was no chance of her getting married any time soon.

'Well, that went off all right,' Mrs Collins said when her son and his new wife had been driven away. 'Winnie looked so happy and my Sam – well, he looks like he reached up and captured the moon.'

No one could have put it better and as the guests began to depart, Susie walked to the door with Timothy, giving him her hand. She'd been surprised to see him amongst the invited guests, but pleased. He'd given Winnie a large box that was very heavy, most probably a china tea service, Susie thought.

'It was kind of you to come,' she said as he looked at her.

'Thank you for your gift. Winnie hasn't opened it yet, but I am sure she will like it.'

'A very boring choice of a tea service,' he said with a sparkle in his eyes that made her heart leap. 'I wanted to come, Susie, why wouldn't I?'

'Perhaps it isn't quite what you're used to?' She arched a fine brow.

'Perhaps it was more fun than I'm used to,' he said, his eyes holding hers. 'May I kiss you, Susie?'

'If... you wish,' she said, her cheeks pink as he reached for her, pulling her in close to his chest. He bent his head, pausing, waiting for her to look up, her eyes searching, and then he touched his lips to hers.

The kiss was soft and yet demanding, seeming to draw her heart from her body, making her lean into his chest and sigh softly as it ended.

She looked up at him. 'Ohhh...' she whispered shakily, her body feeling as if it was blissfully melting; she swayed slightly, but held tight against him she was safe.

'Yes,' he said as if in answer to a question. 'So where do we go from here, Susie?'

'I'm not sure,' she murmured, shaken and uncertain. 'I didn't expect to feel... I've never...' She shook her head, because she was a woman in her thirties and not a young girl. 'So foolish...'

'No, not foolish because I haven't either,' he said and she saw he was smiling. 'I have kissed before – but not like that...'

Susie's eyes opened wide in wonder. He looked a little bemused, as if he hadn't expected to feel so much either. She felt shy and nervous in a way she never had. Footmen had stolen a kiss when she was a parlourmaid – one had wanted to marry her, but Susie hadn't been interested. Now she was completely out of her depth.

'I shall ring you,' Timothy said and touched her cheek lightly. 'Goodnight, my dearest girl. Dream nice things of me, Susie – and don't look so worried. Things do work out sometimes, you know.'

He walked away then to the car he'd arrived in – a small Model T Ford, a far cry from the Daimler his uncle Hugo had loaned him for their dinner at The Savoy. Susie smiled, watching as he started it with the handle and then got in and drove away. She turned and went back into the kitchen.

Her mother was sitting at the table while Lilly, Rosalind and another girl Susie didn't know, but whose name was Sarah, were clearing the last of the dishes.

'You were a while saying goodnight to him,' Mrs Collins said, smiling at Susie. 'It was good of him to come and give Winnie a present. I think it is a china tea service.'

'Yes, I am sure it is,' Susie said. 'He wanted to come, Mum. He likes Sam – and I like him. I didn't at first, but that stand-offish look he has sometimes isn't truly who he is.'

'I suppose it is the way he has to behave in court.' Mrs Collins nodded, looking at Susie curiously, but she didn't pry. The girls had returned from the scullery after finishing the last of the dishes. 'Thank you, Lilly, Rosalind – and Sarah, isn't it?'

'Yes, Sarah Leigh,' the girl Susie hadn't known said and smiled. 'Winnie said I could come this evening because I was working this afternoon; I'm a nurse. I hope you didn't mind. I think this was more for family...'

'Oh, close friends as well,' Mrs Collins said easily. 'Now, how are you getting home, my dears? Lilly, Jeb will take you...' She turned to look at Joe. 'Could you make sure that Rosalind and Sarah get to their homes safely?'

'Yes, Mrs Collins,' Joe replied. 'I don't have a car just a coal lorry, but I'll walk you to the bus stop or get a cab for you...' He grabbed his suit jacket, which he'd removed earlier as they put on their coats. 'See you tomorrow, Lilly. Nice do, Mrs Collins. It was the best wedding I've been to...'

There was silence after they left and then Mrs Collins looked at her daughter. 'I reckon Joe Ross is sweet on that Sarah... did you see the way he was watching her all evening? She seems a nice girl – from a good family, I would think.'

'I hadn't noticed,' Susie replied. 'Are you tired, Mum? I know I am. Do you want a hot drink before we go up?'

'I'm all right, thank you. Lilly made us a cuppa just now.' She looked at Susie. 'Well, my girl, aren't you going to tell me? Just what is that Mr Marsh to you? And don't tell me I'm wrong. I've never seen you look the way you do tonight.'

'Oh, Mum,' Susie said with a laugh. 'To be perfectly honest, I just don't know...'

40

Joe walked the girls to the bus stop Rosalind needed. He asked if she would be OK at the other end and she laughed, saying that she lived in a leafy suburb where nothing ever happened. He and Sarah saw her onto the bus, watching as it was driven away and then looked at each other.

'Sarah...' he began, but she put a finger to his lips and hushed him.

'It's all right, Joe. I got your letter and I understood – so I asked Winnie if I could come to her reception in the evening and she said yes.'

'Shall we walk for a bit and then we'll find your bus stop?' Joe asked and she nodded, slipping her small hand into his large one. 'You look lovely. That colour blue suits you...'

'Thank you.' She smiled up at him. 'I like your friends, Joe.'

He was silent, uncertain of how to answer.

'I know you think I don't belong in your world, Joe, but Rosalind's mother knows mine – she fits in with Winnie and the others, so why not me?'

Joe stopped and looked down at her. 'I work long hours, Sarah.

This summer I've taken on building work as a labourer and I'll do my coal round when I've finished for the day. I might be working until gone eight at night...'

'That's all right. I sometimes work shifts of thirty hours at a time with just a break for meals. I'm a working girl, too. Other times I have three days off and then work nights for weeks on end. It would mostly be on a Sunday or sometimes Saturday that we could meet...'

'Are you sure it's what you want? I'm not sure your father would approve of you dating a coal merchant.'

'It is the person that counts not his job.' Sarah squeezed his hand tight. 'We don't really know each other yet, but I know I want to see you, Joe. Do you feel the same?'

'Of course I do,' he said and gripped her arm, turning her to face him. 'I've never wanted anything more – but I've tried not to push you into something you might regret.'

'Why don't we give it a try?' she asked. 'Take it slowly and see what happens.'

'Yes, all right, if you're sure.' He smiled. 'To be honest, I can't think of anything much but you lately...' He bent his head and kissed her, his lips soft and sweet on hers, reverent, seeking but not demanding. Sarah kissed him back, pressing herself against him so that his arms went round her and he held her close, their hearts beating wildly as they surrendered to the feeling that swept them up in a tide of something so strong that both were left breathless. Their eyes locked and held and then they kissed again, Sarah's arms sliding up around his neck, her face pressed to his shoulder when the kiss ended. She was trembling and so was he. It had been inevitable from the moment they met. It was instinctive, without reason, a pure sensation of love and trust and need that neither could resist.

'Shall we meet tomorrow and talk?' she suggested.

'Yes,' he said and caught her hand, kissing it. 'Tomorrow we will really talk, Sarah. I think we're both mad, but I can't walk away now...'

'You'd better not,' she said, laughing up at him as her bus arrived.

'You'll be all right? Shall I come with you?'

'You wouldn't get a bus home,' Sarah said. 'It's too late. I will see you in the morning at ten...'

* * *

When Joe got in, his mother was sitting dozing by the kitchen range. It was late and she ought to have been in bed ages ago.

'Mum,' he said softly as she stirred. 'You shouldn't have waited up for me. Why didn't you lock up and go to bed? I've got my own key.'

'I had to tell you,' she said, looking at him oddly. 'Sibby has gone. She went this afternoon, took all her things. A man fetched her – looked a bit like a spiv to me, smart suit, oily hair...' She gave a little shudder. 'Didn't like the look of him, Joe. I asked her if she was sure, told her she could stay here even if she wasn't your girl, but she laughed and told me she was sick of sitting with a boring old woman like me and off she went.'

Joe felt nothing but relief. He knew he ought to feel concern for Sibby, but he couldn't. She would just have made things more difficult now that he wanted to be with Sarah. 'She knows what she's doing,' he said. 'She didn't have to go with him. She had a good job and a home here – at least until she found another room.'

'She took your gramophone,' his mother told him, frowning. 'I told her it wasn't hers, but she said you'd given it to her. I couldn't stop her, Joe.'

'It doesn't matter,' he said. 'I'll get another one when I can afford it – but that won't be yet. I want to invest what I can with Jeb. He's looking for a partner in his business. He doesn't need me to do anything, just put up some money to get him up and running in another little project he has in mind. I'll be a silent partner, for now at any rate.'

'And that will be the last you'll see of your money,' his mother said with a snort of disgust. 'Jeb is all right, honest enough – but how can he run yet another business? Do you even know what it is?'

'It's pictures, artwork,' Joe said and grinned. 'He says he's bought some good pictures that are worth quite a bit of money, so he's going to open a little shop for them. He doesn't want them in his curiosity shop because they're too good. Jeb thinks he has a good eye for paintings, because he's made a lot of money out of two he bought and sold to a gallery up West. He says they doubled what they gave him when they put them up for sale, so he reckons he can do the same.'

Mrs Ross shook her head in disbelief. 'You'll come unstuck, my lad. Jeb may have had some luck, but what does he really know about the art world? One of these days he'll pay a lot of money for a fake and then your house of dreams will all come tumbling down.'

'Don't you ever give credit where it's due, Mum?' Joe asked. 'I shan't give him all I earn, just a bit. He only wants a hundred pounds...'

'Only?' His mother screeched. 'And where would you get that, Joe Ross?'

'I haven't got it,' Joe replied honestly. 'I do have some saved – but I'll earn the rest during the summer with my extra work.' He grinned at her. 'Jeb knows what he's doing – he's got the nose, Mum. He can smell a bargain and he's going places. If I can earn enough to buy another lorry and pay a man to drive it, I can expand my business. If I'm earning a bit from Jeb's gallery in a few years, I could buy a nice house in the suburbs – a house with a garden. How would you like that?'

His mother stared at him for a long moment. 'I'm not sure I would,' she said. 'Who is she, Joe? You're not thinking this way for me or yourself – there's a girl. I knew it when you finally told Sibby you wouldn't wed her. Don't think you can lie to me because you can't.'

Joe looked at her for a moment, then sat down. 'She's so far above me, Ma,' he said. 'Oh, we haven't got that far yet, but I think we shall… I love her and I believe she loves me.'

Mrs Ross was silent for a while, then, 'You'd better bring her here for tea then, Joe. Let her see what she's lettin' herself in for… because I doubt if Jeb will ever make your fortune. He's more likely to lose you whatever you've saved…'

* * *

Alone in his room, Joe thought about Sarah, and then he thought about what his mother had said. It was a big step to invest the fifty pounds he'd managed to save by doing every job he could manage to find. His summer of labouring on top of his profits from his own business would bring him in an extra fifty pounds, perhaps a bit more. It would be hard work and he didn't want to throw it all away.

Was he a fool to trust Jeb with his savings? Yet he knew his friend had started with a fruit barrow and now owned two shops: the flower shop Lilly ran profitably and his curiosity shop, which was to Joe's mind full of junk but Jeb said turned a profit every month.

'The real money is in the pictures,' Jeb had confided to Joe as they'd sat having a drink together one evening. 'I earned five hundred pounds from one deal, Joe – and I might have doubled it if I'd sold them myself.'

'But you didn't know they were worth that before you sold them, did you?'

'I knew they were worth a good bit,' Joe had said. 'There's a look about good oil paintings, Joe. I've got the eye for it – and I'll learn. I may make mistakes, but I'm a dealer. I shan't buy if I can't see a profit. It will take time to build, but I'll do it, you see if I don't. I'll have a house of my own and a posh car – and as many shops and businesses as I can...'

Joe had wondered if it was the drink talking, but there was no doubting Jeb had already made money. He'd been surprised when he asked Joe if he wanted to invest in the art business.

'Why do you need money if you made all that cash from those two pictures?' he'd asked.

'Because I've spent most of it already on more stock,' Jeb had replied with a grin. 'Notes in yer pocket ain't no good, Joe. You've got to turn 'em over if you want to make money.'

'I couldn't invest much,' Joe had said doubtfully. 'Fifty now – and the rest when I've earned it this summer.'

'That will do,' Jeb had said. 'I'll need you to help me cart some heavy stuff now and then, bits of furniture and garden ornaments – they weigh a ton. It's part of the deal. I'll make you a full partner in the gallery.'

'That wouldn't be fair to you,' Joe had protested. 'You must be putting in far more.'

'Yeah, well, maybe you'll put in some more as we go on,' Jeb had suggested. 'We'll reinvest your share of the profits for the first year or so and then we'll be equal.'

Joe had agreed. He wondered now if he'd done right, then shrugged his shoulders. He was young and strong. If he lost his money, he would just work harder and make more.

For a moment as he got into bed and turned out the oil lamp on the chest beside him, Joe's thoughts turned to Sibby. He had felt nothing but relief when his mother told him that she'd gone, but now, as he settled down to sleep, he felt a slight unease. Where had she gone in a hurry – and who was the man his mother had thought looked like a spiv?

Joe hoped Sibby hadn't done something foolish and for a moment he was aware of a feeling of guilt. When he'd brought her to his home, Joe had known that she expected they would be courting with the intention to marry – but he just couldn't give her what she wanted. He didn't love her. Yet he'd liked her and he knew he would feel uneasy until he'd spoken to her and made sure she was all right.

* * *

Joe didn't see Sibby on Monday morning, even though he waited for half an hour, so it was that evening when he saw Yvonne leaving the workshops that he asked after her.

'She didn't tell you?' Yvonne said, looking at him in surprise. 'She asked Miss Susie for her holiday money on Friday and her cards. She said she'd been offered a better job somewhere else.'

'She's left her job?' Joe looked at her in shock. 'She moved out on Saturday afternoon when I was at the wedding – but I never thought she would leave her job.'

'It probably has something to do with that bloke she was with the other week,' Yvonne said, frowning. 'I called to her, but she ignored me. She hadn't been into work that day...' She hesitated, then, 'I didn't like the look of him, Joe. He looked... I'm not sure, but not the sort of bloke I'd want any daughter of mine to be seen with.'

'Mum said he looked like a spiv,' Joe said, shaking his head.

'Thanks, Yvonne. I was just worried in case she was in any trouble.'

'If you ask me, Sibby doesn't know what she wants,' Yvonne told him. 'I think there was a secret in her past... something that haunted her. She was restless, never really happy. I hope I haven't upset you. I know you liked her.'

'She was a friend. I looked out for her – that's all...' Joe smiled. 'Don't worry, Yvonne. I'm not bothered. She's made her choice and I wish her good luck.'

He walked off whistling. He'd done what he could and now he could forget Sibby, forget the strange relationship they'd had for a while. His time with Sarah that Sunday had been wonderful and they'd arranged to meet again the following weekend. Life looked good to Joe right now. All he had to do was work hard and start to work his way up the ladder, like his mate Jeb.

41

'Oh, Sam,' Winnie said as they walked along the front at Clacton-on-Sea, past the pier to the pleasure ground, where there were all kinds of rides and arcades. 'I've never been to such a lovely place. The sea looks blue today and... Oh, it is all just perfect.'

Sam held her hand tighter and she looked at him, seeing that he wanted to kiss her but was holding back in such a public place. Things had moved on since the war, manners more relaxed, but it was still frowned on for couples to kiss in public and in full daylight too.

'We're lucky with the weather,' he remarked. 'I've been to Southend-on-Sea a few times, but I like it better here. I was stationed nearby during the war and some of us came in now and then for a bit of fun. The piers were closed at the time, but the cinemas were still open. There's a good film on tomorrow night – shall we go?'

'Whatever you like,' Winnie said and pulled at his hand, tugging him behind a shelter on the promenade. They were out of view of the street and most of the folk on the beach were too busy to notice as she leaned in and kissed him. 'I love you, Sam Collins.'

Sam grinned and drew her in for another kiss but let her go as some passing youths wolf-whistled loudly. 'They're only jealous,' he said and touched her face lovingly. 'I'm so lucky, Winnie. Last night... well, it was good, wasn't it?'

'Lovely,' Winnie said and snuggled into his arm, smiling up at him. 'I wondered what it would be like – but it was nice...' She gave a little giggle of pleasure. 'Better than nice.' A clock struck three then and she looked up at him mischievously. 'It will soon be time for tea – shall we go to our room and get changed for it?'

Sam chuckled. 'You're a minx, Winnie Collins – but just the way I want you. Come on then. We can go for a long walk on the beach tonight when the moon is up...'

Laughing in their happiness, they ran hand in hand to the hotel on the seafront. Funnily, it had the same name as one in London where they went to tea dances, though no dances were held at this Waverly. It was quiet, but there was a games room and Sam had started to teach her to play darts.

'When we go to the pub you can join in instead of watching,' he'd told her. 'But we'll find somewhere to dance while we're here – I want to dance with you for the rest of my life, Winnie...'

Alone in their room that warm July afternoon, Winnie moved into Sam's arms once more. Any shyness on her part had vanished when her gentle and inexpert husband had loved her so sweetly and tenderly the previous two nights of their honeymoon. Neither of them was very good at it yet, as Sam had laughingly told her, but they had the rest of their lives to learn. Something they were both eager and willing to do as they tumbled into the bed together...

Whatever trials and problems the future might hold for them, they would face them together. They knew that they were the lucky ones, their friendship had matured into a deep and abiding love that they both knew would never fade.

'We are so lucky,' Sam whispered to Winnie as he held her close, his hands gently wandering, caressing and adoring. 'It could have been so different, Winnie.'

'I know...' Her eyes were moist with tears of love tinged with sorrow. 'I still can't truly believe you're here with me and not locked in that horrid cell...'

'The reason I'm here is because of Ernie. I don't know why he did it, Winnie. I just pray that Mr Marsh can help him.'

'So do I,' she said and lifted her face for his kiss and there was no more time for talk just then...

42

'You all right, Lilly?' Joe asked when he called in to see his sister that Friday morning. She was making up a basket of flowers and stopped to look at him. 'Jeb is away again at another sale, for two days this time, isn't it?'

'Yes, just one night though,' Lilly agreed and smiled. 'Susie popped in five minutes ago, Joe. She had a postcard from Winnie. She says the weather is lovely and they are happy. But she also had other good news... They've released Ernie on bail pending further investigations, and she says that Mr Marsh, who helped Sam, has arranged for him to stay in a good nursing home. Poor Ernie is very ill and Susie says that Mr Marsh got him out on the grounds of ill health. He says he has more evidence, too, and so he got an order for bail.'

'Well, that is good news,' Joe said. 'I didn't believe he did it, any more than Sam did. At least he will get to die in peace. Sam told me he doesn't have more than a few weeks left to him, according to the doctor Mr Marsh got for him.'

Lilly's eyes were wet with tears. 'I feel so sad for him, Joe. He's had a terrible life.' She sniffed hard. 'It ain't right...'

'No, it ain't,' Joe agreed, looking grave.

'Why do you think he confessed to a murder he didn't do?' Lilly asked.

Joe frowned. 'Not sure. When I told him how important it was that we could prove Sam's hammer had been lost or stolen, he gave me an odd look and said he might be able to help. I thought he might tell the cops he'd seen Derek Norton go into Sam's shop and take it, but I never dreamed he would confess to the crime himself...'

'It seems odd,' Lilly said. 'I mean most of us in the alley have been kind to him in small ways – but that wouldn't make him give up his freedom for the last precious few days of his life, surely?'

'I think there must be a stronger reason. I did see something once, but I don't suppose it means anything...' Joe shook his head. Sam had hinted that he knew why Ernie had confessed to a crime he didn't commit, but he hadn't told Joe anything more and Joe hadn't probed. 'No, I shan't say because I'm probably wrong.' He smiled at her. 'As long as you're all right, Lilly, I'll get going.'

'I'm fine,' she said. 'Are you starting on the building today?'

'Tomorrow. Today I'm fetching stocks of coke and filling sacks, but after that it will be non-stop graft for a while.' He grinned and went out whistling to himself. He was glad that Ernie was being looked after. He'd felt a bit uneasy at first, in case Ernie had done it because of what he'd said to him, but then he'd realised that didn't make sense. It was only recently that he'd remembered seeing Ernie deep in conversation with Nobby Carter. He'd looked upset, defeated, and Nobby had been angry. Joe couldn't shake the feeling that it had something to do with Ernie's false confession, but he had no idea what...

* * *

Timothy rang Susie at the workshop later that afternoon. He suggested that he take her out for a meal that evening. 'I'll be taking you this time and we'll go somewhere quiet but decent so that we can talk.'

'I can't manage this evening,' Susie told him. 'What about tomorrow?'

'If I must wait...' he said and sounded impatient.

Susie laughed. 'My lady is going somewhere special this evening and asked if I would dress her hair for her. Naturally, I said I would. Meg is learning, but she has a way to go with her hair styling yet.'

'You shouldn't be doing that – you're a businesswoman now,' Timothy told her. 'When you marry, you won't be able to be at her beck and call the whole time.'

'I'm not. She asked and I said yes. It isn't work for me. I love her.'

'What about a different kind of love?' he asked. 'I thought about you all day yesterday...'

'So why didn't you come and tell me?'

'Because I was settling Ernie into that nursing home,' he said and laughed. 'All right, you win. We both have other commitments, Susie. I will pick you up tomorrow at seven...'

'I shall be ready,' Susie said. 'I'm glad you rang, Tim.'

'No one calls me that,' he said. 'I like it.'

She heard him chuckling as he replaced the receiver.

Susie smiled. She thought that perhaps like her he'd needed breathing space to think about their relationship. At the moment, they led very different lives. If the feeling she'd had when he kissed her proved true and lasting, they might both have to make big changes. She wasn't at all sure his family would accept a woman like her. Susie might be Lady Diane's partner now, but she'd had the minimum of schooling and what she knew had been learned from life; she'd educated herself, copying her precious lady for manners and a way of speaking that made her fit to be her lady's dresser. She'd read a lot of books and seen a lot of the quality and now she was a different person to the young woman who had begun as a parlourmaid at the age of fourteen.

Whether or not she could ever be good enough for Timothy's family was something that remained to be seen. She was nearly thirty-five and perhaps too old for a family, though to have a child had long been her dearest wish. Susie shook her head. No, she was thinking too far ahead – and all that was for the future. For now she would just get on with her job and leave things to work out as they would.

* * *

Susie wound Lady Diane's hair into a shining coil at the back of her head, securing the French pleat with diamond and pearl pins. Then she teased a few strands out from the sides and across the forehead so that the little curls just framed her lady's face and made the elegant style softer. She held a silver hand-mirror for her to see the back in her dressing mirror.

'Oh, yes, that is perfect with this evening coat,' Lady Diane cried, looking delighted. 'Because of the collar I couldn't wear it as Meg tried in a kind of bun – it would have caught and looked untidy.'

Her evening coat was one she had designed herself to go over a silver sheath that clung to her figure and flared slightly at the back. The short coat of dark blue velvet had a huge stand-up collar. It was bordered with silver braid and very stiff, resembling the kind of ruff worn by ladies in Queen Elizabeth the First's reign and was rather regal. Because Lady Diane's hair was swept up out of her neck, it looked elegant and showed her white skin and her diamond earrings to perfection.

'It looks wonderful on you,' Susie said. 'I love the collar. I think I've seen a dress with a collar like that on one of Lord Henry's ancestors – in the library in the country.'

'Yes, how clever of you,' Lady Diane said. 'That was Lady Henriette. She was French, you know – and rather naughty...' She laughed. 'It is my ball in a few weeks' time, Susie. I want you to come as my guest...'

Susie stared at her in shock. 'Oh no, my lady! It wouldn't do...'

'Why not? You are no longer a servant, Susie. I know I asked you to do my hair – but as a favour. I will provide a dress for you. I have already asked Yvonne to make it for you – so don't say no. It would be such a waste...' She smiled at Susie as she picked up her evening gloves. 'You can ask Mr Marsh as your partner for the evening. I shall send him an invitation. I have always invited Hugo to my special occasions, you know – but poor dear Hugo is still recuperating. So I must ask Mr Marsh instead and since he helped your brother, I thought you could come together. Besides, I've asked Sally and Ben Harper too, and it is a chance for you to socialise with them... and they are your best customers still.'

'What will Lord Henry say?' Susie was still doubtful, but what she was hearing made sense. Susie needed to be able to meet customers like the Harpers on their own ground.

'I doubt he will notice – and if he does, you are my friend and partner. I couldn't have done any of it without you, Susie. You must try to forget that you were my aunt's parlourmaid. For my part, we have always been friends... Oh, please do come, Susie. You've no idea how stuffy some of my guests are, but I have to invite them. To see you there with Mr Marsh will please me so much.'

Susie inclined her head. She was not sure she could have refused her lady if she'd wanted to – but with Timothy as her partner for the evening... It would help her to realise that she had a new life. As yet that had mostly just been a change in her working day. It was perhaps time that she began to have a social life of her own, to see what there was waiting for her beyond working hours.

She had done what was required of her, despite her misgivings at the start. For the time being, she still wasn't sure if Miss Susie would ever make money, but she'd fulfilled her lady's dream for her and perhaps that was all that truly mattered. Though, as time had moved on, the success of the fledgling business she'd begun had become more important to her. Susie wanted it to succeed, to grow and become something truly special, and perhaps it would.

Like her relationship with Timothy, that was for the future...

ABOUT THE AUTHOR

Rosie Clarke is a #1 bestselling saga writer whose books include Welcome to Harpers Emporium and The Mulberry Lane series. She has written over 100 novels under different pseudonyms and is a RNA Award winner. She lives in Cambridgeshire.

Sign up to Rosie Clarke's mailing list for news, competitions and updates on future books.

Visit Rosie's website: www.rosieclarke.co.uk

Follow Rosie on social media here:

 facebook.com/Rosie-clarke-119457351778432

 x.com/AnneHerries

BB bookbub.com/authors/rosie-clarke

ALSO BY ROSIE CLARKE

Welcome to Harpers Emporium Series

The Shop Girls of Harpers

Love and Marriage at Harpers

Rainy Days for the Harpers Girls

Harpers Heroes

Wartime Blues for the Harpers Girls

Victory Bells For The Harpers Girls

Changing Times at Harpers

Heartbreak at Harpers

The Mulberry Lane Series

A Reunion at Mulberry Lane

Stormy Days On Mulberry Lane

A New Dawn Over Mulberry Lane

Life and Love at Mulberry Lane

Last Orders at Mulberry Lane

Blackberry Farm Series

War Clouds Over Blackberry Farm

Heartache at Blackberry Farm

Love and Duty at Blackberry Farm

The Trenwith Trilogy

Sarah's Choice

Louise's War

Rose's Fight

Dressmakers' Alley

Dangerous Times on Dressmakers' Alley

Dark Secrets on Dressmakers' Alley

Standalone Novels

Nellie's Heartbreak

A Mother's Shame

A Sister's Destiny

Sixpence Stories

Introducing Sixpence Stories!

Discover page-turning
historical novels from your
favourite authors, meet new
friends and be transported
back in time.

Join our book club
Facebook group

https://bit.ly/SixpenceGroup

Sign up to our
newsletter

https://bit.ly/SixpenceNews

Boldwood

Boldwood Books is an award-winning fiction publishing company seeking out the best stories from around the world.

Find out more at www.boldwoodbooks.com

Join our reader community for brilliant books, competitions and offers!

Follow us
@BoldwoodBooks
@TheBoldBookClub

Sign up to our weekly
deals newsletter

https://bit.ly/BoldwoodBNewsletter

Printed in Great Britain
by Amazon

49553271R00178